D1202714

THE SONG OF SADIE SPARROW

Kitty Foth-Regner

FaithHappenings Publishers

Copyright © 2017 by Kitty Foth-Regner

All rights reserved. No part of this publication may be reproduced, distributed or transmitted in any form or by any means, including photocopying, recording, or other electronic or mechanical methods, without the prior written permission of the publisher, except in the case of brief quotations embodied in critical reviews and certain other noncommercial uses permitted by copyright law.

Some Scripture quotations are taken from *The Holy Bible*, King James Version. Others are taken from *The Holy Bible*, New King James Version ©1982 Thomas Nelson, Inc. Used by permission. All rights reserved.

FaithHappenings Publishers
7500 E. Arapahoe Road, Suite 285
Centennial, CO 80112

Cover Design ©2017 FaithHappenings Publishers
Book Layout ©2013 BookDesignTemplates.com

The Song of Sadie Sparrow / Kitty Foth-Regner. – 2nd ed., 2018
ISBN (Softcover) 978-1-941555-35-4
This book was printed in the United States of America.

To order additional copies of this book, contact:
admin@wordserveliterary.com

FaithHappenings Publishers,
a division of WordServeLiterary.com

In memory of my beloved friend

Doris A. Zankl

(1919-2017)

CHAPTER ONE

Sadie Sparrow
Saturday, October 22

In all her eighty-six years, Sadie Sparrow had never been as miserable as she was this dreary Saturday afternoon. Not even Ed's death could compare to being cast aside by her only daughter, packed up and stuffed against her will into a tiny room in a place that she'd never even seen, hidden way out here in the country, in—

"Here we are, Mom," Dana said, turning her fancy foreign car onto a gravel road flanked by crumbling pillars and armies of trees in full autumn glory. "The Hickories—isn't this too cool? It's so exclusive that they don't even post a sign outside."

Sadie was silent. Sure enough, there was nothing but a plaque on the right pillar, bearing the numbers 21470, apparently the address of this place.

They drove into the woods. There were no buildings in sight; for just a moment she wondered if there might not be a rest home here at all, if Dana intended instead to do away with her old mother and leave the body here to rot under the leaves. She tried to remember the name of the country road they'd been traveling—Larkspur or Purslane or Rasputin or something like that—and the number on the pillar, but by this time she had forgotten both, and had to give up on her daring escape plan which would have concluded with her leading the police back to the scene of the failed crime.

Miss Marple she was not.

"I really think you're going to love it here," Dana said cheerfully as she steered her way down the winding road. "It's by far the most elegant place I found. Just wait'll you see it. You'll flip!"

"I'm sure it will be lovely." As Sadie's own dear mother would have noted, the icebox door was open, and she had no intention of shutting it anytime soon.

"And I don't know if I mentioned this," Dana added, ignoring her mother's obvious lack of enthusiasm. "They're about to hire someone to write the biographies of any resident who's interested in telling her life story—you know, as a gift to leave her children and grandchildren."

"Isn't that nice," Sadie said curtly. "Since children and grandchildren are too busy these days to get their elders' stories firsthand."

Dana sighed her Nothing I Do Will Ever Be Enough sigh.

The landscape matched Sadie's mood. The little road was lined with craggy old shagbark hickories, white oaks, scrub elms, and wild cherries. They were all junk trees, as far as the world was concerned, although Sadie had always been fond of shagbarks, especially on a day like today, after a good rain had turned their disheveled bark almost black, and especially at this time of year, with their big golden leaves clinging stubbornly to the branches that had held them all summer long.

And then, rounding the fifth or sixth bend in the road, she spotted their destination—and it quite literally took her breath away.

"There," breathed Dana, almost reverently, "isn't it magnificent?"

The Hickories was an enormous stone-and-concrete building nestled halfway up a forested hill high enough to qualify as a mountain in southeastern Wisconsin. As more of the building came into view, Sadie was reminded of photographs she'd seen in a coffee-table book about Wisconsin's own Frank Lloyd Wright: layer upon low-slung layer of white concrete rectangles that looked like a stack of gift boxes set aside after wrappings and presents had been removed. Thick columns of stone seemed to pierce the boxes at perfect right angles, making the trunks of the surrounding trees look wildly contorted in comparison.

"Yes," Sadie conceded, grudgingly allowing her heart to soften a bit. "It really is."

She noticed the fragrance of burning wood then, and sure enough, there in the center of the building she spotted smoke snaking out of a squat stone chimney.

"It's beautiful," she added.

"It's just what the doctor ordered, Mom." Dana smiled for the first time since they'd pulled away from Pine Grove, the retirement home where Sadie had lived for almost a decade. "I just know you're going to love it."

No, what the doctor ordered—the Great Physician Himself, in fact—is a daughter who loves and respects and honors her mother enough to take her into her own home and care for her until she dies.

But short of that, Sadie had to admit, this place looked about as nice as a nursing home could be. It definitely made a good first impression, even when they'd driven beneath the lowest concrete tier into what turned out to be a warmly lit parking garage. It didn't look like the other nursing homes she had visited over the years, as one friend after another had landed in various iterations of this despised last stop before the Great Beyond. This was by far the grandest one she'd ever seen.

As Dana wheeled her towards a pair of glowing copper doors, Sadie found a new reason to worry: How in the world could she afford this place? Had anyone thought to explore the money angle before signing her up to move in?

The copper doors slid open to reveal an elevator car paneled in glossy dark wood and lit by a crystal chandelier. Crystal!

Sadie decided that the finances were Dana's problem.

She makes plenty of money in that job of hers. Let her pay for it.

For the first time since the Fourth of July, when Dana had begun earnestly talking up the virtues of nursing-home living, Sadie felt a flicker of hope in her heart.

The tour was grueling. Dressed in Saturday jeans and a navy turtleneck rather than her usual power suit and with her light-brown hair pulled back in a ponytail that Sadie thought looked a little silly on a fifty-five-year-old, Dana was clearly in a hurry. Her eyebrows were perfectly arched in their perennial imitation of interest. But she asked no questions of Admissions Director Vanessa as they raced through the various lounges and dining rooms and activity areas. Tall and athletic and long of stride, Dana was pushing the wheelchair so fast that Sadie found herself white-knuckling the arm rests, hoping they wouldn't hit a speed bump that would send her hurtling across the room.

What's more, the place was breathtaking, and she would've enjoyed a more leisurely tour. But she wasn't doing the driving.

"And this is where we show movies," gushed the eminently enthusiastic Vanessa as Dana rolled her mother into a windowless room with carpeting so thick that she was forced to slow down.

"It's wonderful," Sadie whispered. The ceiling glowed with dozens of star-like lights, and there was an old-fashion popcorn cart in the corner. She loved movies—and she loved popcorn.

"I'm glad you like it, Sadie," Vanessa said. "Tonight's feature is *Exodus*, if you'd care to see it, at seven o'clock."

It was one of Sadie's favorites, rarely shown on television for some odd reason—not enough sex, probably. The thought of seeing it again almost made her forget that this young woman whom she had just met had called her by her first name without asking for permission. In the good old days people waited for an invitation, or at least asked for the privilege.

But still: Paul Newman and Eva Marie Saint and the rebirth of the nation of Israel. All this plus fresh popcorn! "I'll be here," she said, practically grinning at their guide. "With bells on."

The final leg of their journey took them up another level via an old-fashioned elevator gated in bronze and paneled in wood and wine velvet, then down a long hall lined with enormous windows overlooking the woods—a stunning sight even on such a dreary day.

"We're headed into the North Wing," Vanessa was saying. "As you can see, the resident rooms are set well apart from the common areas. That means you can get away from the hustle and bustle of this place whenever you want. And don't worry about the distance. We have elevators everywhere, it seems, and there's always someone around to give you a ride."

That was good news, and not only because of the distances. Sadie didn't know if she'd ever be able to find her way around this place on her own.

She was feeling cautiously optimistic by the time they made a sharp right into a warmly lit hallway flanked by paneled doors.

"This room's one of my favorites." Vanessa pushed open the second door on the right. "It's a tad smaller than some of the others, but I think that just makes it cozier."

Sadie gasped as Dana rolled her into the room. It was huge, larger by far than the studio apartment she'd just left. Straight ahead, an entire wall of floor-to-ceiling windows overlooked a courtyard garden, its paths already glowing against the gathering gloom.

And these weren't just any windows. "Is that leaded glass?" she asked.

"That's right!" Vanessa cried, as if Sadie had made a totally brilliant observation. "And real stained glass, too. Plus all our woodwork is locally grown maple. It's really a first-class structure."

"It's gorgeous, don't you think, Mom?"

Dana's voice startled Sadie; for a moment, she'd actually forgotten her own daughter's presence.

"It is indeed," Sadie said, gazing around in wonder. Brown velvet curtains, golden paneling, a matching wooden platform bed—could that possibly be a hospital bed?—and a whole wall of built-in closets flanking a desk. "And Tiffany lamps."

Vanessa laughed. "I'll let you in on a secret, Sadie. They're not real Tiffany, just good fakes." She opened a closet door. "As you'll notice, we've already unpacked for you. We'll move things wherever you like as you get settled in, but I've always found that our residents appreciate having this part of their move-in taken care of. And look, we've put your books over here on these shelves: your Bible and address book, plus your Agatha Christie mysteries and these wonderful old Anne Parrish novels. She was my granny's favorite author, too. So you're all set!"

"Tell her about the safe," Dana said.

"Oh, yes!" Apparently delighted with the reminder, Vanessa walked briskly over to a picture on the wall, one of those fuzzy-looking paintings that Dana was so gaga over, a scene of a couple women and children in a field of dead grass dotted with red flowers. Vanessa tugged on the edge of its frame; it swung open like a door to reveal a safe. "This is for your valuables."

Sadie smiled ruefully. "I wish I had some valuables to put in there."

"Well, you may think of something you'd like to safeguard." Vanessa tucked the picture back in place and gestured at the door. "In the meantime, there's a lock on the door, too. Some of our residents like to use it, and others don't. It's up to you. We haven't had any problems with theft for several years, but you never know."

"I'm speechless," Sadie said, working hard to suppress the huffing and puffing that accompanied any sort of excitement lately; it seemed to irritate Dana. The Hickories really did seem too good to be true. She felt a sudden flutter of panic; the situation reminded her of that novel about the law firm, the one where the young lawyer found himself in just such a position before discovering that there was something horribly wrong with the place.

But she could hardly say anything like that without sounding paranoid, so she resurrected an earlier fear. "I can't afford this place, Dana."

"You have insurance, Mom." Dana knelt down before the wheelchair to look her mother in the eye. "Remember? We bought you a long-term-care policy years ago."

"I haven't been paying for anything like that."

"Sure you have, Mom. Or rather, I've been paying for it when I pay your other bills, using your money. A few thousand a year, and look what you're getting in return."

Sadie thought about the dreary little apartment she'd been living in for the last decade and wondered why they'd waited so long.

"It's great coverage," Dana added. "The best that money can buy."

"Would you care to rest for a while before dinner, Sadie?" Vanessa asked. "Saturday night is steak night here, unless you prefer chicken."

"Steak will be just fine," Sadie said, feeling a bit like Mrs. Got-Rocks. "And yes, I'm ready for a nap."

Sadie also had to admit that dinner was outstanding. After a brisk goodbye kiss from Dana and a much-needed nap on the soft platform bed, she'd been whisked down to the dining room by a sweet little aide. Here, she had enjoyed a rib-eye broiled to medium-rare perfection, along with a baked potato, a lovely broccoli-cheese dish, and a nice glass of sparkling grape juice. No dessert. She hadn't left any room for it, although it was a luscious-looking apricot torte.

Her tablemates were very pleasant. One in particular—was her name Evelyn? Or Eva?—well, whatever, she seemed like she could be friend material, perhaps making up for the ones Sadie had just left behind at Pine Grove. And they'd invited Sadie to join their little puzzle-making club, which appealed to her; she'd always loved working on jigsaws, especially as winter set in.

But none of it could make up for her loneliness now that she was back in her room, feeling totally abandoned by her only child and too tearful to even consider going to see *Exodus*. Instead, she wheeled herself to the desk and dialed Dana's number, hoping for an affectionate word. But, as usual, she was greeted by a cheerful recording inviting her to leave a message after the tone.

"Dana," she cried, making no attempt to sound anything less than desperate. "Please call me. I need to talk to you. I need to hear your voice."

Sadie spent the evening sitting at her desk, cradled by the comfortable but costly wheelchair cushions that Dana had procured from some fancy California company. She tried not to stare at the phone—a watched pot, you know—but it was impossible; not even her favorite Christie whodunit, *The Murder of Roger Ackroyd,* could distract her from this paralyzing loneliness.

You devote your entire adult life to your husband and child, to meeting their every need, and then without warning, you find yourself old and sick and completely alone.

Now and then, she would chastise herself for this self-pity. So unattractive, really, and not at all like her. But then her solitude would reassert itself, and she'd be back to feeling sorry for herself.

At eight o'clock, the aide came in and offered to help her get ready for bed. But Sadie waved her off, explaining that she was expecting a very important call.

"I know exactly what you mean," the girl said. She was young and rather homely and Sadie, feeling a little less than charitable just now, could easily imagine her waiting in vain for the phone to ring. "But remember that you have voice mail. If the call comes in while we're in the bathroom, you'll be able to return it right away."

"Come back later, please," Sadie said, just a sympathetic word or two away from tears.

Alone again, it struck her that Dana might have called while she was at dinner. How exactly did this voice mail work?

There was a big red button labeled *Messages* on the phone; picking up the receiver, she poked it. "You have no new messages," said a woman's voice, her tone firm, uncompromising, uncaring.

"I understand," Sadie replied. "'And don't bother me again until someone cares enough to leave one,' is that it?"

But oh—what if just at this moment, Dana was calling, and got a busy signal? Sadie slammed down the receiver and burst into tears, indulging in her first good cry since the specter of a nursing home had invaded her heart last summer.

The phone remained silent. But by nine, Sadie had regained her composure enough to make her aide think all was well.

No, my dear, no loneliness here. Move along, nothing to see but an old lady looking forward to sweet dreams.

She waited until she was in bed, lights out, to let her thoughts wander to the ultimate cause of this ghastly situation.

Because of course, in the end, it was all her husband's fault. Her *late* husband. Surely Ed had known he was sick. Surely he could have done *something* to keep himself from dropping dead, leaving her a widow at the far-too-young age of fifty-six.

Sadie turned on her left side, pulling the covers up over her head.

It had happened a lifetime ago. But on the rare occasion that she allowed herself to remember, it seemed like yesterday.

Being dumped in an old folks' warehouse seemed like a worthy occasion to revisit those memories.

It had been a Saturday afternoon in September of 1982, a gorgeous fall day, and she was making Ed a pie. She had sent him outside with a basket to harvest the best apples from the tree in their back yard. The swing was still there at that time, hanging from the strongest bough; even though Dana had recently turned twenty-five and had plunged headlong into her career and said she had no interest in having children herself, they were holding out hope for a grandchild or two one day, so he hadn't taken it down. And that day, as he walked past it, Ed had given the swing a little push.

Oh, how often she'd replayed that scene in her mind's eye, wondering why he'd done that, if he had been recalling little Dana's passion for swinging or imagining a future granddaughter's delight.

Not that it mattered, really. Sadie had turned back to her dough-making, working the butter into the dry ingredients, adding a well-beaten egg, sprinkling a bit of water into the mixture. As she worked, she sang one of her favorite old hymns, all the while listening for the squeak of the screen door.

When we all get to heaven, what a day of rejoicing that will be.
When we all see Jesus, we'll sing and shout the victory!

She was just starting to roll out the dough when she wondered what was taking Ed so long. Wiping her hands on an old dish towel, she went to the door and called his name.

There was no response, and no Ed in sight.

He was probably talking to Ray next door. But still, her heart beat a little faster as she skipped down the back steps. No, no sign of Ed or Ray. His workshop, then, in the old barn back of the apple tree. It wasn't like Ed to get distracted, but he must have remembered something he meant to do and he knew that Sadie wouldn't be ready for the apples for a few minutes, anyway—

But no, that wasn't it either. Because there he was, lying face down on the far side of the tree.

Sadie ran to him, fell to her knees, turned him over. But he was absolutely still.

The rest was a blur. She must have cried out, because suddenly Ray and Mabel were there with her, and another neighbor shouted that she'd call an ambulance, and—well, that was the end of their thirty years together. Over, just like that, thanks to a bad heart and a stubborn dislike of doctors.

Ed's death was the end of her life's most important chapter. And now the last chapter was coming to a crashing end, too, only this time she didn't have young, concerned, loving Dana to hold her hand and weep with her. She didn't even have the comfort of their fellow church members anymore; she had stopped attending soon after Ed's funeral, and after a couple months the phone calls from concerned members dwindled to silence. She had made some friends at the retirement home, but over time most had gone on to other places, to live with their kids or to nursing homes or to their graves.

She was finally and utterly alone.

Well, then, this was it. The Hickories would be her final home on this earth.

Sadie Sparrow was perfectly ready to call it a life, and that was what she intended to do, just as soon as the good Lord would have her.

CHAPTER TWO

Elise Chapelle
Sunday, October 23

Looks like you have a new neighbor, Papi. She's *very* pretty!"

Elise swept over to her grandfather, who looked as handsome as any wheelchair-bound ninety-two-year-old ever had, and kissed his cheek. Her hugs were gentle these days. His stroke may have numbed his left side, but his entire body was riddled with arthritis; although he never complained, she'd heard him gasp a time or two before she figured out that his bear-hug days were over.

"Wait till you see her," she teased. "She has the bluest eyes you've ever seen, and a gorgeous smile, and she's a tiny little thing, very trim."

"Foolish girl!" Charles "Papi" Chapelle beamed at his best friend in all the world. "You know there'll never be another woman for me."

"I know, Papi, I know," Elise said, straightening the tie he insisted on wearing, even for The Hickories' onsite church services. She would of course never stand in the way of his happiness, but she was secretly pleased that Papi would never in his wildest dreams take up with another woman; seven decades with his beloved Lorraine had forever spoiled him for anyone else. "But Mamie wouldn't want you to be lonely, you know."

"I'm not lonely." He reached for her hand. "I have you, and I'm surrounded by people my own age. Something you might want to consider doing."

Elise grinned. "Been there, done that, and short of a miracle, I won't be going there again. Got that? Now, how 'bout we head down to church?"

Fran, one of the Sunday service volunteers, motioned Elise and Papi into what was shaping up as the front row in the Great Room overlooking the woods. They were as usual very early. They'd always been early for the Sunday morning services at First Baptist Church, too. Papi insisted that the Lord deserved that much respect, and so did any church in this wonderful land of liberty that he and his bride had fled to in 1940, when Hitler set his sights on France. They'd been early on that score, too, he often said, escaping Paris weeks before their gutless leaders had rolled over and played dead.

Elise pulled a side chair next to his and sat down. A hymn CD was playing on the sound system, just loud enough for the early worshippers to enjoy a magnificent rendition of "Be Still My Soul."

When disappointment, grief and fear are gone,
Sorrow forgot, love's purest joys restored.

"I wonder what Mamie is doing right now," she said dreamily. "What do you think, Papi? What are they doing in heaven this morning?"

Papi sighed, but he was smiling. "I don't know, my dear, but I can't wait to find out."

"Me neither." It was true, but Elise wished instantly that she hadn't said it to the man who had tried so hard to give her a happy life.

And indeed, Papi turned in his chair to look at his granddaughter, frowning in pain or concern or maybe a little of both. "You're too young to say that, Elise. You'll meet the right man, and you'll marry and have children. Your Mamie would have wanted that, you know."

"She wanted that for my mother, anyway," Elise said sorrowfully. "Not exactly what she got, was it?" She lowered her voice a bit; no need to talk of such things in front of the growing crowd of worshippers. "You two never even met my father. And my mother? Running off how many days after delivering me?"

He shrugged. It was not a subject he cared to discuss, and he turned eagerly away to greet the resident that Fran was wheeling into place on his right.

"Let's do this, Papi," Elise murmured, knowing he couldn't hear her. "I'll get married if you and I can have a double wedding. Deal?"

"Oh, Charles," Fran said in her Everyone Here Is Hard of Hearing voice, "I'd like you to meet our newest resident. Her name is Sadie Sparrow, and I think she might be your neighbor."

Papi shook Sadie's hand solemnly, stating his full name, and rolled himself back enough to introduce his granddaughter.

She really is a cute little thing, Elise thought, as Papi turned back to the new woman. She couldn't hear their conversation, but Sadie was smiling sweetly at him and nodding and speaking a few words of her own. Elise wondered if she might be witnessing the beginning of an end-of-life romance, and how she would really feel about that.

Delighted, she hoped. And not the least bit jealous.

Elise was smiling when she tucked herself into bed that night. It had been a wonderful day, a classic warm and hazy Indian Summer afternoon spent in The Hickories garden with Papi and sweet little Sadie Sparrow. It turned out that Sadie had been widowed many years ago—a comfort to Elise, because surely Sadie could've captured another man for herself long ago if that had been her objective. No, she just seemed to be kind and a bit confused, or maybe *lost* was a better word, waking up in this strange new world this morning, perhaps realizing that this was likely to be her final home on this earth.

"One more thing, Lord," Elise whispered, "if it's Your will, please let them become fast friends. Use them to comfort one another, to help them both realize the peace that passes all understanding. And use them to comfort others, to point anyone who doesn't yet know You to Your throne of grace. These things I ask in Jesus' name . . ."

Tired as she was from the fresh air and fellowship, Elise knew within moments that it was going to be another one of those toss-and-turn nights, and not, for once, because of the past. No, tonight promised to be a fretting-over-the-future marathon.

Mamie's death two years ago had been relatively easy— one massive, middle-of-the-night coronary and she was in glory. Heartbreaking for Elise and Papi, of course, but Mamie hadn't suffered for even a second, and for that they'd be eternally grateful.

But Papi was another matter. His daily cocktails of morphine and Vicodin weren't quite controlling his pain anymore, and they'd probably have to do something about it sooner rather than later. Upping the dose was not out of the question, but it was apparently already pretty high, and he wouldn't want to be drugged into oblivion.

"For our light affliction," she reminded herself, "which is but for a moment, is working for us a far more exceeding and eternal weight of glory."

She almost drifted off to sleep on that thought, when she heard scratching in the wall behind her bed. Or thought she did. She listened intently, every nerve on high alert.

True, it had been years since any critters had entered the living space of this big old farmhouse, thanks in large part to the fact that most of the neighboring farms had long ago been developed into the restaurants and stores and car dealerships of western Brookfield. But after letting the developers chip away at his land until only ten acres were left, Papi had put his foot down. Never mind that he had already retired his Fleur de Lis cut-flower business and let the fields run wild; there would be no parking lots on his property, not in this lifetime.

Elise supported his stand, except that it left her on permanent edge about mice and chipmunks and squirrels invading her home. And now Papi wasn't even here to do battle for her.

She was on a wide-awake roll now.

Maybe we should go ahead and sell it all. The land's worth a small fortune, enough to pay for Papi's care for the rest of his life, enough to buy me a nice little pest-free condominium and see me through even if I never go back to work.

"But Lord," she said, "it would be better just to skip all of that. Please, come and get me and Papi and bring us home to Mamie. We miss her so much."

But at thirty-two, Elise apparently didn't have a right to feel this way—even though once Papi died, she'd be left behind for decades, perhaps, to fend for herself, to try to fit into a world that, in her experience, treated committed Christians with contempt.

Maybe she'd go back to First Baptist once Papi was gone. Maybe there'd be some other young singles this time, maybe she'd even meet a nice young man who wouldn't try to pressure her into sex as her last two well-churched boyfriends had, proving once and for all that they were more interested in pleasing themselves than pleasing God. Or maybe she'd meet some elderly people who'd be happy to count as a friend an able-bodied young woman eager to lend them a hand and a heart.

Then again, she could earn her CNA certification and work at The Hickories. It probably wouldn't pay too well, but she was Papi's only heir; she didn't need to earn another penny if she didn't want to. Maybe she'd simply become a fulltime volunteer there.

Sleep was definitely impossible. Elise pulled on her worn fleece robe and padded in slippered feet down to the kitchen. She turned on the dim light over the sink, put a battered saucepan of milk on to heat and sat down at the old oak table. The gas glowed neon blue. She remembered sitting in this very chair many times as a young insomniac, allowing herself to be mesmerized by the flame while Mamie fussed over cups and cookies and napkins. She could recall Mamie finally sitting down with her, gently encouraging her to talk about whatever thoughts were keeping her awake, taking even the silliest of them seriously, reminding her at last that not even a sparrow falls to the ground apart from God's will, and that she was surely more valuable to Him than many sparrows.

Was that why she'd felt an immediate affinity for Sadie Sparrow?

Yes, she missed everything about her grandmother. But there was nothing more she could do for Mamie. It was time to get on with her life. She had quit her teaching position at Stonybrook School to take care of Papi, and she could always go back to that job now that he was ensconced at The Hickories. But did she really want to spend the rest of her life trying to convince classrooms of bored students that grammar was critically important to their futures?

Elise thought not. Especially since she was no longer convinced that it was even remotely true.

CHAPTER THREE

Meg Vogel
Friday, January 6

Meg Vogel was fifty-eight years old when she buried first her husband and, shortly thereafter, her freelance copywriting business.

She had no choice with the former. After twenty-five years of living with her, the last five of them as her husband and the last four battling colorectal cancer, Gil had died on New Year's Eve in a hospice just a few miles from home. Meg had been left drained by the high drama of his illness, the hot fear and cold grief of his last hours on earth, and the cotton-headed confusion of yesterday's funeral.

Now came the easy part. She rose early, shared a leisurely breakfast of scrambled eggs and toast with basset hound Touchdown and oriental shorthair cat Sneak, and put Meg Vogel Copywriting out of the misery it had sunk into during Gil's last year.

Even though the business had outlasted her entire relationship with him, shutting it down caused her surprisingly little sorrow. She'd been a decent copywriter, but never great, and she'd had decent relationships with the trendier ad agencies in town, but never great—at least not good enough to warrant a nod of recognition from the chichi creative directors, designers, and account executives who would float in and out of the meetings she was forced to sit through week after week, feigning interest in a hip new clothing shop or big-name exhibit at the art museum, feigning indifference to the way they all insisted on mangling the English language, feigning gratitude whenever someone tossed her a little project or two.

It took her approximately seven minutes to send out emails permanently closing Meg Vogel Copywriting. There weren't too many people left to inform. Most of her clients had drifted to other freelancers as Gil became sicker. She couldn't really blame them; even when she was at her desk to take their calls, she had been distracted. As a result, she had turned in too many final drafts missing client corrections (she'd misplaced them), too many concepts reusing a headline or phrase that the end-client had rejected last time around (she'd forgotten), too much copy pockmarked with careless typographical errors or missing words (her mind had wandered).

There'd been only a few faithful creative directors and copy supervisors who had stuck with her to the bitter end, giving her assignments with loose deadlines or no deadlines at all. She even suspected one of calling in, and paying, a second writer to keep his projects moving while she played Florence Nightingale. If Gil had been right about an afterlife, she figured a special corner of heaven had to be reserved for such softhearted people.

Fighting back a wave of self-pity with a reminder that leaving her business behind was a cause for celebration rather than tears, Meg prepared a single email for every client in her business address book, whether they had been kind or cruel:

Dear Client,
I've decided to close my business and look for a real job. Thank you for being so patient with me over the last year. It was so kind of you to stick with me through my husband's illness and death and I will be forever grateful.
Sincerely,

Meg Vogel, copywriter

She smiled at the thought of the guilt some people would surely feel when they read it—people like Deirdre Mosswright of Brainwashers Inc. and Adlai Brady of Mind Over Matter, Ltd., who hadn't called her in over a year. Reading it over again, she imagined how small it would make them feel.

Good enough.

She added a subject line: "Meg Vogel closes shop. Thanks for the memories."

With a few clicks of the mouse, she sent it off. She then called the phone company and had her home office and fax lines disconnected.

That was it: how to send thirty years of self-employment packing in less than a quarter hour.

She headed upstairs to her bedroom with Touchdown and Sneak and slept until they woke her up for their dinners, just in time for the six o'clock edition of "Jeopardy."

Meg's best buddy Sandra Slocum called her at eight to see how she was doing.

"Fine," Meg said. "Really, I'm okay. Tomorrow starts a new chapter in my life."

"You're sure? I could come over if you want. Or do you want to have dinner tomorrow night?"

"Sure, we'll have dinner. But not tomorrow. Next week sometime, okay?"

Sandra was a Brainwashers copywriter and she would want to talk shop, Meg knew. Or else she'd want to talk about Gil and cancer and sorrow and death. Meg knew she wouldn't be up for shoptalk for a long time. And she didn't think she'd ever be ready to discuss the rest. She wasn't anywhere near ready to think about it yet.

"Meg, have you talked to anyone about this yet? A counselor, I mean?"

"I'm fine." Meg smiled, an old telemarketers' trick for making yourself sound happy. "Gotta run—bye, now."

She hung up and switched the channel to HGTV. A rerun of "Sarah's House" was on. Now that Gil was gone, there was no one she'd rather spend a little time with than Sarah Richardson and her sidekick Tommy. Maybe, Meg thought, she would update the kitchen once Gil's insurance money arrived. This remodeled farmhouse look could be ideal— her big old sink would fit right in, and she could just paint the grungy oak cabinets white with a splash of yellow.

Presto change-o, a rambling Victorian edges into the twenty-first century. Maybe I'll hire Sarah to direct the transformation.

The first official response to Meg's shutting-it-down email was waiting for her late Monday morning when she finally managed to crawl out of bed. It was from her faithful client Bea, the copy supervisor at Morgan Advertising.

"I hope we can get together SOON and talk about ALL of this," Bea had written. "I don't know quite how to say this, Meg, so I'll just say it: A copywriter is who you ARE. You ARE your business. How can you DO this? What ARE you going to do with the rest of your life??!?!?"

"Beats me," Meg typed in reply. "I guess we'll see."

She hit "send." She had deliberately left unanswered the question that Bea had left unasked: *How can you AFFORD to let your business go?*

The fact that Gil had carried life insurance really wasn't anyone's business, she figured. Nor was the amount of the policy, a cool $250,000. After the last of the medical bills were paid, it wouldn't be enough to escape to a South Seas island. It wouldn't even be enough to take one of those magnificent, $65,000 "trips around the world by private jet" whose brochures popped up periodically in her mailbox, not if she wanted to be able to live in genteel poverty for the rest of her life. But it gave her enough of a cushion that she could spend some time looking for something she liked, even if it only paid minimum wage—perhaps something like the lead Gil's hospice nurse Nora had given her a few days before his death.

The identity issue was a little more problematic. In truth, she hadn't really considered it too much over the last six months. It was difficult to think about who you were as you sat there in a cold gray hospice room counting your husband's breaths, wondering if this one would be his last. But it was true, as Betty Friedan had famously written decades earlier, that a woman needs more than a husband and kids and home. Now her husband was gone forevermore and she didn't even have any kids to show for their marriage, thanks to a lifelong commitment to self that took precedence over even the thought of dirty diapers and day care.

So who was this self she had been so committed to?

"Beats me," she told Sneak, who was watching her from the blue plaid snuggle bed sitting on the right leg of her massive U-shaped desk. "Maybe Nurse Nora's idea of the perfect job will tell the tale."

He didn't respond, having settled down for a nice long nap.

Meg stroked his sleek caramel-colored coat for a few moments before heading for the shower. She had lined up an interview with Nora's referral today at four, and it had been ages since she'd hauled out the ironing board. She didn't know if she'd want the job, but she intended to come home with an offer.

The Hickories Health Center turned out to be pretty tough to find. There was no cheerful sign announcing a happy future for those on the cusp of death, just a plaque with a number on it mounted on a crumbling pillar, behind which stood a deep, dense and mostly naked woodland blanketed in the pristine snow of early January.

Meg had driven past the entryway twice before spotting the number. She turned onto what was little more than a one-lane drive and was surprised to hear the crunch of gravel beneath the tires of her trusty old PT Cruiser. This was supposed to be the most elegant nursing home in southeastern Wisconsin; concrete or even brick or cobblestone would have made more sense.

But then, rounding the fifth bend in the winding drive, she saw her destination, so magnificent that she gasped.

The lines of a midcentury masterpiece, a forest that would have made Bambi feel at home, wisps of smoke from several chimneys promising blazing fires within against the five-below-zero out here—it was exactly what she'd been looking for, the sort of place where she could lose herself in natural beauty and lose her sadness in the sorrows of others.

Just what a counselor might have prescribed, if she'd ever consulted one about the emptiness of her life, and the shallowness of everyone she knew, now that the last of her loved ones had "gone on ahead," as those oh-so-solemn funeral directors insisted on saying.

She drove slowly towards the building, scanning its length in vain for a "Parking" or "Entrance" sign. Finding none, she followed the gravel path straight ahead, driving beneath the lowest layer of building into a cavernous lot. She parked and headed for what appeared to be the only way into the building, copper elevator doors flanked by a pair of stairways, all lit by fabulous Craftsman-style lanterns.

For the first time since Gil's diagnosis, Meg felt that there might be some life for her in the wake of his death.

CHAPTER FOUR

Sadie Sparrow
Monday, January 9

The lonely holidays were finally over. On New Year's Eve day, Dana had marched in with her husband Bill and teenaged daughters Amanda and Hannah for a belated Christmas celebration lasting precisely two hours. All very pleasant, all virtual strangers to Sadie; she hadn't seen Bill or the girls since the Fourth of July, and the time before that had been last Christmas. And the meticulously wrapped presents? Other than a tea-making kit consisting of a fancy mug, a sampling of herbal tea bags, and an electric heating coil—the coil being understandably banned from this place, as a potential fire hazard—the gifts were mainly clothes from an upscale discount store. At least she'd be a well-dressed abandoned old lady.

Next on the calendar was a relentlessly cold and colorless winter. And this, a scene from *Murder under the Magnolias*, was one of the toughest mystery jigsaw puzzles she'd ever tackled.

Her companions were not helping the cause. Eva Foster, her newfound friend and dining-room tablemate since her first night at The Hickories, was wearing a sweater with fringed cuffs; the fringes overturned nearly every piece they touched. And as energetically as Eva was working, that meant dozens of pieces were now backside-up.

Then there was Gladys Baldwin. Her vision was not the best, and she kept mixing up the brown pieces with the burgundies that Sadie had just spent a half hour separating.

The fourth member of their little club, the perpetually sleepy Catherine Peebles, was starting to snore up a storm, drowning out the classical music wafting softly through the Great Room. In another minute or two Sadie was just going to give up and head back to her room for a nap.

"And we know that all things work together for good to them that love God, to them who are the called according to his purpose," she thought. It had been one of her favorite memory verses back in junior high, from the eighth chapter of Romans, and the older and lonelier she became, the more she appreciated it.

Is this part of Your plan, Lord, for me to spend my last days doing jigsaws with a gaggle of old ladies in a nursing home?

Not that she had much choice. The hypocrites in Pine Grove's front office were not at all alarmed when she was diagnosed with congestive heart failure, but they'd responded to her third fall with a stern warning that she begin looking for another place to live; her walker obviously wasn't enough for her anymore, the letter said, and they didn't have room for wheelchairs. Nor, it turned out, did any of the other decent retirement homes in the area. Overnight, a nursing home became her only option.

"Do you need some help, Gladys?" asked Eva in her soft little voice. She spoke kindly, her voice trembling with age and effort, and Sadie smiled at her gratefully.

"No thanks." Gladys' head was bobbing up and down as she tossed brown pieces into the burgundy pile and burgundies amongst the browns. Her flashing nails were lacquered in a red matched to her silk kimono, which she said she and her husband had picked up on a trip to the Far East in 1989.

"Maybe you could work on these yellow and orange pieces," Eva said. "I know I'm having a terrible time telling them apart."

Gladys glared at her. "I should say so," she said. "Look at the mess you're making with your fringes!"

Sadie began entertaining some mighty uncharitable thoughts as Eva righted the pieces she'd upended. *You look like a fat old walrus, Gladys Baldwin!*

She hated herself for thinking such things even as she stole a critical glance at Gladys' silly new wig, a near-black number in a style reminiscent of Laura Petrie's 'do on the old Dick Van Dyke show.

Then, suddenly enough to startle her companions, Gladys cried, "Aha! Here we go!"

She shoved a dark brown piece into a sea of deep plum—possibly the shadow cast by the birdbath in the center of the picture—and smiled triumphantly. "Got one!"

Sadie and Eva leaned forward in their wheelchairs to admire Gladys' work. Except the piece didn't really fit. They glanced at each other conspiratorially. They'd take care of it later, after Gladys had left for her semi-weekly shower. And later, maybe tonight or tomorrow, it would be a fun little story to share with dear old Charles Chapelle. It would make him chuckle, which would in turn make her feel like she'd accomplished something worthwhile.

And so it went, with Sadie and Eva making slow progress while Gladys undid Sadie's careful sorting and put pieces where they didn't belong. At one point, Gladys fell into one of her spells where she didn't have a clue where she was or even who she was. But this was one recurrent failing that Sadie and Eva tried hard to ignore; "there but for the grace of God go I," was their unspoken motto, and they both knew very well that they could easily be the next one to fall into a temporary or permanent fog.

Sadie paused from the puzzle to rest her eyes now and then, taking in her surroundings once again. It was the best tonic she'd found yet for the Old Lady Blues. While she'd never been crazy about the Arts and Crafts style, being more of a Queen Anne woman personally, she loved this room's toasty woods and jewel-toned rugs. And oh, the leaded-glass windows lining the room, each one adorned with a rectangle of stained glass in a simple floral pattern—so beautiful!

She also appreciated the golden glow washing over the room on even the dreariest days. The head of the Maintenance department had explained this apparent magic to her last week: clever over-soffit fixtures and warm incandescents everywhere—no fluorescent lights, at least not in the resident areas.

But to Sadie, the most beautiful thing about this enormous room was the freestanding wall that divided it in two, accented on each side by a hand-painted mural, a soft garden scene in corals and peaches and golds. The wall was maybe fifteen or twenty feet wide, and it allowed The Hickories to host events like bingo, sing-alongs, and word games on this side without shutting out or disturbing those who wanted to read or doze or chat with visitors in front of the mammoth stone fireplace on the other side.

It was almost three o'clock and most of the residents were off doing their own thing, leaving Sadie and her friends alone for the time being. There wasn't even a staff member in sight; they had a way of vanishing until they somehow realized you wanted them. If it hadn't been for all the wheelchairs, Sadie might have been able to convince herself she was a luxury-hotel guest back at the turn of the last century.

"Well, lookie here!" Gladys spoke so loudly that she woke Catherine. She snapped down a puzzle piece with authority. "Perfect fit."

"Oh, my." Sadie wondered how Gladys could fail to see that the piece didn't fit at all.

"That piece is brown," said a fifth voice, startling them all. "It doesn't go there."

They looked up to see a youngish woman with short dark hair standing between Sadie's and Eva's chairs. "If you don't mind my saying so," she added.

"Oh, no," the ladies murmured politely, taking the visitor in.

Sadie approved: the woman had a sprinkling of freckles under narrow eyes, and she was wearing a neat black wool pantsuit over a crisp white blouse.

"I'm looking for Lucy Stiles," the woman continued. And, when they didn't respond instantly, "The Activities Director, you know."

"Of course we know, dear," said Eva. "There's only one Lucy working here, that we know of. You just surprised us."

"Are you the new Activities girl?" Sadie asked, thinking she looked a little light to be wheeling around some of the men who lived in this place. She took a closer look and decided this was no girl—she was fifty if she was a day.

"I hope to be," the woman said. "My name's Meg Vogel."

"Nice to meet you, Meg. I'm Eva Foster, and these are my friends—"

"Do you play bridge, dear?" Gladys asked. "It's so boring, living with people without the brains to play bridge."

"Not so fast, ladies," Meg laughed. "I don't have the job yet!"

"Oh, you'll get the job," Eva assured her. "Now, as I was saying, these are my friends Gladys Baldwin, Sadie Sparrow, and Catherine Peebles—oh look, everyone, Catherine's awake—and you'll find us here nearly every day working on our jigsaws."

"Good for you," Meg said. "Good to keep the mind active."

"So they say." It was Catherine this time, to the puzzlers' surprise. She smiled up at Meg, her face round and smooth beneath her perfectly white, perfectly executed Dutch boy hairstyle. "Although some of us feel it's better to let the mind rest."

"The theory being," Sadie added, "that we've each got eighty or ninety years of wisdom packed into our brains, but the librarian who's charged with retrieving it is not as nimble as she used to be."

Which apparently reminded Eva of another Hickories highlight. "Will you be running book group for us tomorrow?"

"Really, I have no idea what will happen," Meg said. "And I think the job I'm applying for will mainly be about writing."

"Biographies?" Sadie asked, recalling that Dana had offered this as something she'd enjoy, to try to make moving here a little more palatable. At the time it had just irritated her, but maybe it would turn out to be fun after all.

"Well, something like that," Meg said. "But I probably shouldn't be saying anything."

"That's okay, honey," said Eva, ever the comforter. "You'll find that we know nearly everything that goes on around here."

"They think we can't hear," Gladys hissed, glancing back over her shoulder to make sure no one was eavesdropping. "But we can. We hear everything, and there are some strange things happening in this place. Not that we'll ever figure it out—in real life, mysteries are never solved. But I'm telling you, we don't miss much."

Gladys' words were proved true just minutes later as Sadie made her way back to her room to take a little nap before dinner. She'd hitched a ride with an aide most of the way but had to navigate the last hallway herself—something she was happy to do, since it gave her the chance to pause and look out at the woods, where someone had gone to a lot of bother to light the craggiest old shagbarks in a display that made her think of Camelot and Merlin and the young Arthur. She took her time traveling the hall, remembering how, later in life, Arthur had wished to fly away from the pain of betrayal.

Sadie understood that all too well.

She paused again at the end of the hallway to scan the feeders for birds, but there were no signs of any at this hour. No signs of life out there at all, in fact.

But there, just beyond the largest suet feeder, was an unusual sight—a tree, gnarled and bowed and dwarfed by its neighbors, its lowest branches dipping almost to the ground as if to help forest creatures too old and weak to scramble up the towering shagbarks.

Swing low, sweet chariot, coming for to carry me home ...

Funny that she'd never noticed this tree before. Maybe it was a trick of the light that made it stand out so now.

She rolled ahead a few feet and made the right turn into the North Wing.

She was disappointed to see that Charles Chapelle's door was still closed, just as it had been for more than a week. She missed him, as well as that sweet granddaughter of his, and so far she hadn't been able to find out what was going on. "Hippa," the nurses kept responding to her inquiries, as if that explained anything.

I looked over Jordan and what did I see, coming for to carry me home?

But real life didn't happen on this earth, or so she'd always been taught. It happened in heaven, after all this pain and drudgery had finally come to an end.

A band of angels coming after me, coming for to carry me home.

She hadn't thought about that song for some time, hadn't understood it when she'd first heard it as a child. But she understood it now.

If you get there before I do, coming for to carry me home ...

She understood the longing behind the words, so much so that it almost broke her heart.

Tell all my friends I'm coming, too, coming for to carry me home.

So much so that—

What was that?

Someone was moaning, that's what it was. Sadie wheeled herself forward towards the first door on her right, the door to the room of a neighbor she'd somehow never met.

She knocked. Hearing nothing but another moan, she pushed the door open and wheeled herself into the dark space beyond.

CHAPTER FIVE

Elise Chapelle
Monday, January 9

Papi slept soundly until almost four-thirty that afternoon, setting a new napping record for himself. When he finally opened his eyes, he blinked hard a half dozen times and looked straight at Elise without seeming to see her. It was another first in this dreadful saga she was enduring, helplessly watching as her beloved grandfather slipped away towards eternity.

She stroked his hand gently. "I'm here, Papi. Can you see me?"

He did not respond.

This was totally unacceptable. The good-for-nothing nursing-home physician had upped Papi's arthritis pain meds until he did little more than sleep. He had gone three whole days without uttering a word to her, and now he seemed to be having trouble with his vision. This was no way to live.

"Papi, please!"

He focused on her then, with apparent effort. But he smiled, too, and spoke, although so softly that she had to lean in to hear him. "Elise, my best girl." That was all, but it was the most he'd said since Friday, and her heart rejoiced.

"I'm here, Papi. How are you feeling?"

He'd lost his focus again, and was struggling to regain it.

"Tired," he said finally. "Time to go home."

She felt a chill, nausea, and a sob of despair rising, all at once.

"It's just the meds, Papi, just the meds. Any pain?"

"No, no pain."

And then he fell asleep again.

That settled it; she would call his old doctor tonight and demand a better solution. There had to be something else that could be done for him.

There just had to be.

CHAPTER SIX

Meg Vogel
Monday, January 9

Sitting in the surprisingly cramped Activities office
amidst balloons, worn song books, and piles of childish
drawings of people, plants, and pets, Meg found herself
longing to be offered the job. Lucy Stiles, the Activities
Director, was nothing like the self-important East Coast
corporate types she'd worked with what seemed like a
lifetime ago, nothing like those painfully hip agency
creatives who had usually looked right through you.

Fifty-something and slightly pudgy, with faded red hair
in long, untidy waves, Lucy seemed like an old friend to
Meg practically from the start. Like Meg, she'd even been
widowed not long ago and seemed to understand Meg's
desire to just chuck the past and pour her heart into people
who might really need her.

Lucy also seemed obsessed with Meg's writing
experience, although it took her long enough to cut to the
chase.

"That's why I called you when your résumé came in,
even though you haven't worked with the elderly," Lucy
said, a good half hour into their interview. "The Hickories'
owner had this idea ages ago of hiring a staff biographer to
write up the life stories of every resident who's capable of
telling it. Isn't that brilliant? But until your résumé landed

on my desk, I hadn't heard from anyone with a writing background."

"What an interesting idea," Meg said, genuinely intrigued. "Tell me about it."

"Well, Mr. Donovan—he's the owner of this place, although we hardly ever see him since he lives in Hawaii— he's been worried about all the residents who never have any visitors." Lucy shook her head. "It's just amazing. Even when their kids live a mile or two away, some of them just can't be bothered. They may take care of the finances, but they're too busy to give their parents the one thing they really need."

"That's so sad," Meg said, her heart aching as she thought of the sweet women she'd just met at the jigsaw table. "How can kids be so cruel?"

"I can't understand it myself." Lucy frowned for a moment before her apparently irrepressible smile popped back into place. "Anyway, Mr. Donovan's idea was to hire someone whose primary responsibility would be spending time with our residents, asking them questions, listening to their responses, and then writing up their stories."

"It really *is* a great idea," Meg said. "And then we could maybe add photos from their younger days and publish the stories somehow—online, or in mini brochures, or maybe entire books . . ."

"Exactly! And in the process, maybe we can help them make sense out of their lives. You know, clarify their purposes."

Meg studied the nearest books on the monstrous wooden desk between them—mostly tomes on activity therapy, it seemed—and nodded, not knowing how else to respond. She personally couldn't imagine what purpose there could be to the suffering that these residents were enduring, and whose purpose it would be, but it didn't seem like a good time to say so.

"So what do you think?"

Meg felt exposed. "Um . . . about what? Their purpose?"

Lucy laughed. "Well, yes, I *would* like to know your thoughts about that, but for the moment I'd just like to know if you want the job. Knowing that you'll have all the other responsibilities I mentioned, too, from running bingo to feeding those who need help."

Meg smiled back, relieved that she wasn't going to have to answer the unanswerable. At least not yet.

"Of course I want the job. When can I start?"

Meg drove home from The Hickories, now officially a nursing home Activities Assistant. She would be earning $10.50 an hour instead of the $75 she had charged as a copywriter, and she faced a fifteen-minute commute each morning instead of nine steps from kitchen to home office. But she would be paying just $200 a month towards her one-person healthcare coverage from now on instead of $2,000 for her own high-deductible policy and Gil's State of Wisconsin high-risk-pool coverage. And she would be banking some paid vacation time, so—if she ever had anywhere to go or anyone to go with—eventually she'd be able to check out some sights more enticing than the third room on the left in the local hospice.

But if she reflected on it too much, she longed to be back there once again, spending hour after hour watching Gil breathe.

She diverted the thought by focusing instead on the fact that the hospice was where she'd first considered making a career change, just days before his death.

Gil's gloomy room hadn't been the sort of place one spent time considering the future. It was decorated with hospital-issue linen cabinets and outlandish silk flower arrangements and samplers embroidered with dear pictures and solemn sayings, presumably Bible verses: "My grace is sufficient," one said. "Absent from the body, present with the Lord," said another. Nothing very comforting in them that Meg could identify, but then she was far from religious. She'd had enough of churches and Sunday school as a kid to last a lifetime and then some, and she had no intention of starting it up again now.

She had been mulling this over when Nurse Nora had come in to check Gil out, jot down his vitals, and verify that his IV pain-med dispenser was just so.

"It won't be long now, Meg." Nora's tone was almost apologetic, as if she were a waitress who was sorry for how long it was taking the food to arrive. "Another day or two, maybe."

Meg appreciated Nora putting a deadline of sorts on their ordeal. Everyone else had refused to, but not Nora, whose predictions about each stage of this horror had been pretty much right on.

"What will you do going forward?" she asked Meg. "Pick up your business again?"

If anyone else had asked, Meg might have been appalled at the intrusion. But Nora had become her friend over the last few weeks, so she simply spoke the truth.

"No, I think I'll close it down, find something different to do."

Nora smoothed the sheets over Gil's incredible shrinking body. "Have you ever thought about going to work for a nursing home? Helping out the old folk?"

Meg stared in amazement. "Actually, I have. How did you know?"

Nora looked up at her, clearly startled. "I didn't know," she said. "But I've seen you with Mrs. Carter next door—you're a natural. And I just happen to know about an opening where my friend Char works. It may not pay much but it's a fantastic place—Char just adores it. Ever hear of The Hickories?"

Meg hadn't, but Nora's enthusiasm was enough to pique her interest. She'd emailed her résumé to The Hickories on New Year's Day, right after meeting with the funeral director. It was a new year and a new life and she hadn't seen any point in procrastinating.

Now, less than two weeks later, the job was hers, and she was feeling fairly excited about it as she turned into the driveway leading to what had been one of old Brookfield's premier homes when it was erected over a century ago, long before the little city had become a suburb of Milwaukee. It was the house she'd lived in her entire life, from infancy through marriage, and now the unfamiliar state of widowhood, and she planned to die there as well.

The critters got the news first. Touchdown was more interested in when supper would be served, but Meg made him sit and listen with the always-attentive Sneak.

"And here's the really great part," she said, pulling the basset's ears up into the goofy topknot that always made her laugh. "Once I settle in, you guys might get to come to work with me. Not every day, of course, but on quieter days. You'll be part of the entertainment!"

Unimpressed, Sneak enjoyed a jaw-shattering yawn before slinking off to the dining-room-turned-office. But Touchdown danced around gaily, no doubt because of the elation in her voice, although she liked to pretend that he understood.

He continued rejoicing his way into the kitchen, where she prepared their suppers and poured herself a glass from a bottle of Merlot that Sandra had brought over months ago in an attempt to cheer Meg up. The scheme had failed, with Meg taking off for the hospice just twenty minutes into the visit. Now she was glad she'd saved the wine; it was five star and deserved to accompany a celebration rather than a death watch.

Except it wasn't much of a celebration, she had to admit as the three of them snuggled on her worn leather loveseat in the little TV room.

The realization that there was no one she absolutely had to call with the news of her new job filled Meg with sadness. But it also reminded her of how much worse she'd felt the last year or so, before Gil had gone into the hospice, when a friend would drop by to share good news with him. More than once she'd held her breath, expecting him to at least react indifferently. But he never did, instead responding with joy, as if he would be around to see whatever supreme milestone the visitor was celebrating—a book to be published or exhibit to open or baby to be born or whatever other happiness was consuming the friend's life at the moment.

"He really meant it," she told Touchdown. "Your daddy was really happy for other people."

Touchdown wagged the tip of his tail, the houndly equivalent of a sad smile.

Whereupon she puddled into the first good cry she'd had since they'd received Gil's death sentence.

CHAPTER SEVEN

Sadie Sparrow
Monday, January 9

H ello? Anyone home? Can I help you?"
It took a few moments for Sadie's eyes to become accustomed to the dim light in her neighbor's room; the drapes were closed against the courtyard lights. But by the glow of the nightlight above the bed, she could just make out a figure lying beneath tented-up bedclothes.

"Help me."

Sadie rolled up to the bed. It was occupied, she could now see, by a woman lying on her back with her hands folded neatly on her chest in coffin-ready pose.

"I'll help you," Sadie said, reaching out to touch the woman's hands. "What can I do for you?"

"Pain," the woman whispered. "Pills, please."

"Okay, dear, let me see what I can do. I'm your neighbor, Sadie, so I don't have any pills myself, but I'll find someone who does."

"Sadie," the woman said. "My Sadie."

"Yes, I guess I'm your Sadie. And what's your name?"

"Beulah Bannister." Her voice sounded a little stronger already. "I'm ninety-three."

"My goodness! And what a lovely name, my dear. It reminds me of one of my favorite songs. Let's just find your call light and then I'll go look for—oh, hello!"

The room was suddenly washed in light as a tired-looking woman with sad eyes and kinky, white-streaked blonde hair pushed her way through the door carrying several large bags. She dropped them on the table at the window wall and, ignoring Sadie, made a beeline for Beulah.

"Mom, it's me," the woman said gently, pulling off her red ski jacket and tossing it on the nearest chair. "How are you today?"

"I hurt," Beulah said. "Sadie's going for help."

They introduced themselves to each other, Sadie and the daughter, whose name turned out to be Bunny, and then Sadie got the scoop: how Bunny had stopped in on her way home from work last Tuesday to find her mother lying in a heap on the bathroom floor, incoherent, and how after what seemed like an eternity they found themselves in the emergency room with a doctor who was absolutely livid, having discovered that both of Beulah's legs were broken.

"It was horrifying." Bunny was speaking in a voice as soft as Eva's, and it made her story all the more chilling. "Just horrifying. And the worst part of it was that he said it could have been a case of abuse. In fact, he called the Administrator here and read him the riot act, right in front of us."

"Do you think it *was* abuse?" Sadie asked, appalled at the very idea. "From someone who works here?"

"Well, that was certainly the ER doctor's thought. But the orthopedist said it was impossible to tell from the type of break. I forget the terms he used, but the x-rays apparently reveal nothing about how it happened. And naturally, the staff on duty that day, and even the night before, deny having anything to do with it."

"Naturally."

"Plus Mom doesn't remember anything about it, so we have no way of knowing what happened, right Mom? She may just have fallen, they said. She can't walk without a walker anymore, but she may have forgotten that. You know how it is when you're sleeping and you wake up and it takes you a few moments to remember something awful? Well, she may have managed the few steps to the bathroom and then—well, I can't even think about it." She shook her head as if to banish the obvious image.

"But you're okay now, Mom, right?" Bunny stroked her mother's cheek lovingly, then punched the button on the call light. "We just need to get you some of that good pain medicine."

Beulah was a slip of a thing, Sadie saw. Her face was a field of washed-out freckles under faded brown eyes and her thinning hair was short and white and straight as a stick.

"Thanks for being here," Bunny said. "It's good to know that Mom has a kind neighbor."

"I'll keep an eye on her." Sadie was almost breathless at the idea that a staff member—an aide or nurse or even a housekeeper—might have deliberately hurt a resident. She started rolling herself towards the door, then paused. "If this happened as you suggest, Bunny, with your mother getting up to go to the bathroom, I wonder how she got around those side rails on her bed? You'd think they would've been enough of a hindrance to wake her up, wouldn't you?"

"There were no side rails then," Bunny said. "Just grab bars. We'd asked for the full rails, but Big Brother said no. Apparently the State is so afraid of even a hint of restraint that you don't get bed rails until you fall and hurt yourself without them. So now we've got them, two broken legs too late."

The Hickories' head cook outdid herself that night, serving up chicken cordon bleu, buttered new potatoes, and green beans, all cooked to melt-in-your-mouth texture for those who had some trouble chewing. And for dessert, out-of-this-world peach pie à la mode.

Sadie practically licked her plate clean, at least in part because she wasn't paying much attention. She was too troubled by all she'd heard from Bunny, and she was busy planning her strategy for learning the truth.

After dinner, Sadie sat for a while before the fire in the Great Room, fleshing out the plan she would put into motion that very night to determine which second-shifters were candidates as abusers. Not that she knew when it had happened, or who'd been on duty, but it would be a start.

"How about something for my back?" she would ask the nurse on duty tonight. Then, lying amidst fresh white sheets and pillows so plump that she really felt very comfortable, she would put on her best grimace and wait.

It was so warm here at the fire, and she'd missed her afternoon nap, and the thought of her cozy bed was making Sadie very sleepy.

Would this night nurse hesitate a little too long? Would she take pleasure in letting her patient suffer?

So warm. So sleepy.

Char was the nurse's name. Was torment her game? Sure, she seemed nice, but who really knew her?

She was gazing down at Sadie now with unnaturally deep blue eyes. "We'll see," she was saying, using a plastic spoon to stir two white tablets into a tiny plastic cup containing applesauce. "But first, you have to take these."

Sadie parted her lips to accept the mixture and swallowed obediently, then tried again.

"Now?" she asked, praying silently for the strength to keep up the act as sleep threatened to overtake her. "A pain pill?"

Or was she already asleep?

Char was staring at Sadie now. She was a tall woman, and painfully thin, with spiky blonde hair and sharp features.

"Tell you what," she said, chuckling. "Let's not and say we did, okay?"

Sadie's heart leapt; her suspicions were confirmed. Miss Marple had nothing on her!

Char wasn't finished. "Guess your God will have to help you out of this one, eh, old girl? You know, the one who made those pathetic little bones of yours?"

Sadie glanced at her call button, its cord wrapped casually around the hand rail at her side.

"Don't bother," *Char said, untying the cord and tossing the call button to the floor.* "I'm all you've got until morning. Or maybe longer. Maybe I'll volunteer for a double shift."

Sadie Sparrow, detective extraordinaire! If only she had this on tape!

"Bet you're sorry now that you have a private room, aren't you, old girl? Because it's your word against mine, and they're used to hearing imaginary complaints from you old birds."

Char laughed as she turned to her drug cart to record her work.

"Let's see," *she said, retrieving a packet from the second drawer and holding it up so Sadie could see it.* "A pain pill was what you asked for, right? And a pain pill is precisely what will disappear from this drawer." *She cackled, dropping the packet into the pocket of her light blue scrub top before pushing her cart back out into the hall.*

"Ta-ta. If you need anything, do use your call light!"

Sadie woke with a start, her heart pounding, only to find herself just where she'd parked after dinner, before the roaring fire in the Great Room. What a dream! She put a hand to her chest to steady herself. Her heart was pounding.

After waiting for a few minutes to regain her composure, she headed back to her room, now even more determined to put her plan into action.

But of course it didn't turn out anything like her dream. When she asked for some pain relief, Char immediately offered Sadie two Tylenol PMs and a call to the doctor if she needed something stronger.

Oddly disappointed—how could she be sorry about a nurse's kindness?—Sadie drifted off into a dreamless sleep.

CHAPTER EIGHT

Elise Chapelle
Monday, January 9

It was almost ten o'clock when Dr. Maglio returned Elise's call. She felt a little guilty when she heard the weariness in his voice; he was not young himself, and if the time of this call was any indication, he was working some pretty long hours.

"Always have," he said when she mentioned it. "I'd be a pretty poor excuse for a doctor if I let my patients suffer while I saw to my own comforts. Now, what can I do for you, Elise? Is it about your Papi?"

She told him all about this latest trial, which seemed to her to be primarily the result of these awful medications.

"What're they giving him?"

She had written it down carefully, asking the evening nurse to tell her exactly the dosages and timing, and now she read every last detail to Dr. Maglio.

"My goodness, Elise, that's quite a cocktail! What was that doctor's name? Buck something? I'll call her first thing tomorrow and have a little talk with her, okay? Now, don't cry, sweetheart. We'll have him back in fighting shape in no time at all."

Relieved, Elise hung up and thanked the Lord for the good doctor. But her relief didn't last; it took her approximately two minutes to remember that sooner or later there'd be other worries, other phone calls, and that

Papi was most likely going to be heading Home himself in the not-too-distant future.

She knew she should be happy for him, but she was—she admitted it—too lonely to manage it.

She headed upstairs to get ready for bed and took a good look at herself in the bathroom mirror. She'd had a number of admirers tell her over the years that she was a natural beauty; she was tall and willowy, with shoulder-length brown hair falling in thick waves, flawless ivory skin, and almond-shaped eyes in an arresting green. She wouldn't personally call it beauty, but then she knew she was far from scary looking.

"You're going to have to make an effort," she told her reflection, a habit that she'd taken up since moving Papi to The Hickories. "You're going to have to get yourself a new life once he's gone."

Face washed, teeth brushed, and dressed in her favorite flannel pajamas, she sat down at the desk in her bedroom and fished stationery and pen out of the top drawer. The blotter was worn, but it had done its job, keeping the creamy desktop unblemished for more than two decades. The desk was French provincial in style, old fashioned even when Mamie had helped her choose it for her tenth birthday. But fashion had never been a big concern around the Chapelle household. And this style had made little Elise feel connected to her mother, the mother who'd given birth to her and taken off for Paris and had never bothered returning, leaving Papi and Mamie to raise her right here at Fleur de Lis on West Bluemound Road.

Elise still wrote her letters to her mother in longhand, taking care with her penmanship because Mamie had taught her to do so.

Dear Helene,

She wrote the words as if they were close friends. It still felt odd to her, but her mother was thoroughly modern and thoroughly artsy and had insisted from the start that Elise call her by her first name.

Just thought you should know that your father is not doing so well. He's still at The Hickories, but he's been in so much pain with his arthritis that the doctor has doped him up. But I talked with Dr. Maglio tonight—do you remember him? He's been Papi's doctor as long as I can remember, and was Mamie's, too. He's going to call over there tomorrow morning to get things straightened out. That is my prayer, at any rate.

She wondered if her mother ever prayed, if she had any relationship with the Lord, if she'd ever repented of anything—say, for instance, of having abandoned her only child. At least, Elise assumed she was the only child; she hadn't heard about any others, but really she wouldn't put anything past Helene.

I hope that this note finds you well, and that you have been able to sell some of your watercolors. We are grateful for the landscape you sent us for Christmas in 2005—it's just lovely. I intend to hang it above my bed as soon as things calm down for Papi.
Love from your daughter,
Elise

"Love from your daughter." Elise knew it was a little unkind to spell their relationship out, as if Helene would be clueless without the reminder, but she couldn't help herself. She would never forget the fact that she had been forsaken; why should her mother get to?

Addressing the envelope to Helene's Rue Baillet apartment and affixing three Forever stamps to it, Elise crawled into bed and fell asleep almost instantly.

CHAPTER NINE

Meg Vogel
Monday, January 9

Meg finally dried her tears, poured herself another glass of wine, and did some serious channel surfing. Finding nothing worth watching, she decided to write out some starter questions for her biography interviews—maybe that would get her mind off her unhappiness.

It worked for about a quarter hour. But the events of the recent past were vying for her attention, making it difficult to stay focused on the future. She finally gave up. Maybe she'd look over the sign-in book from Gil's funeral. There'd been so many people there, most of them strangers to her, or so it seemed; maybe seeing the names would help her get her bearings.

The book was in the big box that the funeral home had sent home with her, still sitting there on the coffee table. She opened it with some trepidation.

With good reason, it turned out: underneath the funeral book was a collection of Gil's possessions from the hospice—toothbrush and paste, a comb whose slightly mangled teeth had once fallen prey to Touchdown, a Bible and a worn spiral notebook with a photo of a craggy wooden gate in a stone wall on the cover. There were Get Well cards brought by Gil's many friends, too, as well as the pajamas and robe that he'd never worn there, apparently finding that putting on a hospital gown required less effort.

Almost sixty years of life, Meg thought sadly, and all he'd needed in the last few weeks of it fit neatly into one box that wouldn't have contained Touchdown's toy collection.

How the funeral home had ended up with this stuff, Meg didn't know, but as much as seeing these things now hurt her, she was grateful that she hadn't been forced to return to that awful room at the hospice to clean it out.

She flipped through the funeral book. Each page contained six names and addresses, and (she counted carefully) almost twenty of them had been filled. Amazing, really—well over one hundred people paying their last respects.

She took a closer look and was ashamed to see that she recognized very few of the names, beyond those of her own friends and a handful of couples they'd socialized with over the years. Gil had probably known some of these people from his last job, but she suspected that most were from this church he'd started going to a few months into his illness.

Sheer foolishness.

Granted, they'd been a faithful group, calling and writing and visiting both here at the house and at the hospice. They'd made him happy, but towards the end he was so exhausted that Nurse Nora had limited visitors, first to five a day, then two, and finally she'd banned them totally.

Meg wondered if she was expected to write to all these people to thank them for showing up at the funeral.

The very thought of it was so overwhelming that she repacked the box and tucked it in the corner. She'd worry about it tomorrow, like Scarlett O'Hara.

What she needed was some comfort reading. She headed upstairs to her bedroom and made a beeline for the bookshelves lining the north wall. They were packed with favorites from every era of her life, including her childhood and teen years—extensive collections of classic Nancy

Drew, Judy Bolton, and Trixie Belden books, seven Black Stallions, a selection of romances by Rosamond du Jardin and Gwen Bristow, and an entire shelf devoted to the early novels of Kathleen Thompson Norris, bestselling female writer of the first half of the twentieth century.

All were tempting, but right now she needed the best, and that meant Norris. Maybe *The Heart of Rachel.* She flipped through the nearly century-old book, letting its dusty scent take her back to the day she'd first discovered it on her mother's bedside table. She'd been twelve or thirteen, and it had been pouring all day—she distinctly remembered the sound of unrelenting rain on the roof as she curled up on her mother's bed with this very volume, and read the first words: "The day had opened so brightly, in such a welcome wave of April sunshine, that by mid-afternoon there were two hundred players scattered over the links . . ."

She hurried through her nighttime toilette and climbed into bed with Touchdown and Sneak. She made it all the way to page fifteen before plunging into sleep.

CHAPTER TEN

Sadie Sparrow
Wednesday, January 11

Sadie ran into Elise Chapelle that morning on her way down to the dining room. They spoke only briefly, but the girl seemed happier than she had the last time they'd met. She said something about the doctor and planned adjustments to her grandfather's medication—great news, she assured Sadie.

To celebrate, Sadie ate a hearty breakfast of oatmeal and cinnamon toast, well-buttered and broiled until it had caramelized; really, the food was so good here that she was going to have to start watching her waistline. She then returned to her post at the Great Room fireplace to give some more thought to Beulah's story and what she could do about it. Try as she might, she couldn't think of anything beyond tricking an aide or nurse into being mean to her. But that wouldn't really be proof, unless she managed to bring out the sadist in one, and even then—

"There you are, Sadie Sparrow!"

Sadie was surprised to see the Activities applicant from Monday afternoon making her way across the hardwood floor and then settling herself on the hearth at Sadie's feet. The woman was wearing a chocolate-colored wool pantsuit and a creamy blouse today; Sadie felt a pang of sorrow that she would never again look that pretty in anything.

"So Sadie," the woman—Meg, that was her name!—was saying, "I got the job! And I'll be working on a lot of activities here, but there's a special assignment that Lucy has given me, and I'm hoping you'll help me out with it."

As a resident with a growing reputation for having most of her marbles, Sadie was already getting used to being called on by the staff. She supposed she should be flattered, but it was usually followed by a request for help where none was really needed—picking the bingo numbers or watching someone decorate a Christmas tree or giving an opinion on a song selection for the next in-house church service. These requests were condescending, somehow; they made her feel like a five-year-old being asked to help Mommy bake a cake by tasting the frosting.

But the askers all meant well, she knew, so she smiled encouragingly at Meg.

"I was a professional writer in my old life," she was saying, "and I've been asked to interview some of the residents and write up their biographies. Lucy suggested that I start with you. It may not be easy, since it's totally new territory for all of us, but I think it'll be fun, and you can be my prototype. What do you think?"

Sadie was so surprised that she forgot all about the Beulah puzzle.

"You know, I think I'd really love to do that," she said. "I don't think I've ever been a prototype for anything."

Meg laughed. "Great! We'll muddle through it together, then."

They made a date for their first interview on Friday afternoon, and Meg gave her a list of starter questions to think through in the meantime.

Ten minutes later, Gladys wheeled herself up to the fireplace, almost crashing her wheelchair into Sadie's in her eagerness to see what Sadie was looking at.

"What's that?" she demanded. "Doctor bill?"

Sadie looked up reluctantly from the list of questions Meg had given her. "No, it's for a project that the new girl is working on. I'm sure she'll be talking to you about it, too, but maybe I shouldn't say any more right now."

Gladys sniffed. "It's about their Spring Fling party, I'll betcha. Well, they can keep their parties, as far as I'm concerned. Waste of time and money."

"But I hear you never miss them, Gladys," Sadie chuckled. "They say you're always the first one there and the last to leave."

"They should spend that money on the food. Food's terrible here, just terrible. Instead of parties they should get someone who knows how to cook."

Meg's questions were definitely intriguing.

That night after dinner—even though Gladys managed to find fault with the carrots and onions, it had been a delicious meal of impossibly tender pot roast and cornbread muffins—Sadie wheeled herself to the built-in desk in her room, flipped on the lamp, and pulled her best pen and her old leather-bound notebook out of the drawer. No notes were needed for the "who, what, where and when" queries of "Part One, The Basics"; but "Part Two, Beyond the Basics" included a number of questions deserving some thought, and Sadie didn't want to attempt to answer them off-the-cuff. Someone—okay, her daughter Dana Sparrow Maxwell, to be precise—might one day read Meg's report, and it might be Sadie's last opportunity to impact a life that had gone tearing down the wrong path, the path to what Sadie called "dead-end careerdom."

The first of these questions was pretty broad. "Why do you live here now?"

Sadie started writing out the answers in her arthritic hand.

1. *Because I have heart failure and need help. Can't even safely transfer into bed or onto the toilet on my own and that means the retirement home won't have me anymore.*
2. *Because living with my daughter was not an option. Her plate is plenty full without adding a helpless old mother to her duties.*

She sat back and thought for a moment. *Does that sound pathetic?* Dana did not suffer whiners gladly. Imagining the eye rolling these thoughts would provoke, Sadie crossed out her second point and substituted a more positive answer:

2. *Because I wanted to live with people my own age, with the same values and experiences and hope for the future.*

She liked that. It was true, Dana would like it, and it might lead to an interesting conversation with Meg.

3. *Because it's a beautiful facility with a dedicated staff and my daughter made sure the bill will be paid to make up for otherwise ignoring me.*

Definitely whiney! Sadie put a period after "staff" and crossed out the rest, sighing. It was pathetic that she was framing her answers in order to avoid irritating her so-often-irritable daughter—especially since said daughter would most likely not see her answers until she was cleaning out this room after the funeral (an event which Dana would probably greet with both relief and more irritation, since it would no doubt interfere with some important business meeting).

Still, Sadie's goal here was to plant seeds with eternal impact, and that meant she'd have to set aside all her personal, earthly complaints. She wanted Dana to put down the biography of Sadie Sparrow thinking, "What a woman! I want to be just like her, and spend all eternity with her! How can I be sure of it?"

Sadie laughed. Okay, then, she'd settle for a "Gee, she wasn't nearly as stupid as I thought. Maybe there's something to this eternity business after all . . ."

That reminded her of a favorite song, and she started singing it in her wobbly old voice: "Softly and tenderly Jesus is calling, calling for you and for me."

She looked over the rest of Meg's questions and decided to call it a night. She was tired, and she still had some time to frame her answers before their meeting on Friday. She tidied up the desk and closed her eyes, letting her thoughts drift heavenward on the wings of the old hymn.

"Earnestly, tenderly, Jesus is calling, calling 'O sinner, come home.'"

The best rendition of "Softly and Tenderly" she'd ever heard was Tennessee Ernie Ford's. He had gone on ahead long ago, she knew, not too long after Ed.

"Oh, for the wonderful love He has promised, promised for you, and for me."

She wondered if they had met, maybe had even sung some hymns together. Ed had always been a big fan of Tennessee Ernie's deep-as-the-ocean bass.

"Though we have sinned, He has mercy and pardon— pardon for you and for me."

Thinking of Ed and Tennessee together was surprisingly comforting. And one day, if the Lord would have her, she would join them.

Which reminded her of another old favorite of Ed's.

"Just over in the glory land," she sang, scrunching up her face just like a Spirit-led gospel singer, "I'll join the happy angel band. Just over in the glory land!"

She was smiling now, almost giddy at the idea of heaven and glory and seeing Ed again.

But oh, in the meantime, it was good to be alive!

CHAPTER ELEVEN

Elise Chapelle
Thursday, January 12

Elise was on the joyful upswing of her life's roller coaster. She knew a precipitous plunge was awaiting around the next bend, but for the moment she didn't care: just a couple days off the hard stuff, and Papi was already back to his usual self.

"I'm going to keep a closer eye on your medications in the future," she promised as she wheeled him into the North Sitting Room just down the hall from his room. "I spent some time looking this drug issue up on the internet last night, and it's apparently rampant among older Americans. But I'm forewarned now. I will *not* let this happen again!"

"It really wasn't so terrible, my dear," Papi said. "After all—a little closer to the fire, please?—after all, I've been sleeping like a rock, and you always complained about my not getting enough sleep."

She grinned, overjoyed to see the mischief in his eyes again.

"Still," she said. "I was worried sick, if you must know."

"You mustn't worry. Seriously. 'Let not your heart be troubled, neither let it be afraid.'"

They shared a smile.

"I hope my room in the kingdom is just like this one." Papi looked around, his mouth puckered in approval. "It's all I need—a nice fire, soft furniture, a little lamp for reading—"

"No need for the lamp. We'll need no candle, for the Lord God will give us light. Remember?"

He beamed with pride.

"You taught me well, Papi."

The fire was dying down. She stirred up the embers with the poker.

"You tend a fire like a pro," he said.

"You taught me that, too."

There's just this one thing you refuse to teach me about.

"Can I ask you a question, Papi?" Elise drew the screen closed and placed the poker back in its stand.

Papi nodded, waiting silently for her to continue.

"Why won't you talk to me about my mother?"

He stared into the now-crackling fire for what seemed like a long time.

"Helene," he said finally, "has been a great disappointment to us. But you knew that."

"Yes, you've said that before. But what exactly happened? Why did she run away?"

He studied his hands. "All I can tell you is what she told us. She insisted she was a free spirit—all these young people were free in those days, or so they thought. Your father was long gone by the time you were born, and Helene said that she was too young to take care of a baby herself, that she didn't know who she was, that she had to find herself, and that, to do so, she needed to return to our family's roots in France."

Elise nodded, having heard this much before. "I don't even know the questions to ask, I guess. How about this: Where'd she get the money to do it?"

Papi shrugged. "We gave it to her. She didn't ask for much—a few thousand, as I recall, and she never came back for more. I suspect that she had someone waiting for her there; she always did go for Europeans in general, and especially the Frenchmen she met in college—she was at Lawrence, you know, and they had a robust foreign-exchange program."

"She needed to find herself." Elise pronounced the syllables with regal disdain. "What exactly is *that* supposed to mean?"

"It was in the waning days of the hippie era, and that's what the kids said in those days." He smiled wryly. "It meant, in my opinion, that they wanted to explore the most selfish desires of their hearts, so they could be sure to build lives that would satisfy them all."

Elise considered this for a moment. "I guess that makes more sense than anything else I've heard."

"It was not uncommon in her generation. Those who were so inclined tossed out all the traditional moral training they'd grown up with and lived to feed their personal pleasures and their pride."

"'In the last days, perilous times will come,'" Elise said, her brow furrowed. "'For men shall be lovers of their own selves . . .'"

"I'd say that's a mighty fine description of what happened to much of the western world in the 1960s."

"And to my mother."

Papi nodded.

"Although," Elise said, gazing at him tenderly, "when she took off and left me with you, it was actually the kindest thing she could have done. You and Mamie have been terrific parents to me, the best possible. You've given me a wonderful life."

"Have we?" Papi was staring into the fire again, speaking softly, almost to himself. "Lorraine and I often wondered. We were no longer young. She was thirty-nine when Helene was born, you know, and I was forty. Made us feel like Abraham and Sarah." He smiled at the memory. "And I was sixty-one when you were born. For that reason alone, we were concerned that you wouldn't have a normal childhood. And then you didn't grow up with the usual neighborhood playmates—"

"We didn't exactly live in a usual neighborhood," Elise pointed out. She remembered clearly how the surrounding farmland had been so suddenly gobbled up by commercial development, and how all the neighboring farm families had just as quickly disappeared into the city. "Everyone was gone by the time I was ten."

"And I suppose that's the point. Lorraine and I could have sold Fleur de Lis and moved to a real neighborhood with children for you to play with. Or we could have gone to a bigger church with many more young families. Or sent you to a parochial school or even a public school instead of homeschooling you." His shoulders sagged as he listed their failings. "I'm afraid we thought we were protecting you by keeping you somewhat isolated. But instead . . ."

Elise was surprised to see a tear trail down Papi's face.

"I turned out that odd, huh?"

"Not odd," he said, reaching for her hand, "unless it's odd to be educated in the only things that matter, or to be godly, and a student of the word of God. I suppose that these things make you odd in the eyes of the world."

"'He is purifying for Himself a peculiar people,' Papi!"

"Yes, Elise, that's exactly right. Hmmmm . . . Romans?"

"Titus—gotcha!" She smiled playfully at her grandfather.

"You run circles around me, my dear." Papi considered her, his own face soft with love. "You always could. But these are all wonderful attributes that you have, attributes of eternal significance. The thing that concerned Mamie and me was that you'd be lonely. I'm still concerned about it."

Elise couldn't argue with him on that point, but she didn't want him to beat himself up over it.

"If that's the worst of my problems, I'd say you did pretty well, Papi. And I'll be okay, if the Lord tarries. I promise you I'll find some friends."

"Once I'm gone."

She hesitated for only a moment. It was time to begin accepting the inevitable.

"Yes, Papi, once you're gone."

That evening, Elise spent an hour looking up each of Papi's medications on her laptop, grateful that her grandparents had made a place in her homeschool curriculum for modern communications technologies. The room was lit only by the fire blazing behind the ancient fieldstone hearth, making it easy to read even the tiniest contraindications, warnings, and cautions on the manufacturers' web pages.

"Man alive," she said every now and then as she encountered another horrible side effect while copying and pasting the information into a master document. She was now doubly relieved that Dr. Maglio had somehow pressured the nursing home doctor—Buckminster was her name—to slash Papi's dosages.

Should I call him back again and ask him to get rid of all these drugs?

Printing out her side-effect information with a few taps of the touchpad—this wireless technology really was amazing, she acknowledged—Elise decided to simply wait patiently while watching Papi like a hawk.

Until he was gone.

Feeling consumed with loneliness, she Googled the names of the two girls she'd been friendly with years ago in the homeschool group at church, the two who hadn't joined the others in making fun of her adolescent gawkiness. Okay, so she *had* been awkward-looking in those days, so tall and skinny and graceless when playing basketball or soccer that she could hardly blame the other kids in their group for calling her "the giraffe." And of course word had gotten around about her mother deserting her; she had seen the others whispering at a distance, had witnessed them silencing themselves as she approached.

But these two girls, Stephanie and Holly, had always been kind to her, probably because they weren't great beauties, either.

Misery loves company. And so does ugliness.

She tried their maiden names, which was all she had to go on. But she got tens of thousands of hits, way too many to sift through. Besides, they'd both probably been married long ago. She tried their parents' names, but struck out again. They too had apparently disappeared to destinations beyond Google's reach.

She switched over to YouTube and skimmed through the videos recommended for her, based on prior visits. Sermons, documentaries, some clips on owls and otters and some of the other critters she enjoyed, but nothing especially compelling for her current mood. But wait— there at the bottom of the page, a video of giraffes playing at a UK zoo.

There are no coincidences in this life.

She clicked on the proffered frame and was instantly enchanted at the sight of God's creatures gamboling about, bucking and kicking up their heels, not caring at all how ungainly they appeared to most people, or how very beautiful they were in her eyes.

And there were others. She spent over an hour immersed in the antics of creatures from foxes and polar bears to monkeys and elk.

Of course, the subjects of these videos all had one important thing in common: they had friends to play with.

So here she was, back at square one. Well, not square one, exactly. She was supposedly pretty now, having outgrown her gawkiness. And she now belonged irrevocably to the Lord.

Still, a friend or two would be nice.

Short of hanging out in bars—she had to laugh at the very idea—giving First Baptist another try seemed like her best shot. And there was always the easy solution, asking Stonybrook for her old teaching job, if indeed they still had need of a grammar instructor by then. Not that there was much in the way of friend material there—the other teachers were all older and married—but it would be one way of occupying herself for a few years or maybe even a few decades.

Elise Chapelle, spinster schoolteacher.

Well, she'd cross that bridge after Papi had gone on ahead.

In the meantime, she had been toying with one idea for the last year, and she was almost ready to move ahead with it: building a website about heaven, the only topic that seemed to her to be endlessly fascinating.

In fact, she had signed up for a no-credit creative writing class at Waukesha County Technical College, and it started next Tuesday night. She'd enrolled in other classes over the years but had never quite managed to make it to any of them. But maybe she'd give this one a whirl. She might make a friend or two, and even if that was too much to hope for, she'd surely learn enough to develop a decent website.

Eternity would of course be the main event on this hypothetical site. But in a nod to the here and now, maybe she'd include some cross-references to mothers who abandon both their parents and their children in pursuit of worldly pleasures.

Elise shut her laptop with a sigh. Would she never be able to forget this decades-old hurt and resentment, or at least file it forever in the past?

CHAPTER TWELVE

Meg Vogel
Friday, January 13

Something was missing, Meg knew. She just couldn't quite put her finger on it.

She scanned her list of interview questions once again, probing her memory in vain for the missing subject that had popped into her head on her way to work this morning.

Not good. She was determined to blow her superiors away with this, her first official assignment as the unofficial Resident Biographer of The Hickories. And she was certainly no spring chicken. As iffy as the writing market had become in recent years, there'd no doubt be plenty of young journalism grads with sharp memories and endless energy waiting in line for her job. But if she could just keep her wits about her, she'd always have one competitive advantage: no young thing could compete with an ex-copywriter who'd spent thirty years interviewing people and crafting readable prose about subjects ranging from medical electronics to building control. All she had to do was demonstrate her skills—and her attention to detail.

What am I forgetting?

Meg opened the online Resident Summary file in search of something to jog her memory. She clicked on "Sparrow, S." and immediately saw a standard-issue Hickories snapshot of the sweet little lady with a wide smile, broad nose, and blue eyes, hooded now with age but still sparkling. She wore her short white hair in a tussled style, wavy rather than curled into the easy-care poodle 'do that was all the rage in this facility.

"Sadie Sparrow," she said softly, already loving the old girl strictly on the basis of her name. "What's your story?"

Filed just a few months ago, the admissions report covered only the basics:

Eighty-six, widowed for thirty years, moving here for the usual reasons—ht. failure, unexplained falls, walker inadequate, no room in dining room for wheelchairs so asked by asstd. living facility to leave. Minor memory loss, needs help with meds and transfers. One daughter, two granddaughters, assorted elderly friends. Baptist . . .

Ah, *that* was the question she'd forgotten to put on her list. *Ask about her religion, dumbo.* Lucy had emphasized the importance of religion to most of the residents, and Meg thought Baptists were among those who took this stuff very seriously.

. . . enjoys reading, jigsaw puzzles, singing hymns, cats— has left her cat Wally with daughter Dana (businesswoman, super busy, married w/ 2 teen girls, won't have time for frequent visits).

It was apparently a familiar story—a life that had somehow gone from essential to useful to useless and had now plunged into the never-never land of being set aside by a child with too many important things on her plate.

And being forced to leave behind a beloved pet as well.

"Does your daughter love Wally, Sadie?" Meg asked, near tears. "Will she bring him to visit you?"

She clicked the Emergency Contacts tab. There she was: Dana Maxwell. Married to Bill, mother of Hannah, seventeen, and Amanda, fifteen. Oddly, there was a photo of her too, or at least it seemed odd to Meg at first. But once she thought about it, it made sense from the security standpoint; an employee might find it useful for subtly verifying Dana's identity before letting her take Sadie out.

"Will daughterly outings ever be an issue for you, Sadie Sparrow?"

Dana must have supplied the photo herself. It was a full-body shot of her standing in a magnificent garden, dressed in jeans and a sweatshirt and leaning on a shovel. She looked to be a very fit fifty-ish and wore her light brown hair in a wavy pageboy. And she was surrounded by oriental lilies, liatris, and coneflowers in their midsummer glory—three of Meg's personal favorites from the dozens of bulbs, perennials, and annuals she had grown over the years.

But the whole thing made her sad—and not just personally sad, but sad on behalf of old people everywhere. When she was a kid, her only living grandparent had lived with them, and it was wonderful. She'd adored Grammy, and Grammy had spoiled her. And, as a built-in babysitter, she had given Meg's parents the freedom to do some traveling that would have been impossible otherwise. Sure, when Grammy suffered her third heart attack, she had to go into a nursing home, where she had died promptly and peacefully; but that didn't happen until she was in such horrid shape that she couldn't be cared for at home.

This was different. Even with the amenities of a five-star hotel, The Hickories was still, at least for some, a warehouse for old folks.

Meg was determined to do all she could to make it up to every last resident.

"Maybe we should do yellow this month," Lucy mused, surveying the kaleidoscope of color in the cabinet in the corner of the office Meg now shared with her. She pulled out a ream of marigold paper. "So is today the day you're interviewing Sadie?"

Meg looked up from the February activities calendar she was filling in on her computer and smiled at her boss. "Yes, at one. I'm really excited! Although maybe I should I take that as a warning? Things never turn out the way you expect."

"Oh, never fear—you're going to have a great time with Sadie. She's an amazing person."

Lucy loaded the printer and sat down at her desk.

"But it's really pretty pathetic," she added. "I've seen a lot of neglect on the part of our residents' kids, but Sadie's daughter takes the cake. I hear that she's been here exactly twice since checking Sadie in last fall, and then only for fifteen minutes at a crack. Oh, except for Christmas. She did bring a meal over around Christmas, I guess. But she lives ten minutes from here, and Sadie's fully capable of taking a car ride over to her house. Can you imagine putting your fairly able-bodied mother in a nursing home and then just leaving her there?"

Meg could not.

"But Sadie never says a word about it. I'm sure it hurts her—it would have to—but you'll never hear her complain."

They sighed in unison and returned to their work.

Meg found Sadie in the snug little North Sitting Room, reading the latest issue of *Better Homes & Gardens*. The room was toasty, but Sadie—wrapped in olive-green velour and a plush lap robe in turquoise blue—had positioned her wheelchair as close as possible to the glowing fire.

"Finding some good ideas for us, Sadie?" Meg asked cheerfully as she slipped into a mission-style leather chair.

"I don't think this place needs any ideas," Sadie said, smiling dreamily as she looked around. "It's flawless, straight out of a magazine." She squinted at Meg. "My, you're pretty. A modern-day Vivien Leigh."

"Wow, really? I'm flattered."

"Just don't end up the way she did."

"Which was . . . ?"

"Mad as a hatter, or so they said," Sadie said, lowering her voice as if she didn't want to be overheard gossiping— even if it *was* about an actress who'd died decades ago. "She even drove Sir Laurence Olivier away, if you can imagine that."

"No, really?" Meg knew the whole story, being a big fan of all things *Gone with the Wind*, but she let Sadie tell her anyway, in gory detail. "So sad that she became mentally ill," Meg said finally.

"Was she?" Sadie frowned. "I wonder. Maybe she was just too pretty and talented for her own good—self-absorbed, as they say these days. When you focus all your love and attention on yourself, you can become impossible to live with."

"Well, enough about me," Meg said, grinning as the old lady laughed. "Let's talk about you. Ready?"

"Shoot!"

Meg had interviewed dozens of corporate executives over the years, and scores of middle managers, but never had she met a better source of concisely delivered information than Sadie Sparrow. Not to mention her truthfulness, a somewhat relative concept in corporate America.

That, at least, was her assessment after they'd steamrolled their way through the "Basics" questions in ten minutes flat. No hesitation, no dithering, no forgetfulness; sitting there before the fire, Sadie was all business, even though she said she hadn't worked much outside her home since her marriage in 1952.

"And even then, I just cleaned houses when we needed a little extra cash." She smiled at the memory. "Brooms and mops and dust rags were my specialty. So if I'm answering your questions correctly, you can thank the good Lord! I'm no genius, and I'm really not sure what you're looking for."

"Me neither," Meg said. "Although—could we talk a bit about what is was like *not* to work a regular job?"

Sadie brushed her bangs back and gazed at the ceiling. "It was wonderful," she said, her eyes crinkling merrily. "I spent my days doing the things I enjoyed most—cooking, tidying up the house, washing, ironing, shopping.

"But I was behind the times," she added. "After all, Dana was born in 1957, and I could have joined the feminists, finding someone to watch her while I worked. But I loved being a homemaker and a mother, and in fact Ed and I hoped to have more children. But that was not to be."

"Tell me about your home." Meg's old tape recorder was still chugging away, so she was just jotting down key words and phrases now and then. "What was it like?"

"Oh, well—I mentioned it was in Green Bay, didn't I? Yes, on the east side near Astor Park, really the only pretty old neighborhood in the city. Our house! Well, it would be considered a shack today, but it was the Taj Mahal to me, and in those days, very respectable. One story, painted white; a big back yard with peonies and irises and an enormous old apple tree—Ed hung a swing from that tree for Dana . . ."

Sadie paused to inspect her expertly manicured nails, done *gratis* every Wednesday morning in the Great Room, and then smiled at Meg once again. Her eyes were moist.

"And a whopping two bedrooms and one bathroom." She laughed again. "But that bathroom would be right in style today. It had a big pedestal sink and a claw-footed tub, and a walk-in linen closet big enough for our rollaway bed— do you remember those? Before sofa beds?"

"Absolutely—we had one, too, in fact," Meg replied with a smile. "I loved it when my mom pulled it out because it meant someone important was coming to visit—they'd get my bed, and I'd sleep on the rollaway. And that was normally at Christmas, which made it a harbinger of everything happy!"

And so it went, Sadie revealing bits and pieces of her past, Meg letting those revelations jog her into sharing her own memories. The arrival of the afternoon nurse finally made them check the time; astonishingly, it was quarter after four.

"We've been jabbering for more than three hours!" Meg was astonished; she couldn't remember the last time she'd so totally lost track of time. "And we've covered everything from wallpaper to sports to great childhood memories. Guess we wandered a bit, didn't we? We'd better try to stick a little closer to the questions next week, or we'll never get done."

"I don't know that I'd mind that at all," Sadie said. Her eyes looked a little dewy again. "I can't tell you what a good time I've had this afternoon."

"Me too, Sadie," said Meg, bending over to kiss one powdered cheek. "I can't wait until next week. If I didn't have to get some others started on this—but I really have to do it Lucy's way, and that means five at a time. So until we meet again."

"Until then, sweetheart."

"Now *that*," Meg thought as she wended her way back to the Great Room, for once oblivious to the magnificent forest views flanking her almost every step of the way, "was a fantastic way to spend a Friday afternoon."

She found Lucy standing atop one of the long tables they used for crafts, hanging Valentine's Day decorations from hooks embedded in the ceiling's coffered tiles.

"Don't tell me you were with Sadie all afternoon." Lucy was smiling, but not warmly. "I thought you'd be back in time to help bring folks home from bingo."

"Sorry. We were just having such a great talk that I lost all track of time."

"Well, it will please her daughter." She stepped back to examine her handiwork. Satisfied, she eased herself down to the floor. "Sadie has long-term-care insurance, but Dana's the one calling the shots on where it's spent. I'll email her about all the time you're spending with her mother. She'll like that."

"What I can't figure out," Meg said, "is why she wouldn't kill to spend time with Sadie. She's fascinating!"

"It's tough to understand, all right. But maybe Dana's one of those 'forever young' kids—doesn't have a clue that she'll be in the same position one day herself, if she lives long enough. Or maybe she knows and doesn't want the reminder."

Lucy gathered up her leftover decorations and tossed them in a plastic tub. "But like I said, even though she's one of the worst I've seen, it happens all the time. You'll never see a busier bunch than the kids of parents in nursing homes."

Once back at home, after pottying and petting Touchdown, Meg headed for her home office to begin transcribing her Sadie tapes. It was going to be a big job, even omitting all her own totally irrelevant comments—comments which had consumed a shameful amount of tape, considering that this was to be the story of Sadie's life, not her own.

Still, they'd had a great time and made a fair amount of progress that day, galloping from Sadie's birth on a farm in north-central Wisconsin through meeting her future husband, Ed, at a movie theater in nearby Shawano after the war.

"You don't really want to know all of this, do you?" Sadie had asked Meg a half hour into their talk. "No one has ever been this interested in me before, and I can't imagine that Dana and her girls will ever be."

But Meg had insisted that they would care very much one day, and so Sadie had continued, gazing into the fire, her eyes misty at times and her face soft. Meg could almost see her new friend as she typed up memory after memory.

S. + sister Esther (died 1995, heart trouble) + neighbors ("Mueller girls") often met at the fence separating their families' farms when their chores were done. "We talked and laughed and sang hymns, the only music we knew." Examples: A Mighty Fortress, Amazing Grace, Battle Hymn of Republic, Whiter than Snow, Great Is Thy Faithfulness.

Meg had heard of some of these songs—"Amazing Grace" and "Battle Hymn," of course, and the others sounded familiar, thanks to Gil and his late-in-life discovery of church music.

Gil.

She'd been studiously avoiding thinking about him all day, shoving memories of him aside with considerable success in spite of this week's foray into the stash from the funeral home. She had really become very good at it: she'd gone through those horrible final hours, the notifications, the funeral and its aftermath, all without giving his death any serious consideration.

"And why should I?" she asked Sneak, who was only now waking from his five-thirty nap, stretching and yawning and working up to a yowl of greeting from his desktop bed. She scratched behind his enormous ears and was rewarded for her efforts by his rumbling purr. "Gil didn't give *us* any serious thought those last months, did he, baby? He cared more about that imaginary new friend of his than he did us, don't you think? That God that he suddenly believed in . . ."

Indeed, it had been horrifying to watch Gil go from a man heroically clinging to life, refusing to even consider death an option, to a wimp who'd lost all his fight, saying he was ready to go to his heavenly home.

"What rubbish, eh, Sneak?"

Gil's caving in had cost him at least a few months of life, she was convinced, and maybe a lot more. He just didn't seem to want to live anymore once his new friends from the cancer clinic got through to him.

"Not that it matters to us," Meg added brusquely. Realizing she was hungry, she saved her document and headed for the kitchen, the cat trotting at her heel. "Just as well to get on with our lives, make the most of what little time we have left, right?"

Now where did that line come from? She gave Touchdown his cup of kibble while searching her old-movie memory bank. But she couldn't place the quote.

"Story of my life these days," she said, putting Sneak's bowl on the kitchen table and finding a dog biscuit to keep Touchdown from objecting; he always forgot about his own lip-smacking dinner just as soon as he'd wolfed it down.

Meg made herself a peanut butter and mayonnaise sandwich—a favorite of hers since childhood, although it had always disgusted Gil—and returned to her typing, marveling at the simplicity of Sadie's life on the farm. She typed up every last detail, from how young Sadie's arms had ached from churning butter to the thrill of seeing Ed walk into the movie theater in little Shawano, Wisconsin, looking incredibly handsome in his Army uniform. Sadie said she'd known then and there, when he'd sauntered up to her counter and ordered a lemonade, that she would marry this soldier, and indeed she had done just that. But she'd left that story for their next meeting.

It wasn't marriage that was on Meg's mind the first time she'd seen Gil at Milwaukee's Summerfest, at the 1985 Bon Jovi concert. She had noticed him during one of the band's endless songs, sitting in the next row with a bunch of long hairs. He was distinctive because his hair was short, very dark, and very curly, and he wore a thick mustache and had big, beautiful smiling bedroom eyes.

With curly eyes and laughing hair, sing Polly wolly doodle all the day . . .

"Oh, he was cute, baby," she told Sneak, absently scratching his head. They were sitting in the TV room, the remote resting lifelessly in her other hand, awaiting a command. "He looked kind of like Jim Croce, you know that singer I love so? Dead, too. I wonder if they exist anywhere, and if so if they've met?"

Meg had gone to Milwaukee's landmark lakefront festival with several girlfriends who inexplicably found Jon Bon Jovi adorable. She personally found him revolting, and couldn't stand the group's music—if it could even be called music, as relentlessly loud as it was, with screeching instead of singing. She just couldn't see the attraction. But she saw the attraction in Gil, and he saw the attraction in her. At the end of the concert they'd agreed to grab a beer together, and the rest was history.

"He felt exactly the same way about the music," she said, stroking Sneak's throat now, enjoying his deep purr. "He'd just gone to the concert because his buddies wanted to, 'cause they were really into rock. Not your daddy. He was more of a pop and folk kind of guy. It was one of the things we had in common, you know. We loved our music, hanging out together, drinking wine and singing along with Crosby, Stills, and Nash and the Moody Blues, that sort of group from the 1970s.

"In fact," she said, looking around the little room, which had once been painted a psychedelic shade of orange but now wore a restful taupe, "this used to be our music temple; the TV was in the living room in those days. Can't tell you the wonderful hours we spent here, your daddy and I."

She'd been crazy in love with Gil then, and he with her. He'd moved in with her in 1987, trading in a hippie-esque eastside living arrangement with three other guys for suburban living twenty minutes west of the city. It hadn't taken him long to land a job teaching biology at the local high school, or to surprise her with a new puppy.

"He was a yellow lab that I named Thumper," she told Sneak. "No cat until 1989, when we found Joe at the pound. Imagine that, kitten, life without a cat."

They'd stayed crazy in love over the years, too, quickly making up after the occasional fight, generally agreeing on the important things, and each willing to let the other decide on the unimportant things—which was just about everything, when you came right down to it. They had no angst over family matters. An only child without even a cousin to her name, Meg had lost both her parents before her nineteenth birthday, her mother to cancer and her father to heart disease; she was twenty-three when Grammy succumbed to her last heart attack. And Gil's family was scattered practically around the world. What was left to argue about? They already owned this house, mortgage-free; they both worked steadily; and they both preferred pets to children. End of story.

"Honestly, Sneak, we were perfect for each other. For vacations, we preferred campgrounds to resorts. For food, we were both pretty much meat-and-potatoes types. For entertainment, old movies. We weren't big on home décor, either one of us—although I *did* get sick of the orange paint in here." She smiled at the memory. "But you know what? It turned out that he was sick of it, too."

The cat poked her stomach with a front paw; she'd stopped petting him.

"Oh, sorry." She resumed her work. "So why, you ask, did we get married? You know, that's a really good question."

She had no particular answer. The subject had simply popped up one warm summer evening almost six years ago, when they were stargazing in the backyard, lying on their cheesy nylon chaises.

"So maybe we should get married," he'd said, after trying in vain to identify a constellation besides the Big Dipper. "What would you think about that?"

Meg had been shocked into speechlessness—and, she had to admit, felt an odd thrill that she'd never before experienced.

"Why?" she finally asked.

"Oh, I don't know," he said, climbing out of his chaise and kneeling next to hers. "Guess I think this trial run has lasted long enough."

"Hmmmm," she said, afraid to even look at him. "Twenty-plus years of unwedded bliss."

"Right. So how about we try the wedded kind?"

Unable to think of a reasonable objection, and feeling inexplicably euphoric, she'd agreed, and two weeks later they'd driven to the courthouse and sealed the deal.

She'd transitioned easily from being Meg Barker to being Meg Vogel. "It was really no big deal," she told Sneak. "Some of my feminist friends were offended that I took his name, but in my opinion, it's a non-issue; we all started out wearing our fathers' names, after all. And anyway, I thought I'd rather be named after a bird than a dog. Just don't tell Touchdown."

Meg had fallen with equal ease into finally feeling really and truly secure about their future together. No more masochistic fantasies about him showing up one day and announcing that he'd fallen for some student who'd graduated ten years ago.

Eleven months later, Gil was diagnosed with Stage 3 colorectal cancer and was given a roughly fifty-fifty chance of surviving it. And four years later, he was gone.

"Just my luck, we were dealt the wrong fifty percent," she said, even now acutely aware of what her mother would have said about her reference to luck.

How dare you say that, Meg? You have led a blessed life, and you should be grateful!

But since her mother was no longer around to set her straight, she said it again. "Just my luck, Sneak old boy. Just my luck."

CHAPTER THIRTEEN

Sadie Sparrow
Friday, January 13

Sadie rolled towards her dining table, amused to see her tablemates fixated on her progress. Their bright smiles and raised eyebrows made her feel like a celebrity.

Gladys couldn't even wait for Sadie to lock her wheels. "Well?" she demanded.

"Did you have a good time, dear?" Eva asked.

"What did you talk about?" This, surprisingly, from Catherine Peebles. Catherine was a Christian Scientist who refused pain medication, being convinced that the arthritis raging through her body was a figment of her imagination. Ordinarily, she was in so much pain that she rarely showed any interest in anything. And when she wasn't hurting or sleeping, she was talking about the late great Mrs. Mary Baker Eddy, the nineteenth century founder of Christian Science.

"How long did you two talk?" Catherine asked now. "Did you have time for a nap before dinner?"

"That's all you think about," Gladys snapped. "Not everyone is obsessed with naps."

Sadie intervened in time to prevent a squabble. "It was really no big deal, girls," she said, borrowing one of Dana's favorite phrases. "No big deal at all."

But it *was* a big deal, and Sadie knew it. Her new friends had given her a lift, no question about that. But she knew she couldn't count on any of them long-term; old people die and their young loved ones disappear forever, even after promising to visit you soon. She'd already been here long enough to see it happen more than once. But Meg's biography-in-progress was different. It had begun changing her attitude from the moment they'd scheduled this first interview, especially once Meg had given her the interview questions.

It was amazing, really. It had always been Sadie's policy to advise complainers to count their blessings. Yet she'd apparently not done a good job of counting her own, as depressed as she'd felt since moving in to The Hickories. But when she started pondering the questions that Meg planned to pose—questions about Ed and their life together, about Dana and her family, about Sadie's best memories and even the worst—it was as if the Lord were playing a movie about her life. And even if it wasn't a magnificent movie, populated by beautiful people, places, and things, it starred people who loved each other, living with all their needs met in a humble but well-kept house.

It had been, she realized, a happy story about a solid American family living out solid American values. So what if there hadn't been more children? And so what if it wasn't ending quite the way she'd envisioned, living with Dana's family as a beloved grandma? Short of that idyllic (and quite possibly romanticized) scenario, you really couldn't beat The Hickories as a place to spend your last days.

But these were not reflections you shared with anyone but your closest friends, Sadie knew. And even if they did have the distinct advantage of still being alive and close at hand, neither Gladys nor Catherine would ever qualify as best friends; Eva might someday, if they both lived long enough, but they still had a ways to go. Sadie, at least, had become adept at hiding her feelings, at downplaying the significance of important things and playing up the importance of the insignificant, at protecting her pride and her privacy against meddlesome minds.

A lady never showed her wounds to strangers, her mother had advised her over a half a century ago—or even to casual friends.

"So tell us all about it." Gladys' cheeks were flushed with impatience. She was wearing her poufy old wig. It was a softer shade of brown than her Laura Petrie style, but still looked unnatural over the jowls and wrinkles.

Sadie shook off these nasty thoughts and focused on the interview with Meg.

"Well, ladies, I'm now free to tell you all about it," she said, trying not very successfully to stifle a note of self-importance. "Meg is going to be writing biographies of us residents—at least, those of us who still have most of our marbles. And that means you girls, too," she added generously. "Eventually, anyway. I'm only her prototype, so it will probably take some time for her to hone her technique."

"How wonderful," Eva said. "So you were her first interview? Did you enjoy it?"

"Oh, it was very nice." Sadie was trying to sound indifferent, but her eyes betrayed her excitement. "It's fun to have someone so interested in every detail of your life, down to the color of the dress you were wearing when you met your husband-to-be. I wasn't even especially interested in that detail, but it was fun trying to remember."

"That sounds a little dull, my dear," Catherine said, apparently oblivious to how tedious it was to hear at length about Mrs. Eddy's theories of animal magnetism and at-one-ment.

"What color was the dress, dear?" Eva asked.

"Blue. It was cornflower blue."

In the end, Sadie didn't tell her tablemates much about her conversation with Meg. Most of it sounded too trivial to even mention. They'd just have to experience their own interviews. Besides, the big takeaway, as Dana would say, was what was happening in her own heart, and that was far too personal to share with anyone.

She didn't sleep well that night. Meg had opened the floodgates of the past for her, and she mainly just dozed off and on between long-dormant memories of the Muellers' neighboring farmhouse and her family's, of the Bible readings and devotions that Papa had led them in each night, of the symphony of crickets and owls on hot summer nights—there were no cicadas in those days, at least that she could remember.

But Sadie woke up feeling optimistic, for some reason. Crazy, she knew. How could memories of a beloved but irretrievable past make you feel anything but despair?

She felt so happy, in fact, that she checked out The Hickories' calendar for the day. It was Saturday, and she could see about getting her hair done this afternoon or maybe take in a two o'clock showing of *Ben-Hur*. And here, at ten this morning, there was a Bible study going on in the Southeast Sitting Room. Maybe she'd go to that, in memory of Papa.

And so she did. An adorable little aide by the name of Piper Drew gave her a ride—a definite blessing, since it was a long trek and since she still got lost regularly trying to find her way around this place, with its multiple wings, all connected by those beautiful woodland hallways and elegant elevators. The Southeast Sitting Room turned out to be on the lower level, in the front of the complex. Here, in a cozy room overlooking the main drive, she found a young man who introduced himself as Jamie Fletcher. He had wavy brown hair and merry eyes and looked at first glance like the kind of person you wouldn't mind being stranded with for hours on end.

"I must be early," Sadie said, introducing herself.

"Not at all—I don't usually get much of a turnout at nursing homes." He smiled ruefully. "In fact, that's why I'm here today. The last place was a total failure. So I'm really very happy to see you, Sadie."

Jamie spoke with an accent that sounded vaguely Scottish to Sadie, warm and rich and full of truth. For a while, they chatted about the weather (dreary), the food at The Hickories (outstanding), her family (or lack thereof), and his job (assistant pastor at Brookfield Bible Church, just ten minutes away). They waited for another student or two to show up, but when none had after ten minutes, he suggested they get started.

"How sad that no one else is here," Sadie said. "And rude."

Jamie shook his head. "It's no problem—it's in the Lord's hands, after all, and maybe He has a reason for wanting us to talk alone today. What's your Christian background?"

"Born and raised Baptist."

"American? Southern?"

"Independent."

"Ah, the hardest to gauge. So let me ask you this: How often do you read your Bible?"

Sadie hesitated for only a moment. "Rarely, to be honest. My eyes aren't so good anymore."

"That's okay." Jamie pulled a navy blue paperback out of his briefcase. "Try this one, compliments of the Gideons. It's a large-print New Testament and Psalms, New King James version. We'll work with this, okay? And I promise you, I'm going to do all I can to make it so compelling that you won't be able to put it down." He smiled at her warmly—almost lovingly, Sadie thought.

She told him that she had loved listening to her father read from the Scriptures when she was young, and that of course she'd learned a great deal at church and in Sunday school over the decades as well as from Ed, and that even though she'd never really spent much time in the Bible on her own, she knew it was the word of God and a guide to living.

"That's good," Jamie said. "Nothing tougher than trying to teach the Bible to someone who's read a chapter here and there and thinks that it's nothing but a collection of myths and contradictions. So how about we start at the beginning, just as a refresher, with an overview of the entire Bible? Then eventually we'll zoom in to individual books. Sound like a plan?"

"Yes indeedy," Sadie said, beaming at the thought of having a standing date with such a nice young man. "This is kind of like having my own personal trainer, isn't it?"

"To get you fit for eternity."

They laughed together. It seemed like a long time since she'd laughed, and now she'd done just that with two relative strangers in as many days.

"But there's a more immediate purpose for our meeting, Sadie. And that's helping you with your ministry here on earth."

"*My* ministry?"

"Well, yeah," he said, apparently surprised by her response. "You may wish you were living somewhere else— on your own, or with your daughter, maybe? But you know that not even a sparrow falls to the ground apart from the Lord's will, right?" He grinned. "No pun intended, Mrs. Sparrow."

"That's right, not even one," she said, returning his smile. It had always been one of the more reassuring of the Bible's claims, that God was in control and cared about even the least of His creatures. It had been way too long since she'd thought about that. "That's in Matthew, I think."

"That's right," Jamie said happily. "And the Bible also tells us that He has you here for a reason. Certainly to glorify Him before others, but also to lead them to Him."

Immediately Sadie's head was filled with the things Dana had said over the years about pushy Christians who wanted to force their views on everyone else. She shifted uncomfortably in her chair.

"Unless you're one of those professing Christians," Jamie said, emphasizing the word "professing" in a way that made it sound like not such a good thing, "who think there are many ways to heaven." His eyes had become very serious and very focused on hers. "Does that describe you, Sadie? Do you believe that you just have to be a good person, in the world's eyes, to get into heaven?"

"No," Sadie lied, knowing that this was exactly what she'd come to think in the years since Ed had died. He'd been her spiritual leader, the one who studied the Bible and, like Papa, had worked hard to keep his very thoughts in line with its teachings.

Jamie took her hand and held it gently. It had been a long time since anyone had touched her for any reason other than helping her transfer from chair to bed or toilet or bath, and it made her uncomfortable.

"There is none righteous, no, not one," she added, pulling her hand away and patting his twice as a consolation prize. "Not in God's eyes. That's why Jesus had to die—the perfect sacrifice paying for all our sins, because we're all sinners and we can't cover even one. Without Him, we'll never see heaven."

Jamie was nodding. Thanks to Papa's instruction and Ed's, she'd answered correctly, even if she didn't necessarily believe it anymore.

How could she believe it, now that Ed was no longer here to answer the tough questions? "How could a good God allow such pain in this world?" had been adult Dana's favorite counterattack whenever Sadie had attempted to get her back into church in order to silence the Sparrows' critics, real or imaginary. And after Ed's death at just sixty-five years old, Sadie had spent many hours silently pondering that very question in her own heart.

At first Ed's confident answer had been there to rescue her whenever despair threatened. She could still see him explaining it one fine summer evening when they were sitting in the backyard on their old metal lawn chairs. "He allows pain to chasten us, direct us, and draw us closer to Him," he'd said, gazing fondly at her with his adorable Roy Rogers eyes. "And whatever His purpose, He makes it all work together to the good of those who love Him." She had trusted in that answer for a full decade following Ed's death before it lost its charm.

"I have always been taught that," she told Jamie. "Straight out of the Bible."

"Let's see if I can't make it real to you, more than just the right answer to a pop quiz. How's that sound?"

Sadie's head was spinning by the time Jamie wheeled her into lunch. He had covered 4,000 years of biblical history in less than an hour, and she'd become very confused around the time of Wycliffe and Tyndale. He'd said that she didn't have to remember any of it, really, that he only meant to show her how the Lord had protected His word over the centuries so that she could trust it today, but she was fascinated by the tale and wanted to know more.

"I'll bring you a video on the subject," he'd promised. "I'd like to cover some different proofs next week, if that's okay. How do you feel about science?"

"It's too bad you didn't go to Bible study," Sadie said to her tablemates after he'd left.

"He limps," said Gladys. "Did you know that? Why does he limp?"

"I don't know," Sadie said, "and frankly I hadn't noticed. What difference does it make?"

"I already know all about the Bible," Catherine said. "I just wish someone would study Mrs. Eddy's writings with me."

"How about that practitioner of yours?" Gladys was looking down her substantial nose at Catherine, not really very interested in ultimate truth herself, but apparently sure that Catherine's idea of it was wrong. "You're always sending her money. How come she never comes to see you if she's so great?"

Catherine blinked hard and stared at her coffee.

"It was very interesting," Sadie said. "He went over the history of the Bible—it's just fascinating."

"How many were there, dear?" Eva asked.

"Just me. I guess I have my own personal tutor, unless someone else decides to take the plunge."

"Oh oh," Gladys teased. "Looks like Sadie's got herself a young man."

They all laughed gaily. Laughter was becoming a habit for her, it seemed, and it made her very happy.

CHAPTER FOURTEEN

Elise Chapelle
Saturday, January 14

Elise was a bit late for her lunch date with Papi. She had gone shopping at Brookfield Square, searching for something a little spiffier than jeans and a sweatshirt to wear to class on Tuesday night, and she had been so overwhelmed by the selection that she lost track of time. She tore into the dining room, almost running into a nice-looking young man who was on his way out the door.

"Whoa," he said, taking her forearms in his hands. "You're breaking the speed limit, young lady."

He looked her straight in the eye and grinned at her. Her stomach did a little flip-flop. He was really cute, not terribly tall, but he had these dreamy brown eyes . . .

"Are you okay?"

She laughed and smiled back at him. "Of course, just running a little late. Sorry that I almost ran you over."

"No problem." His eyes did not leave hers. "Well, maybe I'll see you around. Your mother—?"

"Grandfather. Charles Chapelle."

"Grandfather, then. Maybe he'd be interested in our Bible study?"

Bible study? Cute and *Christian?*

"Oh, I'm sure he would," she said. "When is it?"

The young man shrugged. "It's whenever I can get away, at least for now. Activities will be able to tell you."

"Okay, thanks."

The young man was looking at her so intently that she felt herself blushing.

"You'd be welcome to join us, too, Mrs.—"

"Miss." She smiled again, hoping she didn't look as dizzy as she felt. "My name is Elise."

"And I'm Jamie Fletcher." He shook her hand and stepped back to let her pass. "I hope to see you again soon, Elise."

"Old friend?" Papi asked as Elise slipped into the empty chair at his table. His ancient tablemates, Mort and Joseph, didn't even glance up from their plates. Papi said they'd never uttered a word to him, or to each other.

"Never saw him before in my life," Elise said. "He's apparently the Bible teacher."

A waitress slid a dish onto her placemat—a chef's salad with Thousand Island on the side—and disappeared before Elise could thank her.

"Did you know there was a Bible study here?" Elise asked her grandfather after they'd prayed and started in on their meals.

"I did. But I imagine it's awfully basic."

"I suppose," Elise said, nodding a bit and munching thoughtfully on a chunk of tomato. "Still, maybe we should give it a try."

"We?"

"Sure, why not?" she said, busying herself with a roll.

"Yes indeed, why not?" Papi smiled broadly at her. "Who knows? Maybe one of my most fervent prayers will be answered at last."

CHAPTER FIFTEEN

**Meg Vogel
Saturday, January 14**

Meg had been feeding Mr. Olewinski his luncheon entree of pureed ham salad when she saw a nice-looking young man wheeling Sadie towards her table. For a moment she thought it might be one of the old girl's relatives, but then she remembered the morning Bible study and figured he must be the teacher.

"How about you, Mr. Olewinski?" She leaned close to his ear so he could hear her above the din of the dining room. "Would you like to go to a Bible study sometime?"

He rolled his eyes towards her. Mr. Olewinski couldn't even move his head anymore due to some illness. *Which illness*, Meg hadn't a clue; it was just one of the zillions of diseases plaguing the supposedly perfect world created by this imaginary God. She threw an angry glance at the young man pushing Sadie, as though it were his fault.

Mr. Olewinski wasn't able to speak, either, and Meg wasn't able to read his expression. No one seemed to know if he could even think anymore, and once she'd overheard an aide talking some offensive nonsense to him. It made Meg sick to think that he might understand the girl and be hurt by her words. She had reported the incident promptly, and hadn't seen that aide again.

"I personally don't know how anyone could believe in such myths," she continued, as if they were having a real conversation as they sat there, he in a geriatric chair and she on a stool, alone at their table today because the other residents appointed to Table Three were down with some bug. "When we die, we die, and we get that nice long forever nap we've all been yearning for, with no more nightmares and no more pain. Don't you think that sounds wonderful?"

It crossed her mind that if he *did* believe in divine fairy tales, it might be hurtful for her to pooh-pooh them. Not her intention.

"But I could well be wrong, Mr. Olewinski," she said placatingly, spooning up some orange mush that smelled of carrots. His eyes slid back to their usual, straight-ahead position as he accepted the food. "What do I know? My husband was a true believer. He became one after he was diagnosed with colorectal cancer. Someone at the clinic told him about Jesus, and he . . . well, he decided to believe, even though I could never get on board with him."

Meg used a corner of Mr. Olewinski's terrycloth bib to wipe some mush from the corner of his mouth and gave him another spoonful of the mashed potatoes. It was impossible to tell if he liked the food or not, but he always ate everything they offered him. He was a big man—tall and lanky and very well dressed—and she could picture him thirty years ago, dining with clients in Milwaukee's fanciest restaurants.

Did he ever imagine he'd end up being hand-fed a pureed diet by people who had to be paid to help him? Do I ever imagine myself in this position?

"If you want to know the truth," she went on, "I was pretty irritated by Gil's conversion, if that's what you call it."

Mr. Olewinski's eyes slid over to hers again. Was he interested in what she was saying?

"I guess because he went from having all these normal emotions about his cancer—you know, being angry, and determined to fight it, and reading up on clinical trials to see if he couldn't find something that would save his life—he went from that to suddenly being all peaceful and content and disinterested in any medical news. In the end, he turned down the opportunity to participate in a clinical trial right here in Milwaukee, one that's looking really promising. But Gil just didn't care anymore. He said he was ready to go home to his Savior, if you can believe it."

Mr. Olewinski stared straight ahead again. His eyes looked unfocused, at least on this dimension.

"You can imagine how that made me feel."

"Uh," said Mr. Olewinski. "Uuuhhhh."

Meg was so surprised she didn't know what to do. She looked around frantically for help and was relieved to see the kitchen manager, Betsy, rushing to her side.

"What's up, Bill?" she said, totally ignoring Meg. "Did you enjoy your lunch?"

"He was trying to talk, Betsy," Meg volunteered.

Betsy didn't even look at her. She just bent down and put her hand on Mr. Olewinski's shoulder and looked him straight in the eye. "You ready to go back to your room?"

He was silent. Finally Betsy acknowledged Meg. "I think he just wants to go lie down now. I can take him back to his room. Maybe you could give Muriel a hand with her lunch?"

By the time Meg had finished with Muriel—a different sort of challenge, since she strenuously resisted help but ended up spilling most of her food on the table and floor when she was left to her own devices—Sadie and her tablemates had left the dining room. Meg was strangely disappointed.

Maybe I'm getting softhearted, hanging out with these old gals. Or, more likely, softheaded.

It was almost seven when Meg turned into the parking lot of The Farmhouse, nearly a half hour late for her date with Sandra. Meg hadn't realized she'd be working the Saturday shift alone, and when they'd set the time by email that morning, she'd forgotten that *Ben-Hur* was nearly four hours long, and that she'd have to help bring the moviegoers in to dinner before dashing home to tend to her critters.

Sandra was lost in a book and swept aside Meg's apologies. "Honestly, I would've been a little happy if you'd stood me up," she laughed. "Here I am, sitting in the most adorable restaurant in town, with nothing but a great glass of Riesling and one of my favorite old novels to occupy myself."

She flashed the cover of the paperback at Meg before stuffing it in her enormous purse. It was Theodore Dreiser's *An American Tragedy*, a far weightier novel than one would expect this Twiggy-like creature to be reading.

"They say the film's a lot better than the book," Meg said, remembering being forced to plow her way through it the summer before her junior year in high school. "At least it had Liz Taylor going for it."

"To each his own, I guess." Sandra turned her big round eyes intently on Meg. "So how *are* you?"

"I'm not so fragile that you can't argue with me," Meg replied, donning a smile that was only slightly fake. "Why don't you stand up for Dreiser? You know you want to!"

Sandra smoothed her already fabulously smooth silvery blonde bob. "It's not that important. Tell me how you're doing."

"Really good. You won't believe it but I'm absolutely loving my new job."

"Seriously? Tell me about it."

And so Meg did, pausing only to order a Riesling for herself and then pan-fried brook trout drenched with slivered almonds in melted butter. Apparently wanting to avoid anything smacking of controversy, Sandra copied her order.

"Sounds like this Sadie is one special lady," Sandra said when their food arrived.

"She really is." Meg absent-mindedly pushed the buttery almonds off to the side of her plate. "I don't know what it is, but hearing her talk about her life makes me wish I'd lived mine differently. In the country, maybe, married to some farmer and spending my days cooking and cleaning and milking the cows. No, really, don't laugh at me!"

"You don't seem like the Green Acres type."

"Oh, but I am! But anyway, Sadie and her husband did move to the city eventually, to Green Bay, and—well, we haven't gotten that far yet. But from what she's hinted, it was the same sort of life. He was a carpenter, I think, and she stayed at home with their daughter, so the scene was different but the characters were the same. Two people who loved each other—"

"Madly? Passionately?"

"Hmmm, I don't know about that, but faithfully and respectfully and with their lives rooted in the same values. I have the impression there was very little disagreement in that household."

"She was probably a submissive little wife," Sandra said, her tone taking on a note of condescension. "The type that didn't know she had rights." She laughed mirthlessly. "The type that Marty thought he'd found in me."

Meg shook her head. "You're probably exactly right about that, but I'd be surprised to find out that Sadie had wanted any rights in the modern sense of the word. I think she was totally happy with their old-fashioned life until the day her husband died."

"And then?"

"I don't know. But I can't wait to find out."

Sandra is one miserable woman.

Meg pointed the Cruiser towards home, considering their conversation. On the one hand, Sandra talked as if divorcing Marty Moser a few years back had been the best thing that had ever happened to her, with her copywriting work and position at Brainwashers being a close second. On the other hand, she complained about her unrelenting loneliness at night and, during the day, the tedium of her work and the rash of ungrateful clients the agency had managed to attract in recent years.

Meg readily admitted to having had mixed feelings about Gil when he was alive, especially in the last year or so as his personality had started changing. But whether it was her sense of pride or her need for privacy, she couldn't imagine sharing any of those details with anyone else. Sandra, however, had used their conversation about Sadie to launch into a ten-minute lecture on Marty's failings. It left Meg feeling embarrassed for her; after all, Sandra and Marty hadn't even spoken in a couple of years, yet she was apparently finding it tough to move on with her life.

Once home, Meg took Touchdown for a quick walk, then changed into her favorite flannel pajamas and turned on the fireplace in the living room. They'd had it converted to gas in the '90s. It wasn't as good as a wood-burner but it was so much easier that she lit it almost every night during Wisconsin's long winters; she never would have used one requiring logs and kindling and matches and an occasional chimneysweep.

The critters sat in front of the fire, waiting patiently for her to park herself on the couch so they could join her.

But she hesitated.

"I suppose I should take a look at that journal," she said aloud. Sneak ignored her, but Touchdown cocked his head and watched her open the secretary in the corner and pull out the spiral notebook with the photo of a gate set in a stone wall on the cover. "Come on, guys—I found this in your daddy's things. I didn't have the guts to look at it before."

Even now, her heart skipped a beat when she saw Gil's handwriting once again. The first time she'd taken a peek several days ago, she had shut the cover immediately and stuck the notebook in the secretary. It was still strange to look at it now. Even the date on the first page, September 7th, just months before he'd died, brought back a rush of mostly painful memories.

Still, it was about time she gutted it out. At least it was Saturday, and eyes swollen from weeping would not be an issue tomorrow. She could stay in bed all day if she had to.

She was surprised to see that the notebook was almost full. His writing was handsome—small and square and precisely executed—and easy to read. It started abruptly, as if there'd been a previous volume.

Told Dr. W. to forget the chemo. I've had enough for this lifetime. I've never felt so wretched—

He'd listed a dozen symptoms, most of which Meg had never heard about.

Besides, staying alive isn't exactly my top priority these days.

She reached the bottom of the first page and wondered whether she really wanted to know why living hadn't been his top priority.

For what's left of this life, I'd like to have enough pep for another dinner at Gordon's Supper Club, and to have The Talk with Meg.

The Talk? Meg's stomach grew queasy. They'd never made it back to Gordon's; she had not realized it was a priority for him. And she didn't remember Gil bringing up anything that could be described as The Talk. Unless maybe he meant that awful night a month or so before he died, when he'd brought up the subject of an afterlife, and she'd—well, she'd gone kind of ballistic on him.

"It wasn't very good timing," she told Sneak, who was staring at her, not even blinking his placid green eyes. "He was about to die, for Pete's sake, and he wanted to talk about where he was going? You can hardly blame me."

Sneak looked away. Apparently he wasn't buying it.

"I guess I could've been kinder about it," she conceded. "But it made me so angry, that he wanted to drag me into that whole subject before it was absolutely necessary."

Sneak headed off to his litter box. Refusing to feel slighted, Meg read on.

She's not going to like it, I'm afraid. She won't understand. But there's nothing I wish more for her. It's so glorious, this feeling of being loved absolutely and completely.

The queasiness intensified. Was she about to find out that her dying husband had been having an affair?

It's the kind of security I've been looking for all my life, and I don't think I'm alone in that. The ultimate security, knowing that no matter what you do or say or think, your future is secure. His promises are true.

His? Her husband had been having an affair with another man?

But of course that wasn't what Gil was writing about, and Meg knew it. She knew he was writing about this God of his, the one he'd stumbled across at the clinic, when he was getting a port put in for his chemo and ended up having a long talk with another patient.

An affair with another man would almost have been preferable. Or another woman.

She reached down to stroke Touchdown's velvety cheek, her heart softening as he moaned in basset hound pleasure. Gil had really loved this stinky old dog.

"I suppose it's okay, if it gave him some comfort," she said. "It just bugs me when people try to force their fairy tales on me, you know, Touch?"

But he'd dozed off again, too tired to even wag his tail.

Meg pushed the journal away, suddenly unwilling to read further. She retreated to the TV room and flipped through the channels until she found an old movie. It turned out to be *The Razor's Edge*, one of her favorites; she loved Gene Tierney's scruples-free determination to win back the oh-so-good Tyrone Power. Gene's character was relentless; she liked that in a woman.

CHAPTER SIXTEEN

Sadie Sparrow
Saturday, January 14

Between Jamie and *Ben-Hur*, it had been a great day. And for dinner, fried shrimp and a lovely mini concert by a string quartet! Even though she'd been unable to hitch a ride from an aide, Sadie's heart was singing so joyfully as she wheeled her way home that she couldn't quite keep it in. "O that will be glory for me," she sang softly, her voice cracking with emotion, "when by His grace I shall look on His face, that will be glory, glory for me!"

She decided to stop and see Beulah before turning in, and was delighted to find her new friend looking perky in a fluffy pink bed jacket.

"I *do* feel better," Beulah said, grinning. "They must be giving me some great drugs, 'cause I feel like I could go dancing tonight!"

More laughter for Sadie, this time with an impish old woman who was giggling like an eight-year-old.

"The difference is that you may be able to do that one of these weeks," Sadie said wistfully. "I'll have to wait until heaven."

"Were you a good dancer?"

"Horrible. Fortunately, I married a man who wasn't much interested in dancing. But in heaven, with my glorified body, I'm planning to be exceptionally graceful. How about you?"

"I was okay," Beulah replied. "And Norbert was splendid! What I've never been able to do is carry a tune. That's what I'm planning on doing with my glorified body: sing all those wonderful old hymns at the top of my lungs!"

They discussed their favorite hymns and their respective denominations for a while—Beulah described herself as a fallen-away Methodist of the John Wesley school, unable to stomach the liberalization of her once biblically grounded church—and then said goodnight.

"I have something I want to tell you about one of these days," Beulah said, stopping Sadie halfway to the door. "But not tonight—I'm feeling very happy right now and I don't want to ruin the mood."

"Are you sure? I have time."

Beulah hesitated. "It's just that I remembered something that might be important—I'll tell you tomorrow."

Sadie wheeled herself back to the bed. "Tell me now."

Beulah's happy mood slipped away in one long exhale. "All right, then. It probably has nothing to do with anything, but if I didn't say anything I'd always wonder."

"Go on," Sadie said, suppressing a jolt of impatience—one of her besetting sins.

"It was a couple of weeks ago, just before my legs were broken. I'd been sitting at the fire in the Great Room, right after lunch. It's such a lovely place to take a little nap, don't you think? I'm so glad I learned to nod off in a chair."

Sadie nodded encouragingly.

"I don't know what time it was, but I headed back to my room to use the potty, and just as I was making the last right turn—you know it, Sadie, you do it every day."

"Yes, Beulah, go on."

"Well, I noticed something on the floor. Turned out to be a little white pill, right in front of Dotty Meacham's door. I tried to pick it up, but couldn't reach it. To think I once could touch my toes a hundred times without even getting winded!"

"So what did you do?"

"Oh, well, I saw a nurse just a few doors down with her drug cart. I called to her and when she didn't respond—maybe she couldn't hear me, my voice isn't what it once was—I went to her. It was that young German nurse. Juliet, maybe?

"Julia, I think," Sadie said. An image of the young woman popped into her head. She was petite and dark-haired and pretty, or might have been if she'd smile once in a while. But she was the coldest person in this place, and Sadie did not like her.

"Yes, that's it. Anyway, when I pointed out the pill, she went right back and picked it up. And here's what's amazing: she marched back to her cart and tossed it in the bin where they throw the used paper cups and Kleenex. She threw it away!"

Sadie furrowed her brow, confused. Had Beulah expected the nurse to dust it off and give it to someone?

"Don't you see, Sadie? Maybe someone missed a pill that she really needed. Like Dotty. She has those awful seizures, you know. It might have been one of her seizure pills!"

"I see what you mean. So did you point that out to Julia?"

"You bet I did. And it was so creepy. She turned and looked at me like she was just furious, only controlled fury, if you know what I mean. And then she practically hissed at me!"

Sadie had no trouble at all picturing that particular nurse in a quiet rage.

"She said, 'Don't worry about it. Just go back to your room!'"

Sadie gasped. "Did she really?"

"Well," Beulah sniffed, "that's what her expression said. If looks could kill!"

"She had no right to treat you that way," Sadie said, a tad doubtfully. "And I see what you mean about a missed pill. But maybe they have some way of counting the pills so there's never a problem. Or maybe she recognized it as something like a Tylenol."

"In that case, she could've just told me that."

They sat in silence for a few moments.

"And that was right before—" Beulah frowned, her good mood totally shot. "I'll put it this way. It's the last thing I remember before waking up in the hospital to hear that I had two broken legs."

Sadie didn't know what to do with Beulah's revelation. She suggested that they tell Bunny, but Beulah didn't think much of the idea.

"My daughter would have the police and the FBI here within five minutes." Beulah shook her head, but was unable to suppress a smile of pride. "She's an alarmist."

"This is one case where alarm might be justified," Sadie said indignantly. She hated herself for being jealous of their mother-daughter relationship, but she could make up for it by being enraged on Beulah's behalf. "If Nurse Julia hurt you—"

"That's a big if, of course."

The voice of reason, coming from the victim.

Now, sitting in her wheelchair in her darkened room, sporting her best flannel nighty and quilted robe and gazing out at the elegantly lit garden, Sadie tried to come up with the best solution for everyone concerned. But try as she might, she couldn't get past the conclusion they'd finally come to: "We have to tell *someone.*"

It was almost ten before she decided that the most logical someone was Meg. She just needed to get her ducks in order, scout around a little more, perhaps, and then she'd make her case.

CHAPTER SEVENTEEN

Elise Chapelle
Tuesday, January 17

It took Elise forever to find her classroom. The maps on the Technical College's website hadn't been very helpful, so she'd just headed over to the campus, figuring she'd find someone who knew where Room 0B75 was. No such luck; it was cold and dark and there were no students sauntering from building to building. She finally had to find a parking spot and run into what looked like the main building. And by the time she arrived in the right place—the Business Building, of course, which she'd figured meant the College's business offices when she drove past it earlier—she was late for class.

Fortunately, she wasn't the only one, Elise soon discovered. There was no teacher in sight, and students were still clumping into the classroom in heavy winter boots when she arrived, freeing themselves from hats and scarves and puffy ski jackets as they found seats at the tables near the front of the room. Feeling extraordinarily shy, she set her laptop down on the very last table.

Goose! You aren't going to make any friends this way!

She moved up a few tables and slipped into a seat next to a blonde woman. When the woman glanced over at her, Elise let out a gasp. It was one of Papi's favorite nurses, looking like a million bucks in a scarlet turtleneck.

"Char Davis! What are you doing here?"

"I'm going to write an article or a book or a poem or something." Char chuckled. "Anything that takes a little more creativity than counting out pills. How 'bout you?"

"I'm working on a website," Elise said, feeling strangely confident that she would indeed move beyond her preliminary scribbles, now that she'd taken the giant step of showing up for this class. "Thought this Ms.—what's her name? Slocum?—might be able to teach me to write a little more compellingly than 'See Dick. See Jane. See Dick run.'"

They both laughed.

"So what's your website going to be about?" Char asked.

Feeling instantly shy again, Elise busied herself booting up her laptop. "Oh, well, actually, it's going to be about heaven."

"Heaven! That's wonderful! So do you share your grandfather's faith, too? I sure do! What are you calling it?"

Elise beamed. *A new friend and a Christian to boot!*

"I already bought the name," she said, clicking open a PDF containing some of her preliminary designs and turning the laptop so Char could see the screen. "I'm calling it Everlasting Place."

"Well," said Char, as they headed towards the parking lot after class, "she's really nice, but that was *not* what I expected for a class called 'Creative Writing 254.'"

"Me neither. I didn't know we were going to be talking about advertising at all."

"Maybe that's all she knows about."

"Could be." Elise pulled her keys out of her purse, gripping them the way all those frightening articles told women to hold them in dark parking lots. "But you'd think they would've mentioned that in the course description, wouldn't you? Although—you know, what she said about 'messaging' might matter a great deal to what you and I both want to do."

"How so?"

"Well, I don't want to just write for the sake of writing, do you? Don't you want to *convey* something, and persuade people of your point of view? I know I do."

Char stopped at the driver's door of an old sedan that might have been green or brown; it was hard to tell in this light. "You know, that's a good point," she said. "I need to stop being so negative about everything."

"From what Papi says, you're the most positive person in the world. He said you make him smile."

"Everything makes Charles smile."

"Not so!" Elise had a thought. "Hey, maybe your assignment should be an article on making patients happy. You know, written for nurses."

"What in the world would I have to offer on that score?"

"I'll help you. We'll just compare your approach to other nurses'—you know, like good old Julia's. Why do patients gravitate to you and away from her? Maybe we could interview her."

Char laughed. "Sure. We'll just say, 'Julia, we'd like to talk with you about why no one likes you.'"

"Move over, Diane Sawyer!"

"But that's pretty mean," Char added sheepishly, pulling the back door open and tossing her bag inside. "She's really a nice woman. More shy than anything. She just has the kind of face that makes her look angry all the time. Plus she's practically deaf, so people tend to think she's stuck up. I feel sorry for her."

Elise felt a pang of shame.

I get a new friend and what do I do? Right away, I'm gossiping.

"You're right," she said contritely. "Forgive me, dear Lord."

"Forgive us both, Lord. We should know better."

Elise made herself a cup of rooibos tea and sat down at the kitchen table, notepad and pen in hand, to begin working on next week's homework while Ms. Slocum's teachings were fresh in her mind.

The assignment had sounded straightforward: define your project's objectives, audiences, and messages. But it wasn't as easy as she'd expected it to be. Ms. Slocum had insisted that they be very specific in their thinking. They were not to claim "everyone" as their audience or "just sharing my thoughts" as a message.

Elise realized now that she hadn't really thought through her website, short of sketching out an essay or two. It took some intense thinking to come up with a focus that would satisfy Ms. Slocum:

Objective: lead visitors into the kingdom of God

Audience: the lost, especially those who think science eliminates the need for Him

Messages:
There is a God. Here's proof.
He is the God of the Bible. Here's proof.
Here's what He offers us (the Gospel).
Here's what we need to do to claim it for our own.
Here's what it means in this life.
Here's what it means in the next.
What happens if you refuse Him.

She really couldn't see a flaw in her planning, except that—and here she was brutally honest with herself—weren't there already scores of websites covering these very topics? Was there anything that would set hers apart?

It wasn't until later, when she was drifting off to sleep, that she hit upon a solution: dressing up the information with the testimonies or thoughts of The Hickories' staff—nurses, aides, administrative workers, housekeepers, kitchen workers, all people who'd built their careers around helping people on the cusp of eternity. Maybe even a volunteer or two, like that cute Bible teacher.

Or would that be too self-serving? Manipulative, even?

She couldn't be sure but the fact that it even crossed her mind made her suspicious of her own motives. She might be able to trick herself on that score, but God wouldn't be fooled.

"The Lord does not see as man sees," she whispered into the night. "For man looks at the outward appearance, but the Lord looks at the heart."

Perhaps this, then: it would be an opportunity to share her own testimony. Maybe even to be brutally honest about that, too, admitting that she was a genuine, garden-variety sinner, saved by grace.

Maybe she'd even make it an occasion for public confession. Not to mention godly sorrow.

CHAPTER EIGHTEEN

Meg Vogel
Sunday, January 22

Meg didn't mind working weekends, but she knew she'd never enjoy Sunday morning duty. Not because she'd miss her Sunday morning ritual of poring over the newspaper with day-old donuts and cup after cup of coffee spiked with a little sugar and plenty of cream; she could live without that once or twice each month. No, it was the religious rigmarole of Sunday mornings at The Hickories that bugged her.

Lucy had told her that these gigs would usually fall on a day when a local church sent in the troops to conduct a service or hymn-sing. Then she'd simply have to help the Sunday volunteers gather residents for the big event, wheeling the eager worshippers into the Great Room and recording their names in the tattered "Participants" notebook to show off during the next State of Wisconsin inspection.

But Lucy had also warned Meg that she'd occasionally be assigned to a Sunday when there was nothing scheduled. She would then be expected to conduct an hour's worth of what was billed as "prayers and hymns" on the activities calendar. She wouldn't have to create a talk or anything like that, Lucy had assured her; there was a nice selection of prayer books in the little library adjacent to their office, and at least a dozen hymn CDs in the big black case on the sound-system cabinet, and here, a whole file cabinet packed with song booklets keyed to those CDs. It would be a piece of cake.

Meg hadn't admitted it to Lucy, of course, but it really made her skin crawl to be feeding the fantasies of these dear old people. There were other occasional Activities Assistants who came in to help with specific events; Meg had already met several of them. Why couldn't Lucy use *them* for this crazy assignment, she wondered sulkily as she slipped into the black pantsuit that had become her uniform.

At least it was an easy drive on this cold bright morning. There was almost no traffic on Sunday mornings, with most sane people at home in bed where they belonged. She let her mind wander into what she'd really *like* to say to her old folk.

So you see, ladies and gentlemen, there's no such thing as absolute truth. What's true for you may not be true for me.

and

If you can't see it, it doesn't exist. So forget all those fairies and poltergeists and demons and yes, even those gods. They do not exist.

She didn't dare.

But here was an idea: What if she were to say a prayer, a generic prayer of some sort, and then open it up to a "how do you know?" discussion? Maybe that could be considered a faith-building exercise for the faith-filled—and a taste of reality for those less sure of their beliefs.

The more she thought about it, the more appealing this approach became.

By the time Meg arrived, Sunday morning volunteers Fran and Pamela had managed to gather an astounding forty-seven residents in the Great Room, seating them in compatible groups around the room's collection of great and small oak trestle tables. They had arrived extra early, Plump Pamela explained breathlessly, to spur the aides into dressing those most willing and able to attend, personally wheeling many down to breakfast, and then bringing them in here for the eleven o'clock service—truly a heroic effort.

But their hard work and success simply irritated Meg, so she shut herself in the office and feigned doing paperwork while the women made a last-ditch effort to hit the fifty mark, which would have been half of the entire population at The Hickories. Then, at precisely eleven, with the count at forty-nine, she put on the hymn CD Lucy had suggested and invited everyone to sing the first song; it was "Holy, Holy, Holy," a number that sounded way too familiar to her irreligious ear.

Meg then handed out the lyric booklets that went with the CD. Incredibly, half the residents were singing without benefit of the words. *Big deal,* she thought. If they were singing hits from the 1970s—"You've Got a Friend," say, or "Let's Get It On," or "If You Leave Me Now"—she wouldn't need the words either. It just depended what you were raised on.

She finished passing out the booklets and let them sing two more songs—"Praise to the Lord" and "Rejoice, the Lord Is King"—before stepping up to the cherry podium and switching on the cordless microphone.

"Let us pray," she said, opening the prayer book she'd grabbed from the library. She let it fall open randomly and began reading. It was a Psalm—the twenty-third Psalm, the one about a shepherd and green pastures and still waters. It turned out to be horrible luck. She remembered it from long ago; it brought to mind her beloved parents and Grammy, and losing them all to death, one blow after another, back in the 1970s. The reminder left her heartsick even now, four decades later. Angry, too, but this morning the grief seemed to be winning out over the anger.

"Yea, though I walk through the valley of the shadow of death, I will fear no evil," she read, her voice growing thick. "For thou art with me; thy rod and thy staff they comfort me."

Surprised to realize she was in danger of bawling, Meg forced herself to think about the lox and bagel and cream cheese that were waiting for her at home. She would slice some onion . . .

"And I will dwell in the house of the LORD forever."

Done.

Fran and Pamela were still out trolling the facility for participants, she was glad to see; they were both very religious and might not appreciate what she was about to do.

"So what do you say we try something a little different today?" she asked, smiling brightly at her audience. Other than a few raised eyebrows—including Sadie's, she noticed with a pang of guilt—there wasn't much reaction. "Let's try some role-playing. I'll be the big bad atheist, and you tell me why I should believe in Jesus. How does that sound?"

"Why would we want to do that?" asked a woman at the nearest table, a tiny woman sporting white curls and a baby blue cardigan.

Meg was well prepared to field the question. She'd overheard Lucy talking about this very subject with a volunteer the other day.

"To make sure you're ready to give a defense of the faith, as Peter said in one of his letters. Or maybe it was Paul—I forget which one."

"Let's do it," said a woman Meg thought of as Big Bertha, a strapping hulk of a woman with yellow-white hair and hazel eyes. "It'll be fun."

"Okay." Meg took a deep breath, a little unnerved by her own daring. "So I'll start us out by saying that the Bible is chock-full of errors and contradictions. Who wants to address this objection?"

Silence.

"Oh, come on. Doesn't anyone have an answer for me?"

"I do." It was the skinny volunteer Fran, and she didn't look happy as she marched up to the podium and grabbed the mic. But then she put on what Meg thought of as a sunshine-and-light mask.

"This really *is* a great idea," Fran gushed. "I know that many of you have unbelievers in your families and among your friends, and it would be helpful to summarize the answers to some of the most common questions an atheist might have."

Fran turned and looked Meg straight in the eye, just as she said the word "atheist." Meg hadn't ever discussed her spiritual status with anyone here—there were way too many Christians in these parts and she didn't want to start insulting anyone's beliefs. But apparently her silence on the issue hadn't fooled ol' Fran.

It had been a grueling hour for Meg, sitting through the Q&A session as Fran and Pamela took over question-raising duties. She'd managed to ignore quite a bit of it, focusing instead on things like Pamela's hideous plaid skirt and flat-heeled boots (from the 1980s), the ratio of lap-robe-draped attendees to bare-lapped (22:27) and permed-and-dyed to natural (14:35), and her plans for crashing that very afternoon with Sandra and her pets over popcorn and some old movie.

But enough stuff had slipped through to reinforce her sadness for people who were caught up in this mythology.

Pamela's claims about the historicity of the book of Genesis were just pathetic, for instance. And the nonsense about modern-day Israel fulfilling biblical prophecies—well, sure, you could twist any ancient text to make it support something that's already happened. Bring on Nostradamus and Edgar Cayce, for Pete's sake!

She was looking forward to her upcoming interviews with residents who were not in attendance this morning. People like Gladys Baldwin didn't seem like the sort who tolerated the sentimental *or* the supernatural. And that suited Meg just fine.

Sandra showed up at Meg's front door at three that afternoon, carrying a box stuffed with everything from a popcorn popper and fresh popcorn from the health food store to butter, parmesan, and sea salt, plus an assortment of DVDs.

"Take your pick," she said cheerily, fanning the DVDs out on the kitchen counter. "I love them all."

Meg sifted through the assortment. Sandra was really a sweetheart. Here were all Meg's favorites, from *Gone with the Wind* and *The Sound of Music* to *Stella Dallas* and *This Above All*, the latter once again starring the very hot Tyrone Power. And there, at the bottom, Sandra's favorite, *A Place in the Sun*—the Elizabeth Taylor/Montgomery Clift melodrama based on Dreiser's *An American Tragedy*.

"They just don't make them like this anymore, do they?" Meg murmured, looking up to find Sandra smiling at her hopefully. "Let's watch *A Place in the Sun*. I don't know that I've ever seen the whole thing."

"Yippee! You'll love it! I'll make the popcorn if you'll get the beer from my car—I brought Beck's."

The movie was about a poor young man who hoped to make it big at his uncle's factory, was forgotten on the plant floor, was so lonely that he fell in with a factory girl and got her pregnant, only to be suddenly welcomed into high society by his uncle's family. Whereupon—naturally—he met the heart-stoppingly beautiful girl of his dreams. He tried to get rid of the factory girl's claim on him via abortion, failed, kinda sorta let her drown, got caught, and ended up on death row.

"Well," Meg said over the closing credits. "I'm impressed; that was really gripping. Maybe I should give the book another try."

"I knew you'd love it," Sandra said, picking up her popcorn bowl again after having been too engrossed in the movie to bother with it. "I've seen it about twenty times and it just keeps getting better."

"The mother in the end kills me. You know, when she tries to get George to decide whether he had murder in his heart when Alice drowned?"

"Yeah, so that if the answer is yes, he's going to hell. I'm glad she's not judging me, because I'll tell you, I often have murder in my heart! You can hardly blame me, with the jerks I have to work with every day."

Meg laughed. "Me too—I've had lots of murder in my heart in my day." She paused, wrinkling her brow. "But to be fair, I guess the oh-so-religious volunteers at The Hickories would say that our innocence or guilt on that score has nothing to do with our eternal fates. Want another beer?"

"No thanks, gotta drive home. But what do you mean?"

"Well, Prune Face Fran was saying this morning that everyone's guilty of murder if they've ever hated anyone. And really, who hasn't? She said what gets you into heaven is believing in Jesus. Oh, and of course *repenting* of your sins"—Meg rolled her eyes dramatically—"mustn't forget repentance! Wish I could believe it. Do whatever you want and apologize for it and figure that you're a shoo-in for heaven because this Jesus paid for your sins."

"Sweet deal," Sandra said, tossing Touchdown a few kernels of popcorn.

"No kidding. Hey, no more for him. I don't want him getting fat. Touchdown, go lie down."

Amazingly, he obeyed.

"Impressive." Sandra retrieved her purse—a mammoth bag in slouchy peach leather, a fashionable contrast to her aqua-and-olive sweater—and began fishing for her keys. "There's your next career – training dogs."

They shared a laugh.

"So'd this woman look like Mama in the film, Meg?"

"What woman?"

"You're losing it." Sandra's brows shot up. "Or maybe it's me. I meant your Fran."

"Oh, yeah," Meg said, rewinding her memory a tad. "Totally. Think I'd just stay home if that was the best I could look."

"Hmmmm . . . does that mean there's a new man in the picture already?"

Meg thought that it was in pretty poor taste for Sandra to suggest anything of the kind, but why say so after having such a nice afternoon together? Best to make a joke of it. "No new man," she said, pasting a smile on her face, "not now, not ever. Unless I meet someone fabulously wealthy, who'd be willing to support us both. Then you could retire."

"Don't I wish. Where do you suppose the rich old men hang out?"

CHAPTER NINETEEN

Sadie Sparrow
Friday, January 27

W ho's this?"

Sadie squinted at the snapshot, then remembered to don her reading glasses.

"Ah! That's Ed's mother again. Edna was her name. Isn't that cute? Ed and Edna."

"Yes indeedy," said Meg. "What was her husband's name? Edward?"

"Horace." Sadie smiled mischievously. "Not so cute."

"No, not cute at all. But did you like him?"

"Oh, he was wonderful." Sadie sat back in her chair, warmed by her memories, happy to be sharing them with Meg right here in her beautiful room. "He was a farrier, you know, a blacksmith. If he had any anger in him, I think he probably took it out on all those horseshoes he pounded out all day long. Such a sweet man! But then the whole family was very sweet."

She found a snapshot of him amidst those spread out before them. "Here he is. Nice looking, don't you think?"

Meg nodded, stifling a yawn. "Very."

"Oh, I'm boring you, dear," Sadie said, quickly gathering up the photos.

"No, really, I love getting these glimpses into your life. Really I do! I just didn't sleep well last night, for some reason."

Sadie looked at Meg with concern. "Not anything to do with us, I hope?"

Meg laughed. "Oh, no, not at all. I don't have any worries anymore. I just have insomnia fairly often and I hate to take pills."

"Have you tried warm milk?"

"Of course. And melatonin and a warm bath, not hot! And reading and not reading and every other homegrown remedy that's out there, I suppose. All useless."

She did look tired, Sadie thought, noticing the dark circles underscoring Meg's eyes.

"And prayer? Have you tried prayer?"

Meg smiled sadly. "No ma'am, prayer is the one thing I haven't tried."

"You might want to," Sadie offered, wondering if she was being too pushy or not pushy enough, wondering if a prayer offered up to a God you didn't believe in would do any good at all. "As they say, a few minutes spent with Him leads to eight hours of solid sleep."

"I can see how it could have that effect."

Sadie was pleased with Meg's reply until that evening, when she'd had a chance to review their conversation. It was only then that she realized her friend had not been implying that sleep is an answer to prayer. Instead, she had meant that talking with God, real or imagined, would be so boring that it would put you to sleep.

"Oh Lord, I am so useless to You. Why don't you just take me Home?"

Just two hours later, it seemed that Sadie's prayer was about to be answered.

Face washed, teeth brushed, evening pills taken, and wearing her favorite pink-flowered nightgown, Sadie was snuggling down in her oh-so-comfy bed. It was dressed in fresh sheets and blankets and crowned with an assortment of pillows so she could always find just the right one for the night at hand. She stretched contentedly. She was so sleepy, and there wasn't a place in the world that she'd rather be than right here in her own little nest.

Having done what she considered her "serious praying" all day long, she now simply recited the prayers she'd been saying since childhood: "Now I Lay Me Down To Sleep" and "Dear Jesus in Heaven" and "Ich Bin Klein," the latter taught to her by a little girlfriend's German grandma a lifetime ago.

She thought about that little girl. Ilse was her name, and she'd had the prettiest long brown hair, usually worn in braids, and she often wore those cute little dirndls. She called her grandma Oma, as Sadie recalled. Even though Oma had smelled—well, *old* was probably the best way of putting it—and had had a heavy accent, she was the nicest grandma ever. And she'd taught them this wonderful little prayer that Sadie had never forgotten, even though she wasn't exactly sure of its meaning. Something about—

What's this?

Sadie's left arm had started tingling to beat the band, like it had suddenly woken up from a sound sleep.

And now her left leg.

And the left side of her body, and her head, too.

What is going on?

Now her arm felt like it was in a very tight sleeve that was getting tighter by the moment. Not the rest of her body, though. Just the left side.

And then she realized what it had to be: a stroke, of course. Little Sadie Gottschalk Sparrow was having a stroke.

Not that she seemed to be paralyzed or anything. Yes, her arm and leg still moved as commanded. She forced a smile and felt her mouth—no drooping there, as far as she could tell.

She debated her options silently.

She could hit the call button right now to summon help. That would mean an ambulance trip to the hospital, and hours in the ER, and from what Gladys had told her recently in enumerating her own hospitalizations, a day or two under observation with the doctors doing nothing—absolutely nothing—to make her any better.

Or she could wait a while to see what would happen. Maybe this would all go away and she'd get a good night's sleep and all would be well in the morning. Yes, she'd heard that there was a four-hour window of opportunity for treatment. What treatment, she was not sure, but people were always saying it was important to act quickly with a stroke. So maybe she'd wait a half hour, till eleven o'clock, and decide then.

Or she could do nothing, and point herself towards heaven.

She wasn't sure about that, though. Had she really been a good enough person to get in? What if she got there and they threw her into the other place? What if she could see Ed waiting there at the pearly gates, smiling eagerly until he saw St. Peter shake his head and Sadie's face fall—

Oh, it was too unbearable to think about! And now her heart was really racing.

"Calm down, Sadie," she told herself softly. "Stop thinking about that. You know you've lived a lot better life than most people. You've never murdered anyone or stolen anything and you were certainly never one to swear. You'll be fine."

That logic helped a bit. She thought back through some of the greater kindnesses of her life, the many times she helped their old neighbor Mrs. Grace hang her wash out to dry—no small task!—and the bandage rolling she did during World War II and the time she marched all the way back to Woolworth's because the clerk had given her a dime too much in change. And even today, advising Meg to pray; that would surely count to her good.

She was feeling calmer now, although the tingling hadn't abated, nor had the tightness in her arm.

Besides, Jamie had just said that being a good person was not the issue. Just as Ed had always insisted.

What exactly had Jamie said about that? It was something she'd known on some level, like she knew that five times nine is forty-five and that "we" is the first person plural.

Apparently she wasn't thinking too clearly right now, because that didn't really make much sense.

"Dear Lord," she breathed. "Please—"

Please what, Sadie?

"Our Father, who art in heaven, hallowed be Thy name. Thy kingdom come, Thy will be done . . ."

That was it! That was what Ed and Papa had always prayed for, no matter how dire the circumstances: Thy will be done.

"Please Lord, may Thy will be done with this old body of mine. Whatever you think is fine with me."

And she began earnestly presenting Him with the options, and the likely consequences to others.

The next time Sadie looked at the clock it was half past three, and it had to be a.m. because it was still dark out. Amazingly, she had fallen asleep.

The left side of her body was no longer tingling; now it just felt numb. She tested her arm, her leg. They worked fine, even though they felt like they'd had gigantic shots of Novocain. And her smile still felt normal.

Well, it was too late to do anything about it now.

She switched to her firmer foam pillow and promptly fell back to sleep.

CHAPTER TWENTY

Elise Chapelle
Monday, January 30

"Check this one out, Papi!" Elise handed her grandfather the stereo viewer. He appeared to be getting tired, but they were almost finished looking through slides from his 1957 trip through the French countryside with Mamie, and she was enjoying the vicarious journey enough to selfishly push on.

He peered into the viewer and laughed. "Ah, your Mamie on horseback."

"She looks terrified."

"She was, at first. But what a day it turned out to be! We rode through the woods and picnicked in a secret clearing. At least, our guide said it was secret. It was in southwestern France, in the Landes Forest, and he brought a delicious lunch."

"Wine, bread, and cheese?"

Papi thought hard and finally shook his head. "It's over a half-century ago. I don't remember. But I do remember that it was delicious. And that neither your Mamie nor I could walk for the next day or two; we were *extremely* saddle sore!"

Laughing, Elise replaced the slide with one of a charming little cottage and showed it to Papi.

"Ah, this is the place we stayed in the Landes," he said. "Such memories. It was so inexpensive to travel in those days. I do hope it will be again someday so you can see where we came from."

"This was before Helene was born, wasn't it?"

Papi set the viewer down in his blanketed lap—they were sitting side by side, he in his wheelchair and she on the loveseat, his room cozy on a bleak winter's afternoon—and smiled gently at the memory.

"Lorraine was already carrying her on that trip, although we weren't quite sure. Helene was born just before Christmas." He shrugged. "But that was a long time ago, and there's no sense in looking back, is there?"

"I suppose not. But sometimes you can't help it, you know?"

"I do."

"Especially when you have a mother who abandoned you." Elise cleared her throat. "If I may speak frankly."

"Of course, my dear." Papi turned his chair a bit to face her more directly. "Tell me what you've been thinking."

"Well, it's just this," Elise said, frowning at her hands. "I spoke with Mrs. Macklin after lunch today, while you were in therapy. You know her, don't you? She sits at the table next to yours."

He nodded.

"She was telling me that the discussion last Sunday, in the morning service—"

"If you could call it a service," Papi said.

"Right. It was very strange, wasn't it? I don't think that Meg is a believer."

"Nor do I. We'll have to see what we can do about that; she's quite hostile."

"That's just the word Mrs. Macklin used," Elise said, impressed. "'Hostile.' And she said that the service had really upset her, because it reminded her of her own mother's unwarranted hostility. It was like our situation, apparently: her mother dumped her off with her grandparents when she was little. Except at least they saw each other every year or two, when the mother would show up at the door unexpectedly. Mrs. Macklin said it thrilled her as a little girl, when her mother popped in, I mean, and then it broke her heart when her mother got all crabby and left a few hours or days later."

"Very sad," Papi said. "It's difficult to understand how a woman could do that to her own child."

"And then one day, her mother left and never came back again. Just vanished. Mrs. Macklin said she was ten the last time they saw each other. And she never learned what had happened to her mother, whether she had died or been kidnapped or maybe even had another little girl—a better one—that she had decided to stay with."

Elise looked at Papi, her eyes brimming. "The worst part is that it still bothers Mrs. Macklin terribly. She said that not a day goes by that she doesn't think about all these things, and even wonder if her mother might not still be alive. Which is possible, I suppose, because Mrs. Macklin is only eighty-two."

Elise pulled a tissue out of her purse and blotted her eyes.

"And?" Papi prompted her.

"And she said that it's the one thing in her life that she's bitter about, which is so obviously true. Her eyes became so—I'm not sure of the word, but maybe *hard*—her eyes became *hard* as she talked about her mother."

"Bitterness is a horrible thing," Papi said. "Tears you up, and then, just when you think you're healing, it returns, worse than before."

"And Papi, I don't want that to happen to me. I don't want to nurse this grudge against *my* mother into bitterness. But I just don't know how to get past it."

Papi bowed his head for a long moment, in prayer or thought, Elise didn't know.

"It's really quite simple," he said at last, his voice kind but heavy. "The Lord has told us to love our enemies, to bless those who curse us, do good to those who hate us and pray for those who spitefully use and persecute us."

"I know, but *how*? How do I do that, Papi?"

"My dearest girl, you know what to do." He reached for her hand and squeezed it. "You pray for yourself, and you pray for her—for her salvation especially, because that would change everything. Ask Him to do whatever it takes to bring her into His kingdom. If it's possible, if she is willing, He will answer that prayer. But more to the point, in making your petitions, your heart will soften towards her. And that root of bitterness will die, because it needs a hardened heart to thrive."

Elise was ashamed to admit even to herself that she hadn't already done this. Too simple for a psychology-swayed American girl, she thought.

"You're right, Papi." She hugged him. "You're always right, you know that?"

He chuckled. "It's not me, Elise. It's the Lord. He told us all we need to know to live peaceful lives. We need only listen."

"And obey."

She picked up the viewer again and replaced the cottage slide.

"Maybe I should have another little talk with Mrs. Macklin one of these days," she said, lifting the viewer to her eyes. "Oh, this is a good one, Papi, check it out."

"I think that would be a very good idea," Papi said as he looked into the viewer again. "Ah, yes, a sunset over the Atlantic, near Mimizan . . ."

CHAPTER TWENTY-ONE

Meg Vogel
Monday, January 30

Wait—wait—*ignore the pity of that appeal. And then—then—But there! Behold. It is over. She is sinking now. You will never, never see her alive any more—ever. And there is your own hat upon the water—as you wished. And upon the boat, clinging—*

"Excuse me?"

Meg nearly jumped out of her skin, so immersed was she in the drowning scene in Sandra's copy of *An American Tragedy.* It was unbelievably horrifying for a novel published nearly a century ago, far worse than the watered-down rendering in the movie.

"I'm Elise Chapelle, Meg," the young woman in the office doorway was saying. "I don't think we've met officially. I'm sorry to have interrupted your lunch."

Meg shook her head to dispel the image of Clyde's cold-blooded abandonment of the drowning Roberta. Yes, that's what it was; the movie had made his intentions ambiguous, but the novel made them clear.

"No problem." Meg smiled self-consciously. "Sorry to be such a space cadet. I'm so lost in this book that I think I'm going a little crazy."

Elise looked politely at the cover that Meg was displaying, apparently clueless.

Beautiful and empty-headed, no doubt. Never heard of Dreiser.

"You should read it," Meg said. "It's riveting. Hated it in high school but now—well, it certainly underscores how deadly all that high-minded Victorian morality could be."

Elise's eyebrows popped up but she didn't comment.

"So what can I do for you?"

"Well," the young woman said, casting serious green eyes on Meg, "Sadie Sparrow said you were writing some biographies about the residents, and I wondered if you might do one on my grandfather—Charles Chapelle, you know, he lives right across from Sadie."

"Ah," said Meg, motioning Elise into the other chair. The young woman sat and gazed at her intently.

"Would you be willing to?"

"Well, let's see." Meg made a show of poring over her calendar and a neatly typewritten chart summarizing her interviews. She took her time over each name, blocking out time on the calendar for writing each one, stalling for no reason at all.

It has to be Dreiser's influence. Evil, evil book!

"I think I could fit him in," she said finally, looking up and seeing a smile break out on Elise's pretty face. "It will be a few weeks, though."

"Oh, no problem! I'd just be so grateful. Sadie tells me you're a wonderful interviewer, and it would give him something to look forward to, besides my visits, I mean, and Bible study of course."

"From what I understand, Charles does very well for himself around here," Meg said, surprised at how officious she sounded.

Elise beamed. "I'm so glad to hear that. He's had a rough time of it in the last few years, with his wife dying, and now his own health problems—especially not being able to get around without help. He can't even wheel his chair himself, you know."

She chattered on, apparently running on nerves; her body was still but her fingers danced incessantly over her folded hands. Meg donned her "I'm listening" look and thought about the sinking Roberta, wondered how long it took to drown and what it was like, whether it hurt or not, what one thought about at that last instant . . .

Ooops! Elise had paused her narrative.

Meg nodded encouragingly.

"It's not only his recent history," Elise continued. "There's been heartache for him for a long time, thanks to his daughter—my mother, actually."

"Really?" Meg was perking up now. *This might be good.* "Tell me about it."

"Should I?" Elise tucked her thick brown hair behind her ears, looking like a confused little girl. "He may not want to talk about it at all."

"All the more reason to tell me," Meg lied. "It will help me steer clear of the subject if I know what to avoid."

"Well, okay."

Cautious but obedient. Perfect.

"My mother's name is Helene . . ."

They talked for a good half hour, until Lucy breezed in from another one of The Hickories' frequent in-service luncheons. Apparently delighted to see Meg hobnobbing with a family member, she quickly disappeared into the Great Room.

"Well, I guess that gives you enough of our sad story," Elise said, pulling on her jacket, a funny old brown-plaid wool number that must have been all the rage a century ago. "Sorry to talk your ear off!"

"My pleasure," Meg said, really meaning it. This young woman's apparent innocence and meekness were starting to grow on her. "You should write *your* memoirs."

Any normal person would have laughed at that, she knew. Not Elise.

"You really think so?"

Oh, Elise, don't take everything so seriously, girl!

"Why not?" Meg offered.

"It's just odd that you should say that." Elise smiled timidly. "I'm taking a creative writing course at WCTC, and—"

"Not Sandra Slocum's class?"

"How did you know?"

Meg laughed. "She's my best friend, and she mentioned a couple of very pretty young women in her class. I wonder if you were one of them?"

"Oh, I'm sure she didn't mean me." Elise buttoned her jacket up to her chin, managing to look cute in spite of the nerdy effect. "But yes, I'm one of her students."

"How funny. Small world, as they say."

"Small world," Elise agreed.

"So give that memoir idea some thought."

"I will." Spoken with furrowed brow and complete sincerity.

Meg smiled as she watched Elise disappear into the Great Room. She'd never met anyone quite like this young woman, so shy and pretty and serious and nervous.

Is this what happens to girls who are abandoned by their mothers?

Meg couldn't help but hope that Elise would one day have a chance to turn the tables on ol' Helene.

CHAPTER TWENTY-TWO

Sadie Sparrow
Wednesday, February 1

Gladys was trying to be nonchalant about her upcoming appointment with Meg, but she couldn't quite stop talking about it during the girls' Wednesday morning puzzle-making session.

"I suppose she'll want to know all about my life on the North Shore," she mused as she scrutinized the sea of mismatched pieces she was amassing.

When no one commented, she looked at her puzzlemates one by one, to assure that they were listening. "I was quite prominent socially, you know. The parties I went to—well, everyone who was anyone was there. I'm sure Meg will want to document that."

Sadie and Eva smiled at each other.

"I'm sure you're right, dear," Eva said brightly. "It's not often that someone of your social standing winds up in a place like this."

Gladys looked up suspiciously. "What's wrong with this place?"

"Nothing at all. It's just that people of your class usually stay home with full-time nurses. Or live with a doting son or daughter."

Gladys glared at Eva, with good reason: it was a low blow, given the fact that Gladys rarely saw any of her three children.

It wasn't like Eva to be so snarky. But snarky she'd been, and now Sadie noticed that Eva's eyes were cold above the smile. Or maybe just tired, as if she hadn't slept well in days. Was it a trick of her pale beige turtleneck against a ninety-three-year-old complexion, or were Eva's eyes telling her something?

Sadie followed her hunch. "Did you by any chance have a chat with Nurse Julia last night?"

The smile vanished as Eva turned her attention back to the puzzle pieces she'd been poring over. "A chat? No, I don't think that would be the right word for it," she said, trying a four-tabbed piece in a space clearly made for three tabs. "She's just plain mean, in my opinion. But why do you ask?"

They looked at each other. Was that fear Sadie saw in her friend's eyes? Or relief?

"It's no longer just my word against Julia's"? Is that what Eva is thinking?

Sadie hesitated. She was no good at interpreting expressions; more often than not, she ended up being wrong.

"Maybe we should talk to Meg," Sadie said. "She'll know what to do."

"About what?" Gladys demanded. "Do about what?"

"About the conditions here, dear," Eva said. "The abominable conditions."

"Ah, you don't know what you're talking about," Gladys said, returning to her pieces. "This is a great place."

"On a great lake," Sadie added. "Remember that slogan for Milwaukee, years ago? 'A great place on a great lake.' Some designer came up with it."

"His name was Jack," said Eva. "My youngest worked with him years ago. The only artist she ever knew who cared about words and grammar."

"I met lots of artists in my day," said Gladys, cheered by the memory. "At every party. They always complimented me on my clothes, of course." She smoothed her tunic, a brilliant peacock blue piece with a riot of rhinestones at the neckline. "I had the best wardrobe in town, if I do say so myself."

Sadie was astonished to feel a pang of jealousy when Meg breezed into the dining room to fetch a sweet little woman named Doris who lived in the Southeast Wing, just down the hall from Gladys. Lunch had been terrific—a lovely Asian salad with ginger dressing and hand-rolled sushi called a "California roll," according to the waitress. But now she no longer felt like going to the afternoon movie. So what if it was *The Sound of Music*, her all-time favorite? She now felt like going home and pouting, and by George, that was exactly what she intended to do.

She started rolling herself back to the North Wing but found the going a little strange thanks to her left arm, which remained numb five days after her presumed stroke; the arm seemed to work just fine, thank the Lord, but her entire left side still felt so odd, almost anesthetized. So she was delighted when dear aide Piper appeared out of nowhere to offer her a ride. Sadie accepted gratefully, chatting with the girl throughout the long ride home as if she hadn't a care in the world.

It was a lie, of course, and she abandoned it the moment Piper settled her in her room. She had plenty of cares, starting with this stupid stroke which she hadn't told anyone about, and which now seemed way too late to mention. They would think she was foolish to have remained silent, or maybe entering the early stages of dementia, in which case they'd send that unctuous psychiatrist in to see her and—

Oh, be still, you silly old woman!

But so far her decision to wait had paid off. She could live with this numbness, annoying as it was.

And if it happened again? Her one fear was suffering a stroke that would paralyze her without killing her or leaving her senseless. It would hardly be unusual.

Well, she'd cross that bridge if and when she came to it.

Sadie rolled over to her desk and refocused her thoughts on the afternoon. Maybe she'd spend some time looking up the list of prophecies Jamie had left with her, in preparation for his next visit, while she tried not to think about Meg talking and laughing with little Doris.

Which was absolutely ridiculous. Sure, she was lonely, but so was just about everyone else in this place, at least those with children. The only woman who was satisfied with the number of visits she got from her kids was Catherine Peebles, and charming as she was when she was awake for their arrivals and departures, she normally dozed through the visits themselves.

Dana hasn't been here since New Year's Eve. Not once.

Well, that was true enough, but Sadie had to be honest with herself: Would weekly visits have satisfied her? Daily? Of course not. What she wanted was a close relationship with her only child, the sort of relationship she'd had with her own mother. And that just didn't seem to be in the cards for her.

She sighed. This self-pity was not only unattractive; studying with Jamie these last few weeks had revived memories of her father and Ed reading the word of God to her, and she remembered that Ed in particular had called self-pity sinful. As he would have insisted, the Lord had placed her in this spot for His perfect purpose, and she had no right to complain.

She could almost hear Ed telling her exactly that, in a much gentler manner, of course, reading to her from his worn King James Bible: "I have learned, in whatsoever state I am, therewith to be content." He would look at her and smile at that point, his heart seemingly halfway to heaven. "I can do all things through Christ which strengtheneth me," he would conclude.

It had been one of Ed's favorite passages, and remembering him reciting it made her happy. Hungry for more, she picked up her large-print New King James and turned to the source of the verse, the fourth chapter of Philippians. Ah, there it was, preceded by the lines that had over the centuries been a balm to countless spirits: "Be anxious for nothing, but in everything by prayer and supplication, with thanksgiving, let your requests be made known to God; and the peace of God, which surpasses all understanding, will guard your hearts and minds through Christ Jesus."

Sadie asked the Lord for the grace to be content and for the peace He had promised. She then read the entire chapter, lingering especially over the part about God supplying "all your need according to His riches in glory by Christ Jesus." She remembered Papa talking about that particular verse when she was fairly little and had been desperate for a pony of her own.

"He supplies our need, Sadie. Not necessarily our wants."

Refreshed, Sadie set the Bible down. Maybe she'd go to that movie after all. She powdered her nose and found a ride to the Great Room's movie theater. She was hoping to arrive in time to hear Julie Andrews sing "I Have Confidence." Hoping, too, to speak with Eva alone, to discuss the Nurse Julia problem and plot out a way to voice their "concerns" without running the ever-present risk of retaliation.

Sadie accomplished both goals that afternoon. She joined the others in singing along as Julie Andrews not only delivered her pitch-perfect rendition of "I Have Confidence" but also managed to leap in the air and click her heels together—at the same time! Sadie also joined them in belting out "Climb Every Mountain" with Mother Superior, not worried in the least that their voices had seen better days. And she joined them in softly warbling along as Maria sang "Something Good," until she was so overcome with the emotion of the scene that she had to stop and fish a tissue out of the sleeve of her pink sweater.

Then, after watching the von Trapps escape the Nazis and climb into the breathtakingly beautiful Alps, she and Eva parked themselves at the fireplace in the Great Room to discuss the Julia problem.

"I have reason to believe," Sadie said, so softly that Eva cupped her ear and leaned closer, "that this particular person may be guilty of more than being mean."

Eva looked both shocked and horrified, Sadie was happy to see. If this suggestion had surprised Eva, then she had surely not suffered physically at Julia's hand.

Sadie answered the unspoken question. "Yes, possibly physical violence. Eva, has she ever said or done anything to you that would make you suspect she was capable of—well, of *hurting* you, or another resident?"

Eva didn't answer right away. She fumbled with the locks on her wheels, perhaps considering how much to say.

"No," she said finally, "not if you mean actively hurting someone, as in slapping or shoving a resident. But she has been known to—well, last night she ignored me when I asked for a pain pill." Eva's eyes met Sadie's; they were red. "My back is getting worse with this horrid arthritis. But when I asked for a pill, she just turned on her heel and walked out of the room without saying a word. Like I hadn't even spoken."

"I'm so sorry, my dear. I didn't realize you were getting worse." Sadie remembered her own dream about Nurse Char denying her pain pills. It was much more dramatic, but the outcome was the same. "Unfortunately, as far as Julia goes, it's your word against hers. We don't have any hard evidence."

"Exactly." Eva frowned. "But if you have proof that she has in fact *hurt* someone, then—"

"Well, not proof, exactly. Just a suspicion, really."

Eva looked intently into Sadie's eyes, her brow lifted in question.

"Sorry, Eva, I can't say anything more. Not yet, anyway."

"I understand. But I'm not sure what you *can* do about it. If you report a suspicion, with no evidence, Julia's just going to deny it. And she could retaliate against the person who told on her, you know. She's cold-blooded enough to do it."

"And most likely smart enough to get away with it."

Her talk with Eva sent Sadie's heart into high gear. It returned to its normal plodding only after she was back in her room with her door closed against the world.

When the late-afternoon knock came, she was relieved to recognize it as Nurse Char's. She breathed a silent prayer of thanks. She couldn't have handled having Julia for a nurse tonight.

After dinner, Sadie pulled out her old notebook and made herself a list.

Dropped pill
B's broken legs
Refusing pain pills to E

It really wasn't much. The dropped pill could have been something as innocuous as a Tylenol. Not giving Eva a pain pill could be dismissed as simply being too preoccupied to hear the request. And the broken legs? She didn't have a single eye-witness, not even Beulah herself.

In short, she had nothing but nagging suspicions. And this irritating numbness that just wouldn't go away.

CHAPTER TWENTY-THREE

Elise Chapelle
Wednesday, February 1

*D*ear Helene,
  I had to write you about the most exciting thing that has ever happened to me. I have met a young man who is everything I've ever dreamed of—godly, biblically literate (and not just literate, but a real scholar!), kind, handsome, and single.

  At least I think he is all these things. I don't know him very well, really. He is an assistant pastor studying theology at a solid Bible college near here, and he is leading a little Bible study at The Hickories—you know, where your father is now living. We had our third study with him today, Papi and I, and there is only one other resident, Papi's neighbor Sadie Sparrow. She is a darling old girl and I must say, I think Papi might be a little smitten. Just a little.

  At any rate, Jamie (my young man) is planning to go into the mission field when he finishes school. He plans to go to Munich, interestingly. Who knows? Maybe I'll visit him one day and stop to see you in Paris. What would you think of that?

  We are learning all about the proofs of the Bible's inspiration and inerrancy. I've read it many times, of course—Papi and Mamie raised me in the faith, and it is so clearly true, Helene. But I'm noticing so many things about it now that I never saw before.

This for instance: the fact that the prophet Isaiah wrote about the earth being round a couple hundred years before it occurred to Pythagoras, even though the Greek seems to get all the credit for it. And the fact that the sun has its own orbit: it took scientists 3,000 years to see the truth of what King David wrote on the subject in Psalm 19. There is no way the Bible's writers could have known such things apart from the inspiration of God Himself. And of course as I'm sure you know, the Dead Sea Scrolls prove that scripture recorded these scientific truths, and scores more, long before the time of Christ. So there was no chronological chicanery going on there.

At any rate, back to Jamie, who is taking us on this "tour of truth." I don't know if he cares for me, but I just have a feeling that he might. We shall see. I just thought you might want to know.

Love from your daughter,
Elise

Elise folded the letter and tucked it into the right-hand desk drawer. She would never send this letter, or any of the others in the drawer. Other girls kept diaries; hers just happened to be named Helene. Every now and then she reread a few of them; the oldest ones were especially bittersweet, filled with a child's wonder over the world unfolding before her, with love for her puppy and the seemingly endless Fleur de Lis flower fields, and of course, with longing for her mother.

At first, her unsent letters had merely been drafts, filled with scratched-out lines and inserts and arrows indicating transposed paragraphs. Finally satisfied, Elise would copy each one over carefully on her best stationery, address an envelope with equal care, and seal her letter inside, kissing the flap as if to steal a maternal kiss. She'd then stash the rough in the drawer.

It wasn't until she was a teenager that Elise had discovered the therapeutic value of writing letters with no intention of ever sending them. She continued to write and post some letters to Helene, but others she wrote solely to record her uncensored thoughts and feelings, and to go off on tangents that interested her alone—mostly theological tangents as she puzzled out a particularly compelling and elusive Bible passage. It didn't matter than Helene would not have been the least bit interested in her daughter's reflections on the shepherd's anointing of his sheep in the twenty-third Psalm, or the apostle Paul's statements about the entire creation being freed from its slavery to corruption; Helene would never see her daughter's deepest ruminations.

In point of fact, Elise thought, embracing the bitterness that was rising once again in her heart, Helene apparently wasn't very interested in anything about her daughter. She'd written back rarely, usually sending nothing more than a postcard or birthday greeting with a few words scrawled so hastily that they were almost illegible. Elise had treasured the messages nevertheless; at least her mother had remembered her.

At midnight, Elise crawled into bed thinking about those long-ago messages, then imagining what it might be like to drop in on her mother in Paris one happy day, en route to Munich. In her fantasy, the seedy little apartment (because surely that's what it was in reality) was transformed into a lovely high-ceilinged living space with Persian rugs and golden-hued tapestries and long silk drapes in pale blue.

Helene would be sitting at her writing table, in the midst of dashing off yet another letter to her beloved Elise. She would be lovely in a chunky turtleneck and jeans—no, wait, in a silk kimono in seafoam green—and her hair, still glossy brown, pulled back into a loose bun. And when she finally noticed Elise, she would gasp and, hesitating only a moment, rise gracefully and float into her daughter's arms.

It was a well-rehearsed fantasy, with only a few of the details changing, and it ushered Elise into contented sleep.

Elise spent Thursday afternoon with Papi, going through more old family slides and chatting about yesterday's Bible study. She'd been hoping to see Jamie—she had parked her old navy Taurus next to his even older silver-and-rust Honda, so she knew he was around—but he was nowhere to be found, at least in the usual spots.

Sadie was MIA, too. Maybe he was helping her with some tricky point of theology, Elise thought. That would be just like Jamie, to spend whatever time was necessary to help someone grasp the word of God.

She was on pins and needles most of the afternoon, but she apparently hid it well; Papi didn't seem to notice. It wasn't pleasant, that was for sure.

If this is what love is like, forget it!

Elise left the door open into the hall, supposedly because the room was a little stuffy. But she didn't hear either of the voices she longed to hear. She finally packed up the slides at five and pushed Papi down to the dining room. No sign of Jamie or Sadie there, either.

Her heart sank when she arrived in the garage to find his car gone. He hadn't even bothered to stop and say hello. Thinking that maybe she'd misinterpreted his kindness as interest, she headed for home, and another lonely night with nothing but homework awaiting her attention.

Elise was booting up her laptop when it struck her.

God does not protect us from the consequences of our sin.

Maybe that was why she was struggling to connect with Jamie? She had, in her mid-twenties, been so longing for love that she'd become impatient with the Lord's plan, had stepped outside of it and transgressed His law; maybe she was paying for it now.

But to be fair, it wasn't as if she'd really been a child of God in those days. She hadn't become one until He had crushed her heart with Mamie's death. But long before her mid-twenties, she'd known what God had said about extramarital relationships (she refused to think in coarser terms). And she had ignored Him. That's all there was to it; she had been willfully ignorant and willfully disobedient.

It wasn't as if she'd been swept away by love or passion. She hadn't been.

Just looking for love in all the wrong places.

That really was the extent of it. She'd bought into the cultural lie, and Phil's persistence and his implied promise that a ring was forthcoming, a Christmas engagement and a spring wedding in their church. Not that she'd cared for him especially—which probably made the whole ugly story even worse, she had to admit—but she *had* cared a great deal about marriage and family, and he had at least been both eligible and attractive in a self-possessed, cool kind of way.

Papi and Mamie had been pleased with the arrangement, too, and had trusted the young couple implicitly. But Elise and Phil had broken that trust.

And then? He had cast her cruelly aside. Not that he'd broken her heart, exactly; it was more like he'd smashed her pride and her sense that all would soon be well with her life. She was supremely grateful that there would be divine justice one day; Phil would certainly have a lot to answer for.

Assuming, of course, that he had not yet repented of his sin, and sought forgiveness. If he had, he hadn't bothered to let her know about it.

So that was her story, or at least part of it. She just needed to decide what, if anything, to do with it.

Would a public confession via her nascent website help some other young woman make better choices than she had?

Would it allow her to leave her guilt permanently behind?

Would it free the Lord to send a husband her way, perhaps a husband named Jamie?

Would it so offend Jamie that he'd never talk to her again?

She opened a new document and typed her name and the date in the upper right, then the name of the course: Creative Writing 254.

And there was the solution: *creative* writing, as in fiction.

Another idea popped into her head, and she began typing:

Advice page
Elise's Advice for the Life-Worn.

Dear Elise,
I am 27 years old and I have a problem. I have been a Christian all my life, but am beginning to wonder about some of the commands of God – esp. the ones about not having sex outside of marriage. My boyfriend Phil

That probably wasn't the best idea. With a couple of mouseclicks and a few keystrokes, she changed his name.

My boyfriend Walt is a Christian, too, but he believes that times have changed.

It took her just a half hour to write both the letter and her response—an excellent, godly, and wholly scriptural response at that, she congratulated herself. Then, not wanting to deceive, she composed an italic introduction explaining that this question had been posed to her not in letter form, but was one that she'd wrestled with many times in recent years.

"This is my first column," she added, "so obviously I have yet to be deluged with questions. If you have one for me, please email me by clicking here."

Suddenly, EverlastingPlace.com was looking like it might really turn into something more than a night-school assignment.

CHAPTER TWENTY-FOUR

Meg Vogel
Friday, February 3

Meg's interview with Gladys was not going well. They'd plowed through the Part One "Basics" fairly quickly, except for the eighty-seven-year-old's inability to put her finger on exactly how many grandchildren she had, and where they all lived. But Part Two was proving to be a challenge.

Gladys had responded to "Why do you live here now?" with a slightly haughty "Because it's a magnificent place," waving a hand around her room as if she were presenting Versailles' Hall of Mirrors to a wide-eyed tourist.

It was nice that Gladys felt that way, Meg conceded, but she was looking for something meatier. "Because my wicked children stuck me here" would have at least had some grit. "Because I'm afraid of dying alone in my recliner" would have had the ring of truth.

How could she write anything interesting if all she had to work with was "it's a great place"?

She thought again of all the executive interviews she'd done over the years, preparatory to writing articles for internal newsletters and external news releases. Colorful and flattering phrases uttered by high-powered sources often left her with the feeling that *this* time, she had a great story to tell; how could she miss with "we wanted to make sure we got our tickets punched" and "they grabbed the low-hanging fruit" and "we're going to eat this elephant one bite at a time"?

And then she'd type up her notes to find that, once again, the executive had really said nothing interesting at all. Plain vanilla, with never a whiff of negativity or controversy or an admission of error or need. As if everything in his company, in his market, in his industry— nay, in the entire global economy—couldn't possibly be any better.

"Let's try number two, Gladys. 'Describe the events that led up to your coming here.'"

Gladys gazed out the window at the battalion of naked shagbarks standing guard outside. She appeared to be scowling, but Meg knew by now that this was just the way she looked, whatever her mood.

"It was two years ago last June, ten months after Abe died. One day I looked out at my gardens and decided it was all too much work."

With unsteady hands, she pulled a photo album off the coffee table and offered it to Meg.

"Wow," Meg said, flipping through page after page of spectacular garden shots, mostly roses segregated by color, but each section complemented by generous plantings of daphne, bearded iris, delphinium, clematis and trumpet lilies—nothing particularly low maintenance. And each "room" was framed by meticulously clipped boxwood hedges that, if Meg's experience was any indication, must have required drenching in antidesiccants every winter to look this good. "Are you saying you did your own gardening until just a couple years ago?"

"I should say not," Gladys sniffed, somehow managing to look down her nose at Meg from the depths of her wheelchair. "I never did my own gardening; Abe wouldn't hear of it. But managing the staff was getting to be too much."

You, my dear vulgar Mrs. Baldwin, are the epitome of nouveau riche.

"What exactly did Mr. Baldwin do?"

"He was an inventor," Gladys said, fluffing her wig—she was wearing her blonde pageboy today. "He invented . . . oh, I don't know. Something to do with automobiles."

Meg took a closer look at the photos of the white rose section, which gave the best view of the house. Or, more accurately, mansion. It was neo-classical in style, if she was remembering her college art history correctly, sided in some sort of stone that had been painted butter yellow.

"The house is stunning," Meg said, almost to herself, paging through the album and gaping at the opulent—some might almost say decadent—interiors.

Her comments warmed Gladys up.

"Yes, it's a lovely house," she said, smiling openly for the first time in Meg's experience with her. "It wasn't when we bought it. It was practically a ruin, but Mr. Baldwin gave me free rein in restoring it, and it turned out rather well, I think."

Meg asked a few follow-up questions before glancing back at her list. She was learning that it was best not to wander too far off track with most of these interviews.

"So here's the next one, Gladys: What if The Hickories hadn't been an option? Would you have stayed there, maybe hired some people to give you a hand? Or found another place? Or maybe you would have gone to live with one of your children?"

It was apparently the wrong thing to ask. Gladys' face fell back into its default scowl.

"All impossibilities," she said, glancing at her wristwatch. "Well, I think I've had about enough for today. Perhaps we can talk again."

She'd hit a sore spot in bringing up Gladys' children, Meg knew. And remembering how the old gal's face had fallen, she felt a pang of guilt; her jab had been deliberate.

Not that Gladys didn't deserve it. "Managing the staff was getting to be too much." *Good grief!*

If there was one thing Meg couldn't tolerate, it was a snob, and Gladys was definitely a first-class specimen. She deserved to be reminded that, in spite of all her financial and social success, she apparently hadn't done too well in the "mother" department. If she had, with her apparent wealth, she wouldn't be living in a nursing home, no matter how exclusive and elegant; she'd be the honored matron of the family, surrounded by love, respect, doting grandchildren, and a team of highly paid nurses and aides.

Still, maybe there were circumstances beyond anyone's control at work here. Or maybe Gladys' kids had turned out to be rotters on their own, without help from their queen mother.

Or maybe that's just the way things are today. Elderly parents are as inconvenient as an unplanned pregnancy.

Fortunately, she didn't have time to dwell on this sad state of affairs. Old Mrs. Witherspoon was wheeling her way slowly down the hall, frail hands encased in rough leather gloves to protect them against the wheels. Grateful for the distraction, Meg greeted her and offered her a ride, something no resident in her right mind ever turned down.

Friday was also Sadie Sparrow day for Meg, and she'd been looking forward to their meeting all week. They weren't getting together until three this time; there'd been some mix-up at the beauty shop, and two thirty was the only time they could squeeze Sadie in. But that was okay with Meg.

An hour or two with her favorite old gal to end the week, followed by two full days with Touchdown and Sneak, and all would be right with the world once again.

It was almost two thirty when Meg delivered the last of the fresh popcorn to the residents crowding the movie theater for a maiden showing of the 1967 film *Camelot*. She washed her hands, grabbed her bag, and headed straight for the North Wing. She'd have some time to kill; but after racing around for the last hour, it would be a relief to relax for a while.

She arrived on North just in time to meet Sadie leaving with Renee, the operator of The Hickories' beauty shop. "I'll be done with her in twenty minutes," Renee promised. "She's one of the easy ones. Should I bring her back to her room?"

"Down the hall to the Sitting Room," Meg said, "if you don't mind. And please don't rush on my account—I can use a rest."

Maintenance had let the fire die out but the room was still toasty. Meg collapsed gratefully onto the banquette. "I'm getting too old for this," she said to the room.

"You don't look all that old to me."

Meg's heart stopped, but only for the moment it took her to scope out the room. There, in the computer nook in the corner, was the young man she'd seen pushing Sadie in the dining room not long ago. He was stuffing papers into a geeky hard-sided briefcase.

"I'm Jamie Fletcher," he said, snapping the briefcase closed. "Sadie's Bible teacher. Are you Meg? Mind if I sit with you a bit, if you're going to be waiting here for her?"

"Please do. If we're talking I won't really be loafing, will I? I'll be meeting with a volunteer."

"So you're the biographer," he said, settling himself in the leather club chair nearest her. "I've been hearing some nice things about you."

"Then you know more about me than I know about you," Meg replied in her friendliest tone, although she really could have used some alone time. "What's your story?"

He was younger and less interesting than he'd looked from a distance, she thought as he rattled off the high points of his life—born in Scotland in 1972, family immigrated to the U.S. when he was just a lad, landed in Milwaukee, University of Wisconsin History graduate, started Bible school in Watertown last fall.

"Do you have a girlfriend?" Meg asked. Her original intent was to goad him into granting that he was a sinner like everyone else, but she instantly realized that he'd probably think she was hitting on him. With his dark brown eyes and high forehead and patrician nose, he was probably used to it, even at that Bible college of his.

But he didn't act like it. Instead, he smiled shyly and regarded his hands. "I'm not really good boyfriend material. I'll be heading out into the mission field when I'm done with school, and it would take a pretty special woman to want to join me."

She pictured him building a church in the middle of a jungle. "Africa?" She stifled a yawn. "Or Borneo, perhaps?"

"No stereotyping there," he laughed. "No, no jungle living for me. I'll be going to Munich. These days, Europe's where we find hearts most hardened to the things of God."

"Mmmm, Munich." She smiled a tad contemptuously. "Nice work if you can get it. But why not Paris or Rome? Or will you be taking the grand tour?"

Jamie returned her smile, apparently missing her sarcasm. He had nice cheekbones and a strong jaw, Meg noticed. In danger of blushing, she busied herself with her notebook.

"It's not as easy as you might think," he said. "I've spent some time with missionaries in Paris and Frankfurt—ah, there's the smirk. But it's seriously hard work to try to get through to people who think they're just fine, thank you, and have no need for a Savior. Especially the intellectuals." Feeling contrite for mocking him even subtly, she put on her kindest face. "I'm sure it won't be easy. I was just being a jerk."

"So that's enough about me. What's your story?

Meg felt suddenly self-conscious. Ridiculous, she knew. She was almost twenty years older than this guy; he had nothing on her in the brains or experience department.

"There's not really much of a story," she said, stalling to compose herself. "I was a freelance writer—a copywriter, to be precise—and now I guess I'm a biographer of old ladies." She winced. "That sounded snotty, and I really don't mean to be. I love working here. It's so much better than the world of corporations and ad agencies. So much warmer and kinder and, hmmm, maybe *purposeful* would be a good word for it. I feel like I'm making a difference in some lives now, and that makes me feel like I might finally be on to something, you know?"

It sounded so lame to her that when she finally looked him in the eye again, she was surprised to see him looking at her earnestly.

"How about you?" he asked. "Are you married?"

"Widowed. My husband died on New Year's Eve."

"Oh, wow, Meg, I'm sorry to hear that."

"He'd been sick a long time," she offered, suspecting that it would make him feel more comfortable. "It was cancer."

It did, apparently. They talked a bit about how hard it was to lose a loved one, and how it really can turn your world inside out, and she mentioned Touchdown and Sneak and what a comfort they were, feeling foolish for even vaguely implying that critters might be an adequate substitute for a human being. Her friends would have jumped on her for the suggestion. But not Jamie. He just looked concerned. Interested.

"So it seems like you might be searching for some meaning to your life," he said finally. "Want to talk about it?"

Meg felt a flicker of anger.

"If you're leading up to your religion, I'm really not interested." She pulled her tape recorder out of her bag and focused intently on getting it set up for her interview with Sadie. "I heard it all from my husband."

"I'm sorry," Jamie said softly. "I guess I just sensed that"—and here she glanced up, giving him a chance to look her straight in the eye—"well, that you might be changing your mind about these things. Just the fact that you left the business world in favor of helping the elderly. That looks like a change of heart to me."

She bristled.

A change of heart. Like I'm Dreiser's repentant murderer.

"Not at all. I simply realized that the business world had no real use for me anymore. Whereas the old folk do. They are amazingly happy to see me. I'm sorry if this offends you but working here *feeds* my pride. And it's my understanding that your Bible would find fault with that."

He shook his head amiably. "My apologies." He put on his happy face again. "Oh look, here's our Sadie, looking more radiant than ever . . ."

"I had a dream about Ed last night," Sadie confessed ten minutes into their interview. "It has me a bit out of sorts."

"I noticed," Meg said gently, "but that's okay. Do you want to tell me about it?"

Sadie sat silently for a few moments. "Yes," she said finally, lifting her eyes to Meg's. "I would like to tell you. I haven't been quite honest with you, you see."

Meg flipped off the recorder to assure her friend that this part of their conversation would be confidential. Sadie smiled her understanding.

"I dreamt that I was sitting in my room here at The Hickories," she began, waving a hand in the general direction of the hall. "I was writing a letter to Dana, when suddenly the door opened and Ed walked in like he'd just run out to the hardware store. Well, maybe more than that, because he came over and hugged me, but nothing like you'd expect after a thirty-year absence." She laughed a little. "Although I guess I don't know how that would be, but you know what I mean."

"Sure."

"He looked just the way he did last time I saw him. He was kind of wiry, and his face was lined and tanned, like an old shoe, I always thought, thanks to his work, you know—"

"He was a carpenter, I think you said?"

"Yes, and a handyman. He fixed things and built things and really did whatever needed doing around the house, mainly for the widows and single ladies in our neighborhood and our church. So he spent a lot of time out of doors, sawing and hammering and painting. People don't like sawdust all over their homes, you know."

Meg nodded.

"We never had much money," Sadie said, smoothing her pantsuit. She was in powder blue today, lovely beneath her white hair and pink cheeks. "But that didn't matter so much. We always had enough, and I was quite the seamstress, so Dana always had nice things to wear.

"Although she didn't think so. She wanted brand names from the store, of course. And the styles, oh, they were ridiculous. These big leather boots, and blue jeans of course, and I'll never forget this blue blouse she had to have—it looked like a girl's version of Ed's old chambray workshirts, and it was twenty-six dollars, for a blouse! Honestly, even if we could have afforded it, I wouldn't think of paying that much for one blouse. But I did the next best thing, made her one myself."

"Did she appreciate it?"

Sadie tipped her head, considering the question. "Oh, I suppose she did, but she would have liked it a lot more if it had had some fancy label in it." She laughed again and scooted herself back in her wheelchair. "So. This little detour is relevant, Meg, because I was the one who really resented our financial condition, not Dana. I wanted to be able to buy her nice things, and Ed just didn't seem to care. He thought that if God wanted us to have more, then He'd see to it that we had more."

Meg could certainly understand Sadie's frustration. "And we're talking the 1950s, right?" she asked sympathetically. "It wasn't an era that allowed you to go out and get a great job for yourself."

"Well, by the time Dana became concerned about clothes, it was the 1970s," Sadie reminded her. "But I married Ed in 1952, and in those days working women who made much money were mostly teachers, or nurses, or secretaries. I think I mentioned that I did do some housecleaning for a few wealthy women, really just for pin money. I suppose if I'd gotten an education, I could have done something grander, and earned some real spending money. It just never occurred to me, if you want to know the truth. A cleaning lady didn't think about doing anything professional back then. And I would've hated it, frankly. I loved everything about being a wife and a mother and keeping house."

It sounds so peaceful, Meg thought. *What were we thinking, we liberated women, when we dumped it all for our careers?*

Sadie smiled sheepishly. "So I lied to you when I said that I thought our house was the Taj Mahal. I didn't. It was a shabby little two-bedroom shack. I'd go into these nice homes to dust and vacuum and scrub and I'd hope that the ladies I worked for would never see where I lived. I was ashamed."

"But surely they didn't expect you to live in a mansion?"

"Oh, of course not. I was being silly. And ungrateful, for that matter. That's what I should have been ashamed of, all that ingratitude."

Meg furrowed her brow sympathetically, steering Sadie back to the subject at hand. "But how does that relate to your dream?"

"Ah, yes, the dream." Sadie gazed off into space again. "Ed took me out onto the balcony—in my dream there was a balcony with French doors leading out to it, not just windows—and we looked out at the garden for a while and he stroked my cheek and gazed into my eyes. Oh, his eyes were so wonderful, Meg, so kind. And he was singing 'In the Sweet By and By.' Do you know that song?"

Meg shook her head.

"Oh, you need to know it to understand. It goes like this—"

And she began singing, her soprano supremely wobbly and her pitch occasionally suspect, but so sweet to Meg's ear: "There's a land that is fairer than day, and by faith we can see it afar; for the Father waits over the way to prepare us a dwelling place there."

She paused to catch her breath, smiling shyly at Meg. "And then this is the chorus: 'In the sweet by and by, we shall meet on that beautiful shore; in the sweet by and by, we shall meet on that beautiful shore.'"

"It's wonderful," Meg said, swallowing hard. There was a lump in her throat, even though she knew this was just wishful thinking. "So Ed serenaded you with it?"

Sadie nodded. "It was a favorite of his. And in my dream, he sounded just the same as he did then. Which of course is the problem."

"The problem?"

"Well, Ed was just sixty-five when he died, and that's how he looked. But I was my real age in the dream," she said, blushing prettily. "Here he was, gazing into my eyes, stroking my cheek, and I was old enough to be his mother!"

She pulled a tissue out of her sleeve and dabbed at her eyes. They were red.

Meg didn't know what to say. "It was just a dream, Sadie," she finally ventured.

"But don't you understand, Meg? That I finally realized—thirty years too late—how very kind Ed was? What a wonderful husband and father he was? I never appreciated him properly, and I think he knew it." She paused to blow her nose. "I was not an easy wife."

Meg wasn't quite following Sadie's thinking, but felt a flush of irritation on her behalf. "I'd say you were pretty easy. You could have demanded that he go out and get some job that would've paid more. You could have demanded a great deal more from him, in fact. A lot of women would have back then."

She didn't really know if that was the case, but figured it was a comforting thing to say.

It seemed to help, anyway. "Maybe you're right, Meg," Sadie said, smiling weakly. "I hadn't thought of it that way. After all, it's not like I ever called him a failure. It's just—well, he wasn't a genius, and he didn't earn a fortune, but he was truly a wonderful, godly man. I wish I'd appreciated him when it counted."

"I'm sure he knew you appreciated him, Sadie, even if you didn't always show it." Meg busied herself with her notes. She wasn't sure whether to chime in with her own story. For in truth, a lot of what Sadie had said could have applied to her relationship with Gil, especially after he'd quit his job teaching biology in order to volunteer at the Rescue Mission. Not that he'd done it for very long—suddenly confused, she couldn't remember the timing on any of this—and not that he'd stopped bringing in any income, since he'd had disability insurance through his job, and finally SSI had kicked in as well.

The difference was that Meg didn't regret her ingratitude, if that's what it was. After all, if Gil had hung in there at his job, he might have hung in there longer when it came to his life as well. And he might not have picked up these foolish ideas about heaven and hell, either.

But let's not go there.

"So let's talk more about your family, Sadie. What school did you say Dana went to?"

As usual, Sandra was sitting at a table with a paperback when Meg arrived at Harper's on the Lake, a rustic tavern serving great fish fries. The place was noisy with merrymakers packing the bar and just about every table, many sporting Packer sweatshirts and jeans, but Sandra had managed to grab a table tucked into a quiet nook off the main dining room.

"What'cha reading?" Meg asked as she sat down across from her friend.

Sandra dog-eared the page she'd been studying and flashed the cover at Meg. It was *The Women's Room*, a feminist novel from the 1970s.

"Any good?"

"It's a little hard to say." Sandra tucked the fat volume in her tote *du jour*, a caramel-colored leather bag that looked luscious with her gold-threaded paisley scarf. "The story was probably decent in its day—housewife gets dumped by unfaithful husband and has to make her own way in the world. By now it's been done to death, but do you remember that movie from the seventies, about a woman who gets dumped but ends up with Alan Bates? Jill Clayburgh was the woman."

"Absolutely," Meg laughed. "Talk about silver linings!"

"Right—I'd take the late Alan Bates over just about any man, dead or alive! So anyway, as far as this book goes, I imagine it was revolutionary forty years ago. Not so much anymore, though. And it's got all these ghastly feminist speeches, as if anyone ever talked that way."

It was just six but the middle-aged waitress was already frazzled. She smiled gratefully when Meg followed up Sandra's order of fried cod and a Heineken with "Same here."

"So don't you think it's true?" Meg asked once their beers had been delivered. "The feminist stuff, I mean?"

Sandra looked at her as if she hadn't heard properly. "Of course it's true! Where would we be today without these pioneers? After all, this 'housewife' business was an aberration of the 1950s; as far as I know, it's never been tried before or since. But it was a disaster! How could a woman be fulfilled planning her days around dusting and doing the wash?"

Meg chuckled. "Well, I guess that's what I always thought, too, although now that I think about it, my Grammy never had a real job, nor did my mother, and they seemed pretty happy."

"Your mother died young," Sandra replied, as if the fact proved her point.

"True. But I still say she was 'fulfilled,' whatever that means. She was a child of the Depression, you know, and I think she was happy to be living the good life."

"If she'd outlived your father, or if he'd left her, she might have thought differently."

"You're amazing," Meg said, helping herself to a breadstick. "Ms. Drama Queen."

Sandra crowed. "You're right, I really am! Why let a good plot line go to waste?"

"But the thing is, the women of our parents' and grandparents' generations really did seem satisfied with their lives." Meg chewed thoughtfully on the breadstick and washed it down with a swig of her beer. "They lived and died and accepted life as it came to them. I never heard any grumbling from them, anyway. Whereas our generation expects perfection every step of the way, and if we don't get it, we're angry. Don't you think?"

The waitress bustled into their nook with family-style serving dishes of fried cod and tartar sauce and coleslaw and fresh rye bread with a big slab of butter.

"Mmmm, perfect," Sandra said, digging in to the fish.

Their conversation focused on Sandra's current workload for most of the meal. Then, over coffee, Meg swung the conversation back to women.

"I interviewed Sadie again today," she said, stirring cream and sugar into her coffee as an ersatz desert. "She's so sweet, Sandra; I wish you'd come and meet her one of these days. She said that she loved 'keeping house,' even though she admitted to wishing for more money, so she could have done more for her ungrateful daughter."

"Ungrateful? Do tell!"

"My word, not Sadie's." Meg didn't want to cast her new friend in a negative light. "It's what I've been able to gather from what some of the nurses and aides say about her. She's supposedly some big-shot executive, way too busy to spend any time with her mother. She sounds like lot of the agency types we've worked with over the years. Control freaks, self-important, total snobs, most of them."

"Like my boss, for instance."

Meg smirked. "Exactly. Just like good old Deirdre!"

"You know, she hasn't once asked about how you're doing, and she knows that we're good friends. I even mentioned to her earlier this week that we were going out for a fish fry tonight, and she didn't even blink."

"I am so glad to be out of that scene."

"I wish I could afford to ditch it myself. I've written enough brochures on anodizing services and parking-lot paint to last me many lifetimes."

"Hope you're saving your pennies."

"I am," said Sandra. "I've paid off my condo and I haven't bought anything but scarves for ages. Like this one; pretty, isn't it?"

"Beautiful." Meg tried to remember a time when she cared about her wardrobe. "Guess I should start paying attention to clothes again one of these days."

"Why bother? You'd be gorgeous in a burlap bag. That's why you've always had your choice of men."

Meg snickered. "I sure knew how to pick 'em, didn't I? Imagine me ending up with a Bible-banger."

They grinned at each other.

"Speaking of saving my pennies," Sandra said, "this class at WCTC could really be a goldmine. I thought it would take a lot of time, but I'm only putting in about five hours a week. And get this: on top of my salary, which is nothing to sneeze at, I could be getting fabulous health insurance. For one lousy class! If I can keep this gig, maybe I *will* be able to quit Brainwashers in a year or two. Go freelance, maybe."

"About your class," Meg said, fishing a twenty out of her wallet to cover her half of the meal, "I met one of your students. Elise Chapelle. Her grandfather lives at The Hickories. Nice young woman."

Sandra laughed. "Here you go again, Meg. Elise is working on a website, and you'll never guess what the subject is."

"Hmmmm." Meg squinted as she recalled their conversation. "Mothers who abandon their children for the streets of Paris?"

Bewildered, Sandra shook her head. "No, you dope. It's about heaven, and about your nemesis—Jesus Christ."

"Good grief!"

"You really do know how to pick 'em, my friend."

CHAPTER TWENTY-FIVE

Sadie Sparrow
Saturday, February 18

Eva wasn't feeling up to it, but Sadie managed to persuade Beulah to come along to the next Bible study.

"And then there were five," Jamie rejoiced when Beulah followed Sadie into the Southeast Sitting Room, both of their chairs powered by a brawny blonde aide. "One or two more and we'll have to find ourselves a larger room."

Sadie and Beulah settled themselves at the trestle table across from Charles Chapelle and his sweet granddaughter Elise. Jamie's joviality was contagious; they were soon chatting about everything under the sun, and before long they found themselves engrossed in Beulah's story.

"My life didn't really begin until I became a genuine Christian," she told the group. "My parents were Christian people, so I'd been going to church my whole life. But it wasn't until we attended a revival meeting in 1936 that I repented and trusted in Christ. I was seventeen when I gave my life to Him, and I've never looked back."

Sadie was fascinated. She didn't recall that she had ever done anything so dramatic. She'd always heard people talking about "making a decision for Christ," but she'd never heard a report quite like this one, delivered in such exquisite detail. Why, Beulah was even describing the boots she was wearing on that snowy night.

"And of course, that was the Great Depression," Beulah added with gusto. "My parents were farmers, and we lived on one hundred and fifty acres near Wausau, but we were as poor as church mice. It wasn't long after my conversion that we had to move. We had lost everything, and so we went into Wausau and rented a room in a boarding house and just prayed for the Lord to take care of us as He had promised to."

"I know He promised," Sadie said, embarrassed to reveal her ignorance but desperate to know, "but where exactly did He make that promise?"

"Maybe the best-known passage," Charles said, opening his Bible and flipping quickly to the sixth chapter of Matthew, "is right here in the Sermon on the Mount. That's where Jesus said, 'Look at the birds of the air, for they neither sow nor reap nor gather into barns; yet your heavenly Father feeds them. Are you not of more value than they?'"

"Bravo, Charles," Jamie said, beaming at the Chapelles. "In fact, let's take a look at that subject in one of our next meetings, okay? It's an important one. But please continue, Beulah."

And she did, chattering on and on as if her life depended upon it.

Sadie felt suddenly sleepy—a frequent problem since her secret stroke—and she was having trouble focusing on the story line. But she faded back in when Beulah got to the part about her father passing up a job in the local lumberyard because he didn't feel led to take it. Was that supposed to be a good thing?

"The world would have accused him of being lazy," Jamie said solemnly, "but I know just how he must have felt."

"Oh, yes," Beulah said. "People were very critical of him. And honestly, I was worried myself. I heard my mother and father whispering at night, after we were in bed, about their savings being almost gone. It was hard *not* to hear; we were living in this single room, my parents and me and my two younger brothers." She shook her head at the memory. "I don't suppose people can get much poorer than we were."

But then, suddenly, the Lord opened a door for them, she said.

"Old Lady Grayson invited us to come live with her and run her farm," Beulah hooted. "It sounded awful to most people, and to be honest even to my mother and me, because Mrs. Grayson had a reputation for being cruel to her hired help. But my dad said, 'This is it,' and so we moved into her house. It was enormous, as big as a hotel in those days. I had my own room, and so did the boys, and she had both indoor plumbing and electricity. What luxuries for us farmers!"

Elise expressed amazement that they'd ever lived without the amenities taken for granted today, and they spent some time chatting about the advent of plumbing and electricity in rural America.

But, impressively, Beulah didn't forget the original point of her story. "She put us all to work, even my brothers, and what do you know: two months later I was privileged to lead Old Lady Grayson to the Lord! I've never doubted that this was exactly why He sent us to her, and had my Daddy turn down the job at the lumberyard. And here's the punch line: The following year she died and left everything to my parents. They worked that farm until the late 1960s, growing corn, mainly. They were approaching eighty by then, and He took care of them every passing day."

"What a faithful God," Elise said, her eyes shining.

She was really a very pretty girl, Sadie thought. In fact— she glanced surreptitiously at first Elise and then Jamie, and back again—yes, they'd make an attractive couple.

"I believe that it was exactly what the Lord wanted us to do," Beulah said, interrupting Sadie's daydream, "and He rewarded my parents for being obedient."

"It must have been so hard," Elise said. "I just can't imagine how frightening it must have been to move into that room, all of you, and to know that the money was running out."

Beulah nodded, her brow creased in thought. "But you know, if my father ever had a moment of worry, he never let on. And that gave us confidence."

"He set the tone for you all," Jamie offered.

"Exactly! We trusted him, and if he trusted the Lord, well then, that was that. As far as I know, I was the only one who ever had any fears over our situation."

She stroked the worn Bible sitting in her lap.

"And I've never been really afraid since then. I've had disappointments and sorrows, of course, like anyone else. But no real fear. His eye is on the sparrow."

"And I know He watches me," Sadie chirped happily, not in the least embarrassed by her less-than-perfect pitch.

They covered another huge chunk of Bible evidence that morning, and Sadie's head was spinning by the time they finished. Jamie was always supremely organized in his teaching. But now, with the constant comments and contributions of her classmates (which she was trying valiantly not to consider interruptions), she felt more addled than ever.

There was something about evolution needing time and past—no, time and chance—and proof that there wasn't time. Or chance. Or either. Something about salt in the oceans and river deltas and mousetraps? Was that possible?

Feeling like a stupid old lady, Sadie welcomed Beulah to her room that afternoon to watch a DVD that Jamie had lent them, a documentary entitled *The Indestructible Book.* They had no popcorn, but Beulah brought in a tin of butter cookies and a bottle of sherry that Bunny had given her for Christmas. They weren't so crazy about the sherry—Beulah said Bunny had bought it as a joke, just because it was what little old ladies were supposed to sip when sitting in their parlors together. But the cookies were delicious, they agreed.

So, too, was the movie. They found themselves spellbound by it. It was the history of the Bible, from Mount Sinai to Plymouth Rock, in a four-hour nutshell. They watched the first half that afternoon before stopping to talk about what they'd learned.

"First of all," said Beulah, "they chose exactly the right man to narrate it, don't you think?"

"Jamie said that he wrote a book by the same name, so I guess it's his movie," Sadie said. "Or was his movie. Apparently, he died some time ago. But oh, I love his accent. It sounds kind of like Jamie's."

"Jamie has an accent?"

"Can't you hear it? It's Scottish; he was born there."

"What do you know," Beulah said. "But this narrator's accent is very strong. And soothing."

Sadie nodded. "What I love about it is the whole idea of how God has protected the Bible over the centuries. I hadn't realized that. You know, people are always saying it has changed."

"Evolved."

"Yes, evolved. People love that word, don't they? At any rate, when you think about it, of course He protected it. Any God who was powerful enough to create the entire universe was certainly capable of protecting a single book."

"The only book He ever wrote," added Beulah. "I don't know why people refuse to believe it these days."

"Jamie says it's a heart problem, not a question of intelligence."

"He's a fine young man, Sadie. Is he married?"

"No, he's not." Sadie smiled mischievously. "Not yet, anyway. I was thinking that he and Elise would make a cute couple."

"Hmmmm," Beulah said, grinning impishly. "I wonder if we could be of any help."

"You can't make two people fall in love," Sadie said, her eyes narrowed in thought. "But let's think about it. We ought to be able to make sure they see a lot of each other."

"Matchmaker, matchmaker, make me a match!" Beulah belted out, good-naturedly mangling the melody.

They shared a long laugh before parting to get ready for dinner, promising to watch the rest of the movie the next day.

Sadie had intended to call Dana today, but there wasn't time now. Well, she'd give it a try tonight or tomorrow; it wasn't like her daughter was sitting at the phone, waiting for it to ring.

CHAPTER TWENTY-SIX

Elise Chapelle
Monday, February 20

Having settled Papi in the dining room for his lunch with the ever-silent Mort and Joseph, Elise fairly flew down the stairs towards the garage. She had to present her first rough pass at a complete website tomorrow night, and she'd been struggling mightily with the website builder she'd chosen—Duck Duck Goose, it was called, and it was supposedly the easiest one available. But not for the clueless, she had discovered.

Still, last night she'd somehow cracked the code. With a little luck or some divine guidance, she could probably get the thing done in time for class *and* squeeze in a nice visit with Papi tomorrow afternoon.

She was so intent on her goal that she almost knocked over the fellow on the other side of the door leading into the garage.

Naturally, it was Jamie.

"Whoa," he said. "Where's the fire?"

She had to laugh. It was such an old-fashioned thing to say, and he looked so adorable in his equally old-fashioned tweed overcoat and fedora.

"Just like the first time we met," he added.

He remembered!

"So where are you off to?"

"Home," she said breathlessly, her mind racing to think of something clever to add.

"Ah. I was hoping—well, another time."

"What were you hoping?"

It was cold in the open doorway; he pulled her inside.

"Well," he said, removing his hat. His face was red. *Maybe from the cold. Maybe not.*

"I just wondered if you might like to have dinner with me sometime."

"Oh!"

"But if not, I under—"

"I'd love to."

Elise felt faint. *Please don't let me pass out, Lord. Not right now.*

"Okay then, great. Well," Jamie said, "I'll be seeing you then."

"Sure."

He turned to walk away.

"Jamie," she said.

He spun around, his eyebrows raised in concern.

"When did you want to have dinner?"

"Oh! Well, yes, let's pick a date. I'm busy this weekend—we have a guest pastor coming in, an evangelist, and I'm in charge of hosting him—but how about the following week? Saturday, say?"

Elise nodded thoughtfully, visualizing her calendar.

"The third?"

"Sure, the third. Let's plan on it."

"Great!" She hurried out into the garage before he could change his mind, her heart dancing.

Just like that, I have a date, and it may be with the man of my dreams!

Later, Elise would wonder how she made it home; she was flying so high that she hadn't the least memory of the drive.

CHAPTER TWENTY-SEVEN

Meg Vogel
Monday, February 20

If Sadie had raised her daughter to be a traditional woman, she had failed abysmally, Meg learned early that afternoon.

She was just setting up the Great Room for a rousing game of bingo when a fifty-ish woman swept in sporting a black cashmere coat over an absolutely stunning asymmetrical suit in dove gray.

"Are you Meg Vogel?" the woman demanded. She was a bit breathless, perhaps the result of racing around in heels a tad too high for a woman her age.

"I am," Meg said, recognizing her visitor from Sadie's e-file. "And you are?"

"Dana Maxwell," the woman replied, and then, when Meg didn't immediately fall to her knees—

Okay, Meg, that was nasty.

—when Meg didn't respond instantly, she added, "Sadie Sparrow's daughter."

"Oh, how nice to meet you," Meg said. "Your mother's great."

"That's what I want to talk to you about," Dana said, tossing her coat on the closest chair. "Do you have a few minutes?"

It had turned into one of the more bizarre conversations she'd ever had, Meg thought later, and here she included her chats with residents whose dementia had taken them far down the road to La La Land. But it was certainly interesting to get a glimpse of this particular daughter's point of view; the busy ones ordinarily didn't have time to do more than bark orders at the nurses and aides.

It seemed that Dana Maxwell had lovingly delivered Sadie to The Hickories last October, earning absolutely nothing in the way of gratitude points for her efforts.

"She was miserable, and I knew it, and she knew I knew it," Dana explained almost as soon as they'd seated themselves in the Activities office. "Once she saw the place, and her room, she was happy for maybe three hours, and then she fell back into her sulk. No one sulks quite as dramatically as my mother."

Speaking of dramatic.

"I'm telling you, it's been horrible. It's not like I've neglected her. We talk every week at a minimum, and I visit her at least once a month unless I'm out of town."

Every week? Once a month? By what calendar?

Meg shook off the negativity. "What do you do?" she asked, genuinely curious about what sort of job it took these days to warrant such a drop-dead gorgeous suit. In the ad biz, no one wore suits anymore. Casual Friday seemed to rule all week long even in the largest corporations, at least in the circles she'd moved in.

"I'm SVP-Marketing for SI," Dana said, not wasting a syllable. "Senior VP."

Meg nodded politely. This was one woman in a hurry, no doubt accustomed to paring her reports down to thirty seconds for C-level executives and directors.

"Let me give you an example," she rushed on. "This past Thanksgiving, we brought my mother the most fabulous dinner, with all the trimmings plus her favorite chess pie—I made it myself—and all she could do was pout."

"Really?" Meg had a hard time believing that.

"Well, maybe 'pout' isn't the right word. But the icebox door was open, if you know what I mean. No? She was just cold to us all, hardly saying a word, asking us nothing about our lives. Sulky, maybe, almost surly."

"I'm sorry to hear that," Meg said, not having a clue what else to say. "I guess I haven't seen that side of her at all. She's just been a delight—"

"That's my point. She was like that all through the holidays, but then she started to change. And now I don't even recognize her anymore. She seems happy, in the organic sense. But she also seems distracted. I just dropped in on her and she was putting on lipstick, of all things. She hasn't done that in years! I'd like to know what's going on. Are you drugging her?"

Meg laughed. "I'm sorry, but no, we would never do anything like that. You could ask a nurse if her doctor has prescribed—"

"All right, I'll check into it. Could you email me the doctor's contact information?" She fished a business card out of her purse. "Because I really object to drugging the elderly, you know. My mother-in-law was on antidepressants and they made her much worse. That's one reason I chose this place; it seemed so nice that drugs wouldn't be necessary. But then what could it be? She isn't interested in some man, is she?"

"Not that I know of." Meg donned her most innocent countenance. "We seem to be fresh out of Cary Grants at the moment."

Of course, there's Charles Chapelle, but there's no need to go there.

Dana fingered the rope of pearls tumbling casually over the gray wool. Meg wondered if they were real. She hadn't seen anyone wear pearls of any kind for years.

"Perhaps it has something to do with you," Dana said finally. "She's mentioned you several times."

"I'm interviewing her for her biography. Maybe it's giving her a chance to really think through her life, and maybe she's liking what she sees."

Dana looked at her like she was crazy, then rose and headed back into the Great Room. "I hope that's all it is," she said. "I hope she isn't in early-stage Alzheimer's or anything like that."

"Oh, I don't think so. Although I'm no doctor, of course."

"Well, send me her doctor's email and I'll find out." Dana tossed on her cashmere coat like it was a jean jacket. "And do let me know if you sense anything unusual, would you?"

"I'll do that."

"Good." She smiled grimly and turned to leave, tossing a quick "thanks" over her shoulder.

Meg was feeling vaguely superior to the Danas of the world, all too busy to care for the "less fortunate," as three decades in the oh-so-progressive ad industry had taught her to think of just about everyone. She realized anew how contrary many of her opinions were to those of her ex-colleagues and friends; the fact that she had survived in their world for so long was proof that she hadn't ever cared too passionately about anything.

But Dana and her ilk did have one thing over her, and that was ambition. Meg just didn't seem able to rustle much of it up lately.

Even Lucy had hinted around about it, pushing her to do more interviews—this, even though Meg had barely made a dent in typing up her notes, let alone writing her first biography. "You know," Lucy had said last week, "half of your value to us is the time you spend getting our residents to open up about themselves. I need you to get aggressive with the interviewing."

That was fine with Meg. She really didn't enjoy writing all that much. It was simply what she'd been doing to make a living for her entire adult life. Talking with old people about their lives, on the other hand, often turned out to be a great time.

This afternoon, she'd scheduled her first chat with a resident named Carl Strobel, who lived in the North Wing a half-dozen doors down from Sadie's room. He was largely bedridden, having recently undergone his third hip surgery.

Meg had never talked to Strobel at any length, and she was a little nervous about the session; Lucy had warned her that he could be mean and a bit of a wolf. But as Meg would later tell her, he turned out to be an absolute gas—gruff, opinionated, right wing and ready to argue with anyone who held a different view of the world, and he never gave off a hint of being interested in anything but her mind.

"So what's going on with your hip?" she asked early on in their discussion, trying to concentrate on him instead of his room. It was the biggest one she'd seen yet, and beyond the overstuffed leather furniture and the oriental rugs, the walls were lined with floor-to-ceiling bookcases—each one holding volume after volume, from classics to what looked like complete collections of Stephen King and Tom Clancy. Meg promised herself a close look one of these days, but in the meantime focused on his face. That wasn't too difficult, she decided; he was good looking, square of jaw and dark of eye even in his eighties and must have been a very handsome young man.

"Useless doctors," he was saying. "Had one hip replacement, picked up an infection, had another surgery to remove an abscess, had a third surgery to remove some of the hardware, and I have to have another one as soon as this heals to get new hardware."

"What a mess!"

"That's right, sweetheart, it's a mess." He asked her to grab him another pillow from the armoire. He didn't miss a beat while she tucked it behind his head. "If I thought I could get along without a working hip, I'd tell them to go jump in the lake. These idiots seem to think I should feel lucky for getting all this attention from them!"

He glared at her. "Not what I'd like to call them, but I bite my tongue when ladies are present."

"Oh, you needn't—"

"I've got scars all over it." He pointed to his mouth. "From biting it."

Meg laughed, but he was not amused.

"I'm telling you, this healthcare system is a disaster! I'll give you just one example: cousin of mine from near Bremen, Germany—you've heard of the Bremen Town Musicians? The fairy tale? My cousin Gabriele needed a heart transplant, but they said she was too old for it and she died."

"I'm so sorry."

"You'll be even sorrier when you hear that she was just fifty-nine!"

His face was turning scarlet; Meg wondered if she should summon help.

"That's what Europe's elite are doing to control costs, sending anyone over 50 off to their graves. And we want to be just like them? What absolute garbage!"

She shook her head, racking her brain for a way to calm him down. "I can't argue with you, Mr. Strobel. But what can we do?"

His rage had apparently shut his ears. "And on top of it, it saves Social Security, doesn't it?" He snorted in disgust. "Great way to reduce *that* burden, isn't it? Just let people die!"

Meg recalled reading that euthanasia was on the rise in Europe, too, but she decided it wouldn't be a good time to introduce that topic.

"They'll just be killing us outright one of these days." Strobel peered at her with interest for the first time. "Think it's happening yet in this place?"

"Of course not!"

"No, and it won't happen here as long as the private sector manages to hang on."

"Think we can count on that for a while yet?" Meg asked. "I really hope this place will still be here when I need it."

"Won't your kids take care of you?"

"I don't have any."

"Ah, a modern woman?" He smiled, or maybe it was a sneer.

"Something like that." She smoothed her legal pad and positioned her pen for note-taking. "How about you? Children?"

He laughed. "Six. Three of each. And not one of them can be bothered with their old man. How do you like that?"

Meg left an hour later with a tape's worth of ranting and only a few pages of personal notes about Strobel; he hadn't been as interested in talking about himself as he was in discussing the issues of the day. But according to Lucy's latest marching orders, that wasn't a problem.

Maybe it was time to give Charles Chapelle a whirl, Meg thought. He seemed like an interesting fellow and he had an adorable accent, and anyway, she'd kind of promised Elise that she'd do it.

She poked her head in Sadie's room on the way back to the office. The door was unlocked—while all of the resident rooms had locks to make the residents feel more secure, those locks could be easily opened with the point of a pen—but the room was empty. But then she heard Sadie's lovely laugh and found her next door in Beulah's room, along with Eva. The three were playing some sort of card game at the table overlooking the garden and were delighted to see Meg.

"Great to see you girls, too," she said happily. "And you, Beulah, you're looking terrific! I'll bet you'll be back on your walker again in no time. How's therapy going?"

They chatted for a while about Beulah's progress (excellent), the card game the girls were playing (Dark Lady), this noon's grilled-crab-and-white-cheddar sandwiches (out of this world), the DVD Sadie and Beulah had watched about the history of the Bible (life-changing), and dear Mr. Jamie Fletcher (totally charming).

Meg finally noticed that a full half-hour had elapsed and excused herself, hurrying back to the Great Room to help Lucy return the bingo players to their rooms.

It had been an outstanding day, she realized as she rode the elevator down to the garage. The Hickories was exactly where she was meant to be, metaphysically and emotionally speaking.

It was strangely liberating to be spending so much time with other widows, Meg reflected as she built a salad for herself using fresh greens, packaged feta crumbles and canned mandarin oranges. Their ages didn't seem to matter, nor did their marital bliss or lack thereof; they had all experienced that queasy feeling of being truly alone in the world, of realizing that security had always been an illusion.

Even after adding slivered almonds and two tablespoons of a quite decent, fat-free Italian dressing, it was a pretty dreary dinner; she poured a glass of cheap chablis and promised herself a big dish of ice cream as a reward for eating so sensibly.

Of course, she mused, her loss was more severe than most of theirs from the standpoint of age; to lose a husband in his late fifties was somehow a more profound injustice, it seemed to her. But from the standpoint of emotional dependence, hers was probably easier. After all, she'd really lost Gil to his God long before he actually checked out of this life.

"Don't you agree, Touchdown?" she asked, seating herself at her old farmhouse table and placing a paper napkin primly on her lap. He responded with raised brows and a wag of the tail-tip. "Your daddy was taking a different road towards the end of his life, wasn't he?"

The salad just wasn't doing it for her. She put a pinch in Touchdown's bowl, tossed the rest in the trash, and made herself a gigantic vanilla sundae draped with peanuts (healthful dry roasted!) and drenched in caramel syrup.

"But we still loved him," she said, savoring the first creamy spoonful. "We just kept hoping both of the nightmares would end, right?"

It wasn't at all difficult to remember what he'd been like before his conversion. Sweet and funny with a definite edge. But he'd lost that edge . . .

Exactly when?

"Do you remember?" she asked Sneak, who had appeared out of nowhere, landing silently on the table and now gazing longingly at her ice cream. "Now that I think about it, maybe it happened even before he brought his imaginary friend home."

She remembered the night he had announced his diagnosis. She'd known that he was having some unmentionable problems in the stomach department, and that he'd been to the doctor a couple times and had even undergone one of those awful exams—she'd had to pick him up from it, in fact, because he'd been knocked goofy with some drug or another, and they'd had a totally uproarious dinner before he crashed on the couch to sleep it off.

"It was maybe a week later, or two," she reminded Sneak, "when he told us the news: it was the Big C. Do you remember that? He was so—oh, I'd never seen him like that, I don't know what it was exactly. Fear of dying, I suppose. Or maybe fear of what he'd have to go through along the way. Or both, maybe. Either way, we'd never had to deal with anything like that, and it changed everything."

Eating slowly, she dipped an occasional finger in the melting ice cream and let Sneak lick it off.

"But what difference does it make, in the end?" She finished the sundae and let him approach the bowl for a little feast of his own. "He's as dead as Ed Sparrow and Abe Baldwin and all the rest of them, and the women they left behind are on their own for the duration."

It is better to have loved and lost than never to have loved at all.

"Oh, gag, what made me think of that?" Meg laughed out loud, remembering the poster she'd had hanging in her bedroom back in the days of her first and only real heartbreak over a young man called Moose. She'd sobbed over the quote for weeks—it was Tennyson, if she was remembering correctly—picturing herself as a romantic figure who would never be able to love again.

What an enormous waste of perfectly good tears.

"That's probably enough, sweetheart," she said, taking the bowl away from Sneak. "The truth is, it's better to have loved and been loved in return; maybe Tennyson never experienced it. I guess I can say I had *that* for more years than a lot of people ever do." She gave Touchdown a good ear-scratching. "And now, well, at least I understand what most of my old ladies have been through. Maybe that's of some comfort to them."

CHAPTER TWENTY-EIGHT

Sadie Sparrow
Saturday, February 25

It had been a strange and wonderful day, Sadie reflected as she settled herself in bed.

First, Dana had called, saying she and the girls would be over at noon with lunch. It was an order rather than an invitation, it seemed; apparently it hadn't crossed Dana's mind that her mother might have other plans.

Well, that was okay. It would've been nice to have had some warning, so she could have looked forward to their visit—she had always felt that anticipation was half the fun of any happy event—but she'd be glad to see them even on such short notice.

They'd eaten right here in Sadie's room, sharing a gargantuan chicken Cobb salad from Breeze's Deli. Sadie would have preferred something else, not being especially fond of Roquefort cheese. And there was no dessert. Dana was dieting herself, as usual, and had begun encouraging Hannah and Amanda to watch their weight, too, although they were so tiny that Sadie wondered if this wasn't the sort of advice that eventually resulted in those awful eating disorders.

But she had a nice time nevertheless. The conversation had centered primarily on the girls' futures. Amanda was only fifteen and was pretty enough to be spending her time breaking hearts, but she was focused on her studies, particularly the advanced math courses that she was apparently acing. And at seventeen, the equally attractive Hannah was wrestling with selecting a college on her way to becoming a doctor; cardiology or orthopedic surgery were currently her most-favored specialties.

"I am so impressed with you girls," Sadie marveled. "It never occurred to me to hope for anything beyond marriage and a family, and now look at you both!"

"It's a different day, mother," Dana said with just a note of pomposity. "No one's satisfied with being just a housewife anymore."

"It would be so boring," Hannah said.

"I don't think I could stand it," Amanda added.

"And is working so wonderful?" Sadie asked in as pleasant a tone as she could muster.

They don't even realize that they're insulting me.

Dana frowned. "Well, of course it is. Or it should be, anyway. We all have to do our share, you know, make a contribution to this world."

"And housewives don't make a contribution?"

"Not really, Grandma," said Amanda. "I mean, you can hire people to do your cooking and cleaning, you know. And whatever else women used to do."

"Have babies? Raise children?"

Hannah laughed. "Look at us, Grandma. We turned out all right, wouldn't you say? And we were raised pretty much like all our friends, with our mothers working at big jobs."

"And it's pretty obvious," added Dana, "that our house is nicer than the one you raised me in. We never would have been able to afford it on Bill's salary alone."

Sadie shook her head. "Well, if you're happy, I suppose that's all that matters these days."

It was Amanda's turn to laugh. "What a funny thing to say, Grandma. Of course, that's all that matters today. Being happy is all that's ever mattered."

Not long after Dana had hustled the girls off, Elise had stopped in to say hello, and to ask Sadie's opinion of her upcoming date with Jamie.

"I think it's wonderful, my dear," Sadie said, genuinely happy for Elise and frankly flattered to be consulted on the matter—especially after seeing her entire generation dismissed by Dana and the girls. "He's a fine young man."

"You think so?"

"I'm certain." Sadie then surprised herself by adding, "He is a man of God, and that's really all that matters."

It really is all that matters. Astonishing!

"I think you're right on both counts, Sadie. In fact, Papi said almost the same thing." She blushed. "Now I just have to pray that Jamie likes me, once he gets to know me a little better."

"How could he not? You're sweet, and kind, and in case you hadn't noticed, you're mighty pretty."

Elise smiled gratefully. "And I suppose we all have our skeletons, don't we? Well, we'll see. I'll let you know what happens."

She didn't elaborate, and Sadie didn't pry. She just nodded wisely and squeezed Elise's hand, immensely pleased to be treated as a confidante by this charming girl.

There wasn't time to talk about skeletons or much of anything else, as it turned out; Meg stopped in just then, taking a chunk out of her afternoon off to visit with Sadie and Elise. From the conversation, it was apparent that Meg and Elise were already fairly well acquainted, and it pleased Sadie to see them enjoying each other.

"'Crossing the threshold,'" Meg was saying, "'Alvin was surprised to see his long-lost friend Amos.' Long lost: hyphen or no hyphen?"

"Hyphen," Elise said, without missing a beat. "'Long' modifies 'lost,' not 'friend.'"

"Ha!" Meg said, turning to Sadie. "This girl was a grammar teacher back in the day, and apparently a very good one—I can't seem to stump her!"

Bewildered, Sadie looked at each one in turn.

Elise laughed. "We're both grammar geeks," she explained. "There aren't many of us left, you know."

"So we're keeping each other on our toes," Meg added.

"Just as King Solomon advised," Elise said. "'As iron sharpens iron, so a man sharpens the countenance of his friend.'"

Sadie smiled contentedly as the girls chattered on.

"Well, I guess I'd better get moving," Meg said finally, giving Sadie a quick hug and a peck on the cheek. "It's been a pleasure, ladies—kind of like an eighteenth-century French salon, and you, Mrs. Sparrow, are the most erudite hostess of all time!"

The compliment thrilled Sadie; no one had ever called her a hostess, let alone erudite. She wondered how she could let Dana know about it without seeming to boast.

There was another knock on Sadie's door just before dinner. It was Beulah this time, looking for Sadie's advice on pre-planning her funeral. She had been seen a television advertisement on the subject, she said, and it struck her as a good idea. But what did Sadie think? Sadie didn't have a clue and said so.

And then after dinner, Charles had stopped in to find out what Sadie thought about Elise and Jamie. He seemed delighted to know that she approved of the match.

Strange and wonderful, Sadie thought as she snuggled into her bed, grateful for the double blankets the housekeeper had given her that morning. It felt as if she'd left her old life behind—yes, even Dana and her family, who seemed almost like strangers to her now. But she seemed to have found herself a new family here at The Hickories, a family that would be hers forevermore.

What a strange thought that was. Where did that come from?

Then, as she lay there rehearsing the day's events, it happened again: out of the blue, the ever-present numbness in her left side began intensifying until it felt like her left arm was encased in a tourniquet.

"Lord," she whispered, "is this it? Am I dying? Am I ready for heaven? I know I still think bad things way too often, and I complain all the time, even if it's just in my head. Am I good enough to get in?"

It's not about what you did, Sadie! It's about what He did!

"Is that true, Lord? If only I could believe it!"

But try as she might, she couldn't; it just didn't make sense. But at least thinking about it distracted her from the issue at hand—the possibility that she might be having another stroke—and eventually she fell into a dreamless sleep.

CHAPTER TWENTY-NINE

Elise Chapelle
Saturday, March 3

Elise was a nervous wreck.

It wasn't the fact that she had been dateless for almost two years; she could be dressing for a night out with any of the guys she'd dated in the past without a single butterfly. It was solely because this one was with Jamie, and for once she felt like the stakes were high.

Not that it was a Big Deal date. They were just going over to The Chancery for dinner, and there was nothing fancy about the place. Jeans and a sweatshirt would have been just fine.

But what exactly do you wear on a first date with the man you think you might want to marry?

Elise looked outside once again into the gathering gloom, seeing nothing to help her make up her mind. This weather was amazing, with the temperatures spiking into the low 50s this afternoon. But it could be below freezing by ten o'clock.

She finally chose a peach-colored cowl-neck sweater—it seemed like a good spring color to her, plus she'd read once that peach was one of the best colors for emphasizing green eyes—and paired it with her best brown flannel trousers and her soft pink coral earrings. They'd been Mamie's, and this would be the first time she'd ever worn them.

Excellent. She looked like she'd gone to some effort, with her hair tumbling in gentle waves to her shoulders and these beautiful earrings. But Jamie would never guess that she'd spent the entire afternoon working those waves into her hair. She decided to apply just a tad of the mascara she kept on hand for such a time as this and then, with her eyes looking so nice, to add a little lipstick in a pink that was so close to her natural lip color that it was barely detectable.

They'd had no trouble conversing at The Hickories, Elise reflected as she and Jamie buzzed down Bluemound Road in Jamie's very uncool old Honda, spotless and redolent with the "New Car" scent offered at the carwash down the road. But now that they'd made a conscious choice to spend time together rather than simply letting circumstances intervene, their conversation was horribly strained. He seemed as shy as she felt, stumbling over a description of a paper he was writing on the resurrection, and missing the first turn into The Chancery's parking lot. As uncomfortable as it made the drive, his unease gave Elise some hope; he was clearly no ladies' man.

And the discomfort didn't last. Once they were seated in a booth, coffee poured, and meals ordered, they fell into the chatter they'd been enjoying for the last few weeks, before and after Bible study. They covered all the usual family relationships, Elise being completely frank about Helene's abandonment of her and how sad it had made her as a child, Jamie hinting at a less-than-righteous life before becoming a Christian.

"As a matter of fact," he said, grimacing at the memory, "I did more than my fair share of drinking and drugs when I was in my twenties. And it was a bartender who led me to the Lord."

"Now that's a story I'd like to hear sometime," Elise said. "And not the abridged version."

"You got it. How about on our next date?"

Elise's heart was singing as she watched Jamie's taillights disappear into the night. He had officially called the evening a date and clearly wanted there to be another one. And he had kissed her on the cheek, making them something more than friends.

But later, as she was trying to fall asleep, she remembered that he'd also added something that terrified her.

"You'll have to tell me about your bad old days sometime, too," he'd said. "You've got to have at least a few stories to tell."

She did indeed. And her "bad old days" weren't really all that old.

Elise spent half the night tossing and turning, trying unsuccessfully to cast her past in a more positive light than it deserved.

But there was just no getting around it: she had sinned big time, spending months on end playing the perfect little Christian for Papi and Mamie while living an entirely different life. And while the Lord may have forgiven her this hypocrisy, she didn't know how she could ever forgive herself.

CHAPTER THIRTY

Meg Vogel
Wednesday, March 7

I had the nicest interview with Charles Chapelle today," Meg said, pouring out glasses of a pricey new Cabernet that Sandra had brought as her contribution to dinner. "Give that sauce a stir, would you?"

"Ah, yes, Elise's grandpappy."

"Right. Although if you knew him, you'd never call him a 'grandpappy.' He's very smooth and sophisticated, even for an old fellow. He has this sort of Cary Grant quality that's very appealing. Plus a French accent."

"Watch your step, Meg," Sandra said, smiling mischievously. "He may act like the devil but he's a secret saint underneath all that charm. A veritable sheep in wolf's clothing."

"He's a little old for me," Meg laughed. "But what makes you say that?"

"Just this. Wait a minute." She pulled her laptop out of her bag—this time, an enormous aqua envelope with lime green piping—and powered it up. "Hang on a second."

"What, did you stumble across a picture of him entering a church?" Meg tended the sauce while Sandra tapped away at the keyboard. "Or catch him hobnobbing with some priest?"

"Hardly," Sandra said. "Here, check this out."

And there he was, a handsome old fellow in a semi-profile black-and-white shot that filled up the entire screen. Inserted just to the right of his mouth was a quote rendered in that dopey Papyrus typeface that churchly types seemed to think ideal for conveying ancient wisdom:

> *I have no doubt I'll spend eternity in heaven with the Lord. He paid my sin-debt on the cross, which means I will stand before Him one fine day in the perfect righteousness of Christ. I am forgiven!*

"Et tu, Charles?" Meg groaned. "So is this the website you were telling me about? Elise's?"

"It sure is—Everlasting Place. Here, I'll show you." Sandra pointed her cursor to the menu listings to give Meg a peek at each thoroughly Jesus-soaked page: One Way, About Christ, Science, History, Prophecy, Heaven.

"How do people become so delusional?" Meg asked, glancing at the sub-pages before heading back to the stove to start the fettuccine. "I just don't get it."

"For some reason, they think it's 'truth' with a capital T. I read through her site and it's fairly interesting, but of course it's nonsense. Here, I'll email you the URL and you can read it yourself."

Meg stirred the entire box of noodles into the boiling water. "Maybe I will."

Sandra was looking at her suspiciously, she noticed.

"The subject may be revolting," Meg said defensively, "but I *am* curious about Elise's writing. Plus, I must say I *like* her and old Charles. They really couldn't be sweeter, and they've had a pretty interesting life. What grade are you giving her?"

Sandra laughed. "If she'd written about space aliens, I'd be giving her an A. As it is—well, she's going to have to pay for the foolishness factor. I'm afraid La Divine

Mademoiselle Chapelle will have to be satisfied with a B or a C."

Meg's Alfredo sauce was heavenly, the garlic bread yummy, and the pricey wine quite good. But she was feeling sick to death of Sandra as the evening drew to a close.

She thought about it later, as she was trying to find a comfortable position between her slumbering critters. It wasn't the business talk that bugged her; she was finding that more and more interesting, the longer she was away from it. And the office gossip was something she'd always enjoyed, even when it was about people she barely knew.

It's her arrogance.

Meg rolled that thought around a bit before deciding it was the truth. Once she got started, Sandra would rip apart everyone in her path, present company excepted. And the point of each anecdote was always how stupid, or clumsy, or foolish, or selfish the people involved were, compared with how intelligent, graceful, practical, and tender-hearted Sandra Slocum was in all circumstances.

Not that Sandra ever said that about herself, but the implication was always there. And tonight, perhaps for the first time, Meg found it really annoying.

Maybe we're spending too much time together. I need to find some new friends.

Meg was surprised at the first people to pop into her mind: Sadie Sparrow, followed a split second later by Elise Chapelle.

Real smart, Vogel. An old lady and a holy roller. Sandra's right, you really do know how to pick 'em.

She pictured the three of them hanging out together in a bar, Elise nursing a Virgin Mary and Sadie taking a swig from a can of Ensure.

She was more than a little shocked to find the image inviting.

CHAPTER THIRTY-ONE

Sadie Sparrow
Thursday, March 15

Wonder of wonders, spring was descending on Wisconsin early for once. Splashes of daffodils were already blooming throughout the forest surrounding The Hickories, and even the shagbarks were budding out. *Clear evidence of new beginnings even for the old and decrepit,* Sadie thought as she propelled herself along the windowed hallway towards her waiting breakfast, half hoping no one would come running to her aid and disrupt this feeling of glorious hope that was washing over her.

She would be seeing Jamie after lunch today, and that added to her sense of anticipation. His tendency to choose different days and times for their meetings was a little disconcerting for her, but their studies were definitely changing her life. Transforming her heart, in fact. Last night she'd realized with a start that her moodiness had vanished; she couldn't remember the last time she'd been down in the dumps about daughterly neglect or having moved into what was probably the place she would die. And her suspicions about that awful Nurse Julia? She'd almost forgotten about them as Beulah's legs healed and Eva's latest attack of arthritis subsided.

She was feeling mighty fine today, sporting her favorite coral pantsuit and dangly silver earrings. The stroke-like symptoms of a few weeks ago had vanished overnight, and she hadn't had another episode since then. In fact, she felt almost as good as new today, so chipper that she burst into one of her favorite hymns—"Rejoice, the Lord Is King!" She cared not a whit who might hear her.

It was on this very day, under Jamie's tutelage, that things began to click in Sadie's occasionally befuddled brain.

The previous week, he had wrapped up his long but fascinating "tour of truth," as he called it. He had spent several weeks on science. (Whoever would have guessed that the Bible made scores of scientific statements in passing, millennia before secular scientists made the same discoveries about everything from the sun's own orbit to the mountains and valleys of the ocean floor? And whoever would have guessed that little ol' Sadie Sparrow would manage to follow a fair portion of it?)

Next Jamie had walked the little class—Beulah, Charles, and Elise were now permanent fixtures, she was a little sorry to say—through the Good Book's prophetic accuracy, focusing heavily on Israel's rebirth as a nation in 1948. Not that she had noticed it back then, but Sadie vaguely recalled Ed talking about the situation in the Middle East with great excitement. So now at last she understood what the fuss was all about, and she regretted not paying more attention to him at the time. What fun they might have had discussing these things!

But what fun it was to learn about it now. It wasn't that she really needed proof of the Bible's authenticity as the word of God; she'd always respected Ed's opinion on the matter. But this proof, confirmed continually by Charles' enthusiastic "Amen!", was making a difference in her attitude towards scripture. She was taking it very seriously now, and it was making her look at her life differently, reflect more on her blessed past, and see God's hand in shepherding her along every step of the way.

And today a major piece of the puzzle would fall into place for her at last.

"So," Jamie had said after they'd all exchanged happy greetings, "we've covered a lot of ground, especially in terms of science and history. What I'd like to talk about today is the gospel itself, and how confident you're each feeling that heaven is your eternal destination."

For some reason he was looking right at Sadie.

Am I supposed to go first?

"Why don't we start with you, Sadie?" Jamie said cheerfully when she didn't respond. "Are you confident that you're headed for heaven?"

"Oh yes, I think so. I believe in Jesus, and I've led a good life."

Jamie cocked his head and looked at her expectantly, like a dog that didn't quite understand his master's command. She smiled at him and rubbed her hands together nervously. Of course, it was the wrong answer, and she knew it. She was just nervous about being quizzed in front of these other people, all of whom obviously knew a lot more about the Bible than she did. She racked her brain looking for the right phrase to rescue herself, but it was too late.

"So you're a good person, are you, Sadie Sparrow?"

That question she could handle.

"I try," she said, smiling at the others. "I've learned from the best, after all—my parents, my husband, and now you!"

Jamie's response was totally unexpected. "How many lies have you told in your life?"

"Lies?" She was aghast. How could one even count? "Too many," she replied, after an embarrassingly long delay.

"So you're a liar." Jamie nodded thoughtfully. "How about this—have you ever taken the Lord's name in vain?"

"In vain?"

"Used it as an expression of dismay or anger or just as a casual exclamation?"

"Oh. Well, I suppose I have."

"So you're a blasphemer, too. What about this: Have you ever hated anyone?"

"Oh no," Sadie said, shaking her head. But immediately the image of Herta Teckel popped into her mind—Herta, the busybody neighbor who had repeatedly called the police on the Sparrows because of dear little Cappy's barking. One yip was enough to send Herta shuffling to her phone. And more often than not, the old bat had sparked the barking herself by letting her cat out when Cappy was outside with Ed.

"I take it back," she admitted. "I guess I have hated."

"And yet Jesus said that hating another is committing murder in your heart. So what does that make you?"

"A murderer?" She looked at Jamie hopefully, awaiting some reassurance. Surely a kind word was on the way.

"So you, Sadie Sparrow, are a liar, a blasphemer, a murderer at heart," Jamie said softly. "Just like the rest of us. You're not such a good person after all, are you?"

"No," she said in a small voice, studying her hands. She felt thoroughly ashamed of herself, and hurt that Jamie was being so unkind to her.

But wait: He said, "Just like the rest of us." What does that mean?

"And this," Jamie said, rising and stretching his arms out dramatically, "is why the gospel is such good news. Do you all see? When God the Son died on the cross, He died bearing all the sin this world *has* ever committed and *will* ever commit. He took the full punishment for your sin, in other words, as well as mine—the punishment that would have landed us in hell for all eternity. And all we have to do to get our personal sins expunged is to repent of them and trust in Him instead of in our own goodness."

"Amen," said Charles, as Beulah and Elise nodded in agreement.

At first, Sadie couldn't quite grasp it—it seemed almost too easy. But then something clicked in her heart.

"So my goodness doesn't matter?" she asked.

"Not a bit, at least from the standpoint of getting *into* heaven."

"Jesus paid it all," Elise added, "just like the song says."

"And goodness *really* doesn't matter?" Sadie thought of all the hypocrites she'd known in church over the years and found herself vaguely disappointed that they might well be heaven-bound themselves.

Jamie sat down and explained it all again—how repentance and trust result in being born again, and the indwelling of the Lord in the human heart, and how the new Christian then experiences growing love for, and obedience to, Jesus Christ.

"It just blows me away every time I think about it," Jamie said. "It's so simple, and yet so transforming. It was the only way the Lord could create a people for Himself, loving and obedient by their own choice. No robots needed or allowed!"

Sadie sat quietly, her heart pounding. It all sounded both familiar and totally new to her. On the one hand, it was pretty much what Ed had always told her. But on the other hand, Jamie's harshness with her seemed to have opened a door somewhere deep inside, as if his explanation had finally reached beyond her brain and into her heart. If it was true—and she had to admit that it made some sort of crazy sense—then it changed everything.

"You've given me a great deal to consider, Jamie," she said finally. "I need to spend some time thinking about it."

She was uncomfortably aware that she was probably the only one in the room who hadn't understood these things. But no one else seemed to mind; they were all smiling at her, and Elise came over to give her a big hug.

"I guess maybe it's a bit of information overload, isn't it?" Jamie pulled a couple of little brochures out of his briefcase. "Here are some tracts to help you digest it all— you can look up the verses they cite in your Bible, okay?"

For the first time in her life, Sadie couldn't wait to crack open the books.

The cream of mushroom soup was exquisite that night, the pork chops were moist and tender, and the lemon torte added a tart exclamation point to a lovely meal. When she heard about it, Gladys would be mighty sorry that she'd stayed in her room with a headache and a peanut butter sandwich.

But then a woman at the table next to Sadie's spat out her milk and proceeded to return her whole meal to her dessert plate.

The normal dinner buzz fell silent. Those who could turn their heads stared at the woman in horror as a small army of aides rushed in to wheel the woman out and clean up after her.

"What was that all about?" Sadie asked Eva, as normal conversation resumed.

"Thickened milk," Eva said. "I think she was overreacting a bit, frankly. They gave it to me once by mistake, and it didn't taste all that horrible. It wasn't great—but some say it tastes like someone else's spit, and I don't agree with that at all. It's not that bad. Certainly not worth upchucking."

"But why would they give that to anyone?" Sadie asked, furrowing her brow in concern. "What's it supposed to do?"

"That sweet little aide Piper told me it's to prevent the kind of pneumonia you supposedly get from inhaling your drinks. They say that too many of us old fogies are ending up in the hospital because of it, and that costs society too much, so they figured out a way to prevent it."

"But how?"

"I guess the idea is that if you drink only thickened liquids, you won't inhale your drinks and you won't get pneumonia."

"Is that true?" Sadie did not like the sound of this. "Does it work?"

"Well, they say it does. I've heard that most people on the thickened stuff die of dehydration before they have a chance to develop pneumonia again."

"It sounds like nonsense to me."

"Me too." Eva lowered her voice to a whisper. "Or maybe something even worse."

"Like what?"

"I was thinking more along the lines of murder."

Sadie gasped, quickly glancing around to make sure no one was listening.

"Woe to those who call good evil and evil good," she murmured, her suspicions about Julia bubbling up in her heart once again.

But this time, Sadie didn't entertain those suspicions. She had bigger fish to fry.

That night, while poring over the tracts Jamie had sent home with her, Sadie Gottschalk Sparrow officially repented of her sins, placed her trust in Jesus Christ to have paid the penalty for every last one, and became, as Ed had always said of himself, a heaven-bound sinner saved by grace.

She hoped it wasn't fear or loneliness or old age that had driven her to this point. She didn't think so; this peace and gladness she was feeling was unlike anything she'd ever experienced before, something that went beyond mere relief or day-to-day happiness.

Surely this was the real thing?

Yes, surely it was, because for the first time in her life—in a day replete with firsts—little Sadie Sparrow wept tears of joy.

CHAPTER THIRTY-TWO

Elise Chapelle
Tuesday, March 20

With Papi safely tucked away in the movie theater, Elise retreated to his room to finish her assignment for tonight's class. Lucy was showing *Fail-Safe* today, another one of his favorites; she would never understand the male taste in cinema, but she was grateful to have some peace and quiet. His room was as silent as a tomb even when CNAs were laughing and carrying on right outside the door.

After weeks of intense work, she'd finally finished her website's main pages a few days ago, including her summaries of the gospel and the evidence for the Bible's divine inspiration and inerrancy. Now at last she was free to get back to her advice column, and to share Papi's most excellent guidance on an important topic.

She fired up her laptop, headed straight to her "Advice for the Life-Worn" page, and started typing.

Dear Elise,

Can you help me get past my bitterness? It seems like the most important people in my life have betrayed me. Yes, I am loved by, and love, my grandparents who raised me, but my mother abandoned me as a baby, and my boyfriends have used me. I just don't seem to be able to quit thinking bad things about them. I actually lose sleep over it.

I know I'm not alone in this. I have seen what it does to people over time, and I don't want to go there. Help!
Cathy

Was that too close for comfort? She didn't think so, but just in case, she changed "grandparents" to "aunt and uncle" and "boyfriends" to "friends" before starting in on her response.

Dear Cathy,
I am so glad you wrote. Bitterness is indeed poison, to us and to those around us, and the Bible instructs us to watch for it and rid ourselves of it just as earnestly as we do wrath and anger and evil speech.
How is the question, isn't it?
Seeing this very problem in my own heart not long ago, a wise old man told me exactly how to deal with it. He advised me to pray for the Lord to rid me of the root of bitterness, and to pray for those who have, in my estimation, been cruel to me. He advised me, in particular, to pray for their salvation, I suppose because it would remind me of what they are facing for all eternity if they don't repent; and if we have any compassion at all, we would never wish eternal hell on even our worst enemies, would we?
If we are faithful to pray this way for these people, we will see our hearts softening towards them. And as this old man said to me, "the root of bitterness will die. It needs a hardened heart to thrive."
And you know what? It works, especially when you take your concordance and spend some time meditating on the passages that talk about bitterness. And it is so liberating—I will be forever grateful to the one who gave me this advice, helping me to see beyond my stubborn anger all the way to eternity.
Blessings,

Elise

Not bad, she thought as she read it over. Straightforward and easy to follow.

She wondered if Ms. Slocum would gain anything from this letter. From the things she'd said to her class here and there, especially about co-workers and clients, the teacher struck her as a singularly bitter person herself.

She saved the post and spent some time tweaking her home page before heading out to fetch Papi.

CHAPTER THIRTY-THREE

Meg Vogel
Friday, March 23

It was mid-morning when Meg, heading back to the office after taking the last of the breakfast dawdlers back to her room, saw Sadie and her friends in the Great Room, caught up not in puzzle-making but in some sort of animated discussion.

"Don't be nosy," she told herself, going straight to Lucy's desk to find the DVD for their ten o'clock exercise program. No problem, for once—Lucy had cleaned her desk off a couple days earlier and it was still clear, with just a small tower of papers on one corner.

Meg returned to the Great Room and cued up the DVD to Session Three, Exercise to the Hits of the 1960s. It wasn't the era of the old folk, but it made the simple leg and arm lifts more fun for her.

She didn't mean to eavesdrop, but it was impossible to ignore Gladys' voice.

"I'm telling you, that's what the man said," she shouted indignantly. "Euthanasia! That's what we're headed for and I don't like it one bit! Drug addicts and drunks get all the care they want but those of us who've been paying the bills all along? Oh no, we're too old!"

Sadie and Eva were sitting quietly in their chairs, apparently shocked into silence, their worried eyes riveted on Gladys.

Amazingly, the normally speechless Catherine Peebles was the one who spoke up. "They just want our money," she said bitterly. "And if we don't have any? Then—"

"Exactly!" Gladys roared.

Her face was growing redder by the moment, Meg could see. Time to intervene; she didn't want a heart attack on her hands.

The old girl was spittin' mad, as they used to say.

"I saw it on one of those news shows this morning," Gladys raged, turning on Meg. "They're going to ration healthcare, the man said, and they're going to do it first by taking it away from old people because we cost the system too much and don't put anything back. But I'll tell you, missy, we paid into it all our lives, and I for one don't appreciate it when they say we're getting entitlements. Roosevelt said it was insurance—and I've never seen any kind of insurance that could be taken away just because you're starting to collect on it!"

"Well, to be honest," Meg began, then wisely shut up. This was probably not the smartest time to speak truth into the situation.

"Yes, yes, I know, fly-by-night outfits do that! But not the federal government! What happened to honoring your elders?"

"That's gone the way of hoop skirts and girdles," said Catherine.

"What do you think, Meg?" Sadie asked, turning to look up at her with wide eyes.

"Honestly, I don't know enough about it to comment," Meg said, crossing her fingers behind her back to relieve herself of responsibility for lying to her dear old friend. She *did* know something about this subject, having taken an interest in it back when Gil was still alive—but nothing that would comfort an old person who no longer had much to contribute to the world, at least not financially.

"They're pruning out the deadwood, aren't they?" It was Eva this time. She looked near death herself, Meg thought, her long face weighed down in sadness above a dreary ivory turtleneck.

"I'll see what I can find out when Lucy gets back, okay?" Meg said, wrinkling her brow in concern. "In the meantime, how about joining us for a little exercise?"

"Why should we waste our energy?" Gladys fairly spat out the words. "You're going to quit feeding us soon anyway!"

"So do you think they've got a point?" Meg asked Char, by far the nicest and most approachable nurse on The Hickories' staff.

"Off the record?" Char glanced around to make sure they were alone. The hall was indeed empty, and the residents' doors were closed. Still, she lowered her voice. "Yes, I believe they have a point."

Char was stunning, tall and slim and wearing her blonde hair in a shaggy pixie. She did not look like a serious student of anything, much less the economics of modern medicine. So Meg was surprised when she launched into a lecture-quality discussion of the need to ration supply when it's exceeded by demand, and how evolving government policy was eliminating money as a rationing tool.

"Once money's off the table," she concluded, "there's got to be another mechanism. And you can bet that the elderly will be the first to get cut off."

Meg was astonished. "Seriously? You mean they'll deny treatment?"

"That will be the first step," Char said in a hushed tone, "and it breaks my heart. Just shatters it. But what choice is there? We can't afford to give everyone all the medical care they want."

Meg stared at her in disbelief. "So is Gladys right? Are they going to start killing the elderly?"

"I think we have a way to go before anyone will suggest *actively* killing anyone against his will. But passively? I'm thinking it won't be long now. Look at public sympathy for physician-assisted suicide. And check out what's going on in Holland. Or don't, if you want to be able to sleep at night."

"Mr. Strobel was saying that we always want to be just like Europe." Meg felt queasy.

"We are such fools, aren't we?" Char shook her head dejectedly. "There are probably millions of people who think it's oh-so-kind to put a suffering person out of his misery; after all, we do it for our pets, don't we? And once you've crossed that line, deciding it's okay to play God and kill a fellow human being, then it's pretty easy to broaden your definition of suffering to include just about any state outside of perfect health and happiness."

Meg was a little shocked to find herself agreeing with Char—no doubt because of her growing love for the old folk at The Hickories, but still, it was unsettling to find herself taking what seemed like a Christian position on an important issue.

What is happening to me?

On Saturday morning, after taking Touchdown for a brisk walk through the neighborhood, Meg fired up her computer and got down to business. So much for her supposed friendship with her boss; Lucy had been bouncing back and forth between "More interviews!" and "Where are the biographies?" lately. And she had asked a couple weeks ago when she could expect to see Sadie's bio, considering that Meg had already interviewed Sadie nine times. She couldn't put it off much longer.

Meg opened up the file entitled "Sadie Outline" and stared at it. Yup, there it was, six pages of neatly outlined notes, arranged with indents and roman numerals, complete and logically organized.

Why can't I get moving on this one?

Once Lucy had lit this latest fire under her, Meg had started pounding the copy out almost as fast as her fingers could type. Gladys' biography had been a piece of cake, deftly crafted so that the old gal hadn't even noticed the references to snobbery written between every line. Sylvia Tenpenny's had been equally easy, as were several others she'd already completed through final drafts that seemed to delight everyone concerned. And Marv Steinhart's had been really fun; it wasn't every day that she had the opportunity to write about one of the architects of the first atomic bomb, even if he had really been little more than a water boy for the real brains behind it. Besides, like Carl Strobel, Steinhart had opinions on just about every issue under the sun, and expressing those opinions seemed to bring him great joy.

But Sadie's biography was a struggle.

Maybe I just don't want our interviews to end.

That was silly, since they'd still be friends and Meg could visit Sadie anytime, after work or even on the weekend if she wanted to spend hours with the old girl.

Meg finally resorted to a technique she'd used often over the years, whenever writer's block threatened to torpedo a project: she just wrote, promising herself that she'd make the text sing in her second, third, or fourth round of edits.

Sadie Sparrow was born on a farm near Shawano, Wisconsin, in 1926, to Meta and Albert Gottschalk.

Meg was tempted to stop and massage the sentence into something irresistible, but endless rewriting of the lead had always been a dead end for her. She plunged ahead.

The farm had been homesteaded by her great-grandfather in the 1800s, and it combined dairy farming with crops such as alfalfa and oats. From the time she could toddle, little Sadie helped out, at first in the home vegetable garden and later in the fields.

It wasn't an easy life. The Depression hit the Gottschalks full force in the early 1930s, along with a horrible drought. The Gottschalks and their neighbors were nearly wiped out. But somehow everyone pulled together and survived by bartering. "We were poor, I guess," Sadie said in a recent interview, "but we didn't know it. Everyone was poor in those days."

Meg tried to imagine what it had been like to live like that, never knowing if you'd be able to hang on to your home, never being absolutely sure that you'd be able to put food on the table next week, never being able to buy your kids a new pair of shoes or a warm winter coat.

Sadie said that God sustained them, apparently being unable to put a stop to the Depression or the drought.

Meg deleted the last clause, even though it reflected exactly what she felt about their allegedly almighty friend. This was Sadie's story, after all, not hers.

Their church became a meeting ground, she said, not only for spiritual nourishment, but also for Sunday, Tuesday, and Thursday potluck suppers, which assured that everyone was getting at least a few good meals each week.

"Spiritual nourishment": that was good. Sadie's biography was finally underway. Fingers flying, Meg filled in three Word pages, then four. She was just getting to the good part—Sadie's story about meeting Ed—when the doorbell rang. It was Sandra, right on time, ready to hit the antique mall.

Reluctantly, Meg backed up her work and shut down her computer.

"Look, an early edition of *Nancy's Mysterious Letter!*"

Sandra's voice was muffled, and it took Meg a few moments to find her. But there she was, on her hands and knees at the back of a neglected booth packed with stacks of musty old books and magazines.

"Is it valuable?" Meg was no slouch as a Nancy Drew fan, but Sandra was the real deal—a true fanatic who knew exactly how to gauge each volume's often murky publication date and edition, and to translate this information into dollars and cents.

"Guess I'm no longer a spring chicken." Sandra winced as she worked her way back to her feet. But her face was flushed in triumph beneath a green cloche that she'd found on eBay in November. It was a great look for her; for a moment Meg forgot about her recent irritation with Sandra, letting herself pretend that the two chums had walked straight out of a country tea room not far from Nancy's fictional home in River Heights.

"My heart's pounding," Sandra said, paging carefully through the volume. "Orange title, orange silhouette, and yes indeedy, Meg, we've got three, make that four, illustrations. All in beautiful shape! It's—I can't believe this—from the title listing, it looks like a first edition!"

Intrigued, Meg moved in for a closer look. "What's it worth?"

"Well, it's in great shape. If only it had the dust cover, it'd be worth at least several hundred dollars. Without it, I dunno—maybe a hundred. It's a long shot, but I'm going to see if that dust cover's back here somewhere," she said, disappearing back into the disarray. "You go on ahead."

But Meg lingered, looking through the stacks of hardcovers with familiar spines. Here were a couple of Black Stallion books, several Bobbsey Twins, Hardy Boys galore, and here—*The Voice in the Suitcase*, a Judy Bolton mystery that had mysteriously vanished from her personal collection! She felt a familiar pang of longing for her childhood, for its innocence and optimism and carefree dependence on all-knowing parents. These wonderful books took her straight back to twin beds and sleepovers and pure, worry-free joy. *The Voice in the Suitcase* was in rough shape, but at just $3, it had to go home with her.

"No luck," Sandra said, startling her. "But I'll take it just the same—they only want five dollars for it."

They strolled through the dusty old mall, past booths featuring dolls or stuffed toys, knickknacks or creaky old furniture, exclaiming over this memory or that, telling each other elaborate tales about the neighbor kids who'd had exactly this little fire engine or the dog who'd eaten out of a dish that looked precisely like that one.

They emerged from the mall several hours later, overwhelmed by nostalgia, making Miss Montgomery's Tea Shop in Oak Creek the only logical place to have a late lunch. There, over crustless cucumber sandwiches and pots of fragrant tea, they finally slipped back into the present.

"So you won't believe this," Meg said, pouring herself another steaming cup of Earl Grey, "but Jamie the Bible teacher asked me out the other day."

"No! I thought he was just a kid?"

"He is—forty-ish, I'm guessing! Whoever would have expected me to turn into a cougar?"

"You wouldn't be the first," Sandra laughed. "Barb Willis—you know her, right?—she's dating a very hot writer who's fifteen years younger than she is, if you can believe it. What did he ask you to do?"

"Just to have lunch. Supposedly to talk about Sadie, but I don't buy that. She's fine; she doesn't need any off-site discussion."

"Is he cute? Are you going?"

"I suppose he's cute, but of course I'm not going." Meg gave Sandra one of her I'm Not That Dumb looks. "For one thing, he's moving to Munich soon—"

"Awesome!"

"Not really. He's going to be a missionary there. And I'll tell you, the last thing I need in my life is another Bible thumper. Although I seem to be surrounded by them lately. Ever since Gil went off the deep end on this Jesus thing, it seems like that's all I hear about. And I want nothing to do with it."

Sandra grinned. "Well, my dear, you'll never hear it from me—you can count on it! So you're not going?"

"No, not to lunch, anyway."

"Then what?"

"Breakfast, tomorrow morning." Meg smiled innocently. "At ten, so he'll have to skip church."

CHAPTER THIRTY-FOUR

Sadie Sparrow
Saturday, March 24

S adie stopped in to visit Beulah after lunch and was
pleased to find her deep in conversation with Eva; they
were her best friends here, and it was wonderful that they
were becoming close, too. They were almost like the
Golden Girls!

"It's about time you got here, Sadie," Beulah bellowed.
"We've got a mystery to solve!"

"Why didn't you tell me that Beulah was your other
victim?" Eva looked a little cross, Sadie thought.

"Allegedly," Beulah said. "And Sadie was just trying to
keep our secrets. I admire her for it."

"What in the world is going on?" Sadie asked, rolling
herself over to Beulah's trestle table, an exact replica of her
own. "What victim?"

She was relieved to learn that her friends had figured
out their shared victimhood without any help from her, if
indeed their collective suspicions about Nurse Julia turned
out to be accurate. Sadie had been careful not to betray
their confidences but protecting their secrets had been a
heavy burden—at least, when she remembered to think
about those secrets at all, not such an easy task these days.
Her memory just wasn't what it used to be.

"Has anything else happened?"

"She refused me a pain pill again," Eva said. "Thursday night. I didn't really need it, but I wanted to test her. She flunked."

"And she was nasty to me yesterday," Beulah added. "I was trying to be pleasant and asked her how she was when she came in to give me my pills, and she completely ignored me. Just said 'here,' and shoved them down my throat."

"Shoved?" Sadie was shocked.

"Well, not shoved, exactly, but you know how rough these girls can be."

It crossed Sadie's mind that Julia might just have been preoccupied or extremely busy—she'd seen it so often in Dana over the years. But she didn't say so. Beulah and Eva were out for blood now, and they wouldn't be sympathetic to such a defense.

"So what should we do about this?" Eva asked.

They both looked at Sadie.

Chief Inspector Sparrow to the rescue.

"I don't know, girls. Tell someone? Like Meg? Or do we need to gather more evidence, and then confront her ourselves?"

"I say we confront her and *then* gather more evidence!" Beulah pounded her fist on the table.

They burst into merry laughter.

"You sound just like the Queen of Hearts," Eva chortled, her eyes filled with tears of mirth. "'Off with her head!' Oh, my heart, that's the funniest thing I've ever heard!"

Sadie smiled again as she snuggled into her bed. It was so wonderful to have friends, so wonderful to laugh together!

Her ancient alarm clock was ticking away. Normally it lulled her to sleep, but not tonight. She opened an eye to check the time: half-past eight, and she wasn't even close to falling asleep. There was only one solution.

"Heavenly Father," she said softly, "you know that tomorrow morning Jamie will be meeting Meg for breakfast, right? Of course, you do—I've mentioned it to You several times since he shared the news with me this afternoon, and besides You know everything!"

Silly! Trying to tell God Almighty something about His creation!

"It would be so nice if he could reach her with the gospel, Lord God. She so needs to repent and trust in You alone. Would You please do whatever it takes to make that happen? I know this is Jamie's prayer, too, so You could answer two prayers for the price of one, if you don't mind my pointing that out."

She laughed out loud, thinking of what a chuckle that bit of human advice must have given the Creator of the universe.

"All in Your perfect timing, of course, but I sure would love to see her receive You in my lifetime. But Your will be done, not mine. Don't let me start telling You what to do and when to do it."

Like He's going to do exactly what I say, according to my timetable!

But she knew He understood her better than she understood herself. She asked it all in Jesus' name, and promptly fell asleep.

CHAPTER THIRTY-FIVE

Elise Chapelle
Saturday, March 24

I believe," Jamie said, smacking his lips, "that was the best meal I've ever had!"

Elise beamed. Her face was still flushed from the cooking exhibition she'd just put on for him. Making perfect chateaubriand was not exactly rocket science if you could find a good beef tenderloin but orchestrating its shallot-and-wine sauce along with the chateau potatoes and steamed carrots was quite the feat.

"Mamie taught me everything I know," she said, clearing their plates and whisking the dishes to the counter. "No, no, sit down. I've saved the best for last." She pulled two glass dishes out of the refrigerator and placed one before him. "The pièce de résistance, as she always said."

"Chocolate pudding?"

"It's mousse," she laughed, "and it took me hours to get it right. It's not as easy as it looks. It's tricky to fold in the egg yolk at just the right time, when the chocolate is just the right temperature."

"It's unbelievable."

She had to agree.

"So tomorrow's your breakfast with Meg?"

He nodded. "It's a good sign that she agreed to it, don't you think? She knows where I'm coming from, obviously."

"Not necessarily."

"Meaning?"

"Meaning she may think you're interested in her." Elise felt like a woman of the world presenting him with this insight, even though it came from all the classic novels she'd read rather than personal experience. "You're rather attractive, you know."

And so is she.

"She's a little old for me."

"That's the trend these days. These older women call themselves 'cougars.'"

He considered that idea for a moment before dismissing it with a chuckle. "Anyway, we're on completely different spiritual planes."

So don't you dare even think about her in romantic terms, Jamie Fletcher!

"True," she said. "But she doesn't realize it, you know. The lost don't know anything about spiritual planes."

"Well, I think you're wrong. She knows exactly why I want to talk with her, and the fact that she accepted my invitation means she's somewhat open to it."

"And if I'm right?"

He laughed, pushing himself away from the table. "She's not going to be exactly thrilled with me, is she?"

Too happy to sleep, Elise seated herself at her desk and pulled out a single sheet of her best stationery—cream, with her initials embossed at the top—and began writing.

Dear Helene,

Just a quick note to update you on my young man.

Here's what happened: He kissed me tonight, Helene, so sweetly, without mauling me the way the others have. He kissed me and held me gently for a moment and said goodnight.

He is the one. I cannot wait for you to meet him.

Love from your daughter,

Elise

She tucked the note into the drawer with all the others and climbed back into bed, promptly falling into a contented sleep.

CHAPTER THIRTY-SIX

Meg Vogel
Sunday, March 25

The morning of what she laughingly thought of as her "big date," Meg threw on jeans and a sweatshirt, then decided she looked a little too deliberately sloppy and changed into a gray turtleneck sweater. She skipped the makeup and let her cropped hair dry naturally instead of blowing it out into a smooth cap, which meant it curled up around her face; she thought she looked like a brunette Miss Piggy. Sure that her overall look would telegraph utter indifference to whether or not Jamie found her attractive, she pulled on a worn purple ski jacket and headed out the door feeling quite proud of her disinterest in him.

She'd chosen Pancakes Plus because it was always jam-packed and noisy on Sunday mornings. And indeed, the waiting area was standing room only when she walked in. But she immediately saw him waving at her from a booth near the kitchen.

"You got here early," she said, pulling off her ski jacket and slipping into the booth.

"I came right from the early service. Gave me a chance to think about the sermon—really a good one today, about what the Bible tells us about heaven."

She would not give him the satisfaction of asking a follow-up question. Instead, she opened her menu and pretended to study it, knowing full well that she would be ordering a feta cheese omelet with hash browns and an English muffin. And juice. A large juice, as long as he was paying for it. And coffee, of course.

The young waitress took their order and hurried off without bothering to write it down.

"Show-off," Meg said, smiling to prove that she was just kidding. "She won't be relying on her memory ten years from now."

What are you doing, you idiot? Why are you trying to impress him?

They chatted about the weather and the neighborhood while they waited for the food, then discussed her job and Sadie's wonderfulness over the meal (he prayed silently, she noticed, before digging into his buckwheat pancakes). Amazingly, there were no awkward silences. Every time one threatened, he filled in the gap, asking her about her home and her pets and her former life as a copywriter.

"So where are you politically?" she finally asked, knowing that he would almost certainly give the wrong answer.

"I'm conservative. No surprise there, I suppose."

"So you don't mind government telling you how to run your personal life?"

He looked at her quizzically. "Do you mean like telling me that private property is to be protected against theft and that murder must be punished? Is that the sort of intrusion into my private life you're talking about?" He downed a slice of the amazingly crisp Pancakes Plus bacon. "Nope, doesn't bother me a bit. How about you? What are your politics?"

She gave him her best "gotcha" smile, knowing that her position was the one any sensible person should have. "I'm independent," she said, "but essentially Libertarian. I'm a Rand girl—Rand Paul and Ayn Rand. I want the government and everyone else out of both my pocketbook and my bedroom. And my life."

"That would explain your—well, to be honest, your attitude. You aren't the easiest person I've ever known."

She laughed, surprised at his forthrightness. "Do tell!"

Much to her amusement, he plunged ahead.

"Okay. It's partly that Libertarians tend to take their politics very seriously. Am I right?"

She nodded briefly. She really didn't, beyond griping whenever government threated to impinge on her freedoms, but she didn't want to be thought of as a political lightweight.

"And I'll bet that all you see," he said, "is government interference with virtually every aspect of life. That has to be very frustrating."

She nodded again. She hated to admit it, but it was a decent observation, one that she wouldn't have expected from a man so heavenly minded that he was no earthly good, as the saying went.

"But you have to be pretty frustrated, too," she said. "Slavish morality has gone the way of—what is it my old girls say? Hoop skirts and girdles?"

Clichéd thinking and speech—real smart, Meg! The last refuge of the unimaginative.

He was smiling at her.

He really is kind of cute. What a waste!

"I suppose I *am* frustrated," he said, "but I try to keep my eye on the bigger picture. It's really what we should be expecting, historically speaking."

The waitress refilled their cups and asked if there'd be anything else; the waiting area was packed. They both shook their heads and she gave Jamie the check.

"Do you mean because of the nonsense about nation states lasting on average two hundred years? People seem to use that as an excuse for not paying attention."

"Something like that, I guess." He glanced at the check and pulled out a debit card.

"So, you can tell me if it's none of my business," he said finally, taking a swig of coffee as if for courage, "but I wanted to ask you about your husband's faith."

Meg shrugged. "There's not much to tell. He wasn't a Christian when I married him, and then he got cancer and got scared, I suppose. He met some people at the clinic and all of a sudden I didn't recognize him anymore."

"You didn't like him better?"

"Nope." Meg busied herself with stirring a mega-dose of cream and sugar into her coffee. "Because, you see, I liked him just fine before. But he suddenly lost his will to fight. It was like he wanted to die—not just to get it over with, but because he was looking forward to heaven." She frowned. "You can't imagine how hurtful that is, to have your husband prefer death to staying with you."

"No, I guess I can't imagine that. Although I *can* imagine being in his position, and being really excited for the first time in my life about going home to heaven—especially if I'd been thinking that there was no hope for eternal life, that I'd close my eyes one day soon and just cease to exist. And I'm sure that feeling would be no reflection on the wife I was leaving behind."

"I'm sure you're right," she said coldly.

"But I'll bet you saw some good changes in him at the same time. Like maybe a new level of concern for you?"

"Well, yes, that's true enough." Meg thought that it was kind of creepy that Jamie knew this. Was it so predictable? "The trouble was, his concern was mainly that I should believe what he believed. And like I said, I have no interest in that sort of thing."

Jamie nodded, his brow furrowed as if he were wrestling with a tough logic problem. "Of course, if you don't believe, you can't see that he was paying you the greatest compliment of all—wanting to make sure that you could spend all eternity with him."

"Yes, I understand that." Coldly, again. Did he think she was stupid? "I just don't happen to agree with his starting premise, or yours. And I don't want you to try to convince me of it, okay?"

"Got it," he said, surprising her with his quick surrender. "But I'm glad for his sake that he didn't suffer from any uncertainty at the end, and that he's now in heaven. Whether you choose to believe it or not really doesn't impact whether or not it's true, you know. He knew it was true, and I know it's true, and it's a wonderful thing to head into eternity knowing where you'll wake up."

"I'm sure you're right." She made a show of glancing at her watch. "Oh, my, I've got to run."

She thanked him for breakfast and pulled her jacket on.

"My pleasure," he said. "Let me just leave you with one thought: if you ever want to see Gil again, you're going to have to figure out how to get there. And I'd like to help you do that."

"Thanks again," she said, hurrying out into the parking lot.

But no thanks, Saint Jamie.

She felt like a fool. He hadn't asked her out because he was interested in her beauty or her brain. He was only interested in her soul. And that wasn't for sale at any price.

The phone was ringing when Meg stepped into her kitchen, fighting through Touchdown's leaping welcome.

The caller was, of course, Sandra, wanting to know all about the date.

"Not a great success," Meg said, squirming out of her ski jacket. "Reminded me of a journalism professor I had in college, Professor Ugly. That's what I called him, anyway, because he was singularly unattractive—he was the Sean

Penn type, complete with goatee. But he was brilliant, and I had such a crush on him."

She took a seat at the kitchen table and blocked Touchdown's clumsy advances with a forearm.

"So," she continued, "one day after class he asked me to stop and see him during his office hours later that week."

"Of course, he did," Sandra said. "You're adorable today and I'm sure you were even more so thirty years ago."

"Yikes, thirty years? But you're right—thirty plus!" In danger of wandering down that rabbit trail, Meg jerked her thoughts back to the subject at hand. "But anyway, you can imagine. I skipped my other classes that day because I couldn't get my hair right, and couldn't decide what to wear, and it was hot out and we didn't have air conditioning in those days, and I didn't want to sweat—"

Sandra giggled. "I know exactly what you mean!"

"So I get there, finally, just as he's about to leave, but he takes the time to talk with me about—get this—wanting me to go on and get my master's in Mass Comm."

"No!"

"Yup. He said something like, 'You're such a great student and a really good writer, and we could really use more people like you teaching in our universities. You could go just about anywhere you wanted—'"

"Except out with him, right?"

"Right. So I thanked him and said I'd think about it and left. I found out later that he was dating this gorgeous blonde in my class."

"She was probably a total chicky fluff."

Meg laughed. "I'm so glad to have a friend like you—always on my side."

They chatted about their other early crushes before Sandra brought her back to square one.

"So Jamie was like Professor Ugly?"

"Oh, right," Meg laughed again. "Spaghetti brain, huh? Yes, like Professor Ugly, Jamie has absolutely no interest in my body or brain. Just my soul."

"What rot!"

"I know. But unlike the Professor Ugly Incident, at least I wasn't really interested in Saint Jamie. I just wanted to torment him a little."

"Like a cat batting around a mouse."

"Exactly."

It wasn't 100 percent true—her feelings were a tad bruised, or maybe it was just her pride—but she wasn't about to admit anything of the kind to Sandra.

Jamie's lack of interest in her physical being served at least one good purpose, Meg thought later, as she watched her old LaserJet printer kick out page after neat page: it had forced her to prove her superiority by finishing Sadie's biography and, just as important, doing an outstanding job on it.

CHAPTER THIRTY-SEVEN

Sadie Sparrow
Sunday, March 25

Sadie and Gladys brunched together on Sunday, enjoying a feast of fresh strawberries and blackberries, French toast with maple syrup, bacon that was every bit as crisp as any Sadie had ever had, as much orange juice as they wanted, and coffee that tasted like something you'd get at a fancy cafe.

Gladys shocked Sadie by calling the meal "good" and then shocked her again by pointing out that Marcia at Table Nine was on "the thick stuff."

"Do you mean thickened liquids?" Sadie was ashamed that she'd let that subject slip to the back burner in recent days, her new spiritual life and time with Jamie being foremost on her mind.

"If that's what you want to call it," Gladys sniffed, "although I don't know why you always have to make everything so complicated. Pretending to be something you're not."

"'Thick stuff' is just fine with me," Sadie said, humbled by the rebuke. "So how did you find out?"

One of Gladys' nicer traits was her willingness to leave a hurt behind. "Before you got here, I heard her complaining about it to the servers. But they wouldn't help her. I think it's a crime."

"A crime?"

"Without a doubt." Gladys lowered her voice and glanced back over her shoulders to make sure no one was eavesdropping. "It kills people, you know. If you don't get enough to drink, you get fuzzy headed and then you die. I've seen it happen again and again."

Gladys had lived at The Hickories for several years, and Sadie didn't doubt that she knew a lot more than she let on.

"Have any of your—have you known anyone who's been on it?"

Gladys eyed Sadie up before answering. "My friends, you mean? Were you assuming I haven't had any friends here?"

"No, of course not, I just meant—"

"I'll have you know that I've had plenty of friends here. It's just that they've all died or gone home."

"Of course you have." Sadie felt her face flush; she'd been caught red-handed. She quickly changed gears. "So have any of them been on the thick stuff?"

"Yes, and they've all died within weeks, except for one. Her name was Ida—she lived next door to me. She survived for two years on the stuff, finally had a coronary."

"Well, then, if Ida made it that long, maybe it's not so bad after all," said Sadie, hoping for a silver lining.

Gladys looked around for eavesdroppers again. "It's not so bad if someone is sneaking you water and soda every day," she whispered. "I kept her supplied."

"Why Gladys," Sadie whispered back, impressed. "You really do have a heart, don't you?"

Gladys glared at her. "Don't you dare tell anyone."

CHAPTER THIRTY-EIGHT

Elise Chapelle
Wednesday, March 28

It was Papi's admiration of Charlie Chaplin that gave Elise a personal glimpse into the soul of Meg Vogel.

The Hickories' Wednesday afternoon entertainment was *The Great Dictator*, and though Papi rarely wasted his time on movies, this was one that he treasured beyond reason. Never mind that it was thought by some to be in poor taste, even though it had been released before the world learned of the horrors of Nazi Germany. Never mind that others—Elise included—found it more than a little boring. Papi loved *The Great Dictator* and he was not going to pass up this chance to see it.

Elise settled him in the theater with popcorn and juice and retreated to one of the overstuffed chairs in the Great Room. It was toasty warm here, with the fire blazing in spite of unusually warm temperatures outside, and she could hear the movie's soundtrack. She relaxed and closed her eyes, ready to doze off if the opportunity presented itself.

It did not. Having started the film for a half a dozen diehard Chaplin fans, Meg flopped down in the chair opposite Elise's.

"Your grandfather seems to love this movie," she said.

"Passionately," Elise said, grinning. "He's a crazy old fellow—just wait till you get to know him better."

They chatted a bit about Papi's peculiarities and detoured through Sandra and her teaching style before Meg veered into the subject she apparently wanted to discuss.

"So what do you think of Jamie?"

Elise blushed—did anyone know they were dating?—but Meg was examining her fingernails and didn't see it.

"Jamie? Oh, well, he's a fine teacher, too," she said, trying to steer the conversation back toward Sandra and teaching styles.

"That's good to hear," Meg said. "Even though what he's teaching is—"

"Yes?"

"Well, let's just say 'unproven and unprovable.' How's that? I don't want to offend you, Elise—I know you share his faith."

"I do."

"But what's weird is that you keep it to yourself, pretty much. Jamie—he's different. He seems to feel like it's his duty to shove his religion down everyone else's throat."

Elise's heart leapt. She'd been trying to think of a way to bring the subject up, and here Meg had dropped it in her lap.

Help me, Lord! What should I say to her?

"I just can't stand pushy Christians," Meg was saying. "I was married to one, you know. This Jesus of yours ruined him!"

"There was a time when I would've agreed with you wholeheartedly," Elise said, smiling sympathetically. "But what you need to understand, Meg, about your husband and Jamie and the rest of us serious Christians, is that we *know* we have the ultimate truth about this life and all eternity—not because we're so brilliant, but because we know that scripture is true."

"In your opinion."

"Well, not really." Elise bit her lip, praying silently for wisdom. "It's demonstrable, for anyone who's willing to look at the evidence objectively. I'd love to show you sometime."

"Jamie has already offered. Sort of."

"Okay, well then, if you're ever interested, you've got people standing by to help."

"I'm so glad." Meg smiled and batted her eyelashes.

It took some effort, but Elise managed to forgive the sarcasm. "In the meantime, I wish you'd understand that we pesky Christians fear for the immortal souls of unbelievers. It's true that genuine faith offers wonderful advantages in this life—most of all, an incredible peace and sort of a fearlessness in the face of trial. But the elephant in the room that unbelievers don't want to talk about is what happens to us after we die."

"There are all kinds of opinions on that score."

"Of course there are. But like I said, we know we have the truth. Jesus said 'I am the way, the truth and the life. No one comes to the Father except through Me.' That's either true or it's not true—and if it is, which we are certain it is, that has eternal implications for every last human being. Including you."

"Yes, I understand that perfectly well." Meg was no longer playing the vamp; her eyes were icy. "But I like you, Elise, and I don't want *our* relationship to be ruined over this issue. Could we just drop it? I'll let you know if I'm ever interested."

"Sure." Elise smiled warmly. "You let me know."

Elise called Jamie as soon as she got home to report on her conversation with Meg.

"I'm afraid I didn't have any more success than you did," she concluded, trying to keep the defeat out of her voice.

But Jamie wasn't discouraged. "Planting seeds, Elise, planting seeds!" he rejoiced. "You're doing the right thing—be her friend, be there for her, and be ready for her questions. I believe she'll have some, sooner or later. Good job!"

She hung up, every word of praise making her feel worse.

Hypocrite! Letting him think so highly of you!

She would have to have a talk with him soon.

CHAPTER THIRTY-NINE

Meg Vogel
Thursday, March 29

Meg was not a happy camper. Mr. Olewinski was taking his ever-loving time about downing his breakfast this morning, and she had a ten o'clock date with Sadie to go over more photos for their upcoming biography. She was tempted to stuff the pureed eggs into his mouth until he had to swallow to breathe, and if she'd thought it would work, she might have tried it. But he'd probably just spit it out or croak on her and that would delay her even more.

She gave him another spoonful of egg, ever so gently, and watched him struggle to down it. Tears threatened; she could not help but feel sorry for him, for everyone who'd ever been dealt such a low blow by the fates.

She wrenched her thoughts away from this dreariness and sent them off in Elise's direction. There were things about Elise that Meg really liked—not the least of which was the girl's sunny outlook on just about everyone and everything. Even her teacher Sandra.

If only Elise could hear Sandra talking about Christians!

Which, come to think of it, bugged her. Elise may have been deluded on the religion front, but what right did Sandra have to mock any of her students, the very students who were making her job a reality, and possibly paving the way for her early retirement?

But hold on—do I not do the same thing? Am I a hypocrite?

Another unpleasant subject. Meg turned her attention back to the job at hand. "You done, Mr. Olewinski?" The old man had pinched his lips together against another mouthful of food. "Okay, then, off we go," she said, dabbing at his lips with a napkin and flipping up the locks on his geri chair.

It was really strange, she thought as she pushed the heavy chair towards his room: despite the iciness she'd shown Elise yesterday, she felt almost torn between Sandra and Elise, between the worlds they lived in, the values they held dear, their interests, and their very characters.

She'd heard of being torn between two lovers—there was even a song about it, as she recalled—but never really about being torn between two friends. It was ridiculous, of course; it wasn't as if either one was demanding her exclusive devotion.

Yet that's exactly what it felt like.

Things could change tomorrow, she knew, but at the moment, Elise would win any such battle. At least, she'd win if only she would drop the religious talk. That she hadn't yet was certainly disappointing.

And then there was another disappointment: Sadie's lifetime photo collection was Missing in Action.

"I just have this little album that we looked at weeks ago," Sadie said, handing Meg a small binder covered in worn black cardboard. "These photos are all very old, and I know you're looking for some more recent ones."

"It would be nice," Meg said, "but if this is all you have . . ."

"Oh, I have plenty more. I just don't have a daughter with enough time to run them over. I called her about them again last night, and she promised to drop them off this morning on her way to a big meeting, but either she forgot, or she ran out of time."

"The story of way too many lives these days," Meg said wistfully. "What were we thinking, we feminists, by demanding to be let into this rat race?"

"It certainly doesn't seem to be making everyone happy, does it? Although Dana did tell me not long ago that it's her career that has allowed them to live in their big, beautiful house. She said they couldn't have afforded it on her husband's salary alone."

"She has a point."

"I think it's sad," Sadie said. "I don't think we realize how quickly forty, fifty years fly by. She's going to realize one day that her life on this earth is over, and the house will be all she has to show for it—that, and two daughters raised to be just like their mother."

"Except they'll probably have even wilder ideas of what the bare minimum is for a decent standard of living." Meg remembered what Sadie had said about her own little house. "I wonder what sort of mansion Dana's girls will expect to live in?"

Sadie nodded, then smiled. "This is certainly a dreary conversation, Meg. Let's talk about something happier—unless you have to run?"

"I blocked this time out for you, Sadie, so we're good to go!" She smiled back at her old friend. "Let's talk about . . . I know, how about best friends? Have you ever had any?"

"Oh, of course! A number of them, in fact, over the years. Haven't you?"

"Well, yes, I guess so," Meg replied. "There has always been at least one girl I hung out with, anyway."

"Who is it today?"

Meg leaned back on Sadie's couch, feeling like a patient at a psychiatrist's office. It was not unpleasant to have someone else asking the questions for once.

"At this point I'd probably have to say it's Sandra," she said, wondering why she felt the need to qualify what had been a given just a few months ago. "I have to bring her over to meet you one of these days. I've told her so much about you!"

"That must have been a dull conversation."

Meg laughed. "Not at all! In fact, we've talked about your life—I hope you don't mind, Sadie? I think it's influencing our thinking. Mine, at least. My idea of what's valuable in life seems to be shifting a little. I think you're making me less of a greedy materialist!"

Sadie looked shocked at that. "Oh, Meg, that's not you. You're not greedy!"

"But I am, Sadie, and I'm definitely materialistic. But that's changing now, thanks to you."

"I guess that's good?"

Meg thought for a moment. "Oh, of course it is. At the very least, I no longer have lingering doubts about closing my business and taking such a huge pay cut to work here. I'm glad I did it." She rose and checked the soil in Sadie's philodendron. Plenty moist; these aides really were on top of the peripherals. "But there's a bit of a downside, too, in that my relationship with Sandra is changing, and I feel like I'm in some sort of limbo."

"What do you mean?"

"Guess I feel kind of lonely these days, being stuck between these two worlds—yours and Elise's being the other one, minus all of your religion." She smiled fondly down at Sadie. "I hope that doesn't offend you. I know you're a big believer. It's just that I'm not. Spiritually, I'm a lot more like Sandra. Which is why she and I will continue being friends till the cows come home, going out to eat together and to antique shops and flea markets. But it's not quite the same. Sandra can be unkind about others—I suppose even about me, when I'm not there to defend myself. I used to think she was funny, and I'd join in on it with her, but lately it's bothering me. And I think that's your fault."

Sadie smiled happily. "I'm going to take that as a compliment, Meg. I'm not sure if you intended it to be, but I'll take it as one just the same."

During the lunch hour, Meg watched some clips from *A Place in the Sun* over her blueberry yogurt. She couldn't stop thinking about various aspects of the story, from why they felt compelled to change the names of Dreiser's characters for the movie to how ambition and greed and lust had turned the protagonist into a murderer. And then there were the curious things about the stars chosen to play the leading roles, like how beautiful Liz Taylor had been in this flick, and how attractive Montgomery Clift might have been if only he'd kept his mouth shut.

Kind of like Jamie, right, Meg?

That really was true, for entirely different reasons. With Clift, it was *how* he said things; with Jamie, it was *what* he said that was so endlessly irritating.

What a waste you are, Jamie Fletcher. Getting to know you is like finding out the really cute guy in your Broadcast Journalism class is gay—such a waste!

Sadie was a regular for The Hickories' Headlines and Coffee parties, and that afternoon was no exception. Meg had to smile when she rolled into the Great Room calling out, "What's news, Pussycats?" to the dozen residents already forming a semicircle in anticipation of the arrival of volunteer Elmer and his stack of newspapers. It was pretty impressive, Meg thought, that her old friend—all these seniors, in fact, including Charles Chapelle and Carl Strobel and even crabby Gladys Baldwin—were still interested in what was going on in the world, even though little of it affected them directly anymore. Definitely not members of the "what's in it for me?" generation.

Unlike me, she thought ruefully as she headed back to the office, wishing she'd had more than a container of yogurt for lunch.

Popcorn—wonder if there's any left from yesterday?

She was pretty sure there would be, given how small the turnout had been for *The Great Dictator*. She made a quick right onto the thick carpeting of the theater and saw a large basket of filled-to-the-brim popcorn bags on the table just inside the door; the night staff had forgotten to dump it. So what if it was a day old? Meg's mouth watered.

But just as she was picking up the basket, she noticed someone sitting at a table in the far corner, a couple holding hands. And they apparently noticed her.

"Oh!" she said. "Sorry to barge in on you!"

She was absolutely shocked when the couple turned out to be none other than Jamie and Elise.

CHAPTER FORTY

Sadie Sparrow
Sunday, April 1

April Fool's Day was gorgeous, and Jamie made it even more wonderful for Sadie by sweeping into the dining room for an impromptu visit. She and her tablemates were just finishing up their lunch—a zesty crab salad, fresh strawberries and blueberry muffins—and she couldn't help feeling a little proud that he made a beeline for her.

"How 'bout a drive around the garden this afternoon, Sadie girl?" He was dressed in his Sunday best and radiated the joy of having spent a morning with his Lord.

"With such a handsome driver," she said, giving him her brightest smile, "how could I refuse?"

He took her back to her room and bundled her up so thoroughly that she could hardly move. Even so, once they rolled outside, the brisk air took her breath away.

"The daffodils are amazing," Jamie said happily as they moved along the melt-into-the-garden concrete paths, artfully stained to look like flagstone but luxuriously smooth for easy wheeling. "Look at them, drifts of them all the way up the hill. What are these little white guys?"

"They're called snowdrops," Sadie said, pleased as punch to be teaching him something for once. "Aren't they adorable? Oh, and look over there, Jamie, the witch hazels!"

She pointed a mittened hand to the top of The Hickories' own little mountain, shimmering in red and yellow.

"Wowzer!"

"I've never seen so many witch hazels in bloom before," she said. "They're just stunning!"

They stopped at the pond at the center of the garden, and Jamie sat down on a bench.

"Are you warm enough?" he asked, adjusting Sadie's scarf. "Want me to go find you some cocoa?"

"Oh, no, dear, I'm feeling toasty. But thank you."

They sat in silence for a while, enjoying the early spring sun.

"Jamie," Sadie said finally, letting her curiosity overwhelm her sense of propriety, "why aren't you married?"

Much to her relief—it *was* a nosy question—he laughed gleefully at her.

"My folks would like to know that, too. But it's really very simple. Until not all that long ago, I was a wild child, partying my life away. I was living for myself, and my pleasure, and I wasn't about to let responsibilities ruin my good time."

"Why, Jamie Fletcher!" Sadie was shocked. "What changed you?"

His smile vanished, and he looked away.

"Well, I won't bore you with the details. The point is that, after college, I slowly evolved into an angry, pill-popping drunk. I lost my job, and my friends, and my self-respect."

"I'm so sorry."

"Me too." Jamie nodded, still avoiding her eyes. "But I guess that's what it took to get me back on the track my parents had set me on. It was a bartender who told me about the Lord, believe it or not."

"Really? That's almost funny!"

"It is, isn't it? He changed my life, obviously."

"So much so that you are spending a lovely Sunday afternoon with an old lady. You should be courting a young lady."

"I *am* courting a young lady." He smiled at her fondly. "And a mighty beautiful one at that! It's really funny, isn't it, how the Lord seems to knit hearts together? It might look random to us, but I'll bet anything there's nothing random about it in His economy."

"Anyone I know?" Sadie asked innocently.

"As a matter of fact, it is. It's Elise." Jamie smiled, his cheeks turning just a tad red.

Another answered prayer!

They went inside, finally, and headed for the fireplace in the Great Room with Sadie clutching two covered mugs of cocoa.

"I was just thinking, Jamie," Sadie said when they were settled, "how so many of us seem to need some sort of crisis before we turn to God. It's like He does it on purpose, to get our attention, don't you think?"

"I do indeed—good insight. In fact, as you'll see, it's a relatively major theme in the Old Testament. So what was *your* big crisis? What softened your heart?"

Sadie considered. "There've been so many things, starting with Ed's death," she said, watching the fire. "But my turning point might have been winding up in this wheelchair. When I first came here, after I got over my month-long pity party—oh, yes, I was wallowing in self-pity because my daughter didn't want me! But once I'd begun to settle in here, it became my goal in life to walk again."

"Did you have some therapy?"

"Oh yes—lots of it. Excellent therapy." She waved her hands over her wheelchair. "But it obviously didn't work."

"It's got to be tough."

"It *is*." She nodded absently, remembering the day she realized that she'd never walk again. "And strangely, they were never able to tell us *why* this had happened. But I'm not alone in that. For most of us in wheelchairs, they just don't seem to know. They shrug their shoulders a lot, these doctors."

"I can't imagine what it must be like," Jamie said sympathetically. "I'd feel so clumsy in a chair, for one thing."

"That's it exactly. And—this will sound funny to you—it makes us sitting ducks for evil, if you know what I mean. Maybe it's a result of living through all these wars, and even the cold war with its bomb shelters and the Russian threat, but I always found comfort in the idea that if I had to run for my life, I could do it." She laughed at herself. "I don't suppose that makes any sense to someone your age."

"You know, it doesn't seem all that odd," he said. "Maybe it's human instinct, to want to be able to flee danger."

"You always seem to understand. Thank you for that." She sipped on her cocoa. "It's the strangest feeling, being stuck in a chair. Sometimes I've almost felt panicky over it. Dana said it's just claustrophobia. She wanted me to see a psychiatrist about it, but I'm not sure I believe in psychiatry."

"I'm with you, Sadie. Sure, medicine may be the gift of God in many cases. But for some of us, the most important thing is submitting to Christ, acknowledging that He's in control of everything. And subscribing to Romans 8:28, where it says that He has promised to make all things work *together* to the good of those who love Him and are called according to His purpose. Believing that can take care of just about every kind of trauma."

"I believe it. I really do."

"His eye really *is* on every sparrow—even Sadie Sparrow."

She laughed. "And that's the solution to every problem!"

The afternoon's fresh air had exhausted Sadie, but she had her aide-turned-engine take her to the West Wing to visit Eva on her way home from dinner. Her friend hadn't even been down to the dining room for several days, and that was not a good sign.

They found her sound asleep, snoring softly. A dinner tray sat on her bed table, untouched, and her TV was tuned to Wheel of Fortune—a program that Eva had never cared for, or so she'd said a month or two ago when the puzzlers were debating their favorite game shows.

"Let me hold her hand," Sadie said, and the aide wheeled her to Eva's bedside. "Thank you, dear. If you don't mind, I'll just sit here for a bit."

And she did, stroking Eva's hand and singing to her softly, choosing songs of heavenly glory and home-going. She was midway through "Face to Face" when she noticed that Eva's aide had come in.

"Don't stop, Sadie." And then the aide joined in, in mellow alto tones: "Face to face I shall behold Him, far beyond the starry sky. Face to face in all His glory, I shall see Him by and by."

Sadie gave Eva's hand a final squeeze and smiled at the aide.

"Our eternal home," she said. "It's going to be wonderful, isn't it?"

CHAPTER FORTY-ONE

Elise Chapelle
Sunday, April 1

A re you feeling okay, Elise? You look a little pale."
Leave it to Jamie to notice. No, I'm not feeling okay. You wouldn't either if you were about to say what I have to say.

"I'm fine."

Jamie sat at her kitchen table and watched her put the kettle on to boil and pull out cups and saucers and a tin of loose Irish breakfast tea.

"Domestic bliss," he said lightly.

"Look, I really need to get this off my chest." Elise sat, folding her hands on the table and staring at them. "Although it may ruin everything, but there's no way around it."

He put a hand over hers. "What is it?"

"Remember when you said we'd have to have a talk about our worst secrets? I think it was on our first date. 'Bad old days,' I think you called it."

Of course it was on our first date. Quit stalling.

She stole a glance at him; he was nodding, looking at her with brows raised in concern.

"Okay, here goes." She sighed deeply. "I had a relationship with a man, a guy from our old church. It was— he told me that I was being old-fashioned, that no one would ever want to marry me without making sure we were—compatible. And I believed him. I knew it was wrong, but I went along with it anyway."

"Go on," Jamie said. He didn't remove his hand.

Stalling for courage, she looked up at the ceiling. It was tin, and the paint was yellowed and peeling.

"It went on—oh, for some months. Mamie was still alive, and I was so dishonest with her. She asked me, more than once, if I was remembering who I was when I spent time with—with this man, and I lied to her. It was terrible, Jamie. The person I was closest to in my whole life, and I'd driven a wedge between us. And I think she knew it."

"Why do you think that?"

The kettle was beginning to whistle. Elise rose long enough to turn the gas down.

"Because I wasn't confiding in her about anything anymore. I had nothing to say to her, I suppose."

"And so, what happened? What ended it?"

Here comes the hard part.

"I thought," she said, swallowing hard, "I thought that I was pregnant."

Jamie took her hand again and squeezed it. Encouraged that he was still showing such kindness, she pushed on.

"As it turned out, I wasn't." She gazed at him through eyes of sorrow. "But okay, Jamie, here it is. When I thought I was, I decided that I would have an abortion. I even called a place downtown to find out what it would involve, what it was going to cost."

"Oh, Elise." Jamie leaned over to embrace her.

She pushed him away and looked at him again, tears in her eyes. "You don't understand. I *knew* what I was doing—I knew it would be murder! I was willing to commit murder to conceal my shame!"

"But you didn't do it."

"But only because it turned out to be a false alarm."

The water was boiling. She gratefully busied herself with tea and infuser and Mamie's treasured Limoges pot, pale blue with yellow roses and gold handle and spout. She didn't feel worthy of using it.

"So you've clearly repented?" Jamie asked when she sat down again. He looked her in the eye.

"Of course."

"And you know that the Lord has forgiven you?"

She hesitated, but only for a second. "Yes, of course, I know He has."

"So, Elise, do you have higher standards than God has?"

She shook her head.

"Then, if He has forgiven you, don't you suppose you can forgive yourself?"

"I suppose," she said softly.

"Then?"

She cleared her throat. "Well, but what about you?"

"Me? You think I won't forgive you?"

"Forgive me, yes." She hung her head and studied her hands again. "But—do you still want me in your life?"

"Elise," he breathed, kneeling next to her and taking her in his arms. This time she didn't resist. "Yes, sweetheart, I still want you in my life. How could you doubt that?"

She relaxed for the first time in weeks.

A taste of heaven, Lord—that's what this is. Thank you!

"If it'll make you feel better," he offered, "I'll tell you all about my life before Christ."

She thought about it for a moment before deciding she didn't want to know anything about it. "It wouldn't matter anyway—you weren't a believer when you were rebelling. But I was."

"Were you really?" He moved back to his chair. "You believed intellectually, maybe, but apparently you hadn't surrendered your life to Him."

Elise considered his point. "And that didn't really happen until after Mamie's death, when I came face to face with eternity."

"So I don't know that you need to be so hard on yourself," Jamie said. "We're imperfect creatures, and we will be until we get to heaven. If we believe God has forgiven us, I think we need to put some effort into being grateful and forgiving ourselves."

"Easier said than done." Elise nodded thoughtfully. "But you're right, Jamie—gratitude and forgiveness. Why do I keep forgetting?"

CHAPTER FORTY-TWO

Meg Vogel
Monday, April 2

So, don't you think this is a good idea, to meet early each month to talk about your progress?" Lucy unfurled her napkin and turned her cup upright in anticipation of her morning coffee. She was looking especially spiffy today; she'd had her hair cut to shoulder length and colored to what must have been its original vibrant red, and she had replaced her normal jeans-and-top garb with a neat navy pantsuit.

"Definitely," Meg said, and she really meant it. She wasn't used to working without specific goals and deadlines. "Especially over breakfast!"

"You've probably noticed that I'm a fan of off-site meetings." Lucy tucked a stray lock behind an ear. "You get twice as much accomplished in half the time when you can get away from the interruptions."

Meg nodded politely, although she didn't really agree. It seemed to her that relaxing in a setting as comfortable as this breakfast-and-lunch shop, with tasty food and beverages just a snap of the fingers away, was not really conducive to focus and efficiency.

A sweet-looking young Mexican man appeared with a pot of coffee, followed by a brisk waitress who took their order in twenty seconds flat.

"Now that's efficiency!" Lucy doctored her coffee with generous quantities of cream and sugar. "Of course, I'm glad that *quality* of service is more important than speed in our line of work. Speaking of which," she added, stirring energetically, "I'm getting rave reviews on your initial biographies. How are you coming along on the rest of them?"

Relieved of the need to engage in endless small talk, Meg pulled a file folder out of her briefcase and extracted a carefully typed table summarizing her progress. She was glad that she'd spent an hour working on it on Sunday; some of these stories were so similar in detail that she was having trouble keeping them straight.

"So here's the scoop," she said, handing Lucy a copy of the chart. "So far, I've interviewed twenty residents, completed nine drafts through first or second revisions, and printed the three that you've seen—Sylvia Tenpenny's, Betty Adamski's, and Marv Steinhart's." She looked up and grinned. "What an interesting fellow Marv is!"

"He's a smart guy," Lucy agreed. "The physicist who worked on the first atomic bomb, right? His kids are really happy with what you did. Great job, Meg!"

"Thanks." She was surprised at how easy it was to slip back into deadline mode. "So I'll gather corrections to the outstanding drafts this week." She consulted the list. "Hmmm, except for Mrs. Collinsworth's and Roger Barber's—I assume they're both still in the hospital?"

"As far as I know," Lucy said, making a few notes on her copy. "Boy, I'm really impressed at how much you've accomplished already. I had no idea that you'd done all of this. What a way to start the week. You've inspired me!"

She sure is chirpy for a Monday morning. Wonder if she's got a job interview?

"I'll knock the revisions out as quickly as I can," Meg said, "and start going through photos with the subjects, too—most of them seem to have pretty extensive albums."

"That's great, Meg, but there's no rush. Like I said before, this is one of those cases where the process is even more important than the product, if our goal is to make our residents feel engaged and loved and incredibly important." She beamed at her biographer. "And you are doing a stellar job of accomplishing it all. I'm hearing nothing but good things about you."

Meg wouldn't have admitted it to anyone, but the praise thrilled her. She hadn't felt this proud of her efforts since the first ad she'd ever written earned the applause of a notoriously difficult client. And that had been thirty years ago.

She was just shutting down her computer for the day when Elise slid through the door.

"I owe you an apology, Meg."

"I don't know why," Meg said, turning back to the screen and dawdling over closing the documents and folders and programs she'd used that day. "You have a right to your privacy."

"But that's just it," Elise said, sounding a little whiny, Meg thought. "I should have told you when we talked last week that Jamie and I—well, that we were in a relationship."

Meg shrugged and powered off her PC.

"It was just kind of awkward, you know?" Elise said. "Like there was no good place to say, 'by the way, we're dating.' By the time I realized that I needed to let you know, it was too late."

Meg shot her an icy smile and began clearing the desk.

"Come on, Meg, you've surely been in that position before."

"Not that I can recall."

You were setting me up, Frenchie. And I'm supposed to forgive and forget?

"I feel like I've betrayed you somehow," Elise said.

Bingo.

"But I didn't do it intentionally, Meg. Plus, well, to be honest, I guess I wasn't sure that my relationship with him was the real deal. I'm still not sure. I keep thinking he's going to dump me when he gets to know me better. And then it would be a moot point."

"And then I'd never know that you'd been dumped?" Icy cold.

"I suppose it was something like that," Elise said, sounding really forlorn now. "I'm so sorry. I wanted us to be friends."

Later, snuggled up on the couch with Touchdown and Sneak, Meg thought about the exchange. Elise had really been suffering over their rift.

"I don't get it, Touch," she said, stroking the velvet head. "We barely know each other. Why would she care that much about what I thought?"

She glanced at the night's TV listings. Nothing of interest; she'd be alone with her critters and her thoughts for the night.

"Maybe she's just that lonely? How sad is that?"

Touchdown gazed at her with his droopy brown eyes.

"Okay, Touch. You're right—I'll forgive her. But not that snake Jamie."

CHAPTER FORTY-THREE

Sadie Sparrow
Wednesday, April 4

Sadie woke feeling that all was right with the world; she'd slept through the night without once waking and her numbness seemed to be subsiding.

Sleep is the Lord's cure for just about everything!

She twittered her way through her morning toilette, humming whenever the words escaped her.

She was just wrapping up "The King of Love My Shepherd Is" when her aide Piper Drew swept in. They smiled at each other while Sadie finished the last verse: "And so through all the length of days Thy goodness faileth never; Good Shepherd, may I sing Thy praise within Thy house forever."

"I love that one," Piper said, pulling her gingerbread-colored hair back into a ponytail and snapping on a scrunchy. "It reminds me of the twenty-third Psalm."

"The shepherd songs are so comforting. Just the idea of being as innocent—and dumb—as a sheep and being cared for by a loving Shepherd. We don't have to be smart as long as we're trusting in Him."

"That's right." Piper looked through Sadie's closet and pulled out a pale pink sweater. "Which is what we must be doing today—trusting Him."

There was something about her tone that gripped Sadie's heart. "What do you mean?"

"Oh, you probably haven't heard." Piper turned back to Sadie, frowning. "They took Eva to the hospital last night. I heard the nurses talking this morning—they believe it's pneumonia. But you didn't hear it from me!"

Sadie was silent as Piper helped her dress and brush her hair into place. As busy as she'd been this week, she hadn't visited Eva since Sunday. She felt horrible that she hadn't realized her friend was getting so much worse.

"You look a little pale, Miss Sadie. Would you like some lipstick?"

Sadie stared at her blankly.

Lipstick? What earthly help would that be?

"No, dear. But here's what you could do for me: see what you can find out about Eva and let me know. I promise I won't let on that you're my source."

CHAPTER FORTY-FOUR

Elise Chapelle
Wednesday, April 4

It was silly to make a full pot of coffee for one person, Elise reflected as she spooned another heaping tablespoon of a dark Brazilian Santos into the basket of her twelve-cup coffeemaker. Most days, she ended up gulping down six or seven cups just to prevent waste, and that couldn't be good for you. One of these days she'd have to quit this, her lone remaining luxury, and settle for a cup of strong tea instead. Or maybe hot chocolate.

But not quite yet.

The smell alone perked her up as she considered the lovely day awaiting her at The Hickories—lunch with Papi, an afternoon concert by the children from a nearby Lutheran school, possibly a visit with Sadie and her friends. And tonight? Maybe she'd take Jamie up on his repeated invitations to attend Bible study at his church; they were in Ruth, he'd said, one of her very favorite books for its beautiful demonstration of God's provision for His children. Maybe Char Davis would be able to go with her—that would really help.

Almost intoxicated by the scent of the brew, she began sifting through yesterday's mail; she'd picked it up last night on her way in from class but had been too tired to look at it. No matter, it was the same old story—catalogs, seminar invitations, and three copies of the same invitation to a new church down the road.

Does anyone ever bother to read this stuff?

Tax forms, coupons, a couple of bills, and yet another expensive brochure offering two-week round-the-world tours by private jet for only $65,000 a person.

But then, at the bottom of the pile, was something she'd been awaiting for as long as she could remember—a letter postmarked Paris, with her name and address penned in her mother's bold hand.

Elise's heart was pounding as she poured herself a cup of coffee and sat down at the kitchen table, examining the writing for clues of Helene's condition. But there was nothing. No shakiness, no hesitation, nothing to indicate that years had passed since Helene had last bothered to write to her daughter.

Her hands were shaking as she lifted the flap on the cheap white envelope. *Thirty-two years old and still under Mommy's spell.*

The letter was handwritten on plain white half-sheets; there was no fancy monogram, no watermark, not even the tacky butterfly or flower or Eiffel Tower you'd find in a cheap boxed stationery set.

Dear Elise,

So happy to have heard from you on my last birthday. I do thank you for writing. Please forgive your old maman for being such a poor correspondent. It just seems that there's always something that must be seen to without delay.

How are you, my love? Would you send me a picture of yourself next time you write, and of Papi? I can't believe my baby is a young woman and that my father has become quite elderly.

Elise shook her head. There was just so much wrong with even these few sentences.

My love? My baby? Forgive me for being a poor correspondent, like there's nothing else to be forgiven? Your father is "quite elderly," but you wouldn't want to bother sending him a letter or card?

She sipped her coffee, barely tasting it. There was news of Helene's recent travels—beautiful "Vienne," historic Budapest, and an enchanting long weekend in Prague, whoever would have guessed how lovely it is?

Then there were several pages documenting various jobs she'd managed to land in recent years. She'd been a waitress in a tiny but fabulous Left Bank restaurant, a tour guide at the 17th-arrondissement home of a little-known but magnificent nineteenth-century impressionist, personal secretary to an avant-garde filmmaker, a bicycling delivery girl in the leading-edge La Défense business district, and a clerk in an impossibly chic accessories boutique. Whatever the task, and no matter how humbling it may have been in reality, Helene managed to make it sound romantic and terribly important.

And finally, the real *raison d'être* for her letter.

Alas, my lovely little boutique closed its doors without warning and without paying us, leaving me with a stack of unpaid bills and an empty bank account. It's merely a cash flow problem, as I've never had trouble finding work, but it's weighing heavily on me. I wonder if you and Papi might lend me a little money until I right the ship again? $10,000 would do it, and I would be <u>ever so grateful</u> and <u>totally committed</u> to paying you back just as soon as possible. (I know it may seem like a lot of money, but the cost of living is so high here, and the exchange rate so unfavorable for the dollar right now.)

If I could hear back from you by the first of May, that would be lovely, and it would save my apartment.

With love abounding and hope that you will help your bad old maman, I remain faithfully yours—

Helene

Elise resisted the temptation to rip the letter to shreds—
Papi would want to see it, after all—and instead indulged in
a few moments of silent fury.

*Vienne and Budapest? Oh, yes, and a weekend in
Prague? And you need to borrow money from us to pay
your bills?*

She practically threw her coffee cup into the sink,
sloshing some of it on the counter, and headed to her room
to get ready for The Hickories.

She didn't share the letter with Papi until later that
afternoon, following the concert.

They were back in his room once again, and he was
talking so merrily about the singing—"they sang with the
voices of angels, Elise!"—that he didn't notice her silence at
first.

When he finally asked her what was wrong, she simply
handed him the envelope.

It took him a while to read it. First, he had to find his
reading glasses, and then he asked her to turn on the lamp
on his library table, and then he struggled with the
envelope. She did not help him. She could not do anything
but watch him. It was like seeing a building implode in slow-
motion video.

At first, he was tight-lipped and apparently emotionless
as he squinted his way through page after page. But then,
towards the end, she saw his mouth quiver, and his eyes
puddle up, and she knew that he would indeed forgive his
daughter, would provide her with whatever support she
asked, no strings attached.

Her heart sank.

When he was finished, he fished his handkerchief out of his pocket and pressed it to his eyes. A good five minutes passed, neither of them saying a word.

But then Papi looked up, smiling ruefully, his face flushed.

"It has finally happened," he said, his voice hoarse. "The day I've been praying for thirty years, Elise. Helene may not realize it yet, but she has reached the end of herself. She wants to come home."

Of course, Helene had said no such thing; what she wanted was $10,000.

But perhaps he was right. She was his daughter and perhaps he could read between the lines in ways that her own child could not.

Either way, Elise could not possibly dash Papi's hopes.

"You must write her back right away and tell her we're sending her a ticket home. Will you take care of it, Elise?"

"Of course, Papi. I'll take care of everything."

Char couldn't make it to Jamie's church that night, Elise was relieved to learn. That meant she, too, could head home and get some things straightened out in her own spirit. Jamie would be disappointed, but he would understand when she told him about the battle she was fighting.

Helene had once again sent Elise's heart into overdrive and it was still racing. But this time, it wasn't heartbreak that she was suffering; it was instead horror at her own reaction to Papi's solution.

Once home, she built a fire in the living room and curled up in Papi's recliner with a cup of Earl Grey and her Bible opened to Luke 15—Jesus' account of the Prodigal Son.

She'd read it a hundred times before, finding tragic and uplifting and endlessly fascinating the story of a younger son demanding his inheritance from his still very-much-alive father and then blowing it all in profligate living until his only option was to come home, contrite and humbled. His father welcomed him with open arms and a great celebration. There was just one problem: an unhappy older brother who had stayed home and served his father well in his little brother's absence—an older brother who was supremely jealous over the younger one's lavishly fêted homecoming.

Elise had never forgotten the story's closing verse, spoken by the father to his older son: "Son, thou art ever with me, and all that I have is thine. It was meet that we should make merry and be glad: for this thy brother was dead, and is alive again; and was lost, and is found."

As usual, her heart ached to think of the father's anguish—past, present, and perhaps future—as he tried to reconcile his sons to one another. And as usual, her heart ached for the older brother. People always said that this was a great parable about God's love and mercy and forgiveness, and about the prickly self-righteousness of those who walk the straight and narrow. But she had always felt sorry for the older son. He'd done the right thing all along, but that apparently made him too boring to generate any sort of celebration on the father's part.

It was impossible for Elise to miss the message for their lives. She wondered if the prodigal mother would come home, if the long-suffering father would welcome her with open arms, if the mostly right-living daughter would be more forgiving than the elder brother had been.

Honestly, she knew she would find it difficult to forgive Helene. Maybe impossible, especially if Papi embraced her as his darling, long-lost daughter, forgiving and forgetting all the pain she'd caused.

Elise could just imagine the scene at the airport—because of course Papi would want to meet the plane, even if it meant that she had to push his wheelchair on foot the ninety miles to O'Hare Field.

There would be hugs and kisses and tears.

And there would be Elise, standing back and watching it all, trying desperately to conquer her own bitterness.

She did not think she could bear it. But she could think of no alternative but to disobey Papi and withhold his offer of a plane ticket home.

And that was, of course, impossible.

Another sleepless night. At two forty-five, Elise finally decided to get up and work these issues out via "Advice for the Life-Worn."

Dear Elise,
I know we are commanded to love our enemies. But I just can't seem to do that with those who have hurt me. Any advice?
Beatrice

The question's simplicity startled her.
That pretty much sums it up, doesn't it?

Dear Beatrice,
I imagine that most Christians struggle to love their enemies, but I keep coming back to one simple fact: it's a direct command from the Lord, from the Sermon on the Mount, no less. "But I say to you, love your enemies, bless those who curse you, do good to those who hate you, and pray for those who spitefully use you and persecute you."
A wise man once said that knowledge is knowing scripture's commands, wisdom is knowing their

applications, and understanding is knowing why they're necessary. Let's see how that applies to this verse.

Clearly, we've got the "knowledge" part down pat, in acknowledging what scripture says about loving our enemies. It doesn't get much clearer than this, does it?

And the application? Equally easy. It applies across the board. Jesus did not say, "love your enemies unless they betrayed you in an especially hurtful manner," or "bless those who curse you unless they are total hypocrites."

But what about the understanding? Why are we to do this? I think we will find the key to obedience here, if we meditate on it sufficiently. That's something you need to do yourself, with the Holy Spirit's guidance. But perhaps I can give you a start.

So why should we love our enemies, beyond it being a command of Christ?

Well, one reason would be to point them to Him, right? If we represent Him and our enemies hate us, then they hate Him. And we should share His desire for—as the apostle Paul told Timothy—all people "to be saved and to come to the knowledge of the truth." One of the best ways to support Him in this is to show His love to even those who have treated us like trash.

Here's another reason: like all His commands, obeying this one is good for us.

If I hate, it tears me up inside. It wastes my time. It frustrates me as I go over and over and over the same territory in my mind and heart. It destroys me and does nothing to hurt the object of my hatred.

Whereas if I love this person with the unconditional, self-sacrificing love of Christ, I not only demonstrate God's agape love to him or her, I also see myself set free from all that inner turmoil and torment.

I've only scratched the surface, Beatrice. Try meditating on these things in light of your circumstances and see where *the Lord leads. It's my prayer that you'll find yourself changed.*

Blessings,

Elise

Elise made some edits and posted the column before tumbling back into bed.

Amazing—I do feel free!

She suspected that it was only a temporary fix at this point, that she would need to reflect on this scripture at greater length and flex this flabby spiritual muscle in various tests before the changes could even approach permanence.

But she was already miles ahead of where she'd been just an hour ago, she knew.

As if to prove it, she promptly fell into a luscious sleep.

CHAPTER FORTY-FIVE

Meg Vogel
Thursday, April 5

When she arrived at the Activities office Thursday morning, Meg found Sadie waiting for her, hoping for some news about Eva.

"The nurses won't tell me anything," Sadie whispered, apparently aware that she was asking Meg to bend the rules for her. "She's been in the hospital for two nights now, and you know that's not a good sign; they won't keep us old ladies any longer than they have to these days."

Meg thought Sadie would probably be tortured to death before revealing a source who'd broken HIPAA privacy rules on her behalf. She picked up the phone and called the West nurses' station.

"Well, it looks like pneumonia, all right," she told Sadie a few moments later. "Not that you heard it from me, right? So, can I give you a ride to breakfast?"

Sadie shook her head, smiling bravely. "I think I'll just work on our puzzle this morning until the service begins."

Meg was grateful that Lucy was on Activities duty that morning, since the big event was—surprise!—another in a seemingly endless series of religious programs. She closed the office door against the strains of some dreary song of the Good Friday ilk and lost herself in a final edit on Sadie's biography.

Not bad, Meg old girl. Not bad at all!

She'd spent the last two nights working on the document at home. It was nine-plus typewritten pages (over 4,000 words, according to her word-count function!) and would make a nice little book once she dropped it into a layout and added pictures from Sadie's extensive snapshot collection; Dana had apparently promised to deliver it by Friday morning.

But first, she needed Sadie's corrections to the text, and Lucy's approval. She reformatted the copy in Bookman Old Style, her favorite font these days, bumped it up to an easy-to-read eighteen-point size, and printed out two copies.

She was just stapling the second set in booklet format when there was a knock on the door. To her surprise, it was Jamie.

"Sadie's in the service next door," she said without waiting for him to speak.

"Yes, she is. I thought we could maybe talk a bit, if you aren't too busy."

The success of Sadie's biography was making Meg feel more generous than she would have ordinarily. "I do have work to do, but I suppose I can take a little break. So go ahead, shoot."

Jamie sat at Lucy's desk and started chatting about a lot of nothing, as far as she could tell. He told her that he'd seen some old Frank Lloyd Wright letters and drawings appraised for $75,000 on *Antiques Roadshow* and that his sister had just gotten herself a yellow lab puppy. He then asked her how the biographies were going.

Trying to show me you're just a regular guy, Jamie? You are not, and you're annoying me.

"So tell me this," Meg said, ignoring his question and smiling smugly. "Have you always been so perfectly self-righteous?"

He was shocked into speechlessness, she was pleased to see.

"Wow, Meg," he said finally, looking into her eyes and no doubt finding hostility there. "I almost don't know what to say."

"Then—"

"No, wait. I said 'almost.' I'd really like to address this with you, because you have it all wrong." He grinned at her ingratiatingly, then continued in spite of her refusal to return the smile. "Like any genuine Christian, I'm the antithesis of self-righteousness. That's the whole point of being a Christian, in fact—we know that we're *not* good people in our own right, and never will be, and that the only good thing about us is Christ living in our hearts."

Oh, brother. Why'd I even go here?

"I wish you wouldn't smirk like that. It's pretty rude."

But it won't shut you up, will it?

"In fact, if you look at the subject honestly, you'll find that it's unbelievers who are self-righteous," he said, emphasizing the word "self" and sitting up a little taller as he warmed to his subject. "I used to be like that. I thought I was a pretty good person, and that if there was a heaven, I'd get in by virtue of my good deeds."

"You doubted there was a heaven?" Meg asked casually, genuinely curious but unwilling to show any great interest.

"I was an agnostic at best until I was almost thirty." Jamie leaned back, hands behind his head. "I'd learned to party hard in college and didn't quit after graduating. I sold trucking services—not the most exciting work, but it's a super-competitive business and I did a lot of drugs in those days, uppers to get through the day and downers to get to sleep at night. Then on the weekends I'd drink to escape the pressure and to bury my anger."

He really *was* beginning to sound like a regular fellow, Meg realized. She could identify with anger, anyway, and the need to bury it.

"I was, in fact, a very angry guy. Whenever anything went wrong, which of course is daily in the business world, I'd find someone to blame for it—my boss or a competitor or the waitress who'd blown my customer's order the previous week. If I forgot to get a quote in, it was the secretary's fault, never mine, because she should've reminded me. And I didn't suffer in silence; I let people know they'd let me down. Finally lost my job because I had such a short fuse, and it was getting shorter by the day."

"And all this time you thought you were a good person?"

He laughed. "Yeah, go figure."

"So you turned to Jesus," she said, "and you all lived happily ever after."

"Not exactly." Jamie flashed dimples Meg had never noticed before. "I'd gone into this dive of a bar on Bluemound Road one afternoon—it must've been a weekday, because I was the only customer—and was just starting to get quietly loaded when the bartender asked me if I wanted to talk about it. Turned out that he knew exactly what my problem was. 'I used to be just like you,' he said. And he told me all about his past, and it was like that old song about 'singing my life with his song'—do you know it?"

"Yes, it was a Roberta Flack song. One of my favorites back in the day."

He nodded. "That's the one. So he claimed that he'd investigated the Bible on a dare with his brother, and found out that it was true. Challenged me to try it myself—said the science alone would astound me, but what did him in was prophecy. We talked about that a long time—as I think I mentioned, I was a history major in college, so I found his claims about prophecy pretty interesting."

Meg didn't know what he was talking about but didn't want to get him going on that subject. She just nodded enough to show she was listening, not enough to indicate great interest.

"To make a long story short—and it *was* a long one, since I had a lot of time on my hands at that point—I took him up on his challenge, figuring I'd be able to prove him wrong fairly easily. But I failed. Instead, I found out that what he'd been claiming was the truth." Jamie shook his head, as if he still had a hard time believing it. "To cut to the chase, I finally had to bow my heart to Jesus Christ as Creator and Savior and Redeemer and everything else these born-again types said He was. And at the same time, to address your original point, to acknowledge what a total loser I was, repent of all my rebellion against God, and make amends with the people I'd hurt."

He finally fell silent, his expression deadly serious.

The wall clock said it was almost eleven, time for Meg to help bring residents back to their rooms for pre-lunch preparations. She cleared her throat.

Jamie didn't seem to notice. "And the amazing thing is that everything started changing for me," he went on. "Most notably, my anger vanished. Maybe it was a miracle, or maybe it's just what happens when you quit making excuses for yourself and acknowledge that you're a total jerk. It really humbles you."

"It really humbles you," Meg said mockingly on her way home that night. "Humble" was the hot new verb, it seemed, with every celebrity talking about how humbled he or she had been by the latest awards and accolades. But how could adoring fans possibly humble you?

They couldn't. It's just another lie.

Except that Jamie hadn't been talking about cheers from the crowd. He'd been talking about realizing he was perhaps not quite as good a person as he'd thought he was. Did that make this brand of humility the real deal?

She flipped the radio on to an oldies station and joined Jim Croce in "Bad Bad Leroy Brown." It wasn't her favorite Croce song, but it was better than thinking that maybe this creepy Christian wasn't such a bad guy after all.

Meg's Friday morning assignment was becoming one of her favorites, running The Hickories' semi-weekly exercise class. She simply had to round up as many residents as she could and then take them through a series of very simple stretching exercises. It took only a few hours of her time, racing around to gather people gave her a bit of a workout, and she was able to put on whatever music she liked—even golden oldies, since some enterprising Maintenance man had hooked up a '70s-era stereo to the Great Room's sound system.

This morning she'd chosen an old Glenn Miller Greatest Hits album of her mother's, featuring songs from "In the Mood" to "Ida" to "Fools Rush In." She didn't mind them, and the old folk were crazy about them. Glenn Miller helped her attract a bigger crowd than Lucy ever got with her yucky disco music.

And it worked again today: Meg spread the word to the aides on duty and did her own soliciting and by the ten o'clock kick-off, she had forty-seven aging exercise nuts ready to bump their heart rates up, if only by a few notches.

They covered a full chapter in *Exercises for the Elderly*, with Sadie and her front-row crowd making a particularly heroic effort to keep time with the music. They mostly failed, bursting into laughter time and time again as they realized how funny they must look.

Breathless and happy, they wrapped up the session at ten forty-five, and by eleven each flushed participant had been delivered safely to her room, or to the dining room, or to a knot of friends holding forth on the food lately or Lawrence Welk's best shows or their favorite books.

Meg was still smiling over the old girls' silliness as she hurried back to the office from her last delivery. She was looking forward to the tuna salad sandwich she'd packed this morning and an hour or two with Sadie and the Sparrow photo albums.

She was surprised to find Elise at the office door.

"What can I do for you?" Meg asked coldly, startling her.

"Oh! Sorry, Meg. I just wanted to leave you this." And she handed Meg an envelope.

It contained a greeting card with a sad basset hound on the front—the spitting image of Touchdown, although Elise couldn't have known that—and a handwritten note inside:

Dear Meg,

I'm so sorry if I offended you the other day, by not telling you about Jamie and me. I thought we were becoming friends, but I've never really had any and I didn't know how to handle it. Obviously I messed up. Can you find it in your heart to forgive me?

Fondly,
Elise

Meg felt her heart melting.

"Oh, please don't worry about it," she said, hugging Elise with affection so sincere that she surprised herself. "I can be pretty prickly about offenses, real or imagined. And this one was definitely in the 'imagined' category."

"So could I buy you lunch?"

Meg thought longingly for a moment of her tuna salad. But it would wait. "Sure, why not? Where to?"

They ate at a Bakers Square not far from the Hickories, downing luscious Asian salads and hot tea and chattering about everything from gardening to favorite childhood games.

"Did you ever play wedding?" Elise asked.

Meg shook her head. "What's that?"

"That's when I'd put on these fancy old gowns—there were whole trunks of them in the attic, in every color imaginable—and pretend I was about to get married. Just waiting for my groom, who looked a lot like Cary Grant."

They laughed.

"And the attic was your wedding chapel?"

"No, the attic always scared me. I'd quick find my dress du jour and drag it down to my grandmother's room. There was a full-length mirror there and I would put the dress on and parade around wearing what I thought was the appropriate expression for a bride-to-be, like this—"

She stuck her nose up in the air and closed her eyes and turned her mouth down into a slight frown.

Meg laughed. "So brides are snooty and nasty?"

"Or maybe just fearful of what was to come."

They munched for a bit, smiling at each other. They were an odd couple, Meg thought, with Elise being easily young enough to be her own daughter. Maybe that was what made them a good fit, she realized with a start; she knew that Elise's mother had abandoned her as an infant, and perhaps she'd been secretly longing for a daughter of her own—well, of hers and Gil's own—to make them a real family.

"I'm curious," Elise said finally, "why did you and Gil get married? Why not just live together like everyone else?"

"I suppose it was the security." Meg didn't feel the need to come up with a better answer, not finding the question especially interesting.

"Marriage is a guarantee? In this day and age?"

"Well, it makes it harder for a philanderer to get away."

"Would you want to stay with a philanderer if he wanted to leave?" Elise was apparently dead serious.

"Well, no, of course not." Meg wondered where this line of questioning had come from. "That's one of the great things about feminism: we can support ourselves now."

"So marriage doesn't increase your security?"

Meg bit her lip, thinking. "Well, no, I guess it doesn't."

"Then why get married?"

"Why these questions, Elise? Are you and Jamie—?"

"Oh, no," Elise said, blushing. "He hasn't asked me. I was just thinking about the whole institution the other day. I mean, Christians get married because that's the order God established in the Bible—you get married and have children and treat each other the way He has prescribed, always based on agape love—that's self-sacrificing love, born of the will and not of emotion. It's a real commitment, which is why Christian marriages last. Or *should* last, I ought to say."

Meg considered this. "I guess that's something we messed up on, my generation," she admitted. "We made love and sex more important than commitment, or just about anything else. Which is a little twisted, when you think about it."

Elise nodded. "It makes the whole idea of marriage kind of nonsensical, I think."

"I guess our minds were bent by the spirit of the day— the sexual revolution, the music, the idea of 'if it feels good, do it.' It was chaotic, but somehow the ideas stuck."

"It's really too bad," Elise said. "And look where it's gotten us—I watched a movie on TV the other night that glorified infidelity. It made the husband of an adulteress look like a complete dork for even existing."

"Infidelity and adulteress?" Meg smirked. "What old-fashioned words."

"Maybe so, but old-fashioned isn't necessarily bad, is it?"

Meg had to agree that it wasn't. But she was tired of the subject, and said she had to get moving.

Back in her office, she thought about what a reasonable conversation they'd had. Elise was one cool cookie for a Christian, making her opinion known without making you think you were expected to adopt it as your own.

Maybe they really were becoming friends. Unlike Sandra, Elise at least did not spend all her time building up and looking out for number one.

CHAPTER FORTY-SIX

Sadie Sparrow
Friday, April 6

Sadie could hardly believe the story that Meg had created out of their discussions.

"This is just wonderful, Meg—but you've made me sound too good to be true!"

"You *are* too good to be true! Now help me find the best photos to go with your story."

They were sitting in Sadie's room at the table overlooking the garden, where the daffodils were still holding their own against drifts of coral and golden species tulips.

Dana had somehow carved enough time out of her schedule to drop three fat photo albums off that morning, and Meg seemed to be enchanted by what she was finding in them. Sadie didn't quite know why, but she was thrilled with Meg's enthusiasm and this part of the "life story" process; she hadn't looked at these albums in years, and she was overwhelmed with happy memories.

Here was a very shy young woman wearing a pretty suit, complete with corsage, on her wedding day. And here, a wee white house, the Sparrow home. And here were countless snapshots of little Dana posing for the camera, riding a stick horse, digging in a sandbox, clinging to a swing hanging from the Sparrows' beloved old apple tree.

"Oh, look at this," Sadie breathed, "these pictures in the park are from the day Ed proposed to me." She touched the nearest photo with a heavily veined hand; she could feel her eyes threatening to spill over. "Meg, maybe I should go through these myself first. You know, so I can pick out the best ones. Would that be okay with you?"

"Of course," Meg said. She hugged Sadie, brought her a fresh box of tissues from the nightstand, and left her alone with her memories.

Except for periodic pauses to wipe her eyes, Sadie barely looked up from her albums until her aide came in to get her freshened up for dinner.

"I've been lost to the world this afternoon," she laughed. "Foolish old woman! As if remembering a happy past can make you happy today."

"Oh, I don't know," the aide replied, wheeling Sadie to her desk. Her name was Shelly or Sally or something like that; Sadie couldn't quite remember. "My mom always said that remembering the happiness of the past is like catching sight of the joy awaiting us in heaven. Or something like that."

"Your mother is a wise woman, my dear," Sadie said, dusting her nose with her favorite loose powder. "Thank you for that reminder."

After dinner, Sadie dialed Dana's number and was shocked to hear, on the fourth ring, her daughter's voice rather than a recording.

"Sorry to bother you," she said briskly, the way Dana liked her conversations, "but I wanted to thank you for bringing over my photo albums and tell you that there are so many cute ones of you. You might want to take some of them to put on your computer."

"Oh, sure. Next time I'm over, I'll take a look, okay?"

"Of course," Sadie said, hesitating for only a moment. "Do you know when that might be?"

A longer pause. Sadie pictured her only child counting silently to ten; she shouldn't have asked.

"I'm not sure at this point," Dana finally said. "I'll let you know."

Don't call us—we'll call you.

"Okey dokey. I'll talk to you later, then."

For once, Sadie did not hang up from a call with Dana feeling sad and teary-eyed. In fact, interrogating her heart, she rejoiced to find not a twinge of self-pity. Progress!

Which reminded her of the last stanza of Martin Luther's *A Mighty Fortress*. In honor of the changes taking hold in her heart, she sang the whole hymn, lingering especially over the closing words: "Let kith and kindred go, this mortal life also. The body they may kill, God's truth abideth still, His kingdom is forever!"

On Saturday morning, Sadie tried it the easy way: she asked Char outright if she knew anything about how Eva was doing.

"Now, Sadie, you know I can't tell you that," said the nurse, leaning down to give her charge a peck on the cheek. "Remember what I told you about those nasty old privacy laws? Some of us have already been docked for violating them—not saying who, but just so you know that they're serious about enforcing them. So I really can't tell you a thing."

On to Plan B, then: Sadie headed back towards her room until she had turned the corner onto the North Wing, then turned back, hugging the wall to get as close as possible to the North nurses' station without being seen.

And there she sat, pretending to nap to keep a passing aide from delivering her to some unwanted destination.

It took less than ten minutes for just the right call to come in.

"That was the hospital." It was a man's voice, most likely that of the new male R.N. whose name Sadie couldn't remember. At least, that's what she surmised, since the only other men at this place were residents or Maintenance people or the Administrator himself, and she couldn't imagine any of them announcing a call from the hospital.

"Oh good—I put a call into them a while ago." It was Char. "How's Eva doing?"

"A little better, apparently. Although she may not be home any time soon."

A little better? Good news, indeed—thank you, Lord!

Sadie hummed "What a Friend We Have in Jesus" all the way back to her room.

CHAPTER FORTY-SEVEN

Elise Chapelle
Saturday, April 7

It was almost eleven and Elise was pleasantly surprised to find Sadie in her room, going through an old photo album.

"Taking a trip down memory lane?" she asked, spotting a dozen black-and-white snapshots of what looked to be cakes. "Or are you trying to work up an appetite for lunch?"

Sadie laughed, pushing the album toward Elise to give her a better view. "When you think about how much it cost to print all these pictures, it's amazing we took so many. But we church ladies were so proud of our baking skills." She pointed to the cake in the center of one of the pictures. "This one's mine. It was a white cake with apricot filling and frosting, and toasted almonds on the top."

"Sounds delicious."

"It was! Mmmm, I can still taste those almonds. They were best slightly burned!"

They talked church potlucks and recipes for a bit, and then Elise got to the point.

"I need your advice," she said. "It's about Papi and what a fool he's making of himself over—well, over my mother. Which sounds so silly, doesn't it?"

She then told Sadie the whole story, all about Helene abandoning her as an infant and running off to Paris and hardly ever writing—until now, when she needed money.

"Here's the problem," Elise said. "Papi just ordered me to send Helene his credit card information, so she could charge a plane ticket. But Sadie, she didn't say anything about coming home—that's all his idea. I certainly don't see it!"

"And you're afraid she'll use the card for something else?"

"I know she will."

"Oh, dear." Sadie furrowed her brow. "Did you tell him this?"

"I did," Elise said softly, "as gently as I could. And he said that it was his problem, not mine, and that he thought he knew his daughter a little better than I."

"Does he?"

Elise shrugged. "Maybe so, although it seems like a stretch to me, considering that she's written to him only a half dozen times over the last thirty years."

Sadie nodded, smiling doubtfully. "Well then, I guess you have your marching orders."

"I should do as he says?"

"Yes, dear. If your Papi wanted you to buy the Taj Mahal, I'd say it was time to question it. But he knows what he's doing."

"Which is?"

"He's just loving his daughter, whatever the cost."

"I hope it doesn't ruin him."

Sadie smiled. "Oh, it won't ruin him, Elise. Real love never ruined anyone. Besides," she added, her eyes twinkling, "they still have limits on these cards, don't they?"

Elise spent most of the afternoon composing a letter to Helene, tearing up attempt after attempt. Finally, she got right to the point:

Dear Helene,

Your father is quite sure you would like to come home, and will pay for your one-way ticket from Paris to Chicago O'Hare. Please let us know your flight information and we will meet you there. Here's his Visa card information . . .

As certain as she was that her mother would use the card for anything but coming home, she found it very difficult to write the numbers. But Sadie was right: it was Papi's decision, and it was his problem if Helene once again disappointed him.

Still, Elise was not without resources in this matter: she would jump online every day to watch his credit card balance, and she'd intervene if she had to.

P.S. Please don't try to use this card for anything but a plane ticket home.

She almost added, "or you'll be sorry," but thought better of it. Helene would not be sorry for anything, and there was no real threat; Papi would never prosecute his own daughter should she misuse his credit card. Still, this simple request implied that there might be some consequences. Somewhat comforted by it, Elise headed out to the mailbox to post the letter.

CHAPTER FORTY-EIGHT

Meg Vogel
Tuesday, April 24

It had been a busy day. Meg had officially completed her first sixteen biographies to their subjects' satisfaction, emailed the documents to Lucy, and then raced around the facility to schedule her next round of interviews. And she had accomplished it all before the two o'clock bingo game. Once the excitement of the game itself had ended, with Gladys taking the grand prize of a crisp new one-dollar bill, Meg was exhausted. She had to push herself to pick up the cards and markers and to get the Great Room in shape for anyone who might care to use it that evening.

And then Sandra had called with bad news.

"It's my mom," she said in a shaky voice. "She's at Oakridge Hospital right now—she fell and broke her hip. Will you go with me? Please?"

"I'll pick you up in a half hour."

They were shocked to find Frances Slocum in bed, moaning and writhing in pain. While Sandra tried frantically to talk with her, Meg rushed to the nurses' station.

There was just one woman there, dressed in a sloppy plaid shirt and jeans, and she didn't respond when Meg asked her to call a nurse to give Mrs. Slocum something for her pain. Instead, she typed busily on her keyboard and consulted her computer screen.

"She's already had plenty," the woman said, without looking at Meg. "They're all like this the first day or two, but they don't remember it later—almost like it never happened."

Meg returned to the room, painted a sick mint green and lit by ice-cold fluorescents. She told Sandra what the woman had said and hovered there with her until two aides came into the room and asked them to retire to the waiting area while they cleaned Frances up.

"Mrs. Slocum," Sandra said.

The younger aide looked at her blankly.

"Please call her Mrs. Slocum," Sandra said, raising her voice. "Don't call her by her first name, please. Show some respect."

They both ignored her, calling their patient Frances while Sandra and Meg were still within earshot.

"I hate this place already," Sandra growled as they sat down in the waiting area, done up in the same mint green but with lots of peach accents. "Look at these putrid colors."

"Not great," Meg agreed.

"So I have to tell you what her facility said. Arbor Hills, I mean—that's the name of her assisted-living place."

"Right," Meg said, feeling irritated. Sandra had apparently forgotten the weekend Meg had donated to her cause a couple summers ago, driving all over town in search of just the right assisted-living facility for her mother. She *knew* it was called Arbor Hills.

"The director called me a few days ago to tell me Mom had fallen again—third time—and to say I'd have to move her. Can you believe it? She said they're not set up to handle falls. At which point I asked what good they were." Her irritation melted into fear. "Probably shouldn't have said that, huh? It probably didn't help our cause. I suppose I could try apologizing . . ." Sandra looked miserable.

"I guess she needs better supervision, Sandra," Meg said as gently as she could. "It's time."

Sandra nodded glumly. "She'd like to live with me, of course. But that's impossible. Even if I weren't at work all day—"

"It's a lot to ask," Meg said, the memory of caring for an invalid painfully fresh in her heart.

"So, a nursing home. I've made some calls—The Hickories is way too expensive, but the trouble is, so is every place else. She could swing $3,000 or $4,000 a month for a couple years, but nothing like $10,000."

"But there's Medicaid, Sandra. She'd just have to pay her own way for a year or so and then Medicaid would kick in. She'd probably have to have a roommate, but so what?"

"That's what they tell me." She pulled her compact out of her purse and powdered her nose, unnecessarily as far as Meg could see. In the good old days, they'd be puffing on cigarettes right here in the waiting room. "She'll hate it, you know."

"It's awful, isn't it?" Meg sighed. "It wasn't that long ago that our grandparents lived with us. I don't think there were many nursing homes back then."

"Our mothers were at home then. These days, everyone works."

"I know," Meg said sadly. "Maybe that's part of the problem. Oh, I don't know. I don't have a clue what we should do. It just seems like we took a wrong turn somewhere along the way."

"Easy for you to say," Sandra said sullenly. "You haven't had to deal with finding a home for a sick mother."

Meg spent the following Saturday driving around in Sandra's oh-so-cool BMW X3, helping her inspect a handful of relatively affordable nursing homes in the Milwaukee area. Each one seemed worse than the last from the standpoints of cleanliness, staffing, and resident alertness; in the final place they visited, every last resident they saw seemed to be stoned into submission.

Sandra finally settled on Legacies Long Term Care, the first one they'd toured. It consisted of a dilapidated old mansion fronting a mammoth concrete addition, and it sat out in the middle of what might have once been a cornfield, southwest of the city.

"It's not bad," Meg lied when Sandra announced her decision. "It's got a decent Medicare rating—three stars isn't terrible, you know. It didn't smell. And the price is certainly right."

"Wonder how they came up with the name 'Legacies.' Sounds like a pick-up bar, doesn't it?" Sandra pointed her vehicle towards Meg's house. "I'll stop in on my way to work Monday morning and get everything set up. I can't believe the hospital's already planning to throw Mom out."

"Just think what it'll be like by the time we're her age."

"What do you mean?"

"Oh, what do I know?" Meg opened her window to a cool breeze; trolling the halls of mostly decrepit nursing homes had given her a headache. "But I hear things at work. They say that government reimbursements are falling again. I guess the places that accept Medicaid are losing money like crazy on patients who aren't private-pay, which means those who *are* private-pay have to come up with even more to subsidize the losses."

Sandra considered this. "Do you mean there are places that refuse Medicaid? I would think that would be illegal."

"It's legal. And why shouldn't it be? Why should a business be forced to sell its services at a loss?"

"Ever the entrepreneur, aren't you?" Sandra's tone was not complimentary. "So, you may be right, but still."

"Still," Meg agreed. "But we may not feel that way if these places start closing down because they're losing money. That's what's happening in England, I guess—they can't afford to keep all their nursing homes open. And Germany's shipping its elder poor to ultra-cheap rest homes in eastern Europe and Thailand. I heard some admissions staffers talking about it at The Hickories the other day."

They shared a few moments of silence.

"And it's all happening," Meg added, "just as our generation begins to hit the skids."

Sandra's eyes were filled with tears. "There must be a solution."

"I can't imagine what it would be," Meg said. "We have too many boomers, and not enough young people to support us in our old age."

"And a generation of women who had careers instead of children."

"Guess it's time for us to invest in some nursing-home insurance, huh?"

Sandra nodded. "Would you have time to look into it?"

"Sure," Meg said. "We'll get ourselves some insurance and hope there are still a few nursing homes around to accept it when our time comes."

Meg had just started the Wednesday afternoon movie for the residents when Jamie appeared at the door of the little theater.

She greeted him cordially enough, ushered him back into the Great Room, and asked how she could help him.

"I'm just looking for Sadie," he explained. "She stood me up."

"If you'd stick to one particular day, you wouldn't have that problem," Meg said with a chilly laugh. "She had a doctor's appointment today—should be back around three, if you'd like to wait."

"You wouldn't mind?"

"Suit yourself." Meg tucked her hands in her pockets—she was wearing her favorite denim jacket, perfect for awkward moments. "I'm stuck here for the duration. Have to make sure there are no problems during the movie, you know."

"And you don't want to watch it?"

"No. It's called *The Robe*, and it's about—"

"I know it well," he said.

They sat at the fireplace, he in a club chair and she on the hearth, which gave Meg a direct sightline into the theater. She watched the waning fire idly, too lazy to throw another log on, while Jamie tried to make conversation.

"So tell me more about your husband," he said at last, finally stumbling into a subject she was interested in talking about. Interested, because she'd been thinking a lot lately about Gil's change of heart and blaming Jamie for that change. Not Jamie personally, of course, but people of his ilk.

"Would you like to know about how he deserted me?"

Saying it out loud didn't hurt nearly as much as she'd expected it to, not even to this man who would've been the enemy of her soul if she believed in souls. And from his expression, she could tell that she'd shocked him with her question; it gave her a perverse delight.

"Gil made this conscious decision to switch directions on me, and he changed big time," she added, glowering at him. "He was no longer the man I married."

"Tell me more about it," Jamie said, his brow creased in concern. "How exactly did he change?"

She rifled through her mental complaint file; it was packed. She remembered only too well the day she first noticed a change in him, when they'd gone shopping for a new recliner for the living room, something comfortable for him during this ghastly chemo regimen. They'd been arguing mildly about it for ages—she wanted something sleek and trendy in a modern fabric, he wanted an overstuffed leather monster with plenty of padding. But when they got to the store, he headed straight for the chairs she would like, merely glancing at the ones he'd been coveting. That was definitely not like Gil.

"You'll have to live with it a lot longer than I will," he had said when she questioned his apparent change of taste.

But she couldn't tell Jamie about that episode, especially since they ended up buying a streamlined, contemporary chair in a burgundy and camel paisley fabric—exactly what she wanted. It made Gil the hero and her the villain.

Abandonment, Meg—how did he abandon you? Ah, yes, the gateway to a slew of betrayals!

"Well, for starters," she said sullenly, uncrossing and recrossing her legs, winding up for the onslaught, "he suddenly quit swearing. Not that he'd ever been especially foul-mouthed, but he suddenly started using these wimpy expletives like 'doggone it' and 'nuts.' He also started looking away from me if I said—well, if I used a harsher word."

"Okay," Jamie said, nodding.

"Then this," she continued. "Suddenly he had no stomach for gossip. As long as we'd been together, I'd regale him with stories about colleagues and vendors and clients. And he'd do the same, telling me about the stupidity of most public educators—he was a biology teacher, you know. We made mincemeat of these people. And Gil loved it as much as I did—how we would laugh! At the end of the day, we'd tend to the critters and then sit down with a drink and I'd say, 'So what's the gossip?'"

She told Jamie about the first day Gil had ignored her question, changing the subject to the weather. "The weather, for Pete's sake!" But he had just started his first course of chemo at that point, and she'd figured he was feeling sick.

"Or I thought maybe he was just unable to hold up his end of the conversation," she added. "You know, like he couldn't contribute anything, so he didn't want to go there. He could hardly tell stories about his fellow patients. Not even I would do that."

Jamie smiled at her.

"I wouldn't," she snapped. "I'm not a complete shrew."

"I'm sure you wouldn't. So what else?"

Meg had kind of expected him to say, "Ah, yes, now I see why you felt deserted." But he didn't, so she upped the ante.

"He quit drinking entirely and quit reading the books we always shared—thrillers, mostly—and started spending hour after hour reading the Bible."

Good enough for you, Jamie boy? Got a clue what sort of betrayal that was?

"And you never considered following suit?"

"No," she said, in a tone indicating that he'd just asked the dumbest question she'd ever heard. "Why should I change, just because he did?"

"That's the sixty-four-thousand-dollar question, isn't it? What else?"

"His job. He'd been on a paid medical leave and he suddenly quit."

Jamie looked surprised, she was happy to see. Finally, a change that might have shocked him.

"He said that he wanted to do something important with what was left of his life—as if there's any job that could be called 'important.' It's all just a waste of time."

"'All is vanity,'" Jamie said.

Meg looked at him suspiciously. "I don't know about that, but unless you're saving lives, I don't suppose any job qualifies as critical. Anyway, he decided he'd rather volunteer at the Rescue Mission than teach what he called 'scientific revisionism.' So that's what he did. He gave up the job they were holding for him as well as his disability payments."

Jamie looked at her expectantly. He apparently didn't want to ask the obvious question.

"Could we afford it?" Meg yawned in a display of supreme indifference. "Well, I suppose so. We had decent savings and a couple little inheritances. And there was my income, too, at least at first. But to give up that money!"

"What was his reasoning?"

"He felt that what they had been asking him to teach was dishonest; it was nothing but partial truths and fairy tales, he claimed. And he couldn't in good conscience continue accepting money from the system that promoted that kind of deception."

"I'm liking Gil more and more," Jamie said. "He sounds like a great guy."

Meg glared at him, ready to remind him of her opinion of Christians. But Sadie appeared at that very moment, huffing and puffing excitedly even though she was being pushed by one of the second-shift aides.

"No problem," Jamie said over her profuse apologies. "It gave me a chance to have a nice little chat with Meg."

Meg smiled at Sadie. "Yes, we had quite a talk."

Sadie beamed at them both. "Then maybe my tardiness was providential," she said. "Do you two believe in answered prayer?"

Long-term care insurance turned out to be cheaper than Meg had feared. Between the cut-rate and expensive policies, she found a good middle-of-the-road plan that would set a girl back just $150 a month for several years' coverage, whereupon government assistance would kick in.

Two days later, she and Sandra signed up and paid up, leaving only a simple in-home physical standing between themselves and lifelong security. They then celebrated with an expensive dinner of artery-clogging cheddar and Emmenthaler fondue washed down with copious quantities of an artery-clearing Merlot.

"I'm stuffed, but you only live once," Sandra said as they waited for an utterly irresistible finale of chocolate fondue. "So'd anyone die this week?"

"Not a one. Some hospitalizations, but it's been a while since we lost anyone. I'm beginning to think the human species is evolving into immortality. Heaven on earth!"

"Just so long as we can afford to come back here every month or two," said Sandra, licking her lips as the waiter delivered a plate of fresh fruits and pound cake . . . and then, to their "ooohs," a pot of luscious melted chocolate.

"I take it back," said Meg. "I think we're already in paradise."

CHAPTER FORTY-NINE

Sadie Sparrow
Wednesday, May 9

It was a gorgeous day, warm and infused with the scent of early lilacs. Sadie was riding Papa's big old paint horse Ned bareback, loping him across a field of wildflowers in full bloom, golden Alexander and yellow star grass and prairie smoke bud and a dozen others that Mama considered weeds when they snuck into her garden. She could see the Mueller girls on the other side of the field, just at the edge of the forest, spreading out a blanket for their picnic. She leaned forward and hugged Ned's neck (she had always loved him best of all the horses she'd ever known) and his canter was so smooth that she was barely moving, but her stomach was full of butterflies at the prospect of seeing her dear friends Milly and Grace after all these years—

"Sadie?"

Someone was nudging her shoulder. At first she thought it might be Ned, but then the field vanished and she realized it was her aide Piper, and she was in her bed at The Hickories, and she had wrapped her arms around not Ned's neck but a spare pillow.

"Let me sleep more," she said, closing her eyes tight and trying to summon up the dream again.

But it was no use.

"It's time to get up, Sadie," Piper was saying. "You asked me to wake you at four, remember?"

Sadie moaned. "Yes, dear, I remember. And I thank you."

"Here, let me help you."

Sadie loved the always-gentle Piper and was only too happy to let her help—she'd left the mirage of independence behind when she was forced to trade in walker for wheelchair and had found it supremely liberating to accept such kindnesses.

"And guess what, Sadie? Eva's back!"

"Wonderful! Will she be at dinner?"

"Mmmm, I doubt it. She's pretty weak. Pneumonia can really take a lot out of someone her age, you know. And so can spending all that time in the hospital."

"Then I'll go to her room. I can do that, can't I? I've really missed her!"

"Of course. Let's finish getting you ready and I'll take you. Just don't expect to see her doing any cartwheels."

It wasn't until she was trying to fall asleep that night that Sadie recalled a horrifyingly pertinent movie from the 1950s. She'd seen it on one of those glorious summer nights when Dana was a little girl, when the three of them would climb into the front seat of Ed's spiffy salmon-and-black Chevy Bel-air with a big bag of buttered popcorn and several bottles of grape-flavored soda pop and pillows and blankets and head for the Skylite drive-in theater.

It was one of those alien-invasion movies, and if Dana hadn't fallen asleep early on, they probably would have left—she and Ed had never seen such a movie before, and it would've been too scary for a child. It was in fact kind of scary for an adult, Sadie remembered saying to Ed on the way home that night.

She couldn't remember much of the plot. But she did remember the tell-tale sign that various characters had been possessed by an alien: a mark on the back of the neck. The hero—a little boy, she thought—would talk to these suddenly oddly behaving people and then they would turn away from him and SURPRISE! he would see the mark and know they were goners.

That was how she felt tonight. It wasn't so much how Eva had looked lying there in her bed in a flannel gown, so frail and worn out, her hands trembling and her white face all cheekbone and nose and eyelid. Her silver-white hair, ordinarily pulled back into a neat bun, fell loose to her shoulders; Sadie had never seen it down, and thought it made Eva look even older than her ninety-three years. But she had chatted a bit with Sadie, sounding better than she looked, apparently cured of the pneumonia that had whisked her off to the hospital a month ago.

But then a young man had delivered her dinner tray, and while he was still uncovering the dishes, Eva reached for the juice glass.

"So thirsty," she'd said, taking a sip and then pursing her lips as if she'd just sucked on a lemon. "It's so thick, Jacob."

He'd consulted the meal slip on her tray. "It's supposed to be. Pudding consistency, it says."

"Okay," Eva had said docilely, returning the glass to her tray. "Whatever you say."

Sadie's heart had almost stopped. What was it Eva had said about this very thing, not so long ago?

"Most people on the thickened stuff die of dehydration before they have a chance to develop pneumonia again."

And *"I was thinking more along the lines of murder."*

Yet Eva had barely made a peep when Jacob served the thick stuff to her.

Just like the mark on the back of the neck.

Sadie tossed a bit more before falling into a troubled sleep.

Five days later, Eva slipped quietly into eternity. She had died of "natural causes," Nurse Char told Sadie, whispering this bit of knowledge as if she'd revealed some top-secret information that would certainly lead to a law suit by Eva's family if they found out that Char had spilled the beans. As if Eva's four daughters, now residing in upscale towns in Washington and Vermont and upstate New York, would give a second thought to anything connected with their mother.

Eva had, in fact, died just as she had lived since the year she turned fifty: alone. That's when her girls had left home, she had told Sadie, all within one calendar year, heading off to the coasts to find husbands for themselves and raise children of their own. It was the same year that Eva's husband, a venerated English professor at the University of Wisconsin-Milwaukee, had left her for a pretty young student whose passion for nineteenth century British literature matched his own.

Eva had been awarded their house in the subsequent divorce—a big old stucco bungalow just north of the university, she'd told Sadie. It had lots of crown molding and built-ins and plenty of charm. But apparently that charm was lost on her girls, because they'd rarely visited even before being tied down by their families. So Eva had given herself wholeheartedly to volunteering at and through her church, zeroing in on hospice work early on in a show of solidarity with others whose lives were also ending. It was, in fact, a fellow hospice volunteer who had helped her find and settle into The Hickories once not even a walker could see her safely about the house.

Sadie spent much of the day following Eva's death recalling the conversations they had had about this life, with all its joys and sorrows and disappointments. Somehow sharing those things—especially the disappointments—made everything feel all right again. That was just life, they had agreed time and time again, and a good thing because they were citizens of a better country, an eternal home, and if things had been wonderful on earth they might have resisted going there.

"Friends will be there I have loved long ago," Sadie warbled. "Joy like a river around me will flow!"

As long as she was able to focus on these things, she felt strangely peaceful about this loss. Oh, of course she'd miss Eva. Beulah and Eva would probably prove to be her last real friends on this earth. It was just too difficult to find true soulmates in a nursing home, where so many residents were slipping into either dementia or complete self-centeredness, with every personality flaw magnified many times over.

"Just to be there and to look on His face," she sang out with gusto, "will through the ages be glory for me!"

Knowing that Eva would never suffer again was such a comfort. And Sadie no longer had to worry about being the one to go off into paradise first, leaving poor Eva abandoned once again.

All in all, it should have been a satisfying resolution to her friend's life story, with Sadie simply feeling honored to have spent its finale with her.

But one nagging issue remained.

Did it still matter? Sadie bowed her head in prayer.

Sure, Eva is now home safe with you, Lord Jesus; she is undoubtedly beyond caring about anything as trivial as a cause of death. But who'll be next, Lord? Should Beulah and I continue our investigation?

Sadie didn't hear an audible response. She didn't even feel Him speaking to her heart, the way some people described getting instructions from Him. How was she to know if they should press on with their inquiries?

Well, Lord, how about this: we'll try to find out whether those thickened liquids are healing gifts from You or murder weapons. And if You don't want us to—if it doesn't matter one way or the other—You just let us know somehow, okay?

Truth be told, Sadie was hoping that He'd call a halt to their apparently futile inquiries. Her heart was so set on heaven right now that she didn't want to yank it back into this sad old world.

Besides, what exactly were they supposed to *do?* She had never felt quite so clueless in her life.

CHAPTER FIFTY

Elise Chapelle
Friday, May 11

Elise was not surprised to find another letter from Helene in the mailbox; a $7860.84 charge for a Paris-to-Chicago Air France fare had popped up in Papi's online credit card statement a full week ago. Helene, it seemed, had deliberately chosen a disgustingly expensive flight. Elise had spent hours poring through online fares for this simple route, converting Euros to U.S. dollars until she knew them by heart. Those fares had started at under $900.

She ripped open the envelope. It was just as cheap as the last one, but this time contained a sheet of beige paper with a short note scrawled in Helene's unmistakable hand.

Oh, my darling Elise,
I am so very excited to tell you that I will soon be home with you for good!
I've made a reservation on Air France flight 416, leaving Paris on Tuesday 6/19 at 1:30 and arriving at O'Hare at 3:45 p.m. on the same day! Isn't that absolute madness? I will find you on the other side of Customs, I trust?
With love unending, I remain faithfully yours—
Helene

Fat chance you'll be on that flight, Helene.

Because naturally, that was why Helene had purchased such an expensive ticket. Sure, she could have gone for the $12,000-plus "La Première" class—Elise had scoped out all the possibilities—but even Papi might have balked at that, might have cancelled the charge. No, Helene was shrewd enough to settle for something just under $8K, something that she could sell to the highest bidder, or maybe simply cash in just before takeoff.

Whatever. The most valuable thing Elise had ever stolen was a quarter from Mamie's purse, and she'd been about seven years old. She hadn't kept up with the finer points of embezzlement.

She told Jamie all about it on Saturday night, over a mouth-watering dinner of fried chicken and coleslaw.

"So you don't think she'll show?" he asked, polishing off his second drumstick.

"I'd be astonished."

"And you think she'd sell the ticket? How would she find someone who just happens to want to fly to Chicago?"

Elise shook her head. "I have no idea how any of it would work, and I don't really care. What bothers me is what it'll do to Papi if she's not on that flight."

Jamie started clearing the table in spite of her protests. "You cook, I clean up—sounds like a fair division of labor to me."

"It will break his heart," Elise continued. "He's trying so hard to be nonchalant about the possibility of seeing her again, but you can tell that he's almost beside himself."

"I hope she doesn't disappoint him."

Elise had some serious repenting to do that night; she had to admit, in her heart of hearts, that she really hoped Helene would just stay away.

"I'm still so bitter about her, Lord," she said, gazing out at the starry sky from her bedroom window seat. "I need Your forgiveness again, and I need to ask You once again to change my heart. I thought I was past it, really I did, but now here I am again with my stomach in knots over the very thought of her coming back here."

She pulled Mamie's plaid shawl around her shoulders—she'd opened a window and the spring air was cool—and considered once again what the Bible had to say about her state of mind.

"Let all bitterness, and wrath, and anger, and clamor, and evil speaking, be put away from you, with all malice," she murmured, recalling a passage from Ephesians that she had memorized years ago after yet another disappointment from the long-absent Helene. "And be ye kind one to another, tenderhearted, forgiving one another, even as God for Christ's sake hath forgiven you."

Just think of what He went through so that you could be forgiven.

"I'm so sorry, Jesus," she said softly, her eyes moist. "Please crush my pride and help me to focus on how very happy Helene's return would make Papi. Please."

CHAPTER FIFTY-ONE

Meg Vogel
Saturday, May 19

Eva Foster's daughters arranged for an elaborate memorial service for their mother at Cambridge Infinity Chapel, the most exclusive funeral parlor in southeastern Wisconsin. The place wasn't to Meg's taste; she felt oppressed by its dim lighting and original oils in dark frames and groupings of heavy, overstuffed furniture. It was a mystery to her why anyone would want to be memorialized in this place. But Lucy had assured her that it was the funeral venue of choice for everyone who was anyone.

"Eva may not have been a mover and shaker," she'd told Meg the day before, obviously unimpressed with the posthumous attention the Foster girls seemed to be lavishing on their mother. "But they want to make sure that their childhood friends know that they can afford it."

Meg attended the funeral partly for Sadie's sake; her old friend had really wanted to go, but Dana was too busy to take her, too busy to even sign the forms that would have allowed Meg to serve as her mother's chauffeur and escort. But Meg also wanted to take a closer look at these Foster girls who'd shared this shameful lack of time for their mother. In fact, their only recent visit to The Hickories had been yesterday, when they arrived to scope out what was left of Eva's estate.

She found the Foster gathering in the west wing of an enormous building festooned with columns and broad balconies. The room was inexplicably named The Strand. At its front, framed by impressionist landscapes and dark-stained bookcases, was a massive carved table bearing an iridescent urn and a framed photo of an elegant young woman, presumably Eva in happier times.

If it hadn't been for the urn, Meg might have imagined herself at a cocktail party, with groups of well-heeled, middle-aged men and women chattering animatedly throughout the room. She worked her way up to the table to take a closer look at the photo. It was Eva, all right, plumper then, but with those prominent cheekbones and her blonde tresses pulled back in that familiar bun.

"She was a beauty, wasn't she?"

The voice startled Meg. She turned to see a woman who looked very much like the Eva she had known, slim and dressed in a creamy taupe, but in her sixties. She was smiling faintly, extending her hand to Meg.

"I don't believe we've met," she said.

Meg introduced herself and wasn't surprised to learn that the woman was Eva's oldest, Eleanor Foster-Walsh.

"The urn is lovely, isn't it?" Eleanor said, tracing its curve with a perfectly manicured hand. "It's hand-painted glass, you know. The cherry blossoms are exquisite, don't you think? Mom would have adored it."

"Lovely," Meg agreed, thinking that Eva would have adored an occasional daughterly visit a lot more.

"My sister Madeline will keep this one—she's the baby of our family, and so feels the greatest sentiment about our mother. But we're each taking home keepsake versions for ourselves."

Meg made polite noises about what a tribute this was to a really wonderful woman, and began talking about Eva's life at The Hickories, her friends and her interests and what a delight she had been. But Eleanor wasn't really interested. She nodded a bit and then excused herself to greet a couple who had just walked in the door.

Alone again, Meg surveyed the room. Rows of chairs had been set up to accommodate the crowd. There had to be two hundred seats, and half had already been taken by men and women dressed in black. She wondered how many of them had ever even met Eva, if they had known her as children, running into her kitchen to show her a beautiful bug they'd caught or to wolf down cookies and milk or to get Band-Aids and kisses for skinned elbows and knees.

She found a seat near the back and busied herself looking at the program. It didn't look promising—with several hymns plus a message, it might end up being a long one. The luncheon menu was printed on the back: after the service, there would be Cornish game hen, roast beef, and champagne served in the Garden Room. Meg decided to skip the luncheon; she really had nothing to say to any of these people, nor apparently did they to her. Eva certainly wouldn't miss her.

The service was conducted by a local Presbyterian pastor who'd never met Eva. For most of her adult life, she had been a faithful member of a church near the university. But the pastor from that church apparently hadn't been up to snuff for the Foster girls, Lucy had said, not being prepared to wear the handsome royal blue cassock sported by this fellow. He may have looked spiffy, Meg thought as he led the singing, but he sure was tone deaf.

His speaking wasn't any better, she decided moments into the eulogy.

"I'm told that Eva was a remarkable woman," the pastor was saying to what had turned out to be a full house. His hair was pure white and almost too thick to be real, but if it was a toupee, it was an expensive one. "She was always impeccably dressed, kept a beautiful home, made sure that her daughters received the finest education, and befriended people at all levels of society."

She was good with tradespeople. Just say it, old man.
She was kind to her inferiors.

"She was a good person," he said, "kind to everyone, even to those who served her."

Meg groaned inwardly.

He then launched into Eva's charitable work, took a swing around how perfectly her daughters had turned out and finished his little talk with how much her grandchildren would have loved her if only they'd had the opportunity to really get to know her.

The message's saving grace, in Meg's opinion, was that there was no mention of God or Jesus, even though Eva had certainly been a big fan. The pastor did mention heaven and seeing her again, but he didn't dwell on it. Then two more dusty old hymns, one stodgy, Thou-laden prayer, and it was over. No fond remembrances, not even any tears, as far as Meg could tell.

The crowd then rose and began moving towards the Garden Room.

Meg left without saying goodbye to anyone. She'd barely known Eva herself, and she felt like crying. It seemed tragic to be surrounded, even in death, by people who really didn't care that you'd finally cashed in your chips.

Meg visited Sadie on Monday to give her a full report. They were once again overlooking the garden, now ablaze with hawthorns and azaleas and late tulips, sharing what they both imagined to be a proper English tea, complete with some rather tasteless biscuits.

"Miss Vogel poured," said Sadie. "That's what the local newspaper would have reported about this little party when I was a girl."

Meg chuckled. "Versus what they would have reported if they'd covered the last party we had here!"

"Oh, wasn't that awful? Mr. Patterson should never have had that second martini, not with all the medication he's on."

"It was my fault for not keeping an eye on him," Meg said. "Or on the martini pitcher."

"It's fortunate that he only broke a lamp."

"Two lamps, and apparently he flushed both of his hearing aids down the toilet when he got back to his room. His CNA saw what he was about to do but was just a step too late to stop him."

They looked at each other solemnly for a moment before bursting into laughter.

"Oh, thank you, my dear," Sadie said, drying her eyes with a sweet little lace-edged hanky. "I haven't had such a good laugh in ages."

"Me neither! It really feels good to laugh, doesn't it?"

Not wanting to ruin the mood, Meg told Sadie a few other amusing stories from the last few months—the highlight being Bertha Stravinsky's 911 call to notify the authorities that someone had stolen her winning entry in the Publishers Clearing House sweepstakes.

But finally, she had to address the elephant in the room.

"So you seem to be doing pretty well," she said, "having lost Eva, I mean."

Sadie smiled at her. "I didn't lose Eva, my dear. I know exactly where she is. And that's why I'm doing just fine. Now, tell me all about the service."

Meg gave her a blow-by-blow account.

"I don't blame you for skipping the luncheon," Sadie said finally. "It doesn't sound like anyone was there looking for comfort or fond memories of Eva. But how sad! I'm sure she was a wonderful mother, and I know for a fact that she took care of her own mother till the bitter end—apparently her mother was a little dotty in the last years of her life, and

Eva was always having to run down to the drug store or five-and-dime to pay for things the old girl had shoplifted."

Sadie bit her lip to keep from smiling and Meg laughed again.

"My point being," Sadie added, "that Eva was good to everyone. The young people are always saying 'what goes around comes around,' but it's not really true, is it? Sometimes it seems like the best people are treated the worst by those they love." She shook her head. "But the Bible tells us to expect that, and I guess there's a very good reason that the Lord allows it."

Meg stared into her teacup, hoping that her silence would serve as a roadblock to this line of thinking.

It didn't work.

"But I guess you don't want to hear about that, do you?" Sadie said. "Do you mind if I ask why?"

Was that annoyance Meg detected in her friend's voice? It seemed impossible, but when Sadie plunged ahead without waiting for a response, Meg knew she was witnessing at least some level of gentle frustration.

"It's always puzzled me when people have been hostile to the things of God, and these great truths. Granted, I wasn't so interested in going straight to scripture before Jamie came along. But I've always been interested in hearing what others had to say on the subject. But there are some in your generation—well, I've never seen anything like it. It's almost like some of you are offended by the very idea of God."

Meg tried to look merely indifferent even though she was feeling a little irritated herself.

"I don't know what to tell you, Sadie," she said. She reached for the last biscuit and broke it into pieces. "It's just that science has demonstrated that there doesn't have to be a creator at all. And if I have my choice, I'll take a God-free universe any day—religion is always trying to make people be something other than what they really are, trying to get them to suppress their natural desires and identity, and making them miserable in the process. And I'll tell you, I've known a lot of really good atheists in my life—better people than some of the religious ones I've known."

She snuck a sideways glance at Sadie, who seemed to be staring into space.

"Present company excepted, of course."

"Of course," Sadie said, turning back to Meg and looking her directly in the eye. "But the fact remains that there is truth—"

"Truth!" Meg put her cup and saucer and bread plate back on the serving tray and brushed imaginary crumbs off her lap. "Sadie, there's no such thing as truth, at least not the absolute kind. Unless maybe it's that life sucks and then we die."

"But what brought you to that conclusion, Meg? Seriously, what gave you this idea?"

Sadie's sad expression softened Meg's heart enough to let her consider the question. She thought back to the first time it had occurred to her that this God business was all nonsense.

"I guess," she said, "it started at my father's funeral. My mom had died the year before, of breast cancer, and then he dropped dead of a heart attack, and it suddenly occurred to me that this God they'd been shoving down my throat my whole life might not exist at all. You know what they say, that man created God, not vice versa."

"How old were you?"

"I'd just turned eighteen."

"You poor child." Sadie's eyes were brimming.

"It was a long time ago. My grandmother and I kept living together until she died five years later, and then I was totally on my own. But I had my journalism degree by then, and my first agency job, so it was—well, it was sad, but it was like a clean break from my childhood. I was off on the next chapter of my life and I didn't spend a lot of time looking back."

"So you left all those childish things behind? Like God?"

"Something like that." It had been a long time since Meg had thought of those days; she squinted as if it would help her mind's eye recall the details. "It was a boyfriend who showed me the way, so to speak. I'd just found out that some friends of ours—of his, really, but they'd become my friends too—I'd found out that they were married to other people, even though they were living together. I'd assumed they were married to each other, you know? In any case, when I found out the truth about them, I expressed some shock over it, I guess."

"Sounds reasonable to me."

"Well, I suppose, if you have traditional values. But this boyfriend—they called him Moose and I was crazy about him—he pointed out that these friends were two of the nicest people he'd ever known, and that they made each other as well as all their friends happy, and that they were a lot better people than some of the judgmental religious types we knew. So I guess it was then that I decided that my ethics were closer to Moose's than they were to my parents' values."

"And you never looked back?"

"That's about it." Meg rose and finished tidying up the table. "It was very liberating."

"Well, I must say that I think it's sad," Sadie said, her eyes seeking Meg's, "and if you'd ever like to discuss it more, I'd love to. But in the meantime, I appreciate your sharing your thoughts with me."

"No problem," Meg said, kissing Sadie's incredibly soft cheek and picking up the tea tray. "But I've really got to get going now; Lucy will be looking for me."

She felt slightly guilty for running out on her friend. But by the time she'd returned the tray to the kitchen, she'd convinced herself that Sadie had really had no right to probe on this particular subject, considering where it might have led if she'd hung around for the denouement.

That night, as Meg sat in her living room sipping a hangover-inducing Cabernet and listening to her old albums on her even older stereo, memories of that long-ago ex-boyfriend overwhelmed her.

She put Carole King's *Tapestry* on the turntable, gently placed the tone arm on the first cut, and danced her way back to the couch in time to the music.

I feel the earth—move—under my feet

This song reminded her of Moose. It was exactly how she'd felt about him.

His real name was Howard. He was tall and slim and wore his sandy blond hair about shoulder-length and he was just so incredibly cool, a god-like cross between surfer boy and hippie. They'd met in a no-brainer journalism class and had gone out for drinks after running into each other in the library towards the end of his senior year, when she was a sophomore.

"Get this," she said to Sneak as he snuggled into her lap, "we were both there that night to do research for our Media Ecology term papers. His was on—let's see, I think it was conservative bias in broadcast news. And mine was on the chicky-fluff anti-feminist content of the day's women's magazines. So we had a lot in common, politically speaking. What dopes we were in those days!"

Sneak closed his eyes and purred heartily.

"It was the 1970s," she said, stroking his throat with an index finger, "and I was getting my first taste of freedom—being gone all day from Grammy and from home—this very house, Sneak! Did you know that? Did you know that your mommy has lived here her whole life, even with your daddy?"

He yawned. Meg put her head back and listened to "So Far Away," "It's Too Late," "You've Got a Friend." Listened and remembered.

"Moose took me to see his friends Roger and Laura on the east side. They lived in an old Victorian duplex, and there were always tons of kids there, eating, drinking, listening to music, talking politics or, if they were high, talking garbage. They were mostly hippies—lots of long hair and blue jeans and work boots. It was a whole new world for me, and they were so friendly and loving, acting like I was their new best friend forever."

Meg finished off her wine and set the glass down. She wanted more but couldn't bear to disturb the oh-so-comfortable Sneak.

"I was crazy about the whole scene, you see, my Sneaky boy. But one day I found out that Roger and Laura were married to other people! I was utterly shocked—that's how innocent I was. And I confronted Moose about it."

She remembered all too well her disappointment at his reaction, her fear of losing him, her desperate wish that she'd just kept her mouth shut and gone along with the crowd.

"He treated me like a child, Sneak. Asked where I got the idea that there was anything wrong with this arrangement, since they obviously loved each other and loved everyone around them and made everyone happy. Asked if I'd prefer that they'd stayed miserable apart from each other, living with people they didn't love, just for the sake of some old-fashioned rules that didn't mean anything to anyone anymore."

Sneak yawned again and regarded her with his luminous green eyes.

"So of course, I said no, and tried to erase his idea that I was too much of a prude for him."

Carole King began her plaintive rendition of "Will You Still Love Me Tomorrow?"

"So you want to know what happened? Well, that was the end of Moose. He never called me again, and in those days a girl wouldn't think of calling a man. He'd graduated at the end of the semester when we met, so there was no way I'd see him at school—although of course I spent the whole next semester daydreaming about running into him. He broke my heart, if you must know. I heard that he'd gone off to live up north, but I don't know."

She sighed. "What a fool I was, eh, boy? I guess that was the turning point, and I never even realized it. But he really changed the course of my life. Gave me a real attitude adjustment, as they say, and it changed everything, even my relationship with Grammy."

Sneak had apparently had enough. He leapt gracefully from Meg's lap and trotted off to the kitchen.

"She died just a year later, maybe from a broken heart. So much had happened, first with my parents' deaths, and then essentially losing me . . ."

Meg shook her head. No point in going there. She grabbed her wineglass and followed Sneak. He was sitting in front of the fridge, looking expectantly at the handle.

"You hungry, boy? Well, let's eat, then. Might as well eat, drink, and be merry, for tomorrow we die."

CHAPTER FIFTY-TWO

Sadie Sparrow
Wednesday, May 23

"Coming to work on the new puzzle?" Gladys asked gaily as she backed herself away from the breakfast table. She was wearing a smart deep pink jacket over a white blouse. It was the most conservative outfit Sadie had ever seen on her puzzle-mate, and the outfit had inspired so many compliments that Gladys was glowing. "It's called 'Murder in Madagascar'—so exotic!"

"Can't this morning," Sadie said. "Jamie will be here at two, and I haven't finished studying my passage yet."

That was apparently enough to ruin Gladys' good mood. "Studying, at your age. What nonsense!"

"It's not really studying, it's more meditating on a passage and figuring out what it means. It's really fun. Why don't you join us this afternoon?"

"Because I'm busy, that's why!" Gladys snarled, now firmly ensconced in her normal mood.

Sadie laughed and pointed her chair towards her room, happily accepting a ride home from one of the newer aides. She was excited about the places Jamie was taking her, building on the biblical foundation he'd laid by assigning her readings that he thought would help her with whatever issue was troubling her at the moment.

He had selected this week's passage because of Eva's death, she knew. It was from the apostle Paul's second letter to the Corinthians, and she found it enchanting:

> *Therefore we do not lose heart. Even though our outward man is perishing, yet the inward man is being renewed day by day. For our light affliction, which is but for a moment, is working for us a far more exceeding and eternal weight of glory, while we do not look at the things which are seen, but at the things which are not seen. For the things which are seen are temporary, but the things which are not seen are eternal.*

Back at her desk, she once again opened her worn leather-bound notebook, a gift from Dana the Christmas after Ed died. Which reminded her that they hadn't talked in over a week, so she took a moment to dial Dana's cell number. She wasn't worried about being distracted from her studies, since Dana would be at work and she'd no doubt get voice mail. Which of course was precisely what happened.

Sadie left a quick, cheerful message and turned back to her passage, letting its implications wash over her. She began making notes, writing her main thoughts at the top of separate pages:

> *We should never be discouraged, whatever happens to our hearts or bodies.*

> *If we have Jesus and His word, our spirits can soar no matter what.*

> *Even the worst suffering is only a blink of an eye compared to eternity.*

Our trials make our eternities even better.

Everything physical that we see will soon be gone—it's the things we can't see that are eternal, like love, mercy, and justice—the traits of God!

She then spent the rest of the morning fleshing out each of these ideas. When she'd finished, she realized that this hadn't been anything like work. It had been nothing less than joy to consider what truths the Lord was trying to impress upon her with this brief paragraph of scripture.

She couldn't wait to share her thoughts with Jamie.

"You've become quite the scholar, Sadie," Jamie said approvingly an hour into their discussion. "Are you enjoying it?"

"Oh, yes. And it's making such a difference in my attitude. I really think I'm developing eternal eyes!"

His face lit up. "How so?"

"Well, most importantly, I suppose, death no longer seems even sad to me, as long as you're a genuine Christian. It seems more like—what did Ed call it? Home . . ."

"Home-going?"

"Yes, that's it exactly! I'm telling you, my memory has seen better days." She rubbed her temples as if to jump-start her brain. "At any rate, I know that he and Eva and so many other people I've loved over my life—my folks, too—I know that they've all simply gone on ahead to heaven, and that they're more alive now than they ever were in this life. I really believe it now. It's not just what you would call doctrine."

She was surprised to see that Jamie was tearing up.

"And I have you to thank for this, Jamie." Now she was tearing up, too. "You showed me how I can know that the Bible is true, and how to study it, and it is changing my heart! It's been over two months since I repented and trusted in Jesus and—"

She held up her hand to keep Jamie from interrupting while she collected herself and caught up with her racing thoughts.

"And now I know exactly how Ed felt about it all. If only I'd known then, what a difference it would've made!"

She pulled a fresh Kleenex out of her sleeve to dry her eyes, giving Jamie the chance to give the Holy Spirit full credit for her transformation. She then told him about her discussion with Meg.

"I pray for her," Sadie said, "of course. But how can I help her see what you've shown me?"

Jamie shook his head. "She has to use that free will of hers to seek Him. Hopefully He'll answer our prayers and hedge her in—so that her only choices are trying to fight through her problems horizontally or looking up in search of His truth."

"What do you mean, hedge her in?"

"It's like we were talking about a few weeks ago. Here, let's take a look at Psalm 139. I'm stepping way out of context here, but it has always struck me as a good way of looking at this sort of thing—almost like backing us into a corner so that we're forced to at least consider Him . . ."

Sadie crooned all the way home from dinner that night. Few seemed to pay much attention to her singing, not even the CNAs who pushed her. If they didn't know her, they thought she was goofy; if they did, they seemed to think she was cute. But every once in a while—tonight, for instance—the aide joined her in song. This one, whose name was Rosa, sang in a clear soprano voice that reminded Sadie of the songbirds who used to gather in the old apple tree behind their house.

Why should I feel discouraged,
Why should the shadows come,
Why should my heart be lonely,
And long for heav'n and home?
When Jesus is my portion,
My constant Friend is He.
His eye is on the sparrow,
And I know He watches me.

They both laughed and, without breaking her stride, Rosa bent down and kissed Sadie on the cheek.

"We're sisters in Christ, Miss Sadie," she said, "and one day you and I'll be singing to the King of kings together!"

"I sing because I'm happy," Sadie trilled, and Rosa jumped right in. "I sing because I'm free. For His eye is on the sparrow, and I know He watches me!"

More joyful laughter.

"That's my theme song, you know," Sadie said.

"I can see why. It's perfect for anyone, but especially for someone named Sparrow!"

As they entered her room, Sadie could see that the message light on her phone was dark; apparently Dana still hadn't found time to return her mother's call.

When Rosa left to tend to another resident, Sadie wheeled herself over to the windows to gaze out at the lush spring garden. It was still light out and several women with walkers were easing their way towards her along the nearest walkway. She watched their progress, softly singing another round of "His Eye Is on the Sparrow," meditating on each line. It was really true. There was no reason to despair over anything, least of all a daughter who appeared to have little interest in her.

"Really, Lord, so what?"

She said it right out loud, not even caring if the women outside heard her through the open casement window. It had been an unseasonably warm day, as the meteorologists liked to say, and she'd cranked one of them open that afternoon to let in the spicy scent of the azaleas—White Lights, the oldest of the gardeners had told her when she got her first intoxicating whiff of them. But it was getting chilly now.

"I love Dana with all my heart, Lord, but she clearly doesn't return the feeling."

She cranked the window closed easily, appreciating the care The Hickories' builders had taken to make every last device as simple as possible for the elderly to operate.

And then it hit her.

"I really don't care if she doesn't love me back."

It was a breathtaking realization for someone who had, ever since her husband died, practically lived for her daughter.

"I honestly don't care!"

She felt a little silly then, remembering how Scarlett O'Hara had said something along those lines when she realized that Ashley only loved her as Rhett loved that Watling woman. It was a moment of high drama in *Gone with the Wind*, and Sadie couldn't follow it up by running out of the room calling her husband's name.

"Well, I could, but they'd lock me up," she said, giggling at the very idea. And then an even more joyful thought struck her. "But Lord, I don't need to run after anyone, because You are all I need and You're right here!"

Whereupon she burst into song again with "Great Is Thy Faithfulness" and then, finding Ed's battered old hymnal on the bookshelf, sang hymn after hymn until Rosa returned to help her get ready for bed.

"I'll call Dana again tomorrow," she thought as she snuggled under her fluffy blankets. "Let her know how happy I am."

As it turned out, Sadie didn't have to call her daughter again. Instead, Dana surprised her with a visit to the dining room at eight in the morning, just as Sadie was sprinkling brown sugar over her morning oatmeal.

"I don't have much time," she said breathlessly, slipping into a vacant chair and bending towards Sadie to deliver an air kiss, complete with a loud "Mwah!"

"What a nice surprise, Dana." Sadie noted that her daughter was dressed to the nines in a beautiful dark brown suit and a pale pink blouse, and her tawny hair was pulled back into a slightly messy bun that had probably taken a half hour to arrange so artfully. "Big meeting?"

"Yes, with our most important client." Dana glanced at her watch. "But I wanted to stop in to take care of that paperwork, so you can go to that funeral."

"It was last Saturday," Sadie said in an utterly neutral tone.

"Oh. Well, then, you'll be ready for the next one." Dana flashed Sadie a dazzling smile. "So, how are you? Good?"

"Yes, as a matter of fact." Sadie took a sip of coffee, stalling to flip through all the mental notes she'd made in preparation for telling Dana about how her entire life had been transformed this spring, how truly content she now was, how—

But Dana was already standing up, getting ready to take off. "That's great, Mom—I'm so happy for you! So I'll go find whoever I need to see." She glanced around the dining room, but except for a few other breakfasting early risers, no one was available to point her in the right direction. "I don't suppose you know who? No? Okay, well, I'll check at the front desk—should be someone there by now. Bye, Mom. Talk to you soon, okay?"

Another air kiss and she was gone.

Sadie was tempted to fall into self-pity but pulled herself out of the mood before it had a chance to crystalize.

"Dear Lord," she prayed silently. "Please save Dana, and while you're at it, could you please make this new thinking of mine stick? Thank you, Lord, in Jesus' name."

Her oatmeal was especially sweet that morning. She savored it gratefully.

CHAPTER FIFTY-THREE

Elise Chapelle
Thursday, May 24

Elise spent a chunk of her morning with Mr. Haskell at the bank; he had invited her repeatedly to call him Grant, but he'd been Mr. Haskell to her for thirty-two years and he would always be Mr. Haskell to her.

Everything was shipshape, he had assured her, as he tried to interest her in looking at the ledgers he had so faithfully kept for Papi. It was a task he'd been handling for decades, ever since the year Papi forgot to pay his Fleur de Lis bills and had been temporarily cut off by their bulb and perennial suppliers. But except for that disastrous season, the Chapelles had been both very successful and very thrifty, Mr. Haskell said, putting most of their money into a trust of his own design. The money remained accessible to them—well, more precisely to Charles, he added, recalling with a sad little frown that Lorraine had already passed on—but it would ultimately be Elise's, if that was her concern.

Which it was not. "I just wanted to make sure that Papi wasn't running out of money. I know you're paying the bills, but I'm guessing that The Hickories costs a fortune."

"It *is* expensive," Mr. Haskell admitted. "But there's nothing for you to worry about, my dear. He has enough for many years yet. And even if he were to run out, The

Hickories would never toss him out; it's supported by a foundation, you know."

"I didn't know."

Looking pleased with himself—perhaps he rarely had the pleasure of enlightening a customer on such an important subject—Mr. Haskell straightened his tie. "Oh, yes," he said. "John Donovan is a very wealthy man, and he built The Hickories to make sure that as many people as possible could go to their graves receiving the finest care available. Of course, he has always welcomed those who can pay their own way and then some, in order to subsidize those deserving souls who haven't much money."

"Does Papi know about this?" Elise asked, amazed.

"Of course. Your grandparents were very friendly with the Donovans. Lorraine gave their daughter Gigi French lessons—"

"Gigi?" Elise was flooded with memories of an older girl, a pretty teenager, who came to see Mamie every week for a number of years. The two of them would disappear into the back room for an hour or more, and then—

"Uncle Johnny and Aunt Ruth!" she said breathlessly. "They weren't really related, but that's what Mamie called them. They used to come over to pick Gigi up, and sometimes they'd stay for lemonade and even for dinner." She grinned at Mr. Haskell. "I was pretty little, you know—I'd forgotten. So he's the mysterious man behind The Hickories?"

"Not so mysterious. There's never been any secret about it."

She shook her head, smiling. "But I wonder why Papi never mentioned it?"

"Maybe he thought you knew."

Elise considered this. It was entirely possible; or maybe he didn't think she would remember these people, no matter how nice they were, from the distant past.

"Well, I guess it doesn't matter, does it? But I'll have to ask him about it. And in the meantime, I just wanted to say that we really appreciate all you're doing for him."

"It's our pleasure, Elise," Mr. Haskell said, gathering the papers he'd spread out for her perusal and placing them neatly in a folder bearing Papi's name. "Is there anything we can do for you? Do you need a larger allowance, for instance? Your grandfather has left very generous instructions for you."

She laughed. "What would I do with more money, Mr. Haskell? Travel the world? Dress myself in furs and diamonds? Hire a personal maid?"

He didn't smile; he apparently took his job too seriously to engage in even low-level merriment. "You could probably do all those things and more," he said. "There's enough money there. Goodness knows that he made a fortune on that farmland of his."

"Okay, Mr. Haskell. I'll let you know when I've found just the right way to blow my inheritance."

Papi had had two weeks to get used to the idea of his prodigal daughter's scheduled return, but he was still almost giddy with excitement. Helene's arrival was all he wanted to talk about, with an obsessive focus on the trip to O'Hare Field. What time should he and Elise leave? Where would they park? How would they find the waiting area for international flights? Should they have lunch on the way down? Then maybe they'd better leave earlier.

Elise's queries about the Donovans led to a welcome change in subject that afternoon, as they sat in the garden, enjoying the sun and the scents and the sight of so many happy old residents rolling and strolling among the flower beds. Papi was surprised to realize that she hadn't known about Uncle Johnny owning The Hickories. "I guess I forgot to mention it," he said, clearly embarrassed. But they then had a wonderful afternoon talking about the Donovans, Elise offering her vague memories and Papi filling in the many blanks.

"So do you still hear from them, Papi?"

His face clouded. "It's been a long time. John had just been diagnosed with Alzheimer's, and Ruth was in very frail health. They're living in Hawaii still, as far as I know, but he may be in a nursing home himself by now. And maybe Ruth is there with him. He wanted couples to be able to stay together for life, you know. He made arrangements for that here at The Hickories—"

"There are couples here? I didn't know that."

"Only one or two." Papi smiled sadly. "We men usually die well before our wives. I'm a rare case."

"You're one in a million, Papi," Elise said, leaning over to give him a gentle hug.

"You are too, Elise dear. Say, I was thinking, maybe we should go down to O'Hare the night before Helene arrives, just to be sure. What do you think of that?"

Elise was astounded to find several emails addressed to her at her "Advice for the Life-Worn" address—her first genuine questions from readers, appearing just two days after she had officially published the site, in time for her last creative writing class.

The first two were relatively useless, with one asking about which of two boyfriends sounded like a better bet, and the second proposing that "love your enemies" really referred only to citizens of enemy nations; she would just send these writers quick personal responses. But the third posed a question she had been asking herself for years.

Dear Elise,

I am a single woman and have been taking care of myself for my entire adult life. I have a good job, a nice suburban home, and a few close friends. Sounds perfect, right?

But it isn't, and I don't know why other than to say that I am so afraid of so many things. Crime, rodents, driving in traffic, disease, getting old, not getting old, having too much money to manage, having too little money, being broke, being homeless—the list goes on and on.

I have heard it said that the Bible says "don't be afraid" something like 365 times. I would love to obey—but how?

Emily

Elise poured herself a glass of grape juice and sat down to compose an answer to put both their fears to rest.

Dear Emily,

Boy, do I identify with your question! In fact, I have personally searched the Bible for all the passages saying, essentially, "fear not" and have found it very helpful to spend a little time each day in one or more of these references. (Luke 12:32 is probably my favorite: "Do not fear, little flock, for it is your Father's good pleasure to give you the kingdom." I just love the image of being a poor dumb sheep who is utterly dependent upon her shepherd.)

So that's one important thing to do. The other one is to consider God's nature: He is all powerful and sovereign, He loves each of us enough to have died for us, and He has told us that we are more valuable than the sparrows He tends to with such perfect diligence. In short, He is able to take care of us, He wants to, and He will.

If these things are true—and they are!—why do we think He would do anything less than take care of us perfectly? With the Creator of the universe Himself watching out for us, why in the world would we ever fear anything?

She reminded Emily that God's idea of what's good for us is often quite different from our own, and that we need to learn to trust what Romans 8:28 says about all things working *together* for the good of those who love Him. She then tapped out what would become her standard closing:

Thank you for writing, Emily. Please let me know if you have further thoughts, or if I can help in any way.
Blessings,
Elise

She proofed and posted her reply and then sent the link to Ms. Slocum, to show off her first genuine reader Q&A.

"You may or may not agree with my content," she wrote, figuring that Ms. Slocum was likely as agnostic as her best friend Meg. "But I'm sure you'll be pleased to see that Everlasting Place is already attracting readers in need of spiritual help. Thank you for holding my hand through this process!"

CHAPTER FIFTY-FOUR

Meg Vogel
Friday, May 25

Eleanor Foster-Walsh finally showed up to clean out her mother's room ten days after Eva's death. Lucy was home nursing a bug of some kind—a great advantage of working in healthcare, it seemed, was the industry's insistence on taking the least sniffle very seriously. So it fell to Meg to make sure that Eleanor had all the help she needed.

There actually wasn't much to pack up. Beyond the usual toiletries and books and a sizable stash of greeting cards and stationery, Eva had had little more than a small beige wardrobe of slacks and high-necked tops and sweaters; "turtlenecks for turkey necks," the laundry lady called them.

"I guess that's it," Meg said, checking the built-in drawers one last time. "Your mother certainly lived modestly."

"She did indeed," sniffed Eleanor, who apparently didn't share her mother's frugal ways. She had waltzed into Eva's room wearing perfectly tailored cream pants and a cream-and-coral tunic and had tossed a coat of soft beige suede over the couch—Chanel goatskin, she'd said when Meg could no longer resist passing a hand over it.

"Gorgeous." Meg buried her envy in a flutter of activity, setting the four suitcases and three boxes on the pull cart she'd borrowed from Maintenance. "That's it, I guess. I'll bring this down to your car and you'll be all set."

"Wait," Eleanor commanded. "I need to get the jewelry."

"Jewelry?"

"She said it was behind the Prendergast." Eleanor glided over to a framed reproduction of a Venetian canal scene and pulled the print back to reveal Eva's wall safe. She took a scrap of paper out of her pocket and begin dialing in a combination. She certainly knew what she was doing, Meg thought wryly; she had it open within seconds.

Eleanor stared into it for a long time before turning to Meg and saying, in a menacingly quiet voice, "It's empty."

Meg swallowed. "What do you mean?"

"My mother," said Eleanor, "had a small fortune in museum-quality cameos. They were primarily French and Italian from the Renaissance, although she had several handsome eighteenth-century pieces as well."

"Cameos?" Meg envisioned her grandmother's cameo brooch and earrings. They'd been kind of ugly, in her opinion, and she was surprised that Eleanor seemed upset about anything like that.

"Yes, she collected them. Not to my taste—I prefer gemstones myself—but she liked jewelry that quite literally told a story. The old ones are fairly valuable, you know."

No, I didn't know, you incredible snob!

"They were all right here last time I visited," Eleanor added, glaring at Meg.

"And when was that?"

"Just last summer." She fingered her necklace, six glittering chains dropping from bejeweled golden elephants. "I'm a very busy woman."

Meg shook her head. "Oh, I didn't mean to—I was just trying to figure out when you last saw her cameos. Might she have had them moved somewhere else, like a safe-deposit box at her bank?"

"I don't know why she would have done that."

"I'll tell you what. Let's go see Mr. Immerfall. He's our Administrator and he might know where she put them."

Eva had indeed registered her cameos with the front office, a groveling Mr. Immerfall told Mrs. Foster-Walsh, and they had indeed been insured for a "substantial" amount. He invited Meg to get back to work while they discussed the particulars.

She left, somewhat regretfully—this was probably the first and last time she'd be anywhere near what might turn out to be a criminal investigation, after all—and headed back to Eva's room to fetch the pull cart. She didn't have anything pressing on her plate, and Eva's things would give her an excuse for stopping back at Mr. Immerfall's office; she might hear something interesting.

Meg circled back past the Great Room, noticing Sadie and her friends working on their puzzle, and thought briefly about stopping in on her way back. But when she returned a few minutes later, snooty Nurse Julia was blocking the doorway with her drug cart.

"Hello, Julia," Meg said, clearly enunciating each syllable.

The nurse ignored her. She couldn't even be bothered to look up from the laptop mounted on her cart.

Meg kept going. She'd find Sadie later. Maybe they could have a nice little chat about snobby daughters and stuck-up nurses.

CHAPTER FIFTY-FIVE

Sadie Sparrow
Monday, May 28

Here we go again," Gladys said, sighing dramatically as she surveyed the rainbow of pills in the little plastic cup that Nurse Char had given her. Then, suspiciously, "What's the blue-and-green one for?"

Char bent close to her patient and lowered her voice, but anyone in the vicinity could hear her. "It's for depression, Gladys. It's the new one that your psychiatrist prescribed."

"Well I don't want it!" Gladys picked it out of the cup and threw it on the table, amidst her arrangement of the greenish puzzle pieces that would ultimately fit into a jungle scene packed with lizards and lemurs.

Char retrieved the capsule and tucked it carefully into a drawer on her cart. "I'll let him know."

"You do that, honey. And tell him I don't care to see him again. There's nothing wrong with me. Who wouldn't be depressed at my age?" Gladys scowled at Sadie. "These doctors are trying to poison us, I tell you!"

She spotted an aide passing the doorway. "Girl! Girl! Come here this instant! Take me home!"

Astoundingly, the young woman complied; if Sadie had been in her position, she would have feigned deafness and kept going.

"I'm warning you," Gladys hissed at Sadie as she was whisked away, her chin jutting out regally. "It's all poison!"

Sadie exchanged a sly smile with Beulah, who had finally given in to her urging to fill the vacancy at the puzzle table. For a moment, it was almost like having Eva back; she would have enjoyed this moment, too. But Eva wasn't there; she was right now enjoying fellowship with the Lord Himself.

Well, not "now," exactly, since there may not be such a thing as time in heaven, but—

"You're next, Sadie," Char said, tapping keys on her little computer as rapidly as the best secretary would have done fifty years ago.

But Sadie didn't get her afternoon pills just then, because suddenly Mr. Immerfall appeared in the doorway with three stern-looking men in dark blue suits and white shirts; only their ties distinguished them in any way. He pointed at them—or at Char, maybe, it was hard to tell— and they marched swiftly to the puzzle table.

It took Sadie and Beulah the rest of the day to drag an explanation out of Meg.

"Don't you think we have a right to know what's going on, Meg?" Sadie asked in her best innocent-old-lady voice, tightening her light spring shawl at her throat even though the Activities office was already quite warm. "All we know is that these awful men asked us if we'd seen Eva's jewelry case."

"Which of course we had not," added Beulah.

"Yes, and then they took Char away." Sadie's brow was creased in worry. "Where did they take her? We haven't seen her since they rushed her away."

"Nothing to fret over, girls." Meg patted Sadie's hand. "In the first place, Char's shift simply ended, and she went home after they questioned her. It's Memorial Day, you know. And in the second place, those men were plainclothes policemen. They just wanted to find out if she knew anything about—well, I'm not sure I'm supposed to say."

"Oh, please Meg, tell us!" Beulah said. "We won't tell anyone, will we Sadie?"

"Certainly not," Sadie agreed, enjoying having a companion who was so aggressively nosey. Eva had been a wonderful friend, but she'd always been a little too timid, in Sadie's opinion.

Meg glanced at the door to make sure it was closed tight. "Well, okay, but you didn't hear it from me."

Sadie and Beulah leaned forward in their chairs.

"It seems that some jewelry was stolen from Eva's room," Meg said quietly.

"I never even knew that Eva had jewelry," Sadie breathed, "except for all those cameos." She glanced at Beulah for support. "Not really my favorite."

"Mine neither," said Beulah. "So did Eva have diamonds?"

"No, ladies, no diamonds." Meg smiled mischievously, apparently enjoying their intense interest. "But those cameos were supposedly worth a fortune. And they were missing from the safe in her room when her daughter came to clean the room out."

"The cameos were worth a fortune?" Sadie was stunned. "They were mostly so—well, so *beige*, if you know what I mean."

"I do know," Meg said. "In fact, I have a cameo ring that my mother left me, picturing a little bouquet of flowers. I never cared for it much, just kept it because it had been hers and her mother's before her. But I guess Eva's were museum-quality, according to her daughter. I looked them up last night on the internet and was amazed to find some selling for $25,000 and even more! Mostly the very pricey ones were set with diamonds, but still."

Astounded, they chattered for a while about Eva and her treasures.

"To think that Eva's cameos were valuable," Beulah mused. "I never would have guessed. Except for maybe that black set she had on not all that long ago, before she went to the hospital—"

"Oh, yes, the necklace and earrings with the little pearls." Sadie closed her eyes to picture them. "I remember thinking that they were rather pretty, and that Eva should have been wearing a black sweater to really set them off."

"Well, it sure doesn't matter now, does it?" Meg turned a critical eye on the smart lavender wrap blouse she was wearing. "To think we ever worry about something as silly as clothing."

"Except maybe those kids of Eva's will give her a thought now and then," said Beulah, "if only when they're crying over the fortune they lost."

Meg shook her head sadly. "But they won't lose anything, Beulah. If the police can't track down Eva's cameos, Mr. Immerfall will call in the insurance company. Her kids are going to get every penny they think they have coming to them."

Meg finally excused herself, saying it was time for her to head home, and wheeled Sadie and Beulah back to their puzzle table. Otherwise alone in the room, they smiled pleasantly until she'd disappeared into the hallway, whereupon they both started whispering at once.

"Amazing," said Sadie. "A jewel thief in our midst!"

"You know exactly who did it, too," said Beulah. "Nurse Julia!"

Sadie nodded. "I thought exactly the same thing. Although we have no proof, do we?"

"But I have a good reason for suspecting her. I meant to tell you this, but I kept forgetting to. You know how sidetracked I can get."

Sadie was all ears. "What is it?"

"Well, I went to church with Bunny on Sunday, as usual, but she brought me back early—she wasn't feeling well, she gets those awful migraines, you know."

"No, I didn't know. I'm so sorry to hear that."

Beulah took a detour into Bunny's headache history, pulling herself up short midway through the second-opinion doctor's diagnosis. "But I digress," she said, her volume by now back to a normal decibel level. "Where was I?"

The two traced their conversation backwards to Bunny bringing Beulah back early on Sunday.

"Okay, there we are, then," said Beulah. "So I came in and that lovely aide—you know, the one with the freckles and curly brown hair and such an odd name?"

"Piper Drew?"

"Yes, that's the one. A living doll! Anyway, she gave me a ride back to my room. I got my key out on the way. But what do you know: the door was open a little, maybe a foot or two."

Sadie's heart skipped a beat. Even though she never bothered locking her own door, she knew the Beulah was diligent about it. "Could you possibly have forgotten to lock it?"

"Absolutely not," Beulah said, a little heatedly. "I never forget! I've got all my silver coins here, like I told you, just in case the economy collapses. Remember? I told you all about that!"

"Yes, I remember." And she really did, albeit a little vaguely. It was some doomsday scenario having to do with inflation and martial law. But then Beulah was much more informed than was Sadie, who'd never been very political.

"They're in my safe, of course, and Bunny's the only other person who knows my combination, but still." Beulah shook her finger at the room, emphasizing each word. "I lock my door!"

"So did you check your safe? Is everything still there?"

"Oh, yes, dear, but that's not the point."

Sadie rifled through her memory of their conversation. "So what *is* the point, then?"

"Oh, didn't I tell you?" Beulah tapped her forehead. "I'm telling you, my memory is a sieve lately! The point is that"—and here she leaned forward and dropped back to a whisper—"*she* was in my room. Julia, the nurse."

Sadie gasped. "What was she doing there?"

"She was just leaving. Said that she was looking for her good pen, that she'd left it somewhere on Saturday night, and thought it might have been in my room."

"Is that possible?"

"Yes, it's possible." Beulah took Sadie's hand in her own. "But why did Julia almost close the door? Why wouldn't she just have left it open while she ran in to look for her pen?"

It was an awfully good question, and neither one had an answer.

Sadie had asked that Beulah be moved to her table in the dining room, and that night her friend was finally wheeled directly to the spot that had been Eva's.

"I'll bet you're looking forward to getting back into your walker full time," Sadie commented as two uniformed waitresses tied fresh white linen "clothing protectors" around their necks. "When do you think that will happen?"

"We're going to start doing some distance walking next week," Beulah said. "The goal is tap-dancing by the Fourth of July and ballet by Labor Day!"

They were laughing merrily as Gladys rolled up. "What's so funny?" she demanded.

"Oh, Gladys, Beulah was just talking about how she'll be tap-dancing by Independence Day!" Sadie wiped her eyes with her bib, still chuckling. "I guess you had to—"

She and Beulah noticed it at exactly the same moment.

Gladys was wearing her elegantly simple black silk caftan. And right in the center, just below her collarbone, was a black cameo necklace with tiny pearls.

Eva's black cameo necklace.

Before they could say a word, the waitress reappeared and tied a linen bib securely over Gladys' ample breast.

CHAPTER FIFTY-SIX

Elise Chapelle
Monday, May 28

Weary of talking about the logistics of Helene's alleged homecoming, Elise begged off her usual afternoon visit with Papi on Monday, instead attending a Memorial Day picnic at Jamie's church.

She'd had a great time, she assured Papi that evening.

"Nice people?"

"Very nice. And highly interested in me."

"Of course, they were interested in you, dear. You're a most interesting girl!"

"I think perhaps they were more fascinated by Jamie having a date," she said, laughing. "There was one young woman in particular who peppered me with questions. I think she might have eyes for Jamie herself."

She described some of the characters she'd met at length, surprised that Papi didn't once utter the words "O'Hare Field." But finally, he changed the subject.

"We've had some excitement around here, too."

She felt a flash of fear, but he was smiling. "What happened?"

"It seems that we've had a theft," he said. "My aide told me all about it: it seems that Eva Foster had a priceless cameo collection in her safe, and it's missing!"

"Wow! How amazing that someone was able to steal something from one of these safes, don't you think? Unless Eva gave the combination to someone for some reason?"

"Could be. God only knows, I suppose."

"God and the thief, that is." Elise ran her fingers through her tangled hair, which she hadn't combed since morning. "But you know, Papi, it's really funny what you say about 'priceless' cameos, don't you think? I never knew they were especially valuable."

"Nor did I. But they say the ones Eva owned were very old."

"Huh." She checked her memory. "Funny that you really don't see women wearing cameos today. I can't think of—oh, but wait."

"What is it?"

"On my way in tonight, I ran into Gladys Baldwin leaving the dining room. She was looking almost stunning in a black caftan."

"You're right. I noticed that she looked very nice tonight."

"But the thing is, I think she was wearing a cameo—a black one, a necklace or brooch. If she was into that sort of jewelry, maybe she'd know something about where Eva's might have disappeared to."

"Maybe she's the thief!" But Papi was teasing, she could see.

"A thief hiding the goods in plain sight? Sounds like a mystery story, doesn't it?" Elise squeezed his hand. "But I just meant that women notice things like unusual jewelry, and they may have talked about cameos in particular."

"It's probably a little late to ask her tonight," Papi said, glancing at his watch.

"Oh, I won't ask Gladys. It's not my place. I'll just let Meg know."

CHAPTER FIFTY-SEVEN

Meg Vogel
Tuesday, May 29

Meg heard all about the cameo sightings first thing in the morning, when she found Elise waiting at the office door along with Sadie and Beulah.

"To what do I owe the pleasure, ladies?" she asked once she'd settled Elise in a chair and managed to squeeze both wheelchairs into the cramped space.

They looked at each other, unsure of who should go first.

Finally, Elise spoke. "We're all aware of the missing cameos, Meg—my grandfather told me last night—and we wanted to let you know that we may have found at least one of them."

"No kidding!" Meg was astounded. "Where?"

"You may not believe it," Sadie said, "but we saw Gladys wearing the black one. You remember, the one we told you about."

"At least, we *think* it's the same one," Beulah chimed in.

"You'd have to ask Gladys about that," Sadie said.

"I saw her wearing it when I came in last night," Elise added. "She was just leaving the dining room. She looked so nice in that black caftan of hers, and the cameo looked like it was displayed on black velvet. It's a stunning piece."

"Great detective work, girls!" Meg shook her head in awe. "C'mon, let's go find Gladys."

They found her sitting alone at the puzzle table, her head bobbing back and forth as she searched for just the right pieces.

"Good morning, Gladys," they called out almost in concert as they approached her, Meg pushing Sadie, Elise behind Beulah.

She glared at them. "Why are you looking at me that way? Have I grown a beard?"

She was wearing her blonde wig today, over a navy pantsuit with a somewhat ludicrous sailor collar. So distracting was the get-up that it took Meg a few moments to notice that she was wearing a lacy silver cuff bracelet on her right wrist; at its center was a large gray cameo featuring a woman's profile.

"What do you want?"

She looks scared. Meg felt suspicious for the ten seconds it took them to gather around the table, but then reminded herself that it would take a pretty stupid thief to be wearing her loot for all to see.

"Nothing to worry about, Gladys," she said at last. "We just wanted to talk to you about your cameos."

"What about them?"

Beulah got right to the point. "Aren't they Eva's?"

"Of course, they're Eva's," Gladys said, frowning in confusion. "She gave them to me."

That was not the answer Meg had expected.

"What do you mean?" Beulah peered at Gladys through narrowed eyes. "When did she give them to you?"

"And *why* did she give them to you?" Sadie added.

"Why are you asking me all these questions?"

Meg took control of the conversation then, explaining about the missing cameos and how upset Eva's daughters were.

"I didn't know they were worth anything," Gladys said, her expression softer now. "I have my jeweler coming in soon to re-appraise my diamonds, and Eva asked me to show him her cameos. She gave me a big case of them, to get them appraised." A smile crept over her face. "So they're really valuable?"

"Apparently so," Meg said.

"I thought they were junk. I never would have kept them otherwise."

"Of course, you wouldn't have," Sadie and Beulah murmured, almost in unison.

"Let's just go get them, you and I." Meg positioned herself behind Gladys' wheelchair and flipped back the wheel locks. "We'll bring them right in to Mr. Immerfall."

This will secure my job forever!

"Thanks, ladies," she said as she backed Gladys away from the table. "Case closed, thanks to you!"

Meg was surprised to see Sandra's BMW waiting in her driveway that evening and was even more surprised to find her friend sitting in the driver's seat, weeping.

She hustled Sandra into the kitchen, let Touchdown outside, and pulled a bottle of brandy and two Donald Duck juice glasses out of the cupboard.

"Here," she said grimly, filling Sandra's glass to the top of Donald's tail. "Drink this."

Sandra did, in one quick swallow. She looked like an aging ten-year-old, her face makeup-free and blotchy, her eyes red and swollen.

"Now tell me."

Sandra fished a wad of tissues out of her purse and blew her nose before looking at Meg.

"She's gone," she said, puddling up again. "My mother's gone."

Meg was shocked. There hadn't been anything wrong with Sandra's mom beyond the nicely mending hip and osteoporosis, according to her doctor. Nothing. She put her arms around her friend and let her sob.

Finally, after Touchdown had interrupted them by howling to be let back in, Meg asked Sandra what had happened.

"I dunno. They don't either. They just went into her room to get her for lunch and found her 'unresponsive.' I guess that's the latest euphemism for 'dead.'"

Meg said all the right things—nursing-home duty was making her an expert at comforting the bereaved—and promised to help Sandra at the funeral home the next morning.

"I feel so guilty," Sandra said, pulling her purse onto her lap. "I could have taken her home. I could have paid for a better place."

"No, you couldn't have," Meg said, gently but firmly. "Your savings would have been wiped out in a year if you'd done that, and you couldn't have left her alone at home all day."

Sandra nodded, her eyes fixed on Touchdown. He gazed back at her sadly, slowly wagging the very tip of his tail.

"You did the best that you could do," Meg added. "That's all anyone could expect."

"I suppose so."

"Why don't you stay here tonight? I'll fix us something to eat."

"No, but thanks. Think I'll go home and draft her obituary." She dried her eyes and rose slowly. "I'll see you at nine, okay?"

Meg walked Sandra to her car, surprised to find that it was still light out. It was a gorgeous spring evening, a reminder of the rebirth that was taking place everywhere you looked.

She watched Sandra drive off, wondering if she should have insisted on taking her home.

"Shoulda coulda woulda." She tossed a cup of kibble into Touchdown's bowl. He dug in, not waiting for Sneak to be served. "That's the problem with us humans, Touch old boy. We have to make all these choices along the way, and it seems like we're always making the wrong ones."

That night, Meg dreamt about Gil for the first time since his death.

He was in full health and they were at the Old Brown Otter in Muskego, their favorite place for nibbling at fish fries and downing enough beer to get a good Friday night buzz on, back in the days before getting stopped for drunk driving had become a serious hazard to one's finances and future.

They were sitting at the bar, he in a gray T-shirt and worn jeans, she in a homemade red-and-white sundress, the only thing from her sewing days that she'd ever worn out in public. She was looking at him and at herself in the mirror behind the bar. Her hair was long—so that meant they hadn't been dating for more than a couple months, because she'd chopped it off early on as a test of his love for her. They were smiling, beaming, clicking their glasses together, stealing kisses now and then.

Happy happy couple.

He excused himself and headed for the bathroom while the bartender poured them two more tap beers. Bud, perhaps? Clydesdales crossed her mind.

She finished her beer—it had gone down quickly, or maybe Gil had been gone an awfully long time. She didn't know which but she started feeling nervous and then she noticed the bartender looking at her. He was at the end of the bar talking with a uniformed nurse and pointing at Meg. He was a sad-faced man to begin with and he looked like he was about to burst into tears.

She panicked then, running outside. Why outside? She didn't know, but she had to get away from this place before they caught her.

They who?

She didn't know that either, but she ran as fast as she could down the long gravel driveway. Her speed was incredible, but she couldn't reach the main road. The woods were getting thicker and the driveway narrower until it was nothing more than a footpath, and then suddenly she saw The Hickories in the distance. She ran faster and suddenly found herself in Sadie's room, weeping, telling Sadie that they'd taken Gil away from her.

"Who, dear, who took Gil away from you?" Sadie was asking, one frail arm around Meg's shoulders. They were sitting on the couch, and Sadie's wheelchair was nowhere in sight.

"I don't know," Meg sobbed. "I don't know who took him away!"

"I do," Sadie said. "But I can't tell you because you won't believe me."

Meg woke up then, her face buried in a wet pillow. When the tears cleared enough that she could see by the faint glow of the night light, she found Sneak sitting inches away from her face, watching over her in her distress.

CHAPTER FIFTY-EIGHT

**Sadie Sparrow
Sunday, June 17**

On the surface, this year's celebration of Sadie's birthday—her eighty-seventh—was just like all the others since Ed died: a week late and executed with breathtaking efficiency by people with more important things to do. Dana had descended upon the North Sitting Room at precisely two o'clock, husband Bill and daughters Hannah and Amanda in tow, each setting down bags of food and gifts before, in turn, giving the waiting Sadie Sparrow a peck on the cheek and a squeeze of the shoulders.

They unloaded cold cuts, cheeses, sourdough bread, potato salad, coleslaw, chips, an array of condiments, plus stout paper plates and everyday silverware. ("We didn't have time to polish your silver," Dana explained, launching into a litany of the week's family activities.) There were bottles of soda and beer and a thermos of coffee—"decaf, just for you, Mom"—and a store-bought sheet cake thick with buttercream frosting.

There were also complaints about the blistering heat, so unusual for early summer. And there was the prayer that Sadie and Ed had taught Dana when she was just three, delivered now without even a whiff of reverence: "Come Lord Jesus, be our guest, let this food to us be blessed. Amen."

For Sadie, it was nearly all déjà vu. Besides the location, the only difference this year was in her own reaction: shockingly, her feelings were not hurt, not one bit. All she felt was sorrow for her family, caught up in lives that would never satisfy, and fear that unless their hearts changed, they were headed for a Christ-less eternity. She would not let herself even think about what that would mean for them.

But she probed her feelings as they built their sandwiches and the kids chattered on about their latest highly organized adventures. It was a little like poking at a once-sore tooth and finding, to her utter amazement, that it had healed completely. Conclusions were difficult to reach—she had to respond appropriately to her grandchildren now and then, after all—but she had the feeling it had come down to this: the only One who really mattered, the only One who really loved her and would be faithful to the end, was God Himself. That was what her life was all about now, and it was a wonderful place to be.

"Grandma? Helloooooooo!" It was math whiz Amanda, apparently miffed that she was being ignored. "Have you been listening to me at all?"

"Oh, I'm sorry, dear." Sadie shook her head almost imperceptibly to send her thoughts back into the corner for the time being. "I was just thinking."

"Is something wrong, Grandma?" Future M.D. Hannah this time, her beautiful face expressing serious concern. "Are you feeling sick?"

"No, no, just reflecting on some things. Everything's wonderful."

"Well, I'm glad to hear *that*," Dana said, peering at her mother suspiciously. "More coleslaw?"

And then it was bedtime again, with Sadie back in her room, seated at the desk-turned-vanity and applying moisturizer to her freshly washed face. Sometimes it felt like she was always sitting here, always slathering on the moisturizer, always getting ready for bed. A trick of time accelerating with the years, she supposed. It was usually a good thing, she decided, since she could face just about any unpleasantness with good humor; it would be over before she knew it, after all.

Of course, it also meant that any happiness would be equally fleeting, but it was a fair trade-off. There were no longer many things in her life that made her terribly happy, in the conventional sense of the word. And those that she could think of—meeting with Meg and with Jamie, for instance—were frequently on her calendar.

She inspected her face in the magnifying mirror. The moisturizer didn't do much to fluff out the wrinkles anymore, but that was okay with her, too. Every line brought her a step closer to Home.

"Real 'women's lib,'" she told her reflection, "is not caring how you look, because there's absolutely nothing worth having that good looks can buy you."

My goodness, where did that come from? How profound!

She grinned at herself. She'd have to try to remember this bit of wisdom for her granddaughters, both of them way too pretty for their own good.

Sadie spent a lot of time that week thinking over all the strange events that had been taking place at The Hickories—not only the cameos, but also Beulah's broken legs, Eva's pain pills, and some other things on the tip of her mind. Try as she might, she couldn't quite remember the rest. But she knew that she'd made herself a list at some point, if she could only remember where she'd put it.

My mind is really going. Must be the stroke. But wait— did I really have a stroke? When was that?

Everything was getting so muddled. And these days it seemed to take a Herculean effort to coax her brain back to the subject at hand.

There was a connection among these events, she was sure. Well, in truth she wasn't sure, but she thought there might be. Nurse Julia, to be specific. But *how* this nasty young woman was connected, she hadn't the faintest idea.

Sadie had been pondering these things intermittently since Eva's death. But now that they had cracked the case of the missing cameos, the other mysteries were on her mind almost constantly.

Stymied, she consulted Beulah once again. But they made no progress.

"What do you think, Beulah? Should we take our suspicions to Meg?"

"I don't see that we have any choice; we're getting nowhere fast, as Bunny would say."

"Wait!" Sadie brushed her forehead with the heel of her hand. "Speaking of Bunny, why not ask her? Or wait, maybe we already discussed this?"

Beulah thought on that for a bit.

"It does seem that we did," she said finally, "but I can't remember what we decided, can you? No? Well, I can ask her, but there's a little problem, Sadie. I love her to pieces, and she's so good to me. But she thinks I'm a conspiracy theorist, if you must know. She never really believed there was anything mysterious about my broken legs. Just clumsiness."

Sadie was shocked; that wasn't the impression Beulah had given her. "I thought you said she'd call the CIA if you told her about—oh, whatever it was that was wrong."

"Wasn't it about the pill that nurse dropped? And possibly the FBI?"

"Oh, I remember," Sadie said, "kind of." She really had only the vaguest memory of something about a dropped pill, but it was a little embarrassing to keep acknowledging such forgetfulness.

"Well," said Beulah, "I guess I meant that if she believed that there was something wrong, she would've called the FBI in. I may not have mentioned the part about her skepticism over these things. She says I have a suspicious nature."

"Oh." Sadie felt a little deflated by this news. "Is she right? Are we crazy?"

"I haven't the faintest idea. Let's ask Meg."

"I'm so happy that you are my friend, Beulah. You're the only one who knows how stupid I'm getting and doesn't hold it against me."

"That's only because my mind is going, too, Sadie dear. But someday—oh, someday, we'll be regular Einsteins."

On Thursday, Sadie and Beulah invited Meg to meet them in Beulah's room after lunch. She did, of course—Meg was such a darling about this sort of thing, they agreed—and they laid out their case that something was seriously wrong here.

"So let me get this straight," said Meg, who'd taken careful notes on a steno pad. "There's the missing pill, and Eva's trouble getting pain medication from Julia. And your broken legs, Beulah, and the whole 'thickened liquids' thing, which may or may not be a scam, and may or may not have been a factor in Eva's death." She glanced at her notes. "Oh, and Julia being in your room, Beulah, with the door closed—or almost closed. Does that about sum it up?"

Sadie and Beulah exchanged glances.

"Well, when you put it like that," said Beulah, "I guess it sounds pretty weak, doesn't it?"

Meg ran a hand through her cropped hair. "I'm just not sure, girls. I don't know what to think, or what to do about it. Guess I'll have to talk to Lucy—although somehow I really dread having to do that."

Sadie and Beulah nodded wisely.

"I'll keep you posted." Meg gave each of them a peck on the cheek before leaving them to their speculations.

"Well," Beulah said, dabbing at her nose with her best lace-trimmed hankie, "I'm feeling a little foolish now. It all sounds sort of fuzzy, don't you think?"

Sadie nodded; "fuzzy" was the perfect word for how so much of the world felt to her these days.

"In fact," Beulah added, thoughtfully refolding her hankie, "I think maybe we should scratch thickened liquids off our list. Don't get me wrong, Sadie, there *are* conspiracies out there. But this one would have to be so big and look who'd have to be involved. Not just these corporations, but even our wonderful whatchamacallits— you know, the ones who help people talk again."

"Therapists?"

"Yes, therapists—good job, Sadie girl! Not to mention the dieticians and aides and just about everyone else here. I can't quite believe it. Of course, they wouldn't all have to be *in* on it, but still, it seems too fantastic."

Sadie was only too happy to strike it off their list. At this point, she would have been happy to throw the whole lot out; she now spent more time trying to recall their suspicions than she did puzzling out the solutions.

"So," Beulah said, "we'll let Meg pursue it, but you and I will forget the thickened liquids. The other things, however—I'd say that the jury is still out on them, don't you agree?"

"Yes, I do," Sadie said as brightly as she could. Was it a lie when you were feeling too befuddled to respond truthfully? She sent up a quick request for forgiveness, just in case.

"But meanwhile," Beulah continued, "let's not fret over any of it, okay? I keep forgetting that God is in control of all these things. Anyway, none of it matters in light of eternity; I'll bet Eva would give us a big fat 'amen' to that!"

"That's the wisest thing you've said all day, Beulah dear. Let's 'let go and let God,' shall we?"

"It's a deal!"

CHAPTER FIFTY-NINE

Elise Chapelle
Tuesday, June 19

Elise wasn't sure whether to be irritated or amused by Papi's insistence that they leave for O'Hare Airport by nine that morning. But it was an improvement over his alternate plan of heading down on Monday afternoon and staying overnight.

"Honestly, Papi," she'd told him more than once, "it will only take a couple of hours to get there, and Helene's flight isn't scheduled to arrive until three forty-five. We could leave at noon, stop for lunch on the way, and still be there in plenty of time."

But Papi wouldn't hear of it. So it wasn't much of a surprise, when she pulled his old green Explorer into The Hickories' parking structure at eight forty-five that morning, to find him waiting for her in front of the elevator. With him were two aides whom he had apparently recruited to help get him settled in the vehicle and load his wheelchair into the back.

"My word," she muttered as she pulled up to them. "You've never looked that excited to see *me*, Papi."

He was indeed grinning like a madman, showing off his perfect dentures and glancing back anxiously over each shoulder to make sure that Team Charles was ready to spring into action.

Okay, that was nasty, Elise!

She said a quick prayer of repentance and forced herself into a delighted smile before exiting the SUV.

"Bonjour, Papi!" She swept in to give him a hug and a kiss on the cheek. "Are you ready? Excited?"

"Yes, yes," he said, directing his aides for the ten-foot ride to the passenger door. They were experts; within moments he was securely seated and buckled up and glancing at his watch while they collapsed his chair and loaded it in the back of the Explorer.

"You should be able to handle it alone," said the shorter one to Elise. "It's one of those light chairs. Then just steady him with the transfer belt—you can leave it on him—and you'll be fine."

"Got it." Elise thanked them and jumped into the driver's seat. "All set for the Chapelle's Big Adventure, Papi?"

He nodded like a bobble-head doll. After weeks of planning and waiting, waiting and planning, the moment of departure was finally here, and he wasn't handling it well. Elise wondered if a Dramamine might not have been in order.

Well, too late now. She drove carefully up the gravel driveway and turned right onto Larkspur before trying to engage him in conversation once again.

"You look nervous, Papi. Are you?"

"No." He was keeping his eyes glued to the road and his hands firmly clamped on his knees.

"That's good."

She slipped the first CD of a fifty-hymn collection into the player and turned the volume up, feeling her spirit relax to an extraordinarily beautiful rendition of "Amazing Grace." They barely spoke until the powerful finish of "How Great Thou Art"; they were well into Illinois at that point, just a half hour from O'Hare.

"Well, Papi," Elise said finally, "we're almost there and it's only ten thirty. How 'bout we stop for an early lunch? There are a bunch of restaurants around Half Day Road."

"Yes, good idea." He'd relaxed a bit once they crossed the Wisconsin/Illinois border, apparently relieved that they'd left early enough after all. "I missed my breakfast."

"Really? Exactly how long were you sitting there waiting for me?"

"Not long," he said dismissively. "Eggs would be good."

They ate at a sweet little café in a newer strip mall, savoring cheese omelets and warm cinnamon buns and a rich Costa Rican coffee.

"You know, Papi," Elise said, when the dishes had been removed and their cups refilled, "I owe you an apology. I've been a shrew about this whole thing, and it's all because I'm jealous."

"Jealous!"

"Yes." She looked him straight in the eye. "You've been so overjoyed at the prospect of seeing Helene again that I seem to have become nothing more than a chauffeur to you."

He reached for her hand. "Elise—"

"No, no, I'm fine now, really. I was just acting like the prodigal son's older brother, jealous about the fuss you were making over her, when she'd broken all our hearts by abandoning us."

Papi considered her words silently, staring at his coffee as if consulting it for wisdom.

"And when you had stayed here all these years," he said at last, "taking care of Mamie and me. How could I have been so blind to it?"

"I was being selfish. If I love you—and oh, I *do* love you, Papi!—then I should be rejoicing over your happiness. And hoping and praying that Helene will be on this flight."

Papi apologized tearfully and at length, and she apologized in turn for having caused them this unnecessary distress, and they had a soul-satisfying discussion about Luke 15's parable of the prodigal son and its application to their situation. So engrossed were they with each other that they didn't notice the café filling up with patrons, and then slowly emptying again, until the waitress interrupted them.

"We close at two," she said, pushing the check she'd left some time ago towards Elise. "Will there be anything else?"

"Oh, my goodness! Papi, it's one forty-five!"

"No worries, as my aides say. We've got plenty of time."

Elise and Papi arrived in the waiting area in O'Hare's international terminal a full hour before the flight was due. She positioned his wheelchair perpendicular to her seat, a standard-issue waiting room chair in fake black leather and chrome, more comfortable than it looked. They soon shifted back into a more personal take on the situation.

"I honestly hoped she would not get on this plane," Elise confessed. "I prayed for that, Papi, as much as it shames me to say so."

"But she bought the ticket. We know she bought it."

"But she could have sold it. She could have turned it back in and taken the money. She could have—oh, I don't know, what do I know about how people do these things?"

"I suppose anything is possible," he said, glancing at his watch. "But we'll know one way or the other very shortly."

"Will you be broken-hearted if she doesn't show?"

Papi gazed at the ceiling and said nothing for a few moments. Elise thought he'd never looked so handsome, with his high forehead crowned in snowy white.

"Yes," he said finally, "I admit it will hurt if Helene doesn't get off that plane, if this was all just a way to get money. It will hurt a great deal, but I will recover." He took her hand again. "After all, I have the most wonderful granddaughter a man could ever want. How could I ask for anything more?"

It wasn't until the next morning, when Papi was in physical therapy and Meg was alone in the Activities office, that Elise was able to talk with anyone about the sad denouement of the Chapelle's Big Adventure.

"So," Elise said, flopping down on Lucy's office chair as Meg turned from her computer, "Helene did not show. We sat in the waiting room for almost two hours after the plane landed, figuring—hoping—that she was just stuck in Customs. But she never showed up."

Meg shook her head, looking almost as sad as Elise felt. "So what did you do?"

"Well, of course I tried to find out what happened. You know, to get them to check the passenger list, and tell me if anyone had been sitting in Helene's seat—if she'd even reserved a seat. We really didn't know anything about it except that the ticket charge had come through on Papi's credit card bill, and he paid for it."

"What did they say?"

"She. It was an Air France flight, and the clerk was a snotty French woman who wouldn't tell us a thing. Papi even spoke to her in French and showed her his credit card bill—"

"That was smart of him to bring it along."

"For all the good it did us." Elise dabbed at her nose with a tissue; she was dangerously close to tears. "She refused to tell us anything—gave me a card and said we could contact their corporate office if we wanted any more information."

"Any *more* information? Good grief."

"I know," Elise said, smiling wryly. "Like she'd already told us way too much."

"So are you okay?"

Elise sighed. "Oh, I suppose, other than being furious with Helene and Air France."

And mostly with myself for wishing this heartache on Papi.

"And Papi?"

Elise yawned. She hadn't slept much, and numbing fatigue was finally kicking in.

"He's taking it pretty well. Surprising, isn't it?"

"I'll say," Meg said. "Maybe he's more worried about you; Helene is *your* mother, after all."

"I think that's exactly right. He kept telling me to calm down. And then he said, 'I will write to Helene, and maybe we will find out what happened, and maybe we will not. It hardly matters.'"

"But you said the airfare was almost six grand," Meg pointed out.

"Try eight grand. But he said, 'It's only money, and it was a good lesson for me—'"

"Pretty expensive lesson."

"Exactly!" Elise rolled her eyes. "He said that the consolation prize was a wonderful time with me, that it was priceless, and he'll never forget it." She laughed. "Like a day with me could be worth $8,000."

"You bet it is," Meg said, leaning over to hug her. "You're a peach and Papi isn't the only one who knows it."

Elise rose to leave. "Thanks for listening, Meg. You know, meeting you has been one of the nicest things to happen to me in a long time."

"You aren't forgetting about Jamie, are you?"

Elise shook her head. "No, not forgetting about him. But I didn't want to talk about it over the phone, and I won't see him until Friday." She dropped her gaze to inspect her fingernails. "Get this: I invited him over for dinner with Helene."

"He'd probably rather be alone with you anyway."

"I suppose," she said, lingering in the doorway. "To be honest, I'm kind of dreading telling him about this."

"But why?"

"Well, you know, what kind of a girl must you be if your mother hates you enough to pull something like this on you?"

"Oh, come on, Elise, she doesn't *hate* you."

Elise thought about that for a moment. "You're right, it's not hate. My mother is totally and utterly indifferent to me. What could be worse than that?"

CHAPTER SIXTY

Meg Vogel
Friday, June 29

Meg met Sandra at Harper's on the Lake the last Friday in June. It had been a month since Frances Slocum's death, and Meg was relieved to see her friend looking much better than she had in the aftermath of the funeral. She'd even put a little weight on her teeny frame.

She started to say as much, but Sandra raised a hand to silence her. "Not yet," she said. "I'll let you know when I'm ready to go there."

"Okay," Meg said, nodding sympathetically. "So let's see. How about this: I had the weirdest conversation with my boss the other day."

"Lucy? You hardly ever mention her."

"Honestly, I don't see her all that often. She's always off at this conference or that meeting, it seems. I think she might be looking for another job. One day she'll be the picture of comfort in jeans and sweatshirt and the next she's wearing her best suit."

"What if she gets another job? Would you want hers?"

Meg shrugged. "I think I'm doing a lot of it already, to be honest. But anyway, she was in this week, and I sat her down to tell her what Sadie and her sidekick Beulah have told me about these odd little events that may or may not be connected."

Meg told Sandra about each of the items on the old girls' list of suspicions—the dropped pill, Eva's being denied pain meds, Beulah's broken legs, the nearly-closed-door mystery, and those creepy beverage thickeners. "Odd, don't you think?"

Sandra twisted her mouth, apparently not quite getting it. "Well, maybe, or maybe not. What is it exactly that they suspect?"

"They don't know what to think. And neither do I. It could all be nothing, or it could be something."

"Can't you research at least some of it, Meg? You were always investigating issues online when you were writing copy; you know how to sniff these things out."

Meg frowned. "I *have* been looking into at least the thickened liquids part of it for a while now. I just can't imagine how awful it must be to never again have a drink of plain old water."

"I agree," Sandra said, grimacing. "Terrifying."

"So I've researched it using the standard medical search engines, and I haven't found anything concrete. They all seem to start with the assumption that a lot of this pneumonia is caused by the elderly inhaling their beverages—they call it 'aspiration pneumonia.' And I haven't seen a thing to suggest that there's anything wrong with either that premise or with thickened liquids as a solution."

The subject was making her thirsty. She polished off her beer.

"Drink up while you can, girl," Sandra said, shaking her head. "Hey, there's another pact you and I should make—if either one of us ever gets put on this stuff, the other one smuggles in gallons of water."

"And alcohol," Meg said. "But here's the thing. When I just do a plain old Google search, I do find a little dissension in the ranks. There's one therapist, for instance, who says that the jury's still out on this issue, that thickeners may not help, that they definitely impinge on quality of life, and, on top of it all, that they're pretty expensive. But that's one person saying, 'hold on, they may not be helpful,' versus a whole medical community that sees thickeners as life-saving tools."

"Seems to me that the bottom line is all these old people who can't even have a glass of water. It's outrageous!"

"But maybe that's the price they have to pay to avoid pneumonia." Meg caught their waitress's eye and pointed to her glass. "Well, I'm no expert. Besides which, even if I were, what could I do about it? It's the children of the residents who have the power, or the medical powers-of-attorney. And get this: I've heard stories about kids who question their parents' doctors—and end up getting fired by the doctors! There was one family who went through every physician in the facility."

"Amazing," Sandra said. "Although after what I went through with my mom, I shouldn't be surprised. I sometimes wonder—" She sighed heavily. "Well, I guess we've been through all of that, haven't we? So what happened with this family?"

"The mother died the day after the last doctor dumped them, so it was no longer an issue." Meg smiled sadly. "And I have no idea who was in the wrong in that case. For all I know, the mom was dying, and the kids just refused to accept it."

"Mmmm, I can understand that. You don't want your loved one to die so you make a big fuss, thinking that surely there's *something* the doctor can do."

"Right," Meg agreed, reaching for a breadstick. "So anyway, I don't see how I'll ever be able to come to a conclusion about what Sadie and Beulah suspect. It's really starting to bug me, in fact. You know, you read mysteries, and they're all nicely resolved at the end, with all the loose ends tied up—"

"Well, that's not exactly true anymore," Sandra said. "More and more, I'm running into books that don't answer the questions they raise. It's kind of unsettling."

"Or maybe more true to life. Maybe we wind up without any answers, in the end. How creepy would that be?"

Their fish fries arrived, and they dug in, each lost in her own thoughts.

"Stuffed," Sandra said finally, leaning back and rubbing her perennially flat-as-a-flounder tummy. "So to back up a bit, what did Lucy say about all of this?"

"Oh, that's right." Meg leaned forward and tucked her chin in her hand. "She said something like, 'Why do you listen to these old crazies?' Can you believe it? And here I thought that she really cared about the residents."

"Wow—not exactly what you expected, huh?"

"Not at all. And in fact, she finished our conversation by telling me—ordering me!—not to talk with them about this anymore. 'Don't encourage them,' was how she put it."

They looked at each other, shaking their heads.

"So tell me what you think of this," Meg continued, tracing a finger along the border of her placemat, slightly embarrassed by her train of thought. "I almost have the feeling that Mr. Immerfall—he's the Administrator—that he's gotten to Lucy somehow, threatening her job, maybe. At first, I was able to talk to her about anything, but in the last couple months, she's turned into such a company hack." Another frown. "If that's true, I wouldn't mind so much if she'd just *say* it: 'Hey, look, we're going to lose our jobs unless we put a lid on it.' You know? But instead she suddenly starts insulting my intelligence. Not to mention Sadie's and Beulah's."

"I wouldn't put anything past anyone," Sandra said. "I *do* think it's all pretty odd."

"I guess there's nothing to be done about it unless something more insidious happens. Like the bed rail thing—the State is so paranoid about the *appearance* of restraint that residents can't have bed rails until they've fallen out of bed and hurt themselves."

"Let's make another pact," Sandra said, "to never get old."

"That's your best idea yet."

CHAPTER SIXTY-ONE

Sadie Sparrow
Wednesday, July 11

By July it was warm enough to make afternoons in the garden a real treat for The Hickories' old folk. A straw-hatted Sadie was among them almost every day. She would begin by sitting near the sweetly scented, apricot-washed English rose bushes or, this week, next to the oriental lilies; the fat buds were opening in such force that their fragrance was sometimes almost overpowering, even for her failing sense of smell.

By the end of her first hour, the sun had normally warmed her aching bones so that she would shrug herself out from under the blanket her aides insisted on wrapping her in before taking her outside.

Then, when she became a little bit too warm, she'd retreat along the concrete path to the shade offered by a stand of young hawthorns, eventually cooling off enough to snuggle back into her blanket before returning to the sun.

She especially enjoyed playing the part of a sunbather, closing her eyes, tilting her face back to welcome the warmth, remembering happier times—summer afternoons on the farm, chores all finished, long lazy afternoons spent with her silly mutt, Rebel, leaping into the pond with him, exploring the woods, and then later, meeting up with the Mueller girls to sing and chatter and forget the shyness that plagued her throughout the school year.

Or had they really been happier times? Maybe not. Maybe just more naïve. She hadn't yet learned to worry about the future, hadn't known the heartache that awaited her decades down the road, the grief of losing Ed, the sorrow of watching her friends die, one by one, and the horror of realizing that she was nothing more than an irritant in her daughter's life.

Of course, she hadn't known her Savior then. This was much better, really, knowing beyond any doubt that she was heaven-bound, that she would one day close her eyes a final time on this earth and open them once again to see— amazing thought—Jesus in all His glory!

She was back in her room by three that afternoon, singing along with her favorite hymn CD. Consisting exclusively of songs about, or referring to, heaven and eternity and featuring singers from Jim Nabors to church choirs, it had been a homemade birthday gift from Jamie.

"Heaven's morning breaks, and earth's vain shadows flee," she sang, every trace of sun-induced sleepiness gone, "in life, in death, O Lord, abide with me!"

She was in the midst of the last chorus of "The Old Rugged Cross" when a tenor boomed behind her: "I will cling to the old rugged cross, and exchange it someday for a crown."

It was Jamie, she knew even before she could wheel her chair around. Dear Jamie!

They sang song after song together, joyfully and sometimes tearfully—"Be Still My Soul," "Jesus Paid It All," "How Great Thou Art," and a half-dozen others, finishing with a rousing rendition of "Shall We Gather at the River," with Tennessee Ernie Ford.

"It's a date!" Sadie crowed. "What fun, Jamie. Thank you for singing with me, and for the CD, and for everything."

They talked then about what heaven would be like, according to scripture, and the likelihood that she'd be heading there first, and how much they would miss each other until they met again, one happy day.

"I'll miss you more," he assured her. "If you get there first, I think you'll be a little too busy with heavenly joy to give me a thought."

"Oh, I do hope so, Jamie," she laughed. "I hope 'earth's vain shadows' really will flee."

"I think you can count on that. What I want to know is what we'll look like. The apostle Paul wrote about 'spiritual bodies.' What in the world does that mean?"

"And don't forget the part about our bodies being like seeds that have to die, so that the plant inside can grow!" Sadie's eyebrows were arched over wide eyes. "That would seem to mean that we won't look anything like we do now, wouldn't it?"

Jamie nodded. "It sure would! And yet I'm certain that we'll know each other."

"I can't wait to see you there."

"Me neither, Sadie girl. Me neither."

On Friday, Sadie was too weak to get up and out of bed. She dozed all morning, ate some lunch (it was a favorite, cream of mushroom soup), and fell asleep again.

"What's wrong with you, Sadie?" The voice cut through a dream of Ed and Dana, an adoring little girl once again. "Sadie, wake up!"

She opened her eyes with some difficulty to see Meg standing there, looking very cross.

"I'm just tired," Sadie said. "Just sleeping in today."

Meg dragged a chair to the side of the bed and sat down.

"Oh, I've missed our interview," Sadie said sadly. "I so love talking with you, my dear."

"No, we're done with the interviews." Meg's face softened. "Don't you remember, I gave you a copy of your finished book?"

"Oh, of course I remember." It was a fib, since Meg's words were ringing only the faintest bell in Sadie's memory. Maybe if she sat up a bit. She struggled to push herself up, fumbled for the bed control and finally succeeded in raising the head to a forty-five-degree angle.

"There," she said as brightly as she could, straightening her white cotton gown and smoothing her hair back from her face. "I'm all set."

What was it we were going to talk about? A mystery of some kind?

"You look pale," Meg said. "Are you sure you're okay?"

"Oh, well, I'm fine for the moment, anyway. Long-term, probably not, but then—"

"What do you mean?" Meg narrowed her eyes again. Definitely cross.

"It's really nothing." But seeing that Meg had no intention of moving on to the next subject, Sadie added, "It's just heart failure. Very common, they say; I imagine that half the people here have it."

"You aren't dying, are you?"

Was there an edge of panic in Meg's voice? Sadie couldn't be sure, but it crossed her mind that just once she'd like Dana to react to her mother's trials with something other than indifference.

"We're all dying, you know," Sadie said, yawning. "It's nothing to worry about. So are my friends working on our puzzle today?"

They chatted for a while about this and that, but it was not as lighthearted a visit as all their others had been. Meg was out of sorts and at times almost surly.

"Are you angry with me?" Sadie asked finally. "I don't think I've ever heard you say a cross word before."

Meg drifted to the windows. The sun was still lighting up the garden, and Sadie imagined her wishing she could be outside on such an afternoon.

"If you must know," Meg said, without turning around, "I *am* upset with you. I've had enough loss in the last year to last me a lifetime, and I honestly don't want to lose you."

Sadie's heart fluttered. It was time, then. This was the opportunity she'd been praying for.

"Come here and sit down again, Meg. We need to talk."

And so Meg did. Sadie dove right in. "I know you don't want to do it, but we really need to talk about ultimate truth." She paused to take a few deep breaths before continuing. "About where you'll spend eternity, and how you can be sure that will be heaven, with Gil and with me and, I hope, your parents—"

At this point Meg jumped to her feet in what looked to Sadie like a white rage.

"Don't tell me about truth," she hissed. "You Christians can't even agree on what that truth is. I hear some of you saying that you have to spend time in purgatory to get to heaven and others saying that everyone goes there and still others that only the elect do and if you're not chosen, that's tough. And of course, it's the self-appointed elect who say this with the greatest humility. What a bunch of—of absolute hogwash!"

Sadie's head was spinning. So much misinformation in one little soliloquy, and she didn't have the energy to address a fraction of it. "You could look into it," she started, her voice barely a whisper.

"I've talked with people who looked into it," Meg said, her eyes wet now. "I've been with people earnestly asking the proponents of these views—all these different Christian views, supposedly—I've heard them being asked various questions about this God of theirs. And all I've heard is 'I don't know' or 'we're not told' or 'that's one of God's little mysteries.' Come on, people, get your story straight!"

Sadie summoned up all her strength; this was too important to ignore.

"That's not truth," she said, "it's ignorance. God has told us all we need to know." *Breathe, old girl, breathe.* "When you hear 'I don't know,' it's a sign that—well, that you've asked the wrong person."

"And who's the right person, Sadie? You?"

Sadie smiled ruefully. "No, dear. But I think I have the answers to the big questions. So go ahead, ask away."

Meg glared at her.

"No thanks, Sadie." She made a show of checking her watch. "I really don't have time right now. Maybe another day."

By Monday morning, after an entire weekend of resting, Sadie had found her second wind. She was even able to make it down to the dining room for breakfast, and to pay Beulah a visit on her way home.

"Sadie, you're on your feet again!" Beulah cried with great delight. "So to speak, that is."

Sadie laughed as she rolled herself into the room.

"I've been praying for you, my friend," Beulah said, waving a hand towards her sitting area. "Come on, let's have a nice long talk."

And talk they did, about everything from Beulah's progress on the walking front—"The therapists here are really miracle workers," she insisted—to Sadie's flagging energy and growing weakness. They covered the food and the laundry service (both excellent), the movie selection of late (a little too modern for their taste), the aides serving the North Wing of The Hickories (mostly very good), and the changing garden scene (unsurpassed).

Sadie even presented Beulah with a new theory about why Julia had been in her room with the door closed, ostensibly searching for her good pen. "Maybe she was simply looking behind the door to see if she'd dropped it there the last time she'd been in to give you your medicine. They always close the door when they come in to pill us, you know, I suppose to give us privacy."

Beulah looked confused.

"Picture it," Sadie prompted. "She's retracing her steps, looking for the pen. She unlocks your door, walks in, and the first thing she does is look behind the door. The pen's not there, so she goes into your room to look further. Whereupon you arrive and find her there with the door almost closed."

They stared at each other for a while and finally nodded in unison.

"It could be," said Beulah. "It really could be that simple."

"Not that it changes the other things," Sadie said, hoping she wouldn't be required to list them right now. "But at least maybe this one was innocent."

They sat in companionable silence for a while, letting their minds drift.

Finally, Sadie reached out and took her friend's hands in her own.

"Beulah, my dear, I just wanted to say that you have become my dearest friend in these last few months, and I'm so grateful for you." She swallowed hard; somehow, she hadn't imagined this as being a difficult monologue. "Will you please remember that?"

Beulah's eyes were wide with surprise.

"Sadie Sparrow, are you trying to tell me something? Are you going on ahead?"

"I think so," Sadie said, smiling tenderly at her friend. "I think it will be soon. I feel it in my bones, as my mother used to say."

Beulah squeezed her hands. "Well, that's just fine, Sadie. I will miss you, but it will only be for a little while."

"That's right, Beulah. Just a short time, in light of eternity."

They smiled at each other, not attempting to hide the tears in their eyes.

"Sadie," Beulah said finally, "once you've had a chance to see Ed and your folks and everyone, would you do me a favor? Find my Norbert and tell him that I'll be with him just as soon as I can. And tell him that Bunny's wonderful. Will you do that for me?"

CHAPTER SIXTY-TWO

Elise Chapelle
Saturday, July 14

H*elene,*
It is now almost four weeks since you stood us up at the airport. Almost four weeks since you made it clear that you are not only heartless, but also a thief.

I don't know how you worked it out, whether you sold your ticket to someone else or wrangled Papi's money out of Air France or just wasted the ticket and figured out some other way to get your hands on some money. Papi won't let me pursue the issue; he has been hurt enough, and he simply does not want to know what you have done.

I guess I should add, if you have done anything; I suspect he is holding out hope that you were hit by a bus on your way to the airport. Sadly, I would be happy to hear that myself. Imagine that—your being so evil that your daughter would be happy to hear of your death.

Elise paused in her writing. The sentiment was true enough, but it did not exactly reflect well on the Savior. She struck out the last paragraph with a permanent marker and continued writing on a fresh page:

I am writing today to tell you not to contact us again unless it's to tell us that some disaster prevented you from boarding that flight. As far as I'm concerned, you are dead to us.

Elise

No more loving sign-offs, no more "your daughter" reminders, no more tucking the letter away in a drawer, never to be sent. She was through with it all. She prayed that Papi would soon be, too.

Suddenly, Jesus' Sermon on the Mount teaching about forgiveness popped into Elise's head: "But if ye forgive not men their trespasses, neither will your Father forgive your trespasses."

She crumpled both pages and tossed them on the floor with the three previous versions she'd scuttled.

"You've already forgiven me of so much, Lord," she said. "How can I refuse to forgive my own mother?"

She tucked her pen and stationery into the top drawer of the desk that had made little Elise feel closer to absent Helene. She would write this letter another time—maybe tomorrow, after she'd had a chance to meditate on forgiveness.

Elise found Meg sitting at the Great Room fireplace that afternoon.

"Outstanding movie today," Meg said as Elise slipped into an overstuffed chair. "*Best Years of Our Lives.* Have you ever seen it?"

Elise shook her head.

"Dana Andrews is adorable in it," Meg said. "Of course, Dana Andrews was always adorable. One of my favorite actors."

Elise looked at her blankly.

"His father was a Baptist minister, they say. I don't know if he subscribed to it, but maybe you'll meet him in heaven."

"Maybe so," Elise said. "I hope so."

Are you really interested in heaven, Meg? Or are you mocking me?

"I thought Papi would want to see this film," Meg added. "How's he holding up?"

"Not good. I finally know what people mean when they say someone is a shadow of himself. It's like all his emotions and energy and charm have been turned down to 'low.' Do you know what I mean?"

"I think so. In fact, what you've just said is a good description of someone else." Meg glanced around to make sure they were alone. "Sadie, I mean."

Elise nodded. "I spent some time with her this morning, and you're right, she's not doing very well."

"She'll snap out of it," Meg said crisply, her face suddenly hard. "She just needs an attitude adjustment."

Elise bit her lip. This was not the countenance of someone you wanted to debate.

"Everyone thinks she's so sweet." Meg fixed her eyes on the ceiling. "But she's not. She is one cruel little old lady and I for one wish she'd just call it a life."

"I can't believe what I'm hearing from you."

Startled, Meg turned her eyes back to Elise. "I'm sorry," she said. "I didn't mean that. I'm just feeling abandoned, I guess."

"Poor Meg."

"Ah, I'm okay," Meg said, stretching her arms out. "I am woman, hear me roar, you know. Besides, I've still got Touchdown and Sneak and our house, and a job I like, so all's well. And I've learned a valuable lesson from Sadie."

"Which is?"

"Never to let myself care too much for a woman in her late eighties."

"You know, it doesn't have to be goodbye forever."

"Don't you start, now," Meg said. She was not smiling. "I really can't take any more of that this week."

CHAPTER SIXTY-THREE

Meg Vogel
Tuesday, July 17

Lucy was in again for the entire week, and she had taken responsibility for supervising the morning's Headlines and Coffee party. After helping get the resident newshounds settled and welcoming news-nut-in-chief Elmer, Meg retreated to the office to work on Jeremiah Page's biography. She'd finished their interviews ages ago, but she had fallen into a pattern of doing nothing with her notes until Lucy started asking about a particular resident. It worked; decades in the ad business had made her proficient at churning out decent copy under tight deadlines. And except for her self-imposed high standards for Sadie's write-up, none of these biographies had to be a work of art.

She was able to lose herself for a while in this one. Mr. Page had had a fairly interesting career in industrial sales, and like the other men Meg had interviewed here, he'd given her tons to work with in terms of his political opinions. What's more, he had demanded that she include every last one in her write-up. "I want my kids to know what morons they've been electing!" he'd insisted. "I want them to know that if I'd had my way, they'd be looking at a much more prosperous future!"

It got her mind off of Sadie, anyway. Meg had stopped in to see her this morning and felt like throwing up every time she remembered it; Sadie had been bloated and breathing hard. And according to the morning nurse on the North Wing, there wasn't a thing that could be done about it beyond keeping her comfortable.

And so Meg focused intently on Mr. Page, giving herself a false deadline of noon. It helped: she was just finishing up a final section on the government's role in healthcare—no surprise, he didn't approve—when Lucy called her to help bring the Headlines and Coffee crowd into lunch.

She and Lucy ate lunch together in the office. It had been a while, and Lucy seemed to be in much better spirits than she had been a couple weeks earlier, when she'd berated Meg for listening to Sadie's and Beulah's suspicions about the odd goings-on at The Hickories.

They spent a good quarter hour chatting about unimportant subjects, from their respective to-do lists to their plans for the upcoming weekend, before Lucy segued into the elephant in the room.

"So have you heard anything more from your conspiracy theorists?"

Meg decided to play dumb. "Who?"

"Sadie and Beulah," Lucy said. "Our resident nut jobs."

Swallowing her irritation, Meg finished her soda and stood. "I see them all the time, Lucy." *Unlike you, I have relationships with our residents.* "If you're asking if they've said anything more about their concerns, the answer is no."

"That's good," Lucy said, popping a Lorna Doone in her mouth. "Because I have to tell you that Mr. Immerfall has concerns of his own about their accusations."

"You told Mr. Immerfall?"

"Of course, I told him. These are serious charges."

Meg shook her head. "They're hardly 'charges,' Lucy. Just worries. Suspicions, if you prefer. Not 'charges.' I wish you hadn't taken it to him."

If I'd known you were going to do that, in fact, I would have just kept it to myself.

"Don't worry about it. It's not like he's going to throw them out." Lucy began sifting through the piles of DVDs on her desk. "Hey, would you mind starting the popcorn? We're showing *Random Harvest* this afternoon, so we'll need an extra batch or two."

Meg told Sandra about Lucy's big mouth that night over drinks at Bennett's in Brookfield, the most self-consciously art deco bar in greater Milwaukee. It was all brass and wood, curved corners and golden lighting, making it almost worth $13.50 for a single cocktail.

"Healthcare's like any other business," Sandra said. "Don't trust anyone, least of all your boss."

"Especially if there's even a whiff of a lawsuit—although Sadie and Beulah didn't have *anything* like that in mind."

The bartender delivered their Stoli-and-Cointreau cosmopolitans with a flourish.

"Excellent," purred Sandra, sipping.

"And we look oh-so-sophisticated."

"Men will be flocking to us any minute now. The lighting in here is very flattering, doncha know."

They laughed; the only guys in the place were under thirty and every last one had a date.

"But before we drop the subject entirely," Meg said, "don't you think there should be some way for a nursing-home resident to express her concerns without making a federal case out of it? I just feel like a tattletale, now that Lucy spilled the beans to Immerfall."

"Seems to me that Lucy's the tattletale." Sandra used a cocktail napkin to polish an invisible spot off the bar's brass surface. "But I don't understand why you're so concerned about it. Big deal if he knows about it."

"Yeah, but if he confronts Julia about any of these things, she's going to know exactly who ratted on her. They're as thick as thieves, Sadie and Beulah, and everyone knows it."

"And you worry that Julia will try to get back at them?"

Meg nodded. "That's it exactly. I feel like part of my job is protecting these dear old girls—and I may have set them up for something ghastly."

It had turned out to be a bad day for friendships all around, Meg reflected as she drove home through a light drizzle. As if Lucy's loose lips hadn't been enough, Sandra had spent some time mocking Elise, and Meg didn't appreciate it.

"I've been spying on this website of hers, and it's really something else," Sandra had said. "She's got this 'Advice for the Lovelorn' column on it, only she calls it something like 'Advice for the Love-Worn'—something like that, anyway. And it's just dripping with all the religious garbage you hate. You should look at it."

Meg remained silent, not wanting to get into an argument, especially one in which she would be defending a defender of Christianity. Impossible.

But Sandra didn't miss much; she had looked at Meg suspiciously. "Don't tell me you're buying into this foolishness?"

"No, I am not 'buying into this foolishness.' But I've gotten to know Elise fairly well and she's a really nice person. Very genuine, very honest, and very humble."

Sandra had guffawed at that. "Humble? Is she also 'blessed'? Those words are all the rage today, you know."

"I do know, and I don't use any of them lightly." Meg had refused the bartender's offer of another drink at that point and stuffed her change in her wallet. "Elise is humble in the original sense of the word, meaning that she doesn't think too much of herself, like some people I know."

Meg winced now as she recalled her words, and the look on Sandra's face; it was not a nice thing to say to a woman who had been through some pretty tough times lately.

Maybe she'd call Sandra when she got home, suggest a movie or mall visit this weekend.

Maybe she'd even apologize for being nasty.

Good grief, what's gotten into me?

Meg couldn't remember the last time she had apologized to anyone for anything. It wasn't really her style.

Besides, it would imply that she was in the wrong. And anyone could see that this little spat was Sandra's fault.

CHAPTER SIXTY-FOUR

Sadie Sparrow
Thursday, July 26

Letting Meg help her to breakfast and back had become part of Sadie's routine. Her friend's obvious sorrow made it the saddest part of the day. But Sadie knew that if she lived much longer, these bed-to-chair and chair-to-bed transfers would soon require two aides and a Hoyer lift; it would be easier on these old bones, and at least she wouldn't have to watch Meg fighting back tears.

"They say winter's back," Sadie said as Meg adjusted her oxygen tubing after helping her back into bed.

"Yes, it's pretty nasty out there today. No snow, but it almost feels like it." Meg clipped the call light to Sadie's blanket. "But it's Wisconsin. What else is new?"

"Do you have a minute, Meg? I'd like to talk with you about something."

Meg looked at her suspiciously but pulled a side chair over to the bed and sat down. She looked defiant, Sadie thought—like she expected to hear about the Lord again.

But that wasn't on Sadie's agenda this time, not really. Although if the opportunity arose . . .

She reached her hand out. Meg took it and burst into tears.

"Now, now, dear, everything's going to be all right," Sadie said as Meg pulled a handful of Kleenex out of the pocket of her jacket. "It really is. But I need to tell you this—I don't want it to be a shock for you."

"I know what you're going to say."

"You do?" Sadie smiled. "Then you know that I'm dying?"

"Yes, I know." There was that defiance again, overpowering the tears.

"The doctor said it could be any time now." Sadie swallowed hard, knowing that she'd be having this same talk with Dana soon, knowing that Dana would probably greet the news without even a hint of sorrow. "You may not believe it, but once I draw my last breath, I'll be more alive than I've ever been. I'll be in heaven. And I want you to be happy for me. Will you try?"

Meg nodded.

"Now do me a favor, and call Dana and ask her to come see me this evening. Tell her it's important, without letting on why. Will you do that for me?"

Meg nodded again, refusing to look Sadie in the eye.

"Thank you, dear. Now run along so I can get a good nap in before lunch, will you?"

Dana showed up that evening at seven. She registered barely any reaction to her mother's appearance, even though it had been weeks since she'd visited. Sure, Piper had combed Sadie's hair and helped her put on a little makeup, but she knew she looked like she'd gained fifty pounds, so swollen was she from stem to stern.

"Why are you in bed?" Dana asked as she pecked her mother's cheek.

"Well, that's what I wanted to talk to you about. I have congestive heart failure—my heart's too big, they say," she said with a little laugh that sent her into a fit of coughing.

"Here, drink some water."

"Thank you, dear. Better."

"So you were saying?"

"To get right to the point, I'm dying, Dana, and—"

"You aren't dying!"

"Oh, but I am. Take a look at my legs if you don't believe me."

Dana pulled the blankets back and gasped.

"That's just all fluid retention, they say." Sadie paused, considering whether she should bother trying to explain it, whether she even understood it well enough herself, and decided she didn't. "You can ask the nurse to explain if you want. But I wanted to talk to you about what happens next."

She was surprised to see Dana tearing up. And, she had to admit, pleased.

"There's a booklet in the drawer of this table. Yes, that's the one. It's about the gospel. I know you're not interested, but I'm asking you to read it. Really read it carefully and think about it."

She paused to catch her breath.

"Mother . . ."

Sadie raised her hand to silence Dana. She didn't want to risk losing her train of thought.

"Then at my funeral—my friend Jamie is going to conduct it, by the way. It's all set, everything, including the hymns. At the funeral, I want you to talk to Jamie about where I've gone."

She paused again. The stress of this talk, of being so demanding, was making it even tougher to catch her breath.

"I mean it, Dana. This is my dying wish. Will you promise?"

"I promise," Dana said.

Much to Sadie's amazement, her daughter's face was suddenly awash in tears.

Thank you, Lord. What a gift for a sad old mother's heart!

"Really, Dana dear, it's all going to be okay if you'll just listen to Jamie."

Julia was her nurse that night—a welcome bit of irony, Sadie thought, and an opportunity she would not let go to waste.

Be still my soul, the hour is hastening on, when we shall be forever with the Lord . . .

Sadie was listening to Jamie's "heaven" CD again when Julia slipped silently into her room, leaving the door slightly ajar.

"You're not looking so good, Sadie," the nurse said, peering sullenly at her patient and presenting pill and water cups. "Take these."

"But you are, Julia," Sadie said, swallowing all the pills in one gulp. "You're a very pretty girl on the outside."

A trace of a smile crossed Julia's perfect lips. She pulled a pen and notepad out of her pocket and made a note.

When disappointment, grief and fear are gone, sorrow forgot, love's purest joys restored . . .

"That pen," Sadie said.

Julia looked at it. "It's a Montblanc—my grandfather's."

This was important information, Sadie knew, but she couldn't quite remember why.

So important! Think, Sadie Sparrow, think!

She plunged into another coughing fit, depositing pink foam on a tissue. Julia watched silently, staring at her lips so intently that Sadie wiped them with extra care.

Be still my soul, when change and tears are past . . .

"So tell me," Sadie said when she'd caught her breath, "did you break Beulah's legs?"

She was feeling dizzy. It was tough to keep the nurse in focus.

"Why yes, I did," Julia said. "How did you know?"

Or had she spoken at all? Sadie couldn't be sure.

All safe and blessed we shall meet at last!

"There is ultimate justice, you know. You will pay for this one way or another."

At least, she thought that's what she said.

Oh, well, no matter. She felt such peace. Her biggest question in this life had been answered—well, at least the one she could remember, and the others had slipped her mind so they couldn't be all that important. There was nothing Nurse Julia could do to her now. Not a thing.

"Fear not them which kill the body, but are not able to kill the soul," Sadie added, or may have added; she was unsure. "But rather fear Him which is able to destroy both soul and body in hell."

More coughing.

Then: "I'm leaving, Julia. I'm going to be with my Savior."

Butterflies—she felt butterflies, for the first time in eons. She was going Home.

"I'll miss you more than you'll ever know," Julia said, or may have said. "I love you, Sadie."

But that can't be; it makes no sense.

Sadie saw the nurse take something out of her pocket. The pen again, or a needle perhaps, or maybe a thermometer.

"How 'bout I give you something to help you relax?"

Sadie felt a moment of panic as Julia reached for her arm, but she suppressed it. She would not give her the satisfaction.

If it had really happened. She couldn't be sure of anything anymore, the way her thoughts were piling up on each other.

"Thank you for being my friend, Sadie."

What did she say? Is she holding my hand now? What is going on here?

Almost immediately, Sadie lost her questions in a great swelling chorus of song. She let herself melt into its incredible beauty.

Face to face I shall behold Him, far beyond the starry sky.

Face to face in all His glory, I shall see Him by and by.

A wonderful thought to ride into eternity.

CHAPTER SIXTY-FIVE

Elise Chapelle
Thursday, July 26

It wasn't until Elise got home from The Hickories that night that she became fairly certain Jamie was about to propose marriage.

Although it had crossed her mind more than once lately, as doting as he had become, she hadn't allowed herself to dwell on it. On the one hand, it seemed too good to be true that this wonderful, godly man might love her enough to want to spend the rest of his life with her. On the other, his determination to head for Munich as a missionary meant that a proposal would force her to choose between marrying him and staying here with Papi; how could she possibly make such a choice?

Now it seemed that she might have to give it some serious thought.

This realization was Papi's fault, really. He'd told her about the big mystery of Eva's cameos, said they were the talk of The Hickories even now, after they'd been found in Gladys' safekeeping, and mentioned that Mamie had had a wonderful cameo stick pin—had she ever seen it?

She remembered it well. It was a fine cameo of a beautiful little horse, mounted on an extremely sharp pin that had poked her more than once as a child. And she knew exactly where it was, in the quilted pink jewelry case that had been Mamie's, and that Elise used to this day for the little bit of jewelry she owned.

Wondering if the horse cameo was as enchanting as she remembered, Elise went straight for the jewelry case when she got home, sitting down with it at the kitchen table, magnifying glass in hand.

It was indeed beautiful—a real work of art! It pictured a colt or filly trotting towards the viewer, head up and ears pricked forward. She wondered if it was worth anything. Not that she'd ever sell it, of course, but it would be fun to know.

It had been ages since she had looked through these things. She began examining each piece—an opal necklace and ring set, a silver charm bracelet with trinkets from a tiny chalet to an ivory swan, several rhinestone-encrusted bracelets, and a number of pins, several of them tarnished black. There had been a story behind each piece, she knew, but she had forgotten most of them; she wished that she'd written them down instead of entrusting them to her memory.

Ah, and here was the Swiss dress watch Papi had given her on her eighteenth birthday. She looked at its delicate face under the magnifying glass; it was so simple, so lovely. And her rings: the garnet ring was a real beauty; it had belonged to Mamie's mother. And somewhere here, her pearl ring, a gift from her grandparents on her twenty-fifth birthday—

Where is my pearl ring?

It was missing. And not for long—she had worn it just last Saturday night. Jamie had commented on its beauty. She remembered returning it to the case before brushing her teeth that night, certain that toothpaste couldn't be good for pearls.

On Sunday, he had taken her to church, picking her up early in the morning and bringing her home in the afternoon, lingering for quite some time before heading back to prepare for the evening service.

The case had been sitting out on the little table in the bathroom. He'd had plenty of opportunity to borrow the pearl ring long enough to get a new one properly sized.

An engagement ring, for example.

So seldom did she wear the pearl ring that she wouldn't have noticed it missing if she hadn't been looking for Mamie's cameo pin.

Elise groaned. It looked like she might soon be forced to make an impossible decision.

CHAPTER SIXTY-SIX

Meg Vogel
Friday, July 27

The battery in Meg's alarm clock ran out of juice at three in the morning. Which meant no alarm, no on-time departure; she was almost a half hour late in getting to work. She dropped her purse off in the office and headed for the North Wing to fetch Sadie for breakfast.

But there she found a group of nurses and aides talking in low voices outside her friend's door. Her heart sank.

Sadie's favorite aide noticed Meg first. "She's gone," Piper said quietly, dabbing at her eyes with a wad of tissue. "I'm sorry—I know you two were close."

The oldest nurse said that she'd been about to recommend calling in hospice care. "I knew it was coming. I just didn't expect it to happen so quickly."

"They don't always go so peacefully," added a nurse wearing bright red scrubs.

"It's a blessing," volunteered another nurse, this one sporting a bold fuchsia streak in her blonde hair.

"Kind of makes you wonder what pull she had with the Man upstairs," said the one in red.

Meg needed to be alone. She turned to leave.

"Don't you want to see her?" one of the nurses called.

"No thanks," Meg said. "I've seen enough dead bodies to last a lifetime."

The rest of the day was a blur. Meg spent a few minutes of it talking over the phone with a frighteningly composed and tearless Dana, who said she had a lot on her plate for the next few days but would be in after the funeral to clean out Sadie's room.

The service was held on Tuesday at a modest funeral home in nearby Waukesha. No ornate furniture or original oils here; it was light and airy and reminded Meg vaguely of the austere Protestant church her parents had dragged her to when she was a kid.

Meg donned her "too crabby to care" face and sat on a folding chair in the room with the Sparrow sign, waiting for someone to talk with her or the service to start, whichever came first. She would not let any direct thoughts of Sadie creep into her thinking; she'd do that later, when she was alone. Until then Meg Vogel would shed no tears.

The casket was closed and there weren't all that many people there—just Dana and her family, a few groups of elderly people, and a handful of caregivers who'd been particularly fond of Sadie. And Mr. Immerfall, which struck Meg as a little odd.

Trolling for new business, Mr. Administrator?

Meg wished that Char had agreed to come with her; she was a nice person and would have been a comfort. But she had to work, and anyway she said that Sadie didn't need a goodbye party: "She's already in paradise, and I'll be seeing her there."

But then Elise and Papi came in, followed shortly thereafter by Jamie. He was wearing a dark blue suit and a tie in the powder blue that had been Sadie's best color. Meg wondered if he'd been aware enough of that sort of thing to select the tie in her honor.

She watched him greeting the family and the old people, as more and more toddled in, leaning heavily on canes or walkers. She wasn't exactly trying to catch his eye, not really. And within moments the Chapelles had joined her, so of course if he looked in their direction at all it would have been to lock eyes with Elise. But it turned out to be a moot point; his eyes never strayed from those of the person he was talking to.

It wasn't until Jamie had reached the podium that he acknowledged the three of them with a nod and a smile. His gaze was especially sympathetic for her, Meg thought. It made her tear up; she knew he must've been crazy about Sadie, to have shown up week after week even in the beginning, when she was the only one who attended his sessions.

"Well," he said, straightening out his notes and smiling at the group, "I hope you all realize that we're here today not to celebrate the life of Sadie Sparrow—but instead, and far more important, to celebrate her home-going."

"Amen," said an old man wearing a jaunty (and, in Meg's opinion, thoroughly inappropriate) bow tie.

But Meg wasn't digging it. One sentence into this little talk and she was already thoroughly offended. Jamie was saying, in essence, that they were there to celebrate Sadie's death.

She glared at him.

"Now I know some of you might not like that," he continued, "but I happen to know exactly where Sadie Sparrow is right now. And trust me, she's a lot more alive than any of us could ever hope to be in this life."

"Amen," said the bow tie, and Papi seconded him.

"And when she asked me to handle her funeral service, she very specifically told me to emphasize her current location, and to spend the rest of my time telling you all how you can be sure to join her when your time comes."

Meg quit listening at that point. Instead, she searched around in her mind for something nice to think about, something pleasant that wouldn't make her feel like crying, and that might keep her thoughts occupied for the duration.

But every nook and cranny she looked into gave her a fresh whiff of death. Her parents? Dead. Her husband? Dead. Her career? Almost over. The book she was currently reading? King's *Pet Sematary*. Even Touchdown and Sneak were getting up there in age, and one of these years she'd be faced with making heart-wrenching decisions about their lives.

It seemed that everything pointed to unhappy endings.

"So we will all stand before the Lord in judgment one day," Jamie was booming, his Scottish accent sneaking into his rhetoric, "and we have a choice: try to pay the penalty for our sins ourselves, which is impossible and leads straight to eternal punishment; or let Christ pay our penalty for us and spend eternity with Him in heaven. It's that simple."

It's that simple for the simple-minded.

It was all just wishful thinking, she supposed. Really, who wanted to think that they lived forty, sixty, eighty years and then just disappeared?

But facts are facts, and there's no evidence to support any other conclusion.

"There's plenty of evidence for the truth of the Bible," Jamie was saying. "And Sadie asked me to ask you to examine it. She herself didn't know for sure until fairly recently . . ."

A shameless plug for yourself, Jamie? What a fine thing to do at a funeral!

Meg thought about some of the highlights of her life, the good deeds and the bad, and she sensed that the latter might outweigh the former. Which made it pretty hopeless as far as she could see; so even if this nonsense turned out to be true, it was a little late for someone like her to start racking up good deeds.

"And the wonderful thing is that you don't need to do anything to get there," Jamie said. "You can't, in fact. The only way into heaven is to repent and trust in Christ to have paid for your sins on the cross."

Is he reading my mind?

Meg arched her back and gazed at the ceiling. It was white, like just about everything else in this room, except for the olive-green carpet and blonde woodwork and gunmetal gray chairs.

And Sadie's casket, a burgundy so dark it was almost black. She thought about restaining the cabinets in her kitchen that color, thought about what kind of flooring she might put in, what kind of countertops she might choose if she were to undertake such a project. She was on to something: here was a neutral-to-happy subject she could play with for the duration of this thing.

When she turned her attention back to the funeral, Jamie was apparently finishing up his eulogy, if you could call it that.

"I'll close with this last thought, because Sadie asked me to. She said, and I quote, 'Tell them that I hope to see them all there.'"

He thanked them for their attention, and said that there would be no burial today, that Sadie's remains were to be buried next to Ed's in the family plot near Shawano, but that they were all invited to stay for coffee and cake in the next room.

Meg did stay for a while, mainly as a representative of The Hickories, but also because she wanted to look Dana in the eye to see if there was a trace of sorrow there.

There was, surprisingly: Dana's eyes were bloodshot, and her perfectly made-up face looked like it had aged ten years since she came to The Hickories to complain about how happy her mother was.

Her appearance melted Meg's heart a little, although her aversion to maintaining eye contact was annoying.

They talked a bit about Sadie and the service and the burial plans before falling into an awkward silence.

"How's Wally?" Meg asked to fill the void, remembering Sadie's frequent mentions of her beloved cat. "Did your mom ever have a chance to see him again?"

Dana hesitated. "To be honest, we had to put him to sleep months ago," she said finally. "He refused to use his litter box and we just couldn't tolerate that."

Meg was horrified. "Did you tell her?"

"Of course not," Dana snapped. "She was better off not knowing."

And longing for the day you'd have time to bring him over for a visit?

"I'm really sorry to hear that. Wish I'd known—I would have taken him in."

Dana shrugged. "He was a one-woman cat. He never warmed up to anyone but my mother."

Which reminded Meg of the finished biography she'd brought along; there were several pictures of Sadie and Wally in it.

"You probably haven't seen this yet," she said, digging the little book out of her purse. "It's the biography your mom and I worked on together. You can have this copy of it."

"Oh, thanks." Dana began paging through it but then apparently saw someone important enter the room. "Derek!" she cried, tucking the book into her own purse and leaving Meg's side with a quick "Sorry, but here's my boss."

Meg watched her in amazement, wondering how someone as terrific as Sadie could have produced a daughter like that.

As Dana cozied up to her boss—a thirty-something hotshot who stood a full head shorter than she, with spiked white-blonde hair, heavy black glasses and a day's growth of beard—Nurse Julia suddenly appeared. She approached Meg wearing a simple black dress with a jewel neckline and short sleeves and a slight smile that suggested she knew something no one else in the room could guess.

"I'm a little surprised to see you here," Meg said icily. "I didn't know you cared about Sadie."

But on closer inspection, she was shocked to see that Julia's eyes were red, and the tip of her nose was bright pink.

"No?" Julia dabbed at her nose with a ratty tissue. "Well, I did. She had a big impact on my life. And I like to think that I had an impact on hers as well."

Meg was tempted to reveal just what sort of impact the nurse had had on her old friend—to wit, Sadie's fretful suspicions about Julia's role in several possible cases of malfeasance. Instead, she glanced around the room to make her boredom with the conversation plain.

"But I guess I was wrong about that," Julia added, pulling a fresh tissue from her shoulder bag. "You wouldn't believe what she accused me of right before she died."

That got Meg's attention. "What?"

"She asked me if I'd broken Beulah's legs."

Meg was so shocked that she spoke without thinking. "Well, did you?"

Julia's eyebrows shot up over her beautiful dark eyes. "Of course not! Beulah *fell*, Meg. She was always forgetting her walker, plus she has osteoporosis. The doctor even said they might have been spontaneous breaks."

"Really." Meg couldn't keep the haughtiness out of her voice. "Then I wonder why Sadie thought you had something to do with it."

"I haven't got a clue." Julia's eyes threatened to spill over again. "I'm telling you, I loved her. It kills me that it would even cross her mind that I'd do such a thing. I hope it was just the drugs talking. Or maybe I misunderstood." She touched her right ear. "My hearing isn't the best, and I only picked up my new cheaters last night."

Meg was stunned to see a minuscule leopard-print bauble in the crest of the nurse's ear—one of those snazzy new hearing aids! She murmured something about Sadie's confusion towards the end and watched a somewhat relieved Julia melt away into the crowd.

This conversation had thrown her for a loop. Maybe Julia hadn't refused Eva a pain pill; maybe she hadn't heard the request. And what about Beulah's breaks? Would Julia have mentioned her final exchange with Sadie if she'd been guilty? Then again, maybe leaving Meg with that impression was precisely what the nurse intended to do. Could it have been an especially subtle red herring?

Meg's silent debate was interrupted by a tap on her shoulder. She turned to find Jamie, his brown eyes focused intently on hers.

"How are you holding up?"

She said she was fine, how was he, nice service, good coffee . . .

And Elise is really a lucky girl.

She blushed, fairly sure that she hadn't said those words aloud.

Where did that come from, anyway?

"I have something for you." He extracted a #10 envelope from the pocket of his jacket. "Sadie asked me to give it to you."

She took the envelope from him. It was a little battered, but she could see her name printed carefully on the front. It didn't weigh much but it contained something more than paper.

"It's a tape," he said. "Do you have a tape player? If not—"

"I do. I'm old school. Still tape all my interviews."

"I'll be interested to hear what you think of it."

"You listened to it?" She was shocked.

"I was there when she taped it." Jamie smiled, then turned to scan the room. "I promised Sadie I'd talk to her daughter."

"Good luck with that," Meg said. "You're really going to need it."

After a short bout of broken-hearted weeping and a long walk with Touchdown, Meg spent the evening on the internet, alternately shopping her favorite retailers' summer sales and playing online games from Jeopardy to Mirror Magic.

"A total waste of time," she told the critters. "That's the best thing to do to soothe sorrows away."

But it was a lie; by ten o'clock she was beginning to feel guilty, too, for frittering away an entire evening.

Deciding to try to redeem at least a bit of the night—and here she smiled, remembering that Sadie had once talked about her father's constant reminders to "redeem the time"—she surfed to Elise's website. It wasn't her first visit, although she hadn't mentioned it to Elise; somehow, she felt like a peeping Tom, a heathen spying on the innermost thoughts of a believer in myths. And indeed, the content struck her as pretty desperate, and pretty foolish, in its attempts to prove God's existence.

But she found the "Advice for the Life-Worn" column fairly interesting. Fascinating, in fact, in the way that Elise turned everything inside out and backwards, as if she were viewing life through Alice in Wonderland's looking glass.

Meg wondered if she could submit a question anonymously.

Hmmmm. Why yes, she could. The form required an email address, so she typed in one she hadn't used in years, but had never closed: HoundHugger262@aol.com

Now, what would be a good question for Elise—one that would make her realize how futile this Christian life really is, and help her move back into reality?

"Aha," she said. "Here we go."

Dear Elise,

If your God is so good, how is it that he allows all the suffering in the world?

Your friend,

Betty

It nearly killed her to misspell "suffering," but it meant that Elise would never suspect that the question came from word nut Meg.

She clicked "Submit" and made a mental note to check back in a couple days for a reply.

CHAPTER SIXTY-SEVEN

Elise Chapelle
Wednesday, August 1

The morning after Sadie's funeral, Elise found seven more questions in her "Advice for the Life-Worn" email box. She was already falling behind, and Everlasting Place had only been up and running for two months.

Today's questions covered a wide range of topics: What was a thirteen-year-old to do about catching her father viewing pornography? How could a middle-aged alto successfully sing her part when she was the only one in her choir section who could read music? Where did Elise stand on the issue of infant baptism? Why are there so many denominations?

Thinking that she'd discuss them all with Jamie—maybe he could help her respond to them—she opened the last one. The hands-down winner, this question from "your friend Betty" asked, in essence, how a good God could allow such suffering in this world.

Elise started working on this response right away, building her answer around 2 Corinthians 4:17-18:

For our light affliction, which is but for a moment, is working for us a far more exceeding and eternal weight of glory, while we do not look at the things which are seen, but at the things which are not seen. For the things which are seen are temporary, but the things which are not seen are eternal.

She typed and typed, knowing that she'd have to go back and edit her words ruthlessly to fit in the one-thousand-word limit she was trying to establish.

"And that is why we do not lose heart, Betty," she concluded. "The 'light' affliction the apostle Paul referred to included suffering and all kinds of beatings and imprisonments. Yet he wrote 'even though our outward man is perishing, yet the inward man is being renewed day by day.' And that's a claim you can cling to for the duration!"

It was on Saturday night that Jamie dropped the bomb.

Stuffed from downing ribeye steaks expertly prepared on Papi's ancient grill, plus corn on the cob and pan-patty squash, they did the dishes and retreated to the old porch swing.

"The days are already getting shorter," Elise said. "It's not even half-past eight and it's already dark."

Jamie didn't say anything, just took her hand. He had been pretty quiet the entire evening, in fact. Thinking of Munich, no doubt.

They swung silently for a while, watching the night fall, listening to the crickets' lullaby.

"Elise," Jamie said finally, his face deadly serious in the warm light slipping through the picture window, "we need to talk."

Here we go.

"I've made an important decision," he said. "And I want you to be the first to know."

That was an odd thing to say.

"A decision about what?"

"About going overseas. About Germany."

"I know what you're going to say, Jamie. I've been anticipating this."

"Really?" He turned to look at her, tilting his head in surprise.

"Yes," she said. "Go on."

"Well, if you already know . . ."

"Out with it!"

"Okay, okay. Here's the thing: I'm not going."

She gasped; it was not what she'd been expecting to hear.

"I'm staying here, sticking with my current job, but also launching a formal nursing-home ministry on behalf of the church."

"Why, Jamie," she said, her heart leaping. "But you've been talking about Munich for so long."

"Maybe it was just a placeholder until the Lord was able to show me what He wanted me to do."

"And this is it?"

"Definitely! I've been feeling for a while that this is where I belong, working with the elderly—"

"You *do* seem to have a way with them."

"I love them, even the cross ones. And I'm obviously not the only one; look at all the volunteers there are at The Hickories alone. This culture may not have much use for the elderly any more, but there are an awful lot of people stepping into the breach."

"So what does the church say about it?"

"It was their idea! The deacons proposed it to me a couple weeks ago, and I accepted the offer yesterday."

Elise rejoiced. "I'm so happy for you!"

Happy for me, too. No heartbreak necessary!

Jamie spent the next quarter hour outlining his initial plans for recruiting volunteers and bringing several more nursing homes into the fold. He'd obviously put a great deal of thought into it already; she was impressed, and said so.

"Maybe you'll join us," he said, taking her hand again. "In an official capacity, I mean."

"I just may do that, down the road—when Papi is gone, I mean."

They swung some more, Elise silently thanking God for eliminating her problem.

No wonder I couldn't figure out what Your leading was on this. You knew there was no decision to make.

"There *is* one thing I'd like you to do while Papi is still with us," Jamie said finally.

He pulled a black velvet jewelry box out of his pocket and opened it.

"Marry me, Elise. Would you marry me?"

She'd rehearsed this moment many times in her heart, but it had always included Munich.

Answer him, you bozo! Say something!

"Of course," she whispered. "Of course I will."

He slipped the ring on her finger. The stone was small but it sparkled like the Hope Diamond.

"It's beautiful. And a perfect fit. How in the world did you guess my size?"

CHAPTER SIXTY-EIGHT

Meg Vogel
Saturday, October 27

Meg had mixed feelings about the Chapelle-Fletcher wedding. She had grown awfully fond of Elise; how could one fail to care for such a gentle creature? And then there was Jamie, so blasted sure of his over-the-top religious beliefs.

Oh well, it wouldn't be the first time she'd had a girlfriend whose husband was distasteful in one respect or another, and it probably wouldn't be the last. Nor would it be the first time she'd stood up in the wedding of such a couple.

And in spite of her reservations, she had to admit that it was a lovely wedding. Held in Jamie's church—an austere white clapboard building with an equally austere sanctuary—the ceremony was conducted by his boss, Senior Pastor Micah MacMillan. And it was traditional from beginning to end, even down to the painfully long message on marital harmony and the oh-so-formal exchange of vows.

It didn't hurt that the bride was both a knockout and a throw-back to a simpler day. Elise looked angelic in a fitted cream skirt suit straight out of the 1940s, complete with a fetching veiled-and-feathered hat—and indeed it had been her grandmother Lorraine's wedding outfit, so carefully stored for nearly seventy years that it looked brand new.

As the bride's attendants, Meg and Char had been invited to wear whatever they happened to have on hand, rather than spending money on a new outfit. Meg had dug through her "power suit" closet, the final resting place for the business clothing that had been, just a couple decades ago, mandatory attire for women on their way up in the business world. She'd chosen a dark brown wool suit that had been her favorite back in the day; it was a little snug in the waist, but with its shoulder pads and shaped jacket, its silhouette echoed Elise's.

Char showed up in a russet-colored shirtwaist with a full skirt reminiscent of the '50s. She'd found it for just $2.50 at the Salvation Army store on Highway 164, she said, and it looked great on her.

But the guys out-did them all, looking quite handsome in navy suits and starched white shirts.

It was, in short, about as conventional as an affair could be—and for Meg, a welcome relief from the super-trendy, bare-everything weddings she'd been to in the last decade. Way too much cleavage and tattooing and black silk for her taste.

"It ain't fitting. It just ain't fitting."

Mammy in *Gone With the Wind*. She would have approved of this wedding, that was for sure.

After the singing—totally and inexplicably unrelated to the event at hand—the pastor launched into his talk. Meg zoned out as he droned on and on about wives obeying their husbands and husbands loving their wives, blah blah blah.

Okay, so aside from the fact that this advice is so "yesterday," shouldn't he have gone over this stuff with them in their pre-wedding meetings? Why bore the entire audience to tears?

She looked out into the pews and saw a number of women wiping their eyes.

They're bored to TEARS, pastor!

But finally he got to the vows. Standard issue, of course; heartfelt homemade vows were apparently not welcome in this place. Just as well, however, since the formal lines went straight to the point.

A crisp "I now pronounce you man and wife," a cheerful "you may kiss the bride," and it was over.

Meg puddled up a bit towards the end, mainly because she was thinking how much Sadie would have loved both the idea and the execution of this particular wedding. She ducked her head hoping no one would see—*as if they're looking at you, you narcissist!*—and headed down to the basement for the simple little spread of crustless sandwiches and cookies, coffee and tea.

Meg filled a plate and took a seat at a round, linen-clad table in the corner nearest the door. She didn't know many of the people here—Char and Papi, of course, and a half dozen aides following Piper around the room. Elise had invited all the residents in Papi's wing, but only Beulah, accompanied by Bunny, had taken her up on it; most of the residents really didn't want to leave The Hickories at all, even if they talked longingly about wanting to get out, to go shopping or dining or worshipping in the real world for a change.

That's what you'll be like, too, one day, Vogel. Old and alone and clinging to the facility at first and then letting your world close in slowly to your table in the dining room and finally to your room. Thinking up a rash of excuses for staying put, a new one each day, a headache on Monday, a sore back on Tuesday . . .

Pastor Micah interrupted Meg's daydream by sitting down next to her. His plate was loaded with little sandwiches, his coffee pale with cream.

"Worked up an appetite, did you?" She grinned, to let him know she was simply being friendly and amusing. He was fairly attractive, after all, and these really were nice people, surprisingly warm and non-judgmental compared with the stab-you-in-the-back folk she was used to in the business world. They reminded her of Gil's friends, in fact—men and women who were looking a lot better to her as increasingly distant memories.

Micah inspected her plate and his own and nodded. "You too, I see." He smiled back at her and downed a little sandwich in one bite. "But what I'd really like is a ribeye steak."

"Can't disagree with you there." She wished that she'd powdered her nose.

"We could sneak over to Gordon's Supper Club," he said, raising an eyebrow in invitation.

Her heart skipped a beat. His hair was thinning and gray and worn so short that it was almost a crew-cut, and his eyeglasses had pronounced bifocal half-moons—clearly the man didn't worry much about his appearance. But he had the kind of sturdy features she liked, and his dimples were adorable.

"What would your wife say?"

He laughed. "No wife. She got tired of being married to a pastor and left me years ago."

"Oh, I'm sorry."

"So am I," he said, gulping down half of his coffee. "It doesn't say much for how I ruled my own household."

"*Ruled?*"

"Yup. The Bible's pretty clear on the subject, for anyone in church leadership."

She did an abbreviated eye roll. He noticed.

"You don't care for the Bible?"

"Not really."

Don't make me explain it all again, pastor. I bore myself with my testimony of unbelief.

"Believe in an afterlife?"

That was at least a surprising segue. "Maybe, maybe not. There's really no way to know for sure."

"Says who?"

Another surprise. "Well, me, I guess. And lots of others in my generation."

"Our generation," he corrected her. "I don't imagine I'm much older than you are. Born in 1950. How 'bout you?"

"Fifty-four."

"Perfect. We speak the same language, then. So, tell me about this potential afterlife of yours."

That was refreshing, too: a Christian asking for her opinion of an afterlife. She talked to him about all good people, and all animals, ending up there, living happy lives forevermore.

One of the church ladies offered them wedding cake, sidetracking their conversation for the moment.

"Delicious," Micah said, scraping every last bit of frosting off his plate.

"Yummy," she agreed, following suit.

"So what's your source of authority for this vision of the afterlife?" he asked, wiping his mouth with his napkin and accepting a coffee refill from another church lady.

She smiled. It was the sort of question Jamie asked, and this time she was prepared to field it. "I've given it some thought," she said. "And I've concluded that it can't be just the Bible."

"Why not?"

"It's too—intolerant." Meg sipped her coffee. "God so loved the world and all that, but He's sending most people to hell?"

"So God can't have standards unless they meet with your approval?"

"Of course He can. That doesn't mean I have to accept them, does it? Besides, there are all these contradictions in the Bible."

Micah smiled. "Can you give me an example? Personally, I've never found any that can't be easily answered."

His brow was creased, in what had to be an imitation of sincerity.

Meg sulked. She was too tired to get into this kind of debate again; every way you turned, these Christians had a pat answer for you.

They talked of other things, from homes and pets to the pathetic state of the union.

Then, apropos of nothing, she returned to their earlier theme. "I'm going to prove you wrong. I'm going to find the inconsistencies myself."

"Great," said Micah. "Watch out especially for scientific error—oh, and for historical error related to prophecy. I'll quiz you."

"I'll call you when I'm ready."

"I'll look forward to it."

By mid-November, the temperatures had plunged into the twenties and the sky was wearing its oppressive winter coat of ash gray.

It was time.

Meg was approaching a crossroads with her life, it seemed, and it was about time that she took a good look at where she had been, where she was, and where she might be going in the future. Beyond going to Sandra's for Thanksgiving dinner. And beyond deciding whether she wanted the Activities Director post or not, now that Lucy had surprised everyone but Meg by resigning for a hospital PR job.

Definitely time to take stock, Meg knew. And that meant, first of all, listening to Sadie's tape, sitting right here on the bookcase in the living room.

It was ridiculous for her to be so afraid of listening to it. Why had she put it off all these months? Did she really think Sadie was going to berate her? Or express panic over dying, tearfully begging for Meg's help? Either one would be totally out of character for her dear old friend.

She pulled her trusty old Panasonic recorder out of her briefcase, plugged Sadie's tape into the cassette compartment, and set it on the side table next to her mother's favorite old wing chair—just the right spot for such a momentous occasion.

Ready to go.

Maybe a glass of wine was in order. She headed for the kitchen, Sneak and Touchdown on her heels in hope of getting a second dinner for themselves, and poured herself a glass of a sweet Riesling on the rocks—nothing she'd do in public, but there was no one here to see.

She returned to the living room, sat in the still-comfortable wing chair, took a deep breath, and pushed "play."

Her heart was racing as she listened to ten seconds of paper-shuffling and throat-clearing. Then, that beloved voice, more quavering than Meg remembered.

"My dear Meg, this is your friend Sadie," the voice said. "I'm going to be going home to the Lord soon, and there are some things I need to say to you before I go. It's my prayer that you'll listen, maybe more than once, and point yourself toward heaven so that I can spend all eternity with you."

Meg sipped. It was a lip-smacking wine, but she would take it easy, if for no other reason than out of respect for Sadie.

"I've made some notes, so bear with me."

She could hear papers rustling again, and then some murmuring.

"There, thank you." Her voice was muffled, like she was speaking to a helper. Jamie, no doubt. Then, she apparently turned back to the recorder. "Meg," she said at full volume, her voice stronger now, "this is what you need to know. The Bible is true. Ask Jamie to tell you how we can know that—he spent weeks helping me see the evidence. I'm certain that it's true from beginning to end."

No offense, Sadie dear, but I wouldn't call you the most discerning person I've ever met.

"Because of that, I am sure that what you believe in this life will determine where you spend all eternity."

Sadie coughed, and Meg detected the sound of the tape stopping and starting again.

"God has a right to set the rules for His creation—and it *is* His, which Jamie can also explain to you. The trouble is that we all have broken those rules. That's what sin *is*— breaking God's rules."

Meg moaned.

Here we go again.

"To get into heaven, the penalty for our sins has to be paid. But we can't pay it ourselves—all the good works in the world won't pay for even one sin. Just think about something cruel someone said to you and then apologized for."

She remembered Gil apologizing a lot towards the end of his life.

"Did his apology make the offense go away? Of course not."

You're right.

"The only way to wash away our sins is to let Jesus do it, which He did on the cross. That was especially horrible for Him because it caused the Father to turn away from Him for the first and only time in His life. Jesus actually *became* our sin, which made Him repulsive to His Father. It was horrible!"

Her voice cracked here, and Meg heard the click of the tape being stopped and restarted once again.

"His sacrifice, His payment for your sins—Meg, it's a free gift."

I know. All I have to do is submit to this imaginary friend of yours. I'm so sorry, Sadie, but you've been taken!

"But you don't get this gift just because you were born. A gift is not yours until you receive it."

Well, at least that much makes sense.

"And you can't do that unless you turn from your sin and trust in Jesus. Rather than trusting in your own goodness, I mean. And once you've done that, you're saved forever."

Forever. Fancy that.

"But the first step is believing all of this, Meg. You must believe it because it's true."

Again, the sound of stopping and starting.

"If you won't, Meg—if you refuse—then I will never see you again. And that makes me so very sad.

"Just ask yourself, please: What if the old lady is right? And please think about it."

Okay, Sadie, I'll think about it, just for you.

"Meg, you did something for me that no one has for a very long time: you made me feel important, and so loved. And I have grown to love you. Please don't scoff at me. Please ask Jamie."

A pause, then—ten, fifteen seconds.

Then: "Farewell, my friend, my dear Meg. Until we meet again one day, I pray, beyond the sunset."

And the tape ended.

Meg sat silently for a long time.

What if she's right? That's the question of the hour, isn't it?

"I love you, too, Sadie Sparrow," she said finally, aloud, startling herself and causing the lounging Sneak to cast a suspicious eye on her. "I guess it couldn't hurt to do as you ask."

She poured herself another glass of wine and sat down again.

I could at least listen to what he has to say. After all, Elise's answer to my question about suffering almost made sense to me.

She pulled her phone out of her purse and dialed carefully; she hadn't called this number since the wedding.

She got voice mail, which was a relief; she wasn't quite ready to have this discussion. Maybe after the holidays. But getting the wheels in motion seemed like the right thing to do, for Sadie's sake.

"Hi guys, it's Meg. Hope you're doing well. I'm calling because—well, Jamie, I finally listened to Sadie's tape, and it looks like we need to talk . . ."

The End

DID YOU ENJOY THIS BOOK?

If so, we'd be most grateful if you'd take a few minutes to leave a review on *The Song of Sadie Sparrow* page at Amazon.com. It can be as short or as long as you like. Thank you!

ABOUT THE AUTHOR

In *The Song of Sadie Sparrow*, Kitty Foth-Regner has written what she knows. For a quarter century, she's been closely associated with a nursing home near Milwaukee, both as the daughter of a resident and as a volunteer. A retired copywriter, she is the author of *Heaven Without Her*, an enthusiastically endorsed memoir tracing her intellectual and spiritual journey from feminist atheism to born-again Christianity. Visit her at www.EverlastingPlace.com.

ACKNOWLEDGMENTS

Many thanks to Greg Johnson for his tireless efforts on behalf of this story.

To Keely Boeving for truly outstanding editorial assistance.

To Ruthanne Taylor for extraordinary patience and attention to detail.

To Linda Jack for invaluable feedback on the manuscript.

To Dr. Julie Ellis and Kathie Grant for their insights into nursing home life.

To Brenda Thimke for critical information on O'Hare Field.

To my husband Dave Regner for unfailing support throughout this journey.

To Nancy Berth for sharing her dear mother with me all these years.

To all my friends at Care-age of Brookfield—without you, there'd be no Sadie Sparrow.

And above all, to my Lord and Savior Jesus Christ, who bore my sins and yours on the cross so that we might all live happily ever after.

CPSIA information can be obtained
at www.ICGtesting.com
Printed in the USA
LVHW011912101218
599940LV00001B/125

9 781941 555354